THE AGE OF MISADVENTURE

Judy Leigh completed an MA in Professional Writing at Falmouth University in 2015, leaving her career of 20 years as an Advanced Skills teacher of Theatre Studies. She has had several stories published in magazines, including *The Feminist Wire*, *The Purple Breakfast Review* and *You is for University*. She has also trained as a Reiki healer, written a vegan recipe blog and set up a series of Shakespeare Festivals to enable young people to perform the Bard's work on stage.

Also by Judy Leigh

A Grand Old Time

The Mis AGE OF ADVENTURE

JUDY LEIGH

avon.

This novel is entirely a work of fiction.
The names, characters and incidents portrayed in it are
the work of the author's imagination. Any resemblance to
actual persons, living or dead, events or localities is
entirely coincidental.

AVON

A division of HarperCollins*Publishers*
1 London Bridge Street,

available from the British Library

ISBN-13: 978-0-00-826922-7

Typeset in Sabon LT Std by Palimpsest Book Production Ltd,
Falkirk, Stirlingshire

Printed and bound in Great Britain by CPI Group (UK) Ltd,
Croydon CR0 4YY

Acknowledgements

Grateful thanks to the many people who are with me on this writing journey: there has been so much support in so many ways. Warmest thanks to my brilliant agent Kiran Kataria, whose knowledge and skills are always invaluable. Thanks to the talented and wonderful Avon team: editor Rachel Faulkner-Willcocks, publicist Sabah Khan and marketeer Elke, and to Emma for the gorgeous cover. I'm grateful for their expertise, energy and enthusiasm.

My heartfelt thanks to the writers whose work continues to inspire me, with a special mention for poets Erika Denham, Beau CC, Zach Jackson, Julie Mullen and Peter Blaker; the talented Solitary Writers, the fabulous Dorset Chapter of the RNA and the gifted Jan Gardiner. I'm grateful to the many people who shine thoughts and encouragement in my direction on a daily basis: artists Sarah Eddy, Rach Cornish and Pete O' Sullivan; Sarah and Jim Forbes, Jonno Watts, Tony and Kim Leigh, Erika and Rich Linney, Shaz Godfrey, Shaz Kemp, Angela and Norman Hill, Ellen Simpson, Kay Graymore, Steve Ford, Susie Honnor, Ian Wellens, Ruchi Singh, Slawka G Skarso.

Love and thanks for your warmth, humour and kindness to the Liverpool legends: Jan and Rog G, Jan M, Ken, Trish, Bill and so many more who are in my heart. Special thanks to Katie Holmes Beauty and Massage, to my Spanish teacher Ingrid and to all my wonderful neighbours.

Finally, affection and thanks to Liam and Cait who inspire everything I do and to Big G, who keeps my head in the air and my feet on the ground. Love to you all.

To Liam and Cait, always.

Chapter One

I haven't touched the black coffee I poured half an hour ago, or the scrambled eggs. I really don't have a hangover after Demi's wedding, although it was certainly a day to remember. The string quartet playing Vivaldi was hilarious, Adie raising a champagne glass, acting the distinguished father of the bride, while my sister Bonnie sobbed in the corner and drank too many cocktails. She left him two days before Demi's wedding after finding lipstick smudges on his shirt collar again. I told her it would be a bad idea to go back to him, and she gave me the usual reply: 'But he needs me, Georgie.' So I dragged her on the dance floor to bop to Aerosmith and watched helpless while she threw up outside in the lush grounds of the spectacular Cheshire mansion. Of course, Adie, the brother-in-law from hell, sidled over and led her away, promising to look after her forever, and I was left by myself in the bar.

Then I was accosted by a man with a neatly clipped beard who tried to smooch with me to 'Lay Lady Lay', breathing down my ear like an asthmatic bloodhound. Not flattering, not even for a fifty-five-year-old woman who's been single for almost six years and has hardly had a second look from a decent man in all that time. Not that I'm interested. I ditched the snorting bloodhound on the dance floor, strutted past Demi and Kyle, who were swaying together, their eyes locked, oblivious to the mayhem caused by her philandering father, and took a taxi all the way back home to Liverpool. It was a costly evening all round.

This morning, my head aches so badly because I'm worried about my daughter and my sister. It's ten o'clock and Jade didn't come home last night. She left the wedding straight after the church service, wrinkling her nose and telling me she was going to a proper party where there'd be young people, not ageing has-beens making fools of themselves. Jade's often out until two in the morning but seldom all night, and she's not answering my texts, which is unusual. Bonnie's keeping quiet, too – no reply to my six messages over the last hour. I assume my sister has a hangover and is still asleep. I expect she's gone home with Adie. It wouldn't surprise me if she was stifled in their airless bedroom, lying pale in the four-poster with the curtains drawn while Adie hovers overhead, fangs at the ready, rubbing his hands together with glee.

Jade's twenty-four: she knows she can do as she pleases but I'm becoming concerned. She often comes in late on a Saturday night after hours of non-stop clubbing, but not much gets in the way of her Sunday morning muesli and a 10-k run. Apart from the half-marathon she's preparing for, she works as a personal trainer, so she knows the value of sleep and a good breakfast. I pour more coffee and breathe in roasted beans.

I'm in a soft dressing gown to my ankles and furry boot slippers. I look a mess. My hair's sticking out, dried with hairspray and sweat from last night's dancing. My skin feels slack, like it doesn't fit the bones in my face. I do a reasonable impression of Marge Simpson, but it's nothing I can't fix with an hour in the gym, a shower and a bit of TLC. I check my phone again, and then push the half-eaten breakfast away from me. I wonder why I thought I wanted scrambled eggs. I smile to myself. It's the same thing with men: appetising and desirable at first glance, then too hot, then too tepid and finally unpalatable. I pour more coffee and check my phone again. The screen is blank and I feel the same way.

I go down to the basement where the gym is: *Jade's Gym*, where she brings clients for one-to-one fitness coaching. I close my eyes and remind myself that although I've lost Terry forever, the divorce gave me a four-storey semi-detached house with a huge mortgage, so that I can run my own business and Jade's, too. My salon's on the ground floor with a gravel parking space outside. The kitchen and lounge with the raised garden behind ageing French windows are on the first floor and there are three bedrooms at the top. *Beauty Within* was my choice of name, because it's a beauty salon within my house: 5 Albert Drive. A lovely part of Liverpool: trendy and a little bohemian at the same time. Perfect for me. Jade and I revel in the fact that we don't even have to open the front door to go to work, except to let in clients.

It hasn't always been that way. After all the dives and sweatshops I've worked in since I was eighteen, painting nails and waxing legs all hours of the day and late into the evening, pacifying fretting clients and fussy bosses, I'm grateful to have my own business, even if it's sometimes a struggle to make ends meet.

I spend ten minutes on the exercise bicycle and realise that I did drink too much last night. The wheels are spinning and so are the walls. I heave myself out of the saddle and crawl up three floors to my bedroom, shower, make myself presentable then check the time and the phone for messages. Nothing from Jade or Bonnie. It's 11.30. I have to go out. I throw some things in a shopping bag, pull on a warm coat in dusky pink and some black boots and I'm off, striding across the park. I should make it for midday.

It's glorious outside: a beautiful March morning, early spring, and the park is a flurry of flowers, purple crocuses and a blanket of bluebells. The sky is pale blue and little clouds float across like toy yachts. There are the usual Sunday dog walkers: a black-clad Goth woman with a white wolf on a lead; a couple with a brown mongrel, clearly too in love to notice the dog running in circles and lifting its leg against a tree. I push my hands deep into my pockets, feel the breeze whisk my hair and tickle my cheek, enjoying the satisfying crunch of gravel beneath my boots. I may be fifty-five and unloved, but I try to cut a stylish figure. It's important to me as a beauty therapist to look as good as I can, even if no one's interested. I keep my hair smart, a rich honey blonde, and my teeth are in good working order. I had a smile that could light up a room, once upon a time.

I turn into a row of terraces just five minutes' walk from the park. These houses have a history. Once grand, later dishevelled, they now provide cheap accommodation and a good income for private landlords. I take out my key, ring the bell three times, which is my signal, and open the door.

Nan's in her usual place, by the gas fire, wearing the same old baggy brown cardigan. Uncle Wilf's. She has a dark green woolly hat on and tufts of white hair stick out around her face. She's sparrow-like behind black-framed glasses, with huge watery eyes, baggy tights and fluffy slippers. There's a mug of beer on the table next to her, and a half-empty bottle of Guinness. She struggles to get up, pushing her hands on the chair arms to stand as tall as she can, and despite my protests, she heaves herself upright – five-feet tall now – to give me a hug. I pull her to me and her bones are as light as a chicken's. She smells of Pears soap, beer and something musty like riverbeds.

'How are you, Nanny?' I say.

'Did you remember to order next week's groceries on the line? Did you bring the extra Guinness? I'm getting a bit low.'

I start to empty the bag: beer, biscuits, cake, fruit, chocolate. She grabs my hand. Hers is thin-skinned – purple veins and brown blotches.

'Oh, you're my good girl, Georgina.'

'Cup of tea, Nan?'

'A Guinness'd be better, love.'

'You drink too much, Nan.'

'So the doctor says. But it keeps me company. Besides, Guinness is good for you. They say so on the telly.'

I bustle about and notice the photos on her mantelpiece either side of the loud clock need dusting. Taking a tissue from the box beside her chair, I pick each one up carefully and wipe the glass. There's a black-and-white photo, all smiles: Nanny and her husband, Wilf Basham, who was my mum's elder brother. She's my aunt but everyone calls her nan, never Aunty Anne or even Aunty Nan any more. A few years older than my mum would've been, she's eighty-eight, but made of stronger stuff than either her husband, who died five years ago, or my poor mother, who never made it close to sixty. There are two photos of her wedding in a time when fashions were puffy dresses with petticoats under ballooning skirts. Uncle Wilf has the slicked-back hair of a Teddy boy and a long jacket, his face as serious as an undertaker's.

I pick up another photo of Nan with my mum, Josie,

5

my dad, Kenny and Wilf. Mum's dark-haired, like Bonnie, although Mum's is cut short and backcombed, 1960s style; Dad is fair like me, same straight nose and a too-wide grin. They're laughing, enjoying the caravan holiday Nan is always reminiscing about in North Wales, smiles stuck to their faces as if it were their happiest moment.

I turn back to Nanny Basham. She has froth on her upper lip and is grinning at her Guinness, her eyes shining like a naughty child's behind thick-lensed glasses.

'Your shopping will be here tomorrow first thing, Nan. The supermarket man will bring it in for you but you'll have to put the frozen stuff in the big freezer immediately. And sort out the fridge stuff. I'll put everything else away on Tuesday. And I brought you a Sunday dinner, the ones in the box with the Yorkshires. You like those, don't you? Shall I put it in the oven now?'

She nods and slurps again. 'Put the telly on, Georgina, will you, love? There's a football game on in a bit. My Wilf always loved to watch the Reds on a Sunday afternoon. I like to see all those lads running about in their little shorts with their skinny legs.'

She settles in her chair and I set to making her lunch. The screen rattles in the background and Nan giggles, poised like a queen, waving the remote like a sceptre.

An hour passes quickly, plates clanging and Nan sucking gravy and demanding another Guinness. I glance at the phone screen as I clear away her lunch and wipe up the dishes. There's still nothing from my sister or my daughter. Nanny's performing one of her monologues in the next room, reminiscing, leaving me a split second to answer after each rant. She's still in the armchair, in front of the television, a steaming cup of tea in her hands, warming her fingers.

'Your mother wouldn't have liked it, Georgina. I mean,

Josie's not here to see it but, God bless her, she'd have spoken her mind, that's for sure.'

'I know, Nan—'

'In our day, we thought marriage was for life.'

'Like a sentence for murder?' I shout from the little kitchen. She doesn't hear.

'All this chopping and changing partners. Like a bloody barn dance. At least Bonnie's stuck with her man.'

I mutter, 'He's sticking his arms round other women. She's stuck it for over twenty-five years. It's time they became unstuck, Nan.' Again, she doesn't hear.

'Mind you, I don't like that Adie Carrick. I liked Terry Wood, though. He was a nice lad. Your Jade's just like him, you know.'

I'd been fond of him, too. I breathe out and glance at my phone again. 'Unreliable, you mean?' No texts, no messages.

I dry my hands and go back to the lounge. She's calling to me, her eyes on the television.

'Good-looking, both of them, father and daughter. Fit, well made. She's the image of him. Same violet eyes. You should have hung on to him, Georgina.'

I sit down and shrug. 'He took off with another woman, Nan. Remember? Alison with the little rabbity face. Seriously, she even dresses like Jessica Rabbit. Tight outfits, silly posh voice. She thinks she's sex on legs. He thinks so, too.'

'Where did he move to?'

'Ealing. Where the comedies come from.'

I'm looking at the back of her head. She's still staring at the television.

'He has a little lad now?' she asks.

'You know he does. He must be four years old or thereabouts.'

She turns to me and frowns.

7

'He's called Arran. Like the sweater.'

She nods and drains her tea, puts the cup back on the table and inspects the empty Guinness glass.

'You'll come over on Tuesday then, Georgina?'

'Like always, Nan. I'll bring you a few extra things.'

'I'd like some of those double-chocolate biscuits with the white bits in them.'

'All right, Nan.'

'And . . .' She raises the empty bottle.

'All right, Nan.'

'It's the second half now. We're playing the blue ones and they're losing by a goal. The ones in blue are from London. There's a nice little one though, very cute. Dark hair in a knot on top of his head. He's about to hit the bar. Watch a minute.'

I lean on her chair and stare at the screen. After some nifty footwork, an earnest-looking little man in a blue jersey with his hair pulled back from his face cracks a shot against the post. The ball slams hard and the wood snaps like it might split. The little footballer puts his hands to his head and gazes up at the sky.

'How did you know that was about to happen?'

She grins, her lips wet with the last of the Guinness. 'It's yesterday's game. It's a repeat. They're showing it again. Cheap telly. You off now?'

'Yes, Nan.'

'I'll see you on Tuesday, will I, Georgina? Let yourself out.'

'Righto, Nan.' I turn to go and she fumbles with the empty glass.

'One more of these?'

'You've had two.'

'Another one makes three. I can still count. I'm not drunk yet, am I? Or demented.'

I shrug and go to the kitchen, wave an opener at the serrated lid and bring in a fresh bottle. I kiss the top of her woollen hat.

'You warm enough, Nan?'

'Just about. The heating's expensive so I keep it on low.' She glances up and her eyes narrow, crafty as a fox's 'You don't want to worry about me, Georgina. I'm all right.' She stares right into my eyes. 'I'm not the only one who's lonely, misses a bit of company.'

I shrug on the pink woollen coat, pull my boots on. 'I'm not lonely.'

'Get away with you,' she chuckles. 'I can smell it on you. You think you're independent. But you're getting older and you have nobody to care about you. Jade'll be off soon enough, you mark my words. And you'll be all by yourself, watching telly by yourself every night, cold and thinking about the past and all the opportunities you missed, with no one to talk to. You know, Georgina, what you really need is a bloody good—'

'I'm off now. See you on Tuesday, Nan. Enjoy the football.'

'It's getting interesting now. The little dark-haired one is mustard. He's got the ball again. He's running with it. He's a little whirlwind. He's going to shoot. He gets a goal in a minute. We draw with them, two-all in the end.'

'Bye, Nanny.'

I close the door behind me with a snap, put the key in my pocket and smile to myself. It's the same every Sunday – Nan grumbling about the food and her aches and pains – and Tuesdays and Fridays aren't much better. But she's part of my routine and I'm used to it. I suppose I even like it. Nan's one of those strong women, full of determination and sharp of tongue, although she's becoming frail now. I head towards the park and check my phone but no one's called or messaged. It's ten past three. Nanny didn't say thanks for lunch. But then, she never does.

Chapter Two

As I walk through the park, the sound of a police car siren drifts from the road. I shiver and automatically check my phone. Still no messages – I'm worried. My heart's started to squeeze itself tight like a soft rubber ball in my chest. I give in: I press buttons with my thumb to dial. After a few seconds, Jade's voice is loud in my ear. 'What is it, Mum?' I wonder why I didn't phone her before. Of course, I know why. I don't want another Jade tirade, accusing me of being the embarrassing smothering mother. I hear a sharp intake of breath at the other end.

She says, 'What's the problem?'

'I was just wondering where you are—'

She puffs out air. Her way of telling me I'm exasperating; my maternal concern has annoyed her. 'I'm with friends. But last night I—'

'Last night you what?'

'Never mind, Mum. I'll be home later.' There's a pause; I'm waiting for her to tell me more. 'Is there anything the matter?'

'No, Jade. I just wanted to make sure you . . .' I've already said too much.

'Fine, I'll see you later, okay?'

The phone clicks before I have time to reply. I'm pleased she's all right but there's the sinking feeling that I've interfered where I shouldn't. I play back the call in my head. She's told me nothing, except that she's not happy that I've phoned and that something may have happened last night. At least I know she's all right. I try to infer something from her words: where she was, who she might have been with, and there are no answers. Just my imagination overloading me with worrying images: Jade drinking too much; in clubs with the wrong sort of people; the wrong sort of men; the wrong man. I remind myself she's streetwise; she's at a friend's, staying over, celebrating or sleeping it off. But something wriggles, niggles: mother's instinct, perhaps, or just plain worry. I put my phone back in my pocket and try to put my fears away with it. They stay in my mind, buzzing like flies on a hot day.

I pick up my pace. I'm not far from home and, in my mind, I already have the kettle on. Maybe I'll cook something nice for Jade, for when she comes in. I've decided some nourishing soup will do her good after being out on the town all night. In our house, food has always been part of the family culture: something to share, to nourish, to make with love for those we care about. My grandmother's recipe for Scouse was passed down to my mum and to Nan. There wasn't much money in our house, but my parents would offer a good meal to anyone who came to the door. We'd all sit round the table, chattering and laughing, and I try to keep the tradition: the family who eats together stays together. Of course, that's no longer true in my case with Terry gone, but I try to make sure everyone who sits at my table shares food and drink and feels welcome.

As I approach my house, I walk under a hazel tree.

Little golden catkins are beginning to form. I turn into the drive, my boots crunching on gravel. My car's parked outside and it's comforting to see the sturdy profile, the 2010 black BMW X5. It was an extravagant buy but it always felt safer to be driving alone inside something solid and strong. Like driving inside Iron Man's suit, protected and smart at the same time. A car with status for a woman with status, I told the handsome young assistant at the garage when I bought it second-hand five years ago. Having an ex who works in computers has had its uses although, in truth, once I'd paid the deposit on the house, there was nothing left of the divorce settlement. I struggle to make ends meet each month, but there's always just enough to pay my assistant Amanda and Jade, to meet the mortgage and to put food on the table. I manage: I'm in control of my destiny, that's what's most important. On my own, living off my wits. Which is good, of course – I'm inde-pendent and I'm never short of wit.

There's something on the front doorstep, a package. As I approach, I notice it's a bouquet of flowers: roses – red, white and pink – perfect blooms, expensively arranged. I pick them up in both arms like an old-fashioned prima ballerina and bring them to my nose. They have a light, sweet fragrance and I smile. I consider doing a low curtsey but decide against it in the heeled boots.

There's a card, thick and embossed in gold. I pull it out and stare at the words: *Thank you for looking after my Bonnie last night. Adie.* I push the flowers away as if they've started to stink. In a way, they have. I hold them by the stalks, petals hanging down, heavy as a dead rabbit, open the door and march inside. I throw them in the sink and take out my phone. It rings for a while; Bonnie doesn't answer. I wonder if he's tied her up, gagged her. I make myself a cup of tea.

The steaming liquid comforts me. I think back and the images come quickly, remembering when Bonnie first brought Adie home and he was so well mannered and courteous. She'd been gullible with men before Adie, gravitated towards the overconfident type, had her heart broken a few times but moved on quickly enough with encouragement from me.

Adie was different, cunning: he saw Bonnie as a trusting, good-natured clip-on status symbol. I disliked him the first time I saw him and my views never changed. She was shy with him, but I could tell she was smitten, her heart lost in a moment. And Adie was cardboard-stiff in his best suit, like he'd just stepped down from the witness box, straight-faced and slimy, taking a slice of cake and murmuring, 'You make the best gateau in Liverpool, Mrs Turner.' Bonnie had giggled into her hand and turned shining eyes on him, as if he were a saint.

I was going out with a drummer called Magic who played in The Shipperies every Sunday night, wore eyeliner and looked like a Greek god. I had no time for my sister's creepy suitor. As she poured tea, my mother said, 'And what do you do, Adrian?' His smile was just teeth and no expression in the eyes. 'I buy old property, do it up and sell it on, make money.' Bonnie was all breath and excitement. My mum managed to make it to their wedding, but she wasn't well. She died a few years after that. She'd have hated to see Bonnie now.

I was a godparent at Demi's christening seven years after they were married. Jade was two years old, wriggling and bawling in Terry's arms all the way through the starched service. Bonnie hovered by the altar in a pink fitted suit and heels, nervous with little Demi Adrienne in her arms, the tiny baby swathed in metres of shining silk looking like the Christ child, while Adie shook the vicar's hand and whispered, 'Thanks for letting me have the Saturday afternoon slot at such short notice. I'll give you a cheque for the Orphans of Somalia. Will a grand be enough?' I saw Terry's face. He didn't like Adie either: he found him too competitive, too flash, whereas Terry was laid-back, good-natured, kind.

Then years later, Bonnie became thinner because Adie said he preferred women to be fashionably slim and she started to wear dresses that came to her knees because he said he liked his women tastefully glamorous. He paid for Dad's funeral eight years ago and Terry hung back in the corner staring at guests he'd never seen before, his hands in his pockets, while Adie told everyone he'd given his beloved father-in-law the sending-off he deserved.

I sat with Nanny Basham in a corner while she'd cradled a bottle of brandy and sobbed, telling me about Dad and Mum and Wilf, the good times I'd heard about a hundred times before. Terry grumbled afterwards that he'd never had respect for Adie. That was something we agreed on. Adie Carrick was only out for himself. Bonnie was just a trophy, his in-laws just an opportunity to show how magnanimous he was.

Demi went to a private school, where she was demure in a grey blazer and tartan skirt. Jade was popular at the local comprehensive; it was a good school and she was sporty and bright, but Adie insisted on making comparisons. 'You get what you pay for in this life.'

I always replied, 'I'm not having my child at school with kids whose parents are politicians and gangsters.'

I'll never forget how he looked at me. Eyes like bullets. Then Terry moved out. We'd been arguing a lot. I'd been doing the arguing; Terry retreated into himself: he met Rabbity Alison and the rest is history. I became Georgie Turner again, not Georgie Wood. After Terry left me, Adie

15

squeezed my arm one day when I was making coffee in Bonnie's kitchen, his lips against my ear. 'If you need any money, Georgie, just say. We're family, and family sticks.' But I walked away, stared through the window at the patio and the swimming pool complex, and promised myself I'd manage just fine without his charity.

Meanwhile, Bonnie stayed in the background smiling sadly; years passed and she became quieter, more timid. Then she found lipstick on his collar, not her shade, and suggestive messages on his phone. A year later, there was a lacy G-string in his car. He claimed he knew nothing about it, then he suddenly remembered he'd lent the car to a friend the night before. I'd have left Adie for that, but Bonnie swore it was a one-time incident, she'd been neglecting him, it'd never happen again: he loved her.

Of course, Adie simpered, playing the part of the trustworthy brother-in-law; he told me that now I was by myself, now my man had left me, he'd keep an eye out for me, or lend me money. As he turned away, I pointed down my throat with two fingers and thought I'd rather roll naked in the gutter. I'm not afraid of Adie Carrick. I've never liked him or the way he treats my good-natured sister. I have suspicions about the property he buys and sells, and the money he makes, which seems to slide through his fingers like poker chips.

I put the mug down and reach for my phone. A text has come in: it's from Bonnie. I read it, hoping for the best but expecting the worst. Of course, I'm right. *Adie and I have decided to give it another go. We're off to a spa hotel for a week. See you soon.* I throw the phone on the table and put my head in my arms. I picture them both, driving from Frodsham in his Boxster to an expensive hotel in Cheshire. She'll have a facial there, paying ten times as much as I charge downstairs for a better

16

aromatherapy one; he'll have a full body massage from some young girl in a white overall with make-up as thick as a death mask, who giggles at his anecdotes about how hard he works for his money and how he dines on yachts with film stars.

I imagine Bonnie and Adie at a linen-covered table that evening, fresh from their treatments, him devouring bleeding steak, while she pushes salad leaves around a plate and frets about the four-poster room they'll slink off to after he's guzzled another bottle of Beaujolais. Suddenly I feel tired. Tired and glad I'm single. Tired, glad I'm single and yet not altogether sure. I rub my eyes and a feeling of misery lands on my shoulders and sinks into my muscles like cement. I shake off the loneliness, smear a lipstick smile on my face and set to making some supper for Jade and myself. At least we'll have a pleasant evening together.

By ten thirty, the pan of chowder is cold, a translucent skin settled on the surface. The banana cake I've made is untouched and I'm sitting in front of the television, my glass empty after two gin and tonics. A key rattles in the front door and I jerk myself bolt upright.

Seconds later, I beam at Jade, who's surveying me with arms folded and a frown on her face. She looks cold in the short dress and skimpy jacket she wore to the wedding. Her dark burgundy hair is well cut and hangs perfectly, glossy as glass, framing her face, and her eyes are round, dark velvet and soft as a doe's. I grin, make my voice bright.

'I made some lovely chowder. Sit down, love. I'll bring you some.'

I recognise the glare. She's about to tell me not to bother but she's starving – she probably hasn't eaten all day – so she flops down from full height onto the sofa, ignores me and stares at the television. I know this is the sign for me

17

to bring her food, to wait for the right moment to ask how she is. Or, as usual, I won't wait, I'll ask the wrong questions, she'll bite off my head and then there'll be an argument.

She sits with the tray on her knee, spooning a stream of soup without shifting her gaze from the screen. She's pretending to be glued to the new serial about a cop whose wife has been abducted, determined to ignore me, concentrating on waving the spoon towards her face. She clanks the cutlery against the bowl and starts on the banana cake, her movements automatic, her eyes hypnotised, staring at the television. She finishes eating and I wait for a few seconds.

'Cup of tea?'

She waits a few more seconds.

'Whatever. If you're having one.'

I use the interlude as the kettle boils in the kitchen to decide what to say, how to be subtle and frame my questions. Then I march into the lounge, put the cup between her hands and blurt out, 'So, where the hell have you been since yesterday afternoon?'

I expect her to ignore me or shout at me. Or ignore me then start shouting. I glance at her and I have to focus my eyes to believe what I'm seeing from my usually tough daughter. A tear is rolling down her face. She sniffs and wipes it away with the back of her hand. Another tear tumbles and her voice is tiny.

'I wouldn't expect you to know what I feel . . .'

I rush over to her. 'Jade . . .'

She holds out a hand to push me away. 'Don't start, Mum.'

'What's happened?'

'I've been with friends since this afternoon. I had to talk to someone who'd understand . . .'

18

'Are you in trouble, Jade?'

'No, no, it's all right . . .'

I'm next to her, sitting on the chair arm, trying to hug her. She's twisting away, furious, her hand over her face, making all the signs that she doesn't want me to ask her anything. So, naturally, I persist.

'Jade, what's happened? Where have you been all night? Has something bad happened? Has someone hurt you? If they have, I swear I'll—'

She gulps. 'I'm all right, Mum.'

I put my hands on my hips, stand upright. 'I can see you're not. You're upset. I'm not having this. Come on – out with it. Has someone . . .?'

She stares up and the anger in her eyes dissolves. Her lip trembles and I squat down, take her hands.

'Jade . . .?'

She shakes her head. 'You wouldn't understand, Mum.'

'Why not?'

'You just wouldn't. You're not the type. You wouldn't get it.'

'Try me.' I squeeze her hands in mine. With effort, I make my voice soft. 'What is it, sweetheart? You can tell me anything.'

Her eyes meet mine and I notice tears, huge spheres swelling and tipping over. Then she swallows, takes a breath.

'I've met someone.'

'And?' I lean forwards.

'And nothing.' Her breath shudders. 'I just met someone. I know that he's the right one for me. I'm sure.'

A motor seems to rev and roar in the vicinity of my heart, a loud, fierce engine, and my mind accelerates with it. So does my mouth. My hands grab her shoulders.

'Oh. I see. You've met a man. And I suppose he's married,

19

is that it? He loves you but he won't leave his little wifey? Is that how it goes? Some two-timing, sneaky—'

'Mum.' She wriggles away from me. 'I knew you wouldn't understand.'

I feel my face become hot and I take a deep breath. 'Sorry, Jade. I didn't mean to go off the deep end. I just worry.'

'I'm twenty-four.'

I take a moment, smile, beam, try to make my face resemble an Oscar winner in the middle of paparazzi. 'I'm so glad you met someone, love. So, tell me all about him.' She frowns; her eyebrows cross suspiciously, so I grin even more. 'I'm all ears.'

She waits for ten seconds, another ten, then her voice is quiet. 'I met him at a private party. We spent yesterday evening and the whole of last night together.'

I'm about to jump in with a comment about it all being a bit sudden and then hit her with the follow-up remark about contraception and STIs, but I clamp my lips together and wait. She snuffles.

'We were together briefly this morning. He stayed on to be with me. We talked and talked. He's amazing, Mum. Kind and sweet and really nice. And we both said it together. It's been instantaneous for us both and we both know it's right.' She checks my expression and I make sure I'm not doing my cynical face. I'm doing my happy-adoring-approving-Mum face. She whispers, 'We love each other.'

My cheeks ache with grinning and I need to relax them by speaking, so I say, 'That's wonderful, Jade.' I pause, hoping she notices my full, unswerving support, then I try again. 'So, why so sad?'

The tears tumble again and she's sobbing too hard to find breath to talk. I hug her and she leans on my shoulder.

My neck has become damp and she whispers, 'It's awful, Mum. He's gone back home. I won't be able to see him often. He's away a lot of the time. It's his job.'

I try not to say that absence is a positive, to tell her the cliché that it makes the heart grow fonder. I don't know what to say, so I settle for, 'Is he in the army, then?'

She shakes her head. 'No, Mum. It's worse than that.'

My mind is filling with all sorts of frightening scenarios. She's fallen in love with a gangster. Drug dealer. Long-distance lorry driver. Illegal immigrant. Travelling salesman. Undercover investigator. Tramp.

I opt for something positive and safe and ask, 'Is he an airline pilot?' and wait until her sobs subside.

Then she whispers, 'No, Mum. He lives in Brighton, works in London. He travels all over the country, all the time. He trains every day, all hours, all week, plays games all over the world. I'll hardly ever see him. His job is his life . . . He's a professional footballer.'

Chapter Three

Business is frantic for the whole week in the salon. Although Jade has several clients in the gym each day, she spends most of her time ringing and texting her new boyfriend. I even hear her speaking Spanish to him, although I'm sure that's for my benefit, as I know her Spanish isn't fluent, given her compulsively bad behaviour in modern languages when she was at school. My friend Amanda, who trained as a beauty therapist with me years ago, is my full-time assistant in the salon. She and I are working through a fully booked schedule, doing manicures, pedicures, massages, tanning, waxing. It's non-stop.

By Friday, we've hardly had time for a natter, so I suggest we have lunch upstairs together, especially since Jade is down below in the gym doing one-to-one isometrics with an amateur racing cyclist who's just turned forty and wants to improve his chances of winning races. Amanda and I go up to the kitchen and I make us a salad sandwich and a cup of tea. She holds up her hands and examines her chipped nails.

'I'm owed a manicure on the house, Georgie. Look at the state of these nails. I look like an alley cat.'

I put a coffee down in front of her and smile as she attacks it with relish. She's been my friend since we were at college together and we share so much history. I watch her hunched over the table, her shoes off, wriggling her pink painted toes, her feet stretched out at the end of bright orange-and-black leggings. Her hair is long, wavy and intensely red; although, as she's told me several times, the bottle proclaimed it was cherry copper. She has laughing blue eyes and loves to wear colourful clothes. 'Unless I'm avoiding a fella. In which case it's the SAS jumpsuit and a balaclava.' Amanda's been married twice and she's now living with a firefighter called Rhys, whom she claims is the love of her life. Where romance is concerned, she's a self-proclaimed expert.

She waves a hand. 'The problem is, Georgie – we need more help in the treatment room and Jade's too loved-up to get her backside in gear. I mean, I've worked with you here for what? Five years? How many days have I missed?'

'Two. Both hangovers.'

'I know,' she sighs. 'But, I'm always here to work, always good old Amanda ready to paint someone's nails and dye their eyelashes, spray them fifty shades of orange. We're flat out, you and me. Where's Jade? When she's finished with the client downstairs, she'll be back on the phone again.'

I sigh. 'She's in love.'

'My point entirely.' Amanda holds up an empty plate. I dump a sandwich on it and she tackles it instantly. 'Love should make people happy. If she's in love, why is she so miserable?'

'He plays football in London.' I shake my head. 'She can't stop thinking about him, bless her.' I mimic her low voice and pucker my lips. '*Te extraño cariño*.'

'And what on earth does that mean?'

23

'She misses him, I think. I've heard her say it a dozen times. It's so unlike Jade to mope about a man.'

'I know. And she's always on the phone to him.'

I sigh. 'All the time. She's going to see him later tonight. Perhaps it'll cheer her up.'

'Where's she off to?'

'Brighton. He lives in a little village by the coast. She'll be on the three o'clock train. Then she's going to London to watch him play in a game tomorrow. She's not back until Monday night. I've had to move all of her appointments.'

Amanda shakes her head. 'Let's hope he's good-looking and loaded.'

'Let's hope he doesn't let her down.' I fold my arms. 'Or he'll have me to deal with, Spanish superstar or not.'

'He's called Luis, Mum.'

Amanda and I turn round together and our faces flush like two red lollipops. My daughter's leaning against the doorpost. I wait for hell to break out and mutter, 'Sorry, Jade – I didn't—'

But she's all smiles. 'You'll have to meet him. He's lovely. I know you'll adore him. His English isn't so bad and he's so cute and funny.'

'As long as you don't get hurt, Jade.'

'I'm fine, Mum. I told you. He's the one.'

Amanda chips in. 'Your mum's only saying – it's all been a bit quick.'

Jade throws her head back, laughs out loud. 'And this from the woman who's had how many husbands and affairs?'

Amanda waggles her head. 'When you're a mum, you'll understand.'

'I thought you didn't have any kids, Amanda.' Jade's as sharp as glass this afternoon.

I make the peace by hugging my daughter. 'You have a lovely time this weekend.'

'I'll do my best. I have to travel from Brighton to London in a special car tomorrow. Luis's on the team coach. I won't see much of him all day. But we'll make up for it tomorrow night.'

I stare at her and think about calling her a brazen hussy but I clamp my lips together and try to remember what it was like to be in love. I certainly don't remember being so open about my sex life. I say, 'That's nice, love.'

Jade's beaming. 'Right. I'm going to get ready. I'll take a taxi to the station. Luis'll meet me at the other end. We're going somewhere glamorous over the weekend so I'll need *clothes*.'

She whirls away and Amanda rolls her eyes and murmurs, 'Fair play. You can't blame her for it. What a dazzling lifestyle.'

I nod. 'What are you up to this weekend?'

She purses her lips. 'Rhys and I are invited to an anniversary party in Blackpool tomorrow night, so I'll need to shop for a new dress.'

I contemplate the weekend that I'll spend by myself, a visit to Nanny Basham tonight and on Sunday, and I wonder what Bonnie's up to, if she's back from the spa hotel and if she's happy. I push my salad sandwich away untouched and Amanda looks at me eagerly. I slide it onto her plate.

It's Saturday morning, clean-up-the-house time, and I'm hoovering four floors for all I'm worth. I push the nozzle in all corners, my arms extended as if I'm part of the machine: I am Hoover Woman. I have the radio turned up loud, my hair knotted into a floppy scarf, and I'm wearing a baggy T-shirt, leggings and no shoes, singing at the top of my voice. I climb to the top floor and hoover the three bedrooms, then I clean the hallway and the kitchen on the second floor, as well as the living room overlooking the raised garden.

I work my way down to the salon at ground level, the three little treatment rooms, the tanning booth, the reception area with the soft sofas, the gurgling pebble fountain and the stone Buddha. Finally, I'm in the basement, in Jade's gym with music playing through speakers. Cobwebs have gathered in the corners and the main area smells of fetid sweat, testosterone and men's underpants: a stench that I know hasn't come from Jade. I resolve to spray some sweet pea room fragrance in the air later; although Jade'll sniff it out when she's back and tell me it's highly inappropriate. Most of her one-to-one sessions are either undersized or ridiculously muscly middle-aged men.

I'm hoovering under the gym machinery and I notice a spider or two beneath the benches. They've expired and become crusty and dry, many legs in the air, so I bend down, nozzle arched, to commit them to dust. My back is flexible and it's not hard to reach the corners. I view it as good exercise. My favourite band strikes up the opening chords on the music player. I lift the nozzle as a microphone, wiggle my backside and sing along, bawling at the top of my voice, 'Walk this way.'

Suddenly I freeze. I don't know why. Then I turn round and he's standing there with his arms folded, smiling. Dark hair parted at the side, separated in two thick quiff-shaped tufts, navy jacket, roll-neck sweater, navy trousers. He's pale, shaven so clean his face reminds me of a cricket ball. He's staring at me. I jump and almost scream. I'm so glad I don't.

'How the hell did you get in?'

He smirks. 'The front door was open.'

I glare at him. 'Well? What can I do for you, Adie?'

He looks me up and down and his mouth is half-snarl, half-smile.

'Bonnie sent me over.'

I can hardly imagine that. I lean against the hoover pipe, nozzle in the air, and stare at him like I'm Joan of Arc with my flexible lance.

'Did she?'

He smirks. 'She wants you to come over to lunch. I thought I'd come and pick you up.' He surveys my head-scarf, my bare feet, everything in between. 'You look as if you need taking out of here to somewhere civilised. A light lunch, a chat, two sisters together.'

I wonder why she didn't ring or text. Perhaps I missed it. I close my eyes and think for a moment.

'I can take my own car.'

He shakes his head. 'Bonnie insisted. Have a glass of wine with her. I'll do the taxi-ing. Anyway, I'm here now.' He frowns at the leggings. 'You'll need to get changed.'

I want to see Bonnie. I'll put up with the bloodsucker husband from here to Frodsham. Half an hour's drive.

I nod. 'You can wait in the car, then. I'll be five minutes.'

He sits down on one of the benches, adjusts the back flap of his jacket, makes himself comfortable.

'I'll be all right here.' He sniffs the air around me. 'Make it ten minutes, Georgie. Have a shower.'

Standing outside the oak front door, Bonnie looks pallid and slender in a filmy dress and heels; her hair is glossy, curled in soft ringlets. She smiles and puts her arms round my neck.

'Thanks for coming, Georgie. Adie and I had such a great time at the spa. I was so looking forward to chatting to you about it.'

She glances over my shoulder – I can feel the tension in her arms. Adie's behind us, having parked the car.

He smirks. 'I have a meeting in my office, Bonnie. I don't want to be disturbed. You girls have a nice lunch together. I ordered in the Chablis and the smoked salmon specially.'

He saunters away, snake hips, hooded eyes, leaving the pungent smell of expensive aftershave in the air.

Bonnie takes my hand. 'Come on, Georgie.'

I whisper, 'I thought you were dumping him?'

She shrugs. 'I'm not strong like you. And he needs me. He said so.'

I sigh loudly and we walk into the dining room, with high glass windows, a magnificent carved wood table. The view outside is of a vast clipped lawn, birds swirling around a feeder: blue tits, robins. Huge poplar trees frame the windowpane, and the steady dark roof of the swimming pool and leisure centre. I frown at my plate, slivered salmon and rocket. Bonnie fills two crystal glasses with pale wine. We both poke at the fish with silver forks, two mirror images. I break the silence.

'So, tell me about the spa hotel, Bon.'

'It was lovely.'

'What treatments did you get?'

She sighs. 'A pedicure, a massage. A facial where they put little needles in the skin.'

I nod. 'Abrasion therapy. I've seen the machines they use. I'd love one but they're expensive.'

She shakes her head. 'I felt like I'd hugged a hedgehog by the time the therapist had finished with me.' She lifts her head. 'Does my skin look better?'

'Marvellous.' I wonder if she should've had a tan. She's pale as a gravestone. I gulp some wine and ask the question. 'So, did Adie behave himself?'

She frowns, a little crease between her eyes. 'How do you mean?'

'Oh, for God's sake, Bonnie. How many other women have there been? You left him. Why the hell did you go back?'

She stiffens, looks perplexed, as if I've made a huge mistake or history has been rewritten. She nibbles a small portion of smoked salmon.

'He apologised. He'll never do it again.'

I put my fork down, sigh, reach for the Chablis. It's cold and I feel the anaesthetic properties start to calm me, making me feel a little bolder and more protective.

'I don't know why you stay with him. He just wants you here as his trophy. The Barbie doll syndrome. Someone to dress up and keep indoors while he's out money laundering.'

She breathes out so loudly it's like a sharp gust of air. 'Georgie, how can you say that?' She clutches the knife and fork with white knuckles. 'Adie worships me. Anyway, when you have a man who'll do for you what he does for me – when you have a man at all, in fact—'

'Don't be naive.'

'I'm not naive. You're jealous.'

'Jealous? Of you living with Shady Adie with the wandering womb weevil? I don't think so.'

'You've never liked him, Georgie.' She's going to cry.

'Right first time. Because he's no good.' For her sake, I'm not holding back.

'Why can't you support me?'

'Because he's dishonest, Bonnie.' There. I've said it: she needs to know.

She pouts. 'He's a successful businessman. A property developer.'

'Have you ever seen any of the properties he dev—'

There's a cough behind me and we both turn. A man in overalls is holding up a paintbrush. He's short, stocky, fifty-something. He raises bushy eyebrows.

'Excuse me, Mrs Carrick. Mr Carrick said I had to ask you about the feature wall in the bedroom. Did you want the new shade of Addiction or the Aubergine Dream?'

She sniffs. 'Addiction.' The decorator turns and shuffles off. 'Adie's left me in charge of Demi and Kyle's extension.'

I gasp. 'They're living here?'

'As soon as they're back from the honeymoon. Just for a while. Until Adie finds them a house on the Wirral.'

'I can't imagine Kyle liking that. Or Demi.'

'Adie said it'll be nice for us all to stay together. They'll have their privacy. And I'm in charge of the decorating.'

I stare at my sister and wave my fork in triumph. 'You just can't see it, can you, Bonnie? He has you all where he can control you. You're just his little pawn.'

'He bought me this.' She whisks up her sleeve.

There's a gold charm bracelet, loaded with shiny charms. She pushes her hand under my nose and I stare at the delicate gold shapes swinging: numbers, a flower, a crown, a mass of other tinkling trinkets.

I shake my head. 'That wasn't cheap.'

She looks directly in my eyes. 'He said I'm worth the expense.'

I exhale. 'It must give you a carpal tunnel problem . . .'

'He made me promise never to take it off, Georgie. It's a symbol of his love. Eternal and precious.'

I snort. 'Did he get it in one of his dodgy deals?'

She opens her mouth to reply but her phone rings. She clutches it like a weapon and walks into another room. I breathe out sharply: I'm annoyed with myself. I should've convinced her calmly to leave him, kept my temper. My concern for my sister has made me outspoken. She's too

30

good for him, trusting and loyal. And here I go again, arguing with her, when all I really want is to protect her. Bonnie's always been good-natured, but she used to have her own personality, a sparkiness, humour. I wonder when she became so dependent, so gullible. What happened to her self-confidence, her self-respect? I drain my glass and pour myself more wine.

Chapter Four

I finish a second glass of Chablis and the sound of heels makes me look up. Her voice is high, aghast, panicking.

'Georgie, I can't believe it.' Bonnie rushes back into the room, waving her phone. She grasps my arm and I'm amazed at the vice-like squeeze. 'Something's happened. I need your advice.' She propels me towards the huge patio doors, heaves one open and thrusts me out into the garden. 'That was Demi.'

I shiver. The grass is damp and my boots sink into the softness of soil. There are snowdrops on the lawn, creamy white, pale orange, a patchwork of colour leading to the swimming pool complex. I imagine how nice it would be to be in their sauna – my skin is suddenly gooseflesh.

Bonnie's eyes are wide. 'Demi rang me.'

'From the three-month Thailand honeymoon?'

She takes my wrist, squeezes the skin.

'She's phoned me to say that she's having such a good time in Thailand, they might go on to Australia and stay for a bit. Isn't that awful? What do you think?'

'They're young. They have no ties. They don't need to rush back.'

'Adie'll be furious – she didn't ask him first.'

'There'll be plenty of time to finish off the decorating in their extension, to paint the feature wall in the new shade of Addiction. Perhaps that's why Demi and Kyle are extending their honeymoon. Perhaps they want to stay away from Adie.'

She wails, 'What about me? I'll miss her. She said they might be away for another three months. What shall I do?'

'I think they've made a good decision, Bon.'

She's staring at me.

'Adie paid a fortune for the refurbishment of the extension for them in time for the summer. A new kitchen, a bathroom suite. He'll be livid.'

I watch my sister and wonder why she's so loyal to him.

'Demi and Kyle want to be together. By themselves. They just got married. It's a good thing, Bonnie.'

Her face crumples and she starts to snuffle. 'My baby's gone . . . All grown up and gone away. Now there's just me.'

I hug her again. I'll give her a few seconds and then I'll suggest she comes to my house, moves into the spare room and starts a new life for herself. Or that she starts to think for herself; that she becomes her own person rather than a cardboard cut-out wife.

I'm about to tell her that it'll all work out for the best, but she pushes me out of the way.

She announces, 'I have to tell Adie,' and her heels are tapping through the breezy patio windows; she's sashaying through the dining room and towards the steps down to the next level, down to Adie's lair below.

I belt after her, leaving the patio door wide and the draught swirling, the cold air wafting above the warmth of the underfloor central heating. I catch up with her at the bottom of the steps, by the big oak door, which is ajar. She's about to knock.

Voices rattle inside. Adie's hushed tones and another voice, a more throaty bark. My fingers close over Bonnie's wrist, stopping her from knocking, and I hold my breath. Adie's said something about handing over money. He won't be able to do it for a week or two. The guttural growler tells him a deal is a deal and there's no room for negotiation. He then raises his voice and I recognise a Scottish accent.

'This is a big investment. You owe me – with interest, Adie.'

The reply is sycophantic, slippery as syrup.

'I won't let you down, Duncan.'

Bonnie's hand has fallen from my grip. She raps softly on oak, then she pushes the door wide. I stare over her shoulder. Inside, the office is all white walls and polished wood. Adie's standing behind his desk, his shoulders hunched. The other man is opposite, staring. He's short but broad-shouldered, around sixty years old, in an expensive checked brown suit, pale red hair curled close to his head. His hands are in his pockets and, as he turns to us, his face hardens for a moment and then relaxes. He surveys Bonnie and beams.

'Well, who do we have here?'

Bonnie is all breath, gushing. 'Demi rang. She and Kyle have some news. Adie, she wants to extend the honey—'

Adie stiffens. 'Not now, darling.' His teeth come together. There's no affection in the endearment. 'I'm busy right now.'

The red-haired man opens his arms wide, palms up, taking over, his expression expansive. He turns to us and smiles. His face is broad, craggy, and his teeth are even. I notice thick eyebrows, red wiry hair, ice blue eyes as he stares from Bonnie to me and back to Bonnie.

'So, you're Mrs Carrick, I presume?'

She extends a hand. 'Bonnie.'

She's done this many times before, the practised smile, the tinkling laugh. Adie's reliable showpiece. I frown and feel protective again.

The man chuckles, his accent strong. 'Bonnie by name and bonnie of face.' He holds her small hand in his large fist. 'Charming. I'm Duncan Beddowes, by the way. I'm sure Adie's mentioned me?'

Bonnie nods, unsure whether it's polite to say yes or be honest and say no.

Beddowes raises his eyebrows towards Adie, who's squirming for some reason.

'You didn't tell me you had such a lovely wife, Adie. You must be proud of such a treasure.'

She shakes her long curls and Adie mumbles something about Mr Beddowes being a business partner. Beddowes is staring at her wrist.

'May I?' He lifts her sleeve and the bracelet gleams underneath. Bonnie stands poker stiff and the man says, 'Oh, well now. Look at this. What a lovely piece. Solid gold.'

'A present from my husband.' Bonnie flushes but Adie has blanched, his face the colour of the walls.

'How very generous of you, Adie. What a wrist full of symbols.'

Adie's about to say something.

The Scot turns to me. 'And are you a friend of the family?'

Something makes me want to say no, just ignore me, I'm the Invisible Woman, but Bonnie's still holding his hand and her eyes dance.

'This is my sister, Georgie. We're having lunch. Would you like to come up and share some smoked salmon? There's plenty left.'

35

The probing blue eyes stare into her face a moment too long, then he says, 'I'd like to stay but, unfortunately, I have to go home.' He nods. 'My wife's expecting me for dinner.'

Adie's hunched behind him, frowning, awkward. Bonnie doesn't notice. Duncan Beddowes delves into his pocket and produces a mobile phone.

'Would you mind if I took your photo, Bonnie, standing here with me? A selfie? And your sister, too? I know my wife would love a picture of you both. She'd be fascinated by your lovely taste in clothes, not to mention that gorgeous piece of jewellery. She'll be very jealous. She's always asking me where I've been, who I've met during the day, and I'll be able to show her.'

Adie shakes his head, just a little, but Bonnie's already posing, beaming, and the man holds his phone in place. He raises his eyebrows and I sidle behind my sister. He sticks a grin on his face and snaps away.

'Oh, that's a nice one. I know Jeanette'll love to see that. Well, Adie, I'll take my leave. It's a long drive back. But I'll be in touch soon. As we agreed.'

They grasp hands for a fleeting moment. Bonnie's delighted; she fingers the charm bracelet and giggles. I bite my lip. I never heard of a man who'd want to show his wife a picture of himself flanked by two unknown women. I take a step back, my instincts shouting that I shouldn't be there at all.

Adie's silent on the journey home. I ask him if he enjoyed the spa hotel and he grunts. I ask about the Scottish man, if he was a regular business partner, one he'd worked with before, and Adie grunts again. For some reason, we drive through Norris Green, although it's not on the way home, and he stops the Boxster outside a terraced house. The sky is splashed with grey, the street lights like soft haloes.

It's late now and the light has faded to a watercolour wash. The terraced houses have bay windows, closed curtains with dim lights, and the road is silent apart from a passing kid on a bike who veers too close to the car.

'I'll only be a minute. I need to see someone. It's business. Keep an eye on the Porsche. Perhaps no one'll steal it if I leave you in it.'

He lifts a small leather case from my footwell and steps outside, moving with fast strides. He rings a bell at a plastic door with no lights inside and someone opens – a tall, slim man in his twenties in a thin T-shirt and cargo pants. In the time it takes me to look at the telegraph wire running between the roofs, where someone has abandoned a battered pair of trainers, their laces tied, swinging from the line in the wind, Adie's back. He shuts the car door with a clunk, pushes his case behind him and starts the engine. We speed away.

'Everything okay?' I ask.

His brow's knotted. 'No, not really. It was to do with my business partner, the one you met, Duncan. I was expecting a payment from the man who lives in that house. I'll have to call back later in the week. A nuisance, that's all.'

I glance out of the window as we turn into another side street. 'Do you have many business partners round here?' I offer my best smirk.

He doesn't glance at me. His eyes are on the road and then, furtively, behind him through the mirror. I try again.

'It's good news about Demi extending the honeymoon and going to Australia.'

He doesn't answer, or even acknowledge that he's heard me. The sky's darker now. Car headlights swerve towards us from the road and I blink. We reach Aigburth and he pulls at the handbrake sharply as we stop outside number 5, Albert Drive. I hope he won't ask to come in, but he's absorbed in something: he seems to be completely uncommunicative. He barely looks at me, so I slither out of the Boxster, bend towards the window from the pavement and say, 'Thanks, Adie.'

He nods once. 'Don't be a stranger, Georgie,' and he's off, leaving me standing with exhaust fumes whirling round my ankles.

I raise my hand, but it isn't to wave goodbye: I clutch my keys. Indoors, I climb the steps to the kitchen and put the kettle on. On my phone, there's a text message from Amanda about a bargain cocktail dress. Nothing from Jade and nothing from Bonnie. I make a cup of tea and put my head in my hands. I'm not really sure what happened today in Adie's office, but my instincts are buzzing like crowding bees and I'm not feeling comfortable. Adie's clearly out of his depth.

The sink is cluttered with bowls: the one I used to make the Yorkshire pudding mix, the one I used to make gravy, plus the saucepans for potatoes and carrots and peas, which are cooked and steaming in a colander. The meat is resting and the Yorkshires have risen. I'm trying to wash the dishes before the hot water runs out.

'There's a lot of clanking about in my kitchen, Georgina.'

'Yes, Nan.'

'And it smells. And there's steam everywhere.'

'I know, Nan.'

'You should've just bought me a dinner in a box again.'

'I thought we could eat Sunday lunch together. I've made Yorkshire puddings from scratch.'

'I'm used to the dinners in a box.'

I sigh. 'I'm just about to bring it out, Nan. Proper gravy. You'll love it.'

'I liked the old food we had best, me and Wilf together. A proper pan of Scouse. I used to make mine with beef, though, not lamb. Lamb hasn't had a life. Carrots, onions, potatoes, an Oxo cube. Lovely. This modern food doesn't taste of anything.'

'I'll bring your roast.'

'Get me a Guinness first, there's a good girl.'

I wash the last of the saucepans in tepid water then lean over to the fridge, pull out a bottle and flip the top. I carry the glass through as I pour and deposit it, full and frothy, in front of Nan, lifting the empty one. She gazes up, her eyes glinting through thick glasses. She has a brown circle, a wide froth of beer, across her top lip.

'Where's this dinner you've been promising me for an hour?'

'Just coming, Nan.'

'I won't eat it if it's cold. I can't stand cold dinner.'

I rattle about in the kitchen, cut meat, pile vegetables and Yorkshires, pour gravy and return with a steaming plate on a tray, settling it on her knee. She sups a noisy mouthful of beer and replaces her glass carefully.

'I can't eat all this.'

'Try your best, Nan.'

'All these Yorkshires.'

'Two?'

'It's not gone cold, has it?'

'Don't burn your mouth, Nan.'

'I don't know why I couldn't just have a dinner in a box.'

I bring my plate and a fork and sit in the other armchair. The television's blaring. It's a sports pundit giving his views on all the clubs in the league table. I fork a piece of Yorkshire pudding to my mouth and chew. It's crispy on the outside and fluffy in the middle.

'Anything good on TV, Nan?'

'The game's on now. London boys against the Southern Saints.'

I wrinkle my nose. 'Will it be any good?'

She has a mouthful of potatoes, making a soft sucking sound.

'I saw it yesterday. The Londoners win three nil. It's a good game. One of the Saints gets sent off. The one with all the yellow hair. He kicks the goalkeeper.'

'You've seen it already, then?'

She ignores me and snuggles back into the chair, chewing.

'This meat's a bit tough, Georgina.'

She hasn't touched the meat yet. I roll my eyes. 'Best beef.'

We chew quietly for a while. Nan's half cleared her plate.

'I'm used to the dinners in a box.' She reaches for the pint glass, slurps and leans forwards. 'Kick-off now, Georgina.'

Nan's almost finished all the dinner and her glass is empty. The big clock on the mantelpiece ticks loudly. She clanks her cutlery, a sign that she's making an effort with my substandard cooking. I close my eyes and listen to the commentator's voice rise in pitch, speeding up, his voice cracking with excitement. I ease myself to stand, feeling bloated, and pick up Nan's tray.

'Nice Sunday lunch?'

She grunts. 'I got it down me.'

I pile our plates, turn towards the kitchen. 'Cup of tea?'

'Guinness'd be nice.'

'I'll make us a pot of tea.'

I take a pace forwards and she calls out, 'Wait. This is the first goal. Watch. It's a good one.'

I turn back to the screen and blink. A small player in a blue jersey is running alone down the pitch at full pelt, his body bent forwards. He weaves past two tall players and one falls over. He has nifty legs, an agile body, and his face is determined. His fringe is tied in a knot on the top of his head and the rest is longish, dark and straight. He has deep-set eyes, thick brows and a handsome face. Another player, the one with the yellow hair, tackles him and the little player pushes the ball behind him. He twists, leaps into the air with it on the end of his toe and, with a deft overhead scissors kick, he launches it, a crack shot into the back of the net.

'Goal!' yells Nanny from the chair.

The little player runs, a wide grin on his face, and blows a kiss to somewhere in the seats at the front of the stadium.

The commentator shrieks, 'And it's a superb goal from the Spanish striker, Luis Delgado,' and the camera pans to the cheering throng, to glimpse for a second a burgundy-haired young woman in a smart new cream-coloured coat, smiling and blowing a kiss back, before the camera whirls back to the player running on the pitch. I almost drop the tray. It's Jade.

Chapter Five

On Tuesday morning, our first customer arrives in reception just before nine o'clock. It's Sue McAllister – freckled, forty, tall, always smiling – for her leg wax. Amanda breezes in and asks if she'll follow her to the treatment room. I sign the first customer in the appointments book and hear the front door open and close. A young woman in a bright green ski jacket and leggings stands in front of me, carrying a green sports bag.

I hold out a hand. 'I'm Georgie Turner. Can I help?'

She has a charming American accent.

'Good morning. I have an appointment with Jade Wood. Personal training. Nine o'clock.'

I scratch my head: Jade's not back from her weekend in Brighton yet. I texted last night as I thought she'd be home that evening and received the curt reply: *Don't fuss, Mum – back first thing.* I smile at the American woman. She has long fair hair in a loose plait that loops over her shoulder. She's in her late twenties, a smooth face, pale and earnest. I check the appointment book.

'Heather Barrett?'

She nods.

'Can I offer you a cup of coffee?'

The woman looks alarmed. 'I never drink coffee. Perhaps a glass of water.'

I move over to the water dispenser and fill a cardboard cup. The young woman takes it from me, frowns and sips. I glance at the clock: 9.05. My first appointment is 9.15, an aromatherapy facial. I smile at the American woman and I'm just about to make some vague excuse, when the door clicks opens and Jade's standing in reception, grinning, glossy hair, dark sunglasses, a cream-coloured wool coat over her workout gear.

'Sorry I'm late. It's Heather, isn't it? Shall we go straight down to the gym?'

Jade turns to go, whips off the sunglasses and winks in my direction. I know she's had a good weekend. I beam back and mime drinking a cup of coffee. She nods and mouths, 'Later.' I breathe out relief.

We're busy all day, ships passing. I have an appointment with a bride-to-be and her mother, planning make-up for two hours, then I pop over to Nanny Basham's for an hour while Jade and Amanda have lunch separately. It's almost six o'clock by the time we lock eyes again.

'Shall we have a cuppa?' I wave a mug hopefully.

'Sorry, Georgie, love. Rhys has a dose of man flu and he's working the late shift. I want to see him off.'

Amanda shrugs on a heavy green coat and, when she leaves, a chill breeze weaves through the door, cooling the warmth of the reception area. I turn to Jade, who's in a Lycra crop top and leggings and looks exhausted. We lock the door and go upstairs to the kitchen. I put the kettle on and inspect a couple of potatoes to bake, making an effort to keep my voice light.

'Nice weekend, Jade?'

She rolls her eyes, grins and nods.

'He's a talented lad, your Luis Delgado.'

She jerks her head and I think she's about to come back with a cutting reply, but her face breaks into a smile.

'He is.'

'He was on TV at Nanny's. He scored a great goal. And he blew you a kiss.'

'Did you see it, Mum?'

I nod. 'You were on telly, in the crowd.'

Her face has taken on a dreamy look.

'I'm going up again on Thursday night. I've only one appointment on Friday so I'll move it. He has a big game this weekend. It'll be lovely.'

I chew my lip and hold back all the comments about love in haste, regret at leisure, and I ask, 'Does he have a place in London?'

'No, I told you, Mum. Didn't you listen? He has a beautiful flat overlooking the sea in a little village outside Brighton. He and his friend, Roque, live on different floors. The view's spectacular. Two bedrooms, en suite: Luis has sauna facilities. He has a driver, too, for when he and Roque don't want to use their cars or the train. It's in his contract. We don't need to go out, really. But there's so much to do in Brighton, which isn't far away, and we're only a couple of hours from London. It's perfect.'

'You'll soon want to move down there, then?'

She shoots me a guilty look. 'He's special, Mum. I can't wait for you to meet him.'

I move the conversation forwards. 'How do you get on with the language? Is his English good?'

'Not bad. Much better than my Spanish. And we have the language of love.'

I sigh and stick a skewer through the jacket potatoes, throw them into the oven. I shift my position to stand opposite Jade, lean against the worktop and decide I should speak frankly to her, tell her to be careful and not get hurt. I pull a bag of salad leaves apart and take a breath.

'It must be very glamorous, being a footballer's girl-friend.'

She pulls a face. 'He's my boyfriend first, Mum. Luis won't be a footballer forever but we plan on being together—'

'Jade, this is all very sudden.'

'It's called love, Mum.'

'But you're young and carried away by the passion, the excitement . . .'

'That's what love is.'

'No, it's hard work and communication and coping with the tough times.'

'You're just talking about you and Dad. Luis and I are different.'

'That's what everyone says, but it always ends in the divorce courts.'

'Don't you dare, Mum. Dad says you were the one who wouldn't communicate.'

'What?' I hold up the knife I've just chopped tomatoes with. 'He said that?'

'He said you were bad-tempered and cold – you shut him out.'

'So he sought love elsewhere?' Tears spring to my eyes. Of course, it's because of the onions I'm hacking to pieces.

'He was lonely.'

I sweep the salad into a bowl and shake it like it's Terry's neck. I squeeze mayonnaise on top, like I'm throt-tling his wife, Alison's, throat. I wonder why I'm still bothered. It was years ago.

'Well, I'm just saying, Jade, be careful. Take your time.'

'Like you're doing? No relationships at all since Dad?

45

You're cynical, Mum, and you're unhappy, so you just don't want anyone else to be happy.'

My teeth snap together. She's right. Over the last few years, there's been no one. I hurl the empty mayonnaise bottle towards the bin. It skims the metal top and clatters on the floor. I know I should say nothing but the words bubble out.

'Well, don't come to me, Jade, when you're broken-hearted and—'

I realise I've gone too far. Jade's staring, her mouth open.

'Mum. Don't you want me to be happy?'

I rush over and hug her. She holds her arms out away from me, as if I smell. I sigh.

'Of course I want you to be happy, Jade. I'm sorry, love. I'm being too protective, aren't I?' I feel her nod. 'Sorry. I'll start again.' I move away, go over to the cupboard and pull out a bottle of red wine. 'Shall we break our no-alcohol-in-the-week rule and crack a bottle open? Toast you and Luis. To love and good times?'

She pulls a face, raises her arms, stretches lean limbs, and for a moment she looks just like Terry.

'Okay. We need a bit of bonding time, don't we? But, trust me, Mum. I know what I'm doing. And when you meet Luis, I know you'll love him.'

I pour wine into two glasses and the soft liquid glug is calming me already.

'I'm sure I will,' I tell her, raising the glass and swallowing a huge gulp of Merlot.

The following week flies by. Jade returns on Tuesday, deals with a dozen clients midweek and on Thursday, she's back on the train to Brighton. On Friday morning, Nanny Basham has an early doctor's appointment for her heart check-up, so I drive her to the surgery, where she manages to upset the receptionist and antagonise a woman with a fretful baby. I apologise to everyone in the waiting room, and she nags all the way home about the slack state of modern parenting and how the child only needed a comforter to stop it screaming. I nod and concentrate on the road. Nan and Uncle Wilf never had children.

Then we're busy all day, hardly a moment to stop for breath. Amanda leaves at six, excited about a romantic evening she has planned, and when I go to lock up at seven o'clock, I notice a hunched shape sitting on my front step. Bonnie looks up, her face in shadow, and I open the door and propel her inside. She's quaking with cold, huddled against her handbag. I shut the front door behind us.

'Bonnie, what's the matter? What's Adie done now?'

She's shaking. Her eyes leak and her make-up is smudged; the blusher shines livid against the pallor of her face, but the worst thing is the haunted expression in her eyes.

'He was out until three last night. He said he was at a meeting but he smelled of perfume. I asked him if he'd been with someone else and he said no, but when I kept on nagging him, he said it was just some random woman at a business party and it didn't matter. He said I shouldn't make a big deal of it . . .'

I hug her. 'Well done for walking out, Bonnie. You're staying here with me now. How did you get here?'

'I got a taxi.'

'From Frodsham?'

'He has my car keys. He told me I couldn't leave him. He wouldn't let me.'

An engine roars and Adie's car turns into the drive. There's hardly room for him to park next to my X5, so he leaves his Porsche at a diagonal and throws the door open, marching towards us, his head down like a bull, his bald spot shining pink.

Bonnie hides behind me and he moves towards her but I bar his way.

'No, Adie.'

It crosses my mind he could simply push me to one side and I've no idea why I'm standing between my cowering sister and her tall, smug husband. I put my hands on my hips, lean forwards and impersonate an orangutan. The Alpha female.

'We can go inside to talk, but I'm telling you now, if you make a scene, I'll call the police. We do this my way or not at all.'

The blood drains from his face and I breathe out slowly. He nods. His hand clutches a mobile phone. His knuckles are white. He looks at Bonnie.

'Are you all right, love?'

She nods. I fumble for my keys and stare at him, then her.

'She's obviously not all right, Adie. You've cheated on her. It's not acceptable . . .' I shake my head. Not acceptable? It's worse than that.

'Bonnie, I've been so worried. I mean, all this fuss over a silly woman. It was nothing, I swear . . .'

He ignores me, standing with my hands on my hips, and rushes over to Bonnie, wrapping his arms around her. His fingers move to her wrist, over the gold charms on her bracelet, and back to her face. His shoulders are hunched and I can see the tension in his spine through his coat. Bonnie stands stiffly, gripping her handbag, her eyes reflecting her misery.

'Come in, both of you.' I sound like an ancient schoolmistress. 'We have some things to talk about, don't we?'

In the kitchen, we sit down. Adie takes off his coat, puts his phone next to him on the table and scans the screen, head bent. I make coffee. Bonnie sips from a mug, inhaling steam; she looks washed-out. I hand her a tissue and begin the conversation.

'Right, Adie. What's going on? It'd better be good.'

I bite my lip and stifle a smile. I could be a United Nations special envoy. But this is serious. Adie wipes his face with his hands. His brow furrows, sweat lodged in the deep seams.

'Bonnie, I'm so sorry.'

I thump the table with my fist. 'I'm sure you are, Adie. But it's not the first time you've played away, is it?'

Bonnie looks from his face to mine and her expression is blank. He focuses on me.

'I love her, Georgie. Other women don't matter. I can't be without her.'

I wipe my mouth on the back of my hand. 'How much did you love her when you had your arm round another woman last night?' I notice Bonnie's eyes start to fill up again.

He sighs. 'There are some things happening in my life right now – things I can't talk about.'

'Philandering is not one of them.' I sip coffee. 'You have a lot of explaining to do. You won't cheat on her again, Adie. I promise you that.'

He turns a glare on me and his eyes are bitter. 'You're just angry because Terry cheated on you. You don't understand.'

I lean forwards and keep my gaze straight, my eyes boring into his. 'Try me.'

He turns a tender gaze on Bonnie, reaches out and puts his hand over hers. Her face softens. He takes a deep breath.

'I'm a businessman, Georgie. I make a lot of money so I can keep my wife in a plush house. We have nice things. But sometimes I have to take risks and—'

'What does that have to do with other women?' My voice booms like a politician, retaliating during *Question Time*. I'm taking no prisoners.

Bonnie's holding his hand. He brings it to his lips. Suddenly, I'm terrified he's winning her round.

'It was a business party. There were all sorts of women there, you know. I had to fit in: it would have been rude not to. It's all a bit difficult at the moment. I'm having some temporary cash flow problems. A client of mine is pressing for a deadline and I didn't want to say no to hospitality and offend him. It'll take me a week to sort out the funds but then it'll be fine. It was just the once, a woman I'll never see again. I don't even remember her name.'

I face him, square on. 'Bonnie's your wife, Adie. You can't just go with other women and pretend it doesn't matter. It's disrespectful to everyone. And it's not the first time. Why do you think she left you just before Demi's wedding?'

Bonnie winces but she's still gazing at Adie. I look from her to his face – he's staring at her, all apologies, pretending to be sorry, and her lip trembles as she whispers his name. Love is blind. And stupid.

He puts a thumb to her cheek, brushes the skin as if it's delicate silk and sighs. 'Bonnie, please forgive me. I'll never look at another woman again. I promise.'

She sniffs and a tear rolls down her face, then another. He has her where he wants her.

He takes her face in his hands. 'Let's go away, you and me. Let's take a long trip. Goa, Sri Lanka. Let's go tomorrow, stay for three months. Georgie can keep an eye on things.'

I snort loudly. He doesn't notice.

'A second honeymoon. Just think – we could renew our vows. We could stay as long as we like. Away from this awful place. Just you and me. What do you say, Bonnie?' He pauses and then goes in for the killer persuader line. 'Bon-Bon?'

I open my eyes wide. Bon-Bon? The chair scrapes and Bonnie staggers to her feet, snuffles and runs away. I hear her gasp and sob.

Adie glances at me, his face full of loathing, and then he chases her down the steps to the reception level below.

I rub my hands across my face and through my hair. I long for a shower, a piece of toast. I squint at the clock. It's half nine. I wonder if she'll leave with him. I hope not. I remind myself that on Sunday I'll go to Nanny Basham's to make her lunch. Bonnie could stay here and we could go together.

Below, I can hear Adie's voice talking, lilting with emphasis. There's a brief pause, a soft whisper, so I assume she's sobbing and then he starts again, all syrup and persuasion. I try to ignore them, breathe deeply, but instead I pick up a paper napkin and shred it between my fingers into a hundred pieces.

His phone is across the table. I glance towards where Bonnie and Adie have gone downstairs. There's no one around, so I reach for it and flick it open. I know I shouldn't, but I wonder how many other women he's in contact with: his phone could have evidence of his philandering.

I check his most recent phone call – there are no details of a number, but he's spoken to the same unidentified caller three times today and five times yesterday. I look back through his other calls. He's tried to phone Bonnie a dozen times, more. Then I notice he has an unopened text, and I press the button and catch my breath. There it is, the photo of Bonnie and me and the man, Duncan Beddowes, taken in Adie's office. Bonnie's posing, smiling for the camera, and my face is twisted in annoyance. Just below it, the message reads: *I never make empty threats.* The phone nearly slips from my fingers.

I hear voices becoming louder, Adie's protesting and Bonnie's petulant tones. I thrust the phone to the other side of the table and start to play with the shredded napkin, sip cold coffee. The happy couple appear, holding hands, Adie cheerful again, Bonnie looking sad. She can't meet my eyes. Adie's smirking, triumphant. He speaks first.

'We're going home now.'

'Bonnie?' I stare at her. 'Bon, are you sure?' She shakes her head, nods and shrugs. I stand. 'I want you to ring me later, Bonnie.' I stare at Adie, who's wrapped an arm round her and is now helping her into her coat, a true gentleman. 'Seriously, Adie. I want to know she's all right.'

He lifts his coat, turns his back and points her towards the stairs. 'You don't need to worry, Georgie. But thanks for your help. We're all fine now.'

He's eradicated his infidelity in one sentence. I glare at him. He remembers his phone, scoops it from the table and pushes it in a pocket. Bonnie looks over her shoulder as she's ushered away.

'Georgie, I . . .'

'Ring me.'

He steers her down the stairs and the last thing I see is her staring over her shoulder, a round-eyed gaze and smudged make-up. I breathe in and out like a seething dog and clench my fists. An image is soaking into the screen of my mind and words follow: the picture of Bonnie and me either side of a man we don't know and the warning underneath: *Remember . . .*

52

Adie's made a very real enemy and he's definitely in trouble above his head. I wonder what sort of corrupt business he's involved in. A shiver goes through me, from my shoulders right down to my toes.

Chapter Six

The next day, Nanny's surprisingly quiet during my visit. She picks at her roast dinner for one and leaves most of it on the side of her plate. When she gazes at the television, she hardly hears me talking to her. I sit on the rug, snuggle against her knees and gaze up at her as she sips the last of her beer. The music booms and a smooth voice proclaims today's news headlines. There's a politician who's in trouble. He's made a crass remark and other politicians are calling him a buffoon and demanding that he resign. A woman from some fiscal group at a university talks about 3 per cent inflation, how prices are going up, and that it's going to be a hard summer for investors. Nanny tuts.

Then the local news: the screen moves to a street I recognise in Norris Green. A man's voice narrates that the police have staged a big coup to do with money laundering in which a large amount of cash was involved: the first man was arrested in what's expected to be a sequence of arrests. I stare at the screen, at a plastic door with no lights on inside. I remember the same view from Adie's Boxster. An old pair of trainers hangs from the telegraph wire. It's the same house.

Nanny Basham adjusts her glasses and sucks her teeth. 'This city is full of scallies. It never used to be like this.'

I shake my head and wonder if Adie has anything to do with the crime on the television. When we stopped outside the house, he said someone owed him money. For a second, I wonder if he's lost it all. I know he is a wheeler-dealer, but it's possible he's involved in something worse.

I mumble, 'I shouldn't be surprised if it's connected to Adie. Who knows what he does? It's probably not legitimate. Bonnie's best away from him, Nan.'

'I agree, Georgina. But it can't be easy for her.'

'Of course it is. You just walk out of the door.'

'Splitting up, like you did with Terry Wood? Some women find it difficult to be by themselves all the time.'

'I don't.'

'Perhaps Bonnie's not like you, Georgina. Perhaps she doesn't hold with your ideas about women's lubrication.'

'Liberation, Nan.'

The voice on television talks about the arrest and how further arrests will be made.

Nanny shakes her head. 'They want locking up, all of them. And the key throwing away.'

Nan looks tired. I ask her if she's all right and she tells me she's fine, she's just worried about Bonnie. We both are. I can't stop thinking about the text messages; burned in my mind is the photo of us standing either side of the man called Beddowes and I can't rid myself of the image of Adie's fading pallor as he watched his business contact take the selfie.

Bonnie doesn't call me. I text her three times on Sunday night and by midnight I'm so worried, I ring. She answers me with a faint voice. She's in bed with a migraine.

On Monday, I leave her alone and decide she should

have time to herself. She can call me if she needs me. For all I know, she's in Sri Lanka on a second honeymoon.

On Tuesday, my feet don't touch the ground. Amanda and I are busy all day and we spend lunchtime advertising for a new beauty therapist. Now Jade is away so often, we need help and business is good enough to try out a new pair of hands.

I rush to Nan's at lunch to put her groceries away and during the afternoon, I move from client to client. Diane Morris, now Diane Morris-Kandeh, arrives at 3 p.m. for a facial and spends an hour chattering about her husband, twenty-five-year-old Lamin who by all accounts is descended from a Mandinka warrior. He's especially warlike in the bedroom. I roll my eyes because hers are closed, make my voice light and coo, 'Lovely.'

Amanda and I are still busy at five o'clock. Jade texts me that she'll jump in a taxi at the station when she arrives back from Brighton just before midnight. She has a client first thing tomorrow, at 7.30. I check my email and we have two applicants already for the therapist's job: seventeen-year-old Lexi and twenty-three-year-old Ella-Louise, both claiming to have experience in treatments I've never even heard of. The younger one has apparently invented new nail-art designs and Ella-Louise has qualifications in intimate waxing for men, so I decide to interview them both on Thursday morning.

My last client of the day, Mrs Gaffney, whose first name is really Daphne, arrives for her pedicure at five fifteen. She's seventy-seven and sprightlier than I am at the moment, given my thumping headache. She entertains me with a catalogue of raunchy tales about her first three husbands, so I always enjoy those sessions. She seldom talks about the fourth, who died last year, except to say, 'He was the love of my life, God rest him.'

We finish just after six o'clock and Amanda stares out of the window. Beyond the frame, all is grey – the sky is dishwater dark outside, and then a splattering of rain hits the glass and she shudders.

'Rhys's working the late shift. It looks horrible out there. Am I up for a twenty-minute walk home in a freezing downpour through the park?'

I take the hint. 'Stop for a cheeky glass of wine, a bite to eat. I'll get you a taxi home later. We've worked hard today.'

She sits at the kitchen table and smiles. I uncork a bottle of Merlot and it splashes into two large glasses with a familiar glug. I'll make beans on toast. The company will be nice.

Half an hour later, the Merlot bottle is half empty. Or half full. Amanda's chatting about the coming summer and a holiday in the sun.

'When we first met, Rhys and I spent July on the Algarve in a villa. We had a pool outside, rolling hills, no neighbours. He used to stroll around naked all day in the sunshine . . .'

I wrinkle my nose. 'Sounds like a fire hazard to me.'

She misunderstands my cynicism.

'Oh, definitely. I believe in keeping our relationship hot. I mean, I didn't choose a firefighter for nothing. Sometimes I even get him to keep his yellow helmet on.'

I'm ready to join her in spluttering laughter, but her face is serious. I giggle anyway.

'Rhys and I have everything we want, though. This year, I've asked him if we can spend money on experiences. I need a holiday. I've always wanted to go to Hawaii.'

I imagine the beaches, the surf, the cocktails, the garlands; lei placed round my neck by a welcoming islander with a huge smile.

'I'll have to get the calendar out and look at holidays. It'll be easy if we can appoint one of these new applicants.'

'I hope we find someone.' Amanda wrinkles her nose.

'We'll interview on Thursday. I've invited Lexi and Ella-Louise.'

'We have plenty of work for at least one of them.' Amanda scrapes her fork on the plate. 'We both work far too hard.'

I agree and reward us both with a top-up from the wine bottle.

'In fact, Georgie, you need a holiday, too.'

I think of Bonnie and wonder again if she's at the airport with Adie.

I nod. 'It's been a while.'

'When did you last have a break?'

I think about it.

'I went to Paris eighteen months ago for a weekend. And before that I went to Palma for ten days. That was ages ago, though.'

She folds her arms across her chest. 'By yourself?'

I nod. 'I don't mind travelling alone. It's always an experience. I talk to people and I go to places where it's safe, and there's either a lot of sightseeing, or shopping, or a nice beach or a pool.'

'What about a man?'

'Oh, you can get one of those anywhere. You don't have to go abroad.'

She giggles, humouring me. 'No, really, Georgie, when did you last have a proper relationship?'

I trot out an easy answer. 'I'm too busy.' Then I stop to think. 'No, I'm not interested in men and they're not interested in me. Not the nice ones. There was the sleazy man with the clipped beard at Demi's wedding. That's the sort of man who tries to chat me up – the unpleasant ones. You can smell the desperation – they'll sidle up to anything in a skirt. I don't get many offers nowadays but I'm not at all worried.'

She leans forwards and pats my hand. 'You're still young, Georgie. You look good.'

I shake my head. 'No, that's all over with now.'

'What is – love?'

'I'm too independent, too old for love and all that nonsense. Men. Sex. The hassle. Having to compromise. Do what they want to do, go where they want. "Yes, dear – whatever you say, dear." Sharing a bed with a snoring, sweaty bloke with a beer gut. Having to lend him money for the next bet or wondering if I'll find frilly knickers in the back of his car that belong to the woman he's seeing behind my back.'

'You're cynical.'

'Not at all.'

'Terry must've really hurt you.'

'I'm well over him. He did me a favour. I'd rather have this place and the business, to be honest.'

'But what about the company? Someone to cuddle up to? Someone to love who loves you back?'

'I'm happy as I am. Besides, I'm past all that.'

'Is it dating that bothers you, Georgie? I mean, after all these years, do you think you'd still be able to get excited about going out with a man?'

'No.' I shake my head. 'I've had two dates since Terry, both disasters. It put me off completely. What would be the point? I'm too set in my ways. And anyway, men only want a younger, prettier version after a few years . . .'

'You mean like Rabbity Alison?'

I push the memory away, finish my wine and grin at her. 'Okay. It's big decision time.' Amanda looks hopeful: she thinks I might agree to start dating. Instead, I offer her a mischievous grin. 'Should we open another bottle or have a coffee?'

She glances up at the clock on the wall. 'It's nearly nine. Coffee, please. I'd better get off soon.'

I pick up the empty plates. The prospect of a bit of quiet, even an early night tucked up with the hot-water bottle, looms in front of me like an old friend. Jade'll be home around midnight, but she has a key. I'll see her at breakfast time. I don't want to appear the fretful, needy mum.

An hour later, the kitchen is clean, with the plates put away, and I'm curled up in bed reading a book about a man who's lived for hundreds of years but who's lonely and can't adjust to the present time. I'm immersed in the middle chapters. The radio is a tinny rattle of music in my ears. The eleven o'clock newsreader mutters something about rising crime rates and the high price of an average family house. I push my feet against the furry warmth of the hot-water bottle beneath my toes and I feel sleepy. I place the book gently on the floor on its front, switch off the radio and reach for the light. My phone buzzes an in-coming call and I pick up.

'Hello. Bonnie. How are you?'

Her voice comes back as a whisper. 'Georgie. I'm scared. There's someone in the house.'

'Huh? Tell Adie . . .'

'Adie's out. There's someone downstairs. I'm in the bedroom.' I can hear her breathing, a shallow rasp. 'What shall I do?'

I sit upright, wide awake. 'Are you sure? Did you Skype Demi?'

'Yes, a few minutes ago. Then I heard someone moving about in the lounge and something fell or smashed. I don't know what happened but someone's definitely here. I'm scared.'

My thoughts race. 'Are you on your own?'

'Yes. Adie's out until midnight, at a business meeting.'

I make up my mind at once. 'Are you dressed?'

'Yes.'

'Can you get to the back door safely?'

'No, but I could climb out of the window and onto the garage roof, grab the drainpipe, drop down to the lawn.'

'Go now. Take your bag. Keep talking to me.'

'Then what?'

'Run to the road across the garden. Get in a taxi, drive into town. Call me.'

I hear her breath in ragged gasps. 'Okay, I'm doing it, now.'

She's left the phone on and at first I hear nothing, then a soft dragging sound, perhaps a window opening or a leg stretching, Bonnie climbing outside. A soft bump, silence, then she's running. I'm holding my breath.

She gasps into the mouthpiece, 'I think something awful has happened, Georgie. Someone's broken in. I'm on the drive, my feet are wet – I'll put my shoes back on . . .' There's silence, soft sounds, then she's whispering into the phone: 'I'm on the road now, looking up and down, but there's no taxi. I was all on my own, Georgie. Adie left hours ago and said he'd be back late; there was a banging noise downstairs and . . . hang on. Taxi!' There's a pause, an engine. 'Please, yes, the city centre – yes, of course, all that way. Please, quick as you can.'

There's the gritty sound of a male voice in the background and her reply.

I whisper, 'Are you all right, Bonnie?'

She breathes out. 'Yes. I know someone was in the house. I could hear them moving. I can't talk now.'

'Bonnie. Do you have money?'

'I have my card in my handbag. I don't have a coat, though. I'm freezing.'

An idea pops in my head.

'Go to the station. Jade's coming back from Brighton. I'll call her, tell her what's happened. The station'll be busy and it'll look like you're getting a train somewhere. Jade'll meet you and you can come back here together. You'll be better with people round you. Ring me as soon as you're at Lime Street.'

'Okay.' Her voice trembles and then she's gone.

My hands shake as I ring Jade. It takes her a while to pick up and at first she's irritated with my babble, but I take a deep breath and explain.

She says, 'Oh my God, Mum,' and is silent.

'Keep in touch, will you, Jade? And get back here as soon as possible.'

'Right, Mum. I'll be back soon with Aunty Bonnie.'

I breathe out. 'I'll get the kettle on.'

There's a pause then Jade says, 'That'd be nice. I could do with a chat before we go to bed.' I can hear her thinking. I wait and then she says, 'I have some news for you too, Mum. I think it's going to be one of those nights.'

Chapter Seven

It's past one o'clock. Bonnie's hunched over a glass of brandy in the lounge. She's in my favourite armchair, staring out of the French windows at the patch of lawn outside, wrapped in a thick dressing gown, my striped pyjamas and a pair of my old fluffy slippers. The bracelet still encircles her wrist, the little charms winking in the light. Jade's in her cream coat, standing by the windows, frowning with her arms tightly folded. She reminds me so much of Terry.

'Go on then, Mum. Tell me I'm being stupid.'

Bonnie's face is anxious and tired, stripped of make-up. She bites her lip.

'You have to follow your heart, love. It's the only thing.' She thinks for a moment. 'But look where that's got me. Well, maybe you'll have more luck, Jade. Of course you will. I mean, Demi's happy. She and Kyle are in Phuket. She sent me some pictures. I'm so glad she's away from all this . . .' Her face freezes. She's thinking of Adie, of her escape in the taxi.

I stare from Bonnie to Jade and realise I haven't spoken. I don't know what to say to my daughter, which is unusual, so I just mutter, 'I'll support whatever you want to do, Jade.'

Her face clouds. I've said the wrong thing. 'Can't you just be happy for me, Mum?'

I slide from the chair and go over to her, wrap my arms round her. Her shoulders stiffen.

'I'm happy for you, love. It's only . . .'

'You think it's too soon?' She pulls back and her eyes blaze.

I start to yawn and wish I hadn't. She'll think I'm bored. I'm so tired my bones ache.

'Jade, you and Luis love each other. I can see why you want to move to Brighton to be with him. Of course. You're smart, talented, sophisticated, beautiful.' She rolls her violet eyes. 'You'll have a great life there. Of course I'm happy for you.'

Bonnie gives a dry laugh, but her face is sad. 'You'll be fine. You won't mess up like your mum did. Like I've done.'

Tears start and she sucks the dregs from the brandy glass. I fill it halfway and she brings it to her lips. I offer a small glass to Jade and pour one for myself.

Jade sidles over to her. 'You'll be okay, Aunty Bonnie.'

Bonnie takes a breath and forces a smile. 'I hope you'll be lucky in love, Jade.' She breathes out. 'You're off to start a new chapter of your life with your lovely young man. And I . . .' A tear tipples from her eye and she dabs it away. 'I'm about to end a chapter with my wicked old man.' A laugh bubbles in her throat. 'So, cheers to you and to me. In fact, cheers to all three of us.'

'Bring it on,' I grin and our glasses chime together.

Suddenly, there's a rap at the door, loud and insistent. It can only be one person. Bonnie leaps up and runs off like a wild-eyed rabbit to hide upstairs, swiping her handbag from the table and, as an afterthought, taking her glass of brandy with her.

I tweak the door open. His face is grey in shadow.

'Let me in, Georgie.'

I keep the door slightly ajar.

'I'm in my pyjamas, Adie. For God's sake.'

'Where's Bonnie?' Then he's in, looking round the reception area for signs of her. 'Is she here?'

He charges up to the kitchen. Jade and I are behind him. I check that Bonnie hasn't left anything and breathe out.

'No, Adie, she's not here. Do you never talk to her? Wherever would she be at this time of night?'

Jade stands behind me.

Adie stares round the room. 'She must be here . . .' He rushes from the kitchen to the lounge, stares out of the French windows at the raised garden.

I follow him.

'She's not.' I make my voice low. 'What the hell's going on, Adie?'

He shakes his head: I think he's going to cry. I hope not.

'She's gone.'

'Where?' I put my hands on my hips in a Haka stance and think about thrusting my tongue out but decide against it. 'Where's my sister?'

He says nothing so I grab his arm.

'Adie, I'm going to call the police.'

He snatches at my wrist and holds it too hard.

'No. Don't do that.'

Jade says, 'Get off my mum.'

I pull my arm away. 'Where is she, then?'

His face blanches even more.

'She's not at home. I'm worried about her. Something's happened.'

'To Bonnie? What have you done, Adie?' I raise my phone, a sign of intent.

'Georgie, I'm in a bit of trouble. I owe a man some money. I think he came to the house . . .'

I gasp. Jade does the same behind me. I'm suddenly relieved that Bonnie's upstairs. I breathe out.

'You should phone the police.'

'I can't. I have to find Bonnie.'

'Do you have any idea where she might be?'

He's miserable. 'I hoped she might be here. I got home an hour ago. Someone had broken in, been through the things in my office, and Bonnie was missing.'

I fold my arms. 'I'm worried now, Adie.'

He nods, licks thin lips. 'She hasn't taken her coat but her handbag's gone. I'm just worried. I'm having a few problems with a business deal and now she's missing.'

'Adie, what on earth have you done?'

'Nothing I can't sort out.'

His elbows move out from his body, he stands taller. He's recovering his poise.

I wonder what to do, how to get him out of the house. Then his phone buzzes and he grabs it from his pocket.

'It's a text. From Bonnie.'

Jade puts a steady hand on my shoulder.

I frown. 'Where is she, Adie?' My mind's accelerating. She's probably under the bed.

'At the airport. She's telling me to meet her there. We can catch a plane somewhere – get away together.' He gapes at me for a moment. 'She's okay. Thank goodness. She said she heard someone downstairs and knew instinctively we'd need to get away for a bit. My clever little Bonnie. I'll go back to the house quickly, pack a bag and we'll be gone.'

He turns away. He's not interested in me any more.

He's off, through the kitchen and reception, towards the door.

'I'll be in touch, Georgie.'

He flips the bolt and is outside, letting chilly air whoosh into the house. He slips into the darkness and he's a shadow. I hear the clip of his car door, the growl of an engine. Then he's gone. I close the door and lock it.

'And good riddance to Adie. Well done, Bonnie. She played a genius card there.'

Jade's face contorts. 'But when he gets to the airport, she won't be there. What then?'

'It buys us time.' I shrug. 'But we'll have to think of something.'

I go back to the lounge and Bonnie's standing in the doorway, holding her phone in her fist.

'In an hour or two, I'll message him again. I'll tell him I was nervous, I imagined someone was following me and I took a cab to Edinburgh Airport. I'll send him on a goose chase.'

'You heard it all, Bon?'

Her brows are knit in a frown. She's clearly furious.

'I snuck down and listened. Adie's messed up one of his deals. I tiptoed back upstairs and texted him. I'm not being frightened out of my own house by his dodgy friends. I want out.'

Jade links her arm through Bonnie's. 'What are you going to do?'

Bonnie's new resolve and determination fills me with optimism. She'll be better away from Adie. I plaster a smile on my face and launch in.

'We have to avoid Adie until he's out of trouble. We need to think carefully and come up with a plan.'

I gaze from my daughter to my sister. Jade's face is calm, her skin luminous. She's off to Brighton to start a new life with her Spanish beau. Bonnie's pale, anxious. I have to get her away from Adie. I think of what might have happened to Bonnie if she hadn't left the house in Frodsham and my mind shuffles thoughts about what to do next.

Jade leans back in her seat and stretches her arms out, flexing the muscles. I'll miss her when she's in Brighton. The feeling of loss is already starting to squat on my shoulders and clutch at my heart. Then an idea flashes in my mind, perfectly formed. It's an opportunity, exploding in front of me like a firework. In one move, I can persuade my sister to leave her philandering husband and stay close to my daughter at the same time. Adie and his criminal capers are the perfect excuse.

My mind moves to Nanny, all alone in her cold home. At once, I know how to resolve all of our problems in a single checkmate move. And we can have some fun at the same time. It's the perfect opportunity to be together, to bond, three generations of women celebrating independence. A wide grin stretches across my face and, quick as lightning, I change it to a serious frown.

'Bonnie, Jade – I know what we have to do. It's as clear as daylight. We can't stay here and wait for Adie to find out we've sent him on a goose chase. We'll take things into our own hands, be in charge of the situation. Until this problem with Adie blows over, we have to put ourselves first. So, we'll all go away together, tonight. And I know the perfect place.'

Chapter Eight

The sky is full of stars, little diamonds set in metres of black velvet. It's almost three in the morning and the cold has started to bite at the exposed bits of my flesh. Bonnie's helped herself to items from my wardrobe; she's wearing a long faux-fur coat and matching hat and she looks like a movie star. Jade's on the phone to Luis, multitasking at the same time, packing cases and boxes into the back of my BMW. Her movements are smooth and athletic.

I raid the till for the unbanked day's takings, text Amanda that I'll be away for a few days and promise to ring her soon with the details, but please could she hold the fort. Then we lock the front door, leave a light on in the hallway and drive through empty roads to a terraced street on the other side of the park. There are no lights on anywhere: the row of little houses is all in spongy darkness, behind scratchy hedges as straight as sentries.

I slip the key in and open the front door. The three of us are in blackout, walking on our toes, hunched over in a line like the kids in *Scooby Doo*. I flick the kitchen light on and suggest Bonnie and Jade wait downstairs. Nanny's not going to like being disturbed. I'm scared about waking her. What if she has a heart attack?

I creep upstairs, stand on the top step and a floorboard creaks. I hold my breath for ages, thinking what to say.

Then an old lady's voice rasps, 'I have a shotgun in here. And if you don't believe me, you burgling bastard, try me. Come in here and I'll blow your bloody head off.'

'Nan?' I whisper as loudly as I can. 'Nanny, it's me, Georgie.'

I hear the expletive under her breath. Then she calls, 'I haven't got my teeth in. Don't come in yet.' I wait, staring in the dark, then she says, 'All right. You can come in.'

I tiptoe into her bedroom and she switches the bedside lamp on. The room floods with orange light. She sits up in bed in a duck-egg blue winceyette nightie with ruffles at the neck and blinks. Her hair's dishevelled, tufty and tucked under the green woolly hat. I glance round the room. The old wardrobe with the silver mirror reflects our shapes back to us: a ghostlike sliver of a woman sitting up in a bed with rumpled blankets and another woman in a bulky coat, shivering. The room's bare except for the wardrobe, a pile of old books and newspapers in the corner, and several cardboard boxes full of junk. There's a pervasive smell of dusty old clothes and stale piss.

I take a breath. 'You haven't really got a shotgun, have you, Nan?'

'Don't be daft. You think I'm mad? What do you want here at this time of night? Your house burned down, has it?'

I move to the edge of the bed and sit down next to her, taking her hand. Her fingers are stone cold.

'Nan, I have some news for you. I don't want you to worry.'

She leans forwards and her lip trembles. 'Bonnie, is it? Is she all right?'

'She's downstairs. With Jade. We've got the car outside. We have to go away.'

It takes her a while to take this in. She frowns, her face a creased map of the tropics, and her eyes glitter.

'What about me?'

This is it, I think. Here we go. 'You're coming with us. To Brighton.'

'Over my dead body, Georgina. I'm not going anywhere.'

'I can't take care of you here, Nan. Not now. Please, trust me on this. It's not good for Bonnie to stay here. Adie's done something stupid; he owes money and he's made some enemies.' I take a deep breath, finding the right words to coax her to leave the house she's lived in for over sixty years. 'We have to go, Nan. All of us. Jade's going to Brighton to live with Luis. Bonnie needs to get away, just for a short while. We'll all go with Jade.' I stop there: I'm about to say 'to keep an eye on her', but it's best to say nothing.

Nanny stares, her mouth a straight line, and I wonder how I'm going to persuade her. Then she eases her legs out of bed, feet encased in hairy socks, and turns to me.

'We'd better get packing then, Georgina. I can't do it myself, can I? I'm in my eighties. You make sure I have plenty of warm clothes. My own towel. Plenty of Guinness. And I'll need to take my heart tablets and my arthritis tablets. And some photos – Wilf and the one of us and our Josie and Kenny at the caravan site in Wales.'

I must have my mouth open, because she says, 'Stop staring, Georgina. Come on. You can tell me about it as we go. I hope you've brought some sandwiches and a flask for the journey. I like my tea sweet. And I'm not sitting in the front seat. I don't like all those blinding headlights. They give me a headache.' She struggles to her feet. 'Well, I suppose it'll be an adventure. I don't get out much.' She pushes me away with her hand. 'Go on with you, then. I'm going to get dressed. I don't want you staring at my bits and bobs. Get packing. I'm going to Brighton.'

It takes us two hours to pack to Nanny's satisfaction. I do most of it. Nanny spends the time patting my faux-fur coat with Bonnie in it and asking Jade what Spanish men are like between the sheets and whether sex is banned the night before a football match. Jade replies with deliberately outrageous comments.

'We have this game, Nanny, where I wave a red sheet at Luis and he puts his fingers on his head like bulls' horns and chases me naked round the bedroom.'

Nanny believes her. Her eyebrows shoot up under her woolly hat like circumflexes.

By five o'clock, we have her strapped in the back of the car next to Bonnie. She's still stroking the arm of the faux-fur coat like it was Blofeld's white cat. Jade's next to me, chatting to me to keep me alert. Bonnie looks miserable.

'What's the plan, Georgie?'

The idea came to me straight away, before we collected Nanny, and it seems like a good strategy for escape.

'We'll make sure Adie doesn't know where we're going. The plan is to drive north for a bit, to take money from a bank and a cashpoint in Edinburgh, so that we put him off the scent. You text him you're going to the airport there, Bonnie. He'll believe you because we'll leave a trail of evidence. Adie'll follow you north. We'll have a rest in Edinburgh for a few hours, then join the M1, find a bed and breakfast or a hotel off the motorway, where we can sleep properly and recharge our batteries.'

'Edinburgh? I thought we were going to Brighton?' Jade's eyes blaze.

'We *are* going to Brighton. Via Edinburgh.'

'That's mad, Mum. This whole thing is ridiculous.'

I hope my daughter doesn't wake Nanny, who's snoring.

'It's just a few hours, Jade. Bonnie can't risk Adie following us.'

'Then what?' Jade's voice is sulky: she's tired and, just as she did when she was a child, she becomes moody.

'Then we'll go on to Brighton. You can meet up with Luis and we'll lose ourselves somewhere, find a place to stay for a bit until we can sort all this mess out with Adie.'

Jade tuts loudly. 'You're not staying with Luis and me. Couldn't you just drop me off and go somewhere else? East Anglia? Or Cornwall. That's a long way away.'

I decide to say nothing. She must already feel that I'm trying to be a gooseberry. And it's true: it's a case of two birds with one stone. Bonnie'll be safe from Adie and I'll check my daughter isn't moving in with a rampant Lothario. She turns a shoulder away from me, sulking.

It's half past five, but the traffic's starting to build. I turn onto the motorway and glance at other cars, to see if Adie's following us. Several heavy lorries lumber past. I blink to keep alert. The sky is tinged with pink and the light gradually lifts the darkness away.

Nanny and Bonnie nod off on each other's shoulder and Jade keeps me awake by talking non-stop about Luis and his footballing history.

After an hour and a half we're on the outskirts of Leeds, and I know the age and background of every member of Luis' family, his team and all the details and permutations of the offside rule. She plies me with coffee from the flask and I drive into a dappled crimson dawn. The wheels thrum on the tarmac and the dancing red brake lamps swirl in front of me, blurring away into the distance. I yawn. Jade puts rock music on the radio and the powerful sounds of The Disturbed fizz through my brain and my focus improves. My limbs feel heavy and my ankle on the accelerator aches with stiffness.

It's well past past eleven o'clock as we drive through the Old Town part of Edinburgh. It's a beautiful city and I wish I was awake enough to enjoy it. I concentrate on the shuffling traffic. Jade's in a bad mood; she's turned away from me and she's texting with a passion. I pull up outside an ATM, lean over to the back seat and shake Bonnie awake.

'We're here.'

She sighs and opens one eye. 'Brighton?'

'Edinburgh. Bonnie, have you got your bank card, the one from your joint account with Adie?'

She looks puzzled. 'Yes . . .'

'Right. The maximum you can take out is £300. When the bank opens, you can take another £500 over the counter.'

'I thought you had money from the till, Georgie?' She's still half asleep.

'I do. It'll keep us going for a while. But if Adie traces the transaction, which he will, and he thinks we're heading north, then we'll send him the wrong way if he decides to follow us. And the £800 will be useful when we're in Brighton.'

'So why aren't we going further into Scotland then?' Bonnie frowns. 'I've never been to the north of Scotland. It's supposed to be really nice there.'

'It's not a holiday. We're going to Brighton. I've arranged to be with Luis. I'm moving in with him. I'm not going to the north of bloody Scotland.'

Jade folds her arms and I instantly worry that I'll lose her. We've been so close and I wonder what Luis must be like, to be able to lure her away, and if it's only a glamour thing, a passing fancy. I clamp my lips together to stay silent.

'I need breakfast. I'm hungry.' Nan's awake, her voice sharp and insistent.

'Okay,' I sigh.

I feel like a frazzled mum, trying to cope with a badly behaved group of youngsters. But this crazy situation was my idea and I focus sharply on the purpose of it, keeping my mind on the prize. I'll be with Jade, making sure my daughter isn't throwing her life away on some frivolous relationship, and, in the same smart move, my sister'll be miles away from her devious, cheating husband.

I wave my hands, all smiles. 'I'll find us a café after Bonnie's been to the ATM, then we'll come back when the bank's open. Are you all fine with that?'

By half past twelve, Nan's finished a hearty breakfast and everyone else has pushed away food they've hardly touched. Jade's in a foul mood.

We drive ten miles out of Edinburgh and I find a quiet car park and pull in. Nanny's slurping the dregs of a chocolate milkshake through a straw. Bonnie immediately takes out her mirror and checks her make-up. Jade turns an angry face to me.

'What are we doing?'

'I need to sleep, Jade. I'm really tired.'

She blows air through her mouth. 'Oh, for God's sake. Why don't I drive for a bit?'

'I'm not keen on you driving, Jade. It's a long journey

and you're not used to this car. I'd rather drive.' The excuse sounds weak in my mouth. 'I'll just sleep for a few hours. I'll be fine.'

I keep my thoughts to myself. I wish we could go north, have a fun time in Scotland, the four of us. It'd be lovely to have a break together. I consider suggesting it, but she's already impatient to go south. Once Jade's in Brighton, in Luis' flat, I won't see so much of her.

She breathes out a loud sigh and goes back to her phone. I snuggle down in the seat and close my eyes. The radio rattles and I think about switching it off. The midday news comes on and I listen, half expecting a story about Adie. It's the usual politics and sport.

As I start to drift off, I hear Bonnie saying, 'I wonder what Adie's doing now.'

Nan says, 'Good riddance.'

There's a pause, then Bonnie sniffs. 'Demi'll be in Thailand. I'd like to go to Thailand.'

Jade huffs. 'I'd like to go to Brighton.'

There's a sniff at the back. Bonnie's tearful. 'Do you think I'll ever see Adie again?'

Nanny's voice is firm. 'He needs sorting out, that Adrian Carrick. No man should cheat on his wife. Wilf and I were married for fifty years and some. He never looked at another woman.' She giggles. 'Except once.'

Bonnie cheers up. 'What happened, Nan?'

Nan's laughing; I can sense her rocking backwards and forwards and I know her eyes hold an evil expression.

'We were in The Bluebell with your mam and dad. It was New Year's Eve and I'd had a couple of port and lemons. This drunken woman kept waving mistletoe in Wilfie's face, pursing her big red lips, trying to get him to kiss her. I was livid.'

Jade's suddenly interested. 'What did you do?'

'I followed her to the toilets, got her by the scruff of her neck and told her to keep her hands off my Wilf or I'd poke her eyes out.'

Bonnie laughs. Her voice is too high.

'Then I got Wilf home and I asked him if he fancied her. He'd been on the whisky and he said he thought she had nice legs, so without thinking, I slapped him in the face with a smelly dishcloth.'

Jade's mouth must be hanging wide open. 'Nanny . . .!'

'He was so drunk, I thought he was going to keel over. The next day he couldn't remember anything. He never touched the Jameson again.'

It's quiet inside the car and warm. I breathe out and sleep for what seems like an age. Then Jade's shaking me.

'Mum, can we go now?'

I sit up. I'd slumped right down in the seat.

'What time is it?'

'Nearly six. Everybody's been asleep.' Jade's face looms in front of mine. 'We won't make Brighton today, will we?'

Nanny wakes up and grumbles, 'I'm hungry. And tired. What's going on?'

I blink my eyes and realise that everyone's staring at me. I examine the satnav.

'Okay, how does this sound? We'll drive to Kendal. That's in the Lakes. We'll find a B & B and stay overnight.' I look at Jade and smile hopefully. 'I'll have us all in Brighton tomorrow.'

Bonnie murmurs, 'I don't mind.'

'Is that where the mint cake comes from, Kendal? I like mint cake but it sticks to my teeth. What sort of bed and breakfast will we stay in? I can't abide those places with nylon sheets.'

'No one has nylon sheets nowadays, Nan.'

'And I want proper home-cooked food, Georgina. I can't stand food if it's not cooked properly. I don't like burned meat. Or soggy vegetables that taste like sponge.'

'All right, Nan.'

Jade's voice is low. 'Can we just get going? I'll have to text Luis and tell him I'll be even later. I'll tell him I'm a prisoner in a car with my mad mother who's doing her best to keep me from getting to Brighton and I might not make it at all if my uncle Adie has anything to do with it.'

Bonnie interrupts, her voice defensive. 'Adie's got a heart of gold, Jade. If your Luis loves you as much as my Adie—'

Nanny cackles out loud. 'Adie Carrick's nothing more than a criminal. You're too good for him, Bonnie, love.'

Jade nods. 'You're right, Nan. Everyone knows about Uncle Adie.'

Bonnie's aghast. 'What do they know?'

'He's always up to something. Sorry, Aunty Bonnie. My friends in town all laugh about it.' Jade shrugs. 'I've always stayed well away from him. He keeps bad company. I've heard he's into all sorts: flipping houses, dodgy deals. I'm sure even Demi knows.'

Through the mirror I see Bonnie's little face start to crumple. I turn on the ignition and the engine rumbles.

'Right, let's get us all to Kendal. We'll stop somewhere nice. We have money.' I smile at Jade. 'By tomorrow, we'll all be in Brighton. Let's make the most of this little jaunt, shall we? A nice soft bed, early start after breakfast. It could even be fun.'

'Not my idea of fun,' Jade mumbles and stares out of the window.

I think about patting her arm, but I know she'd shrug me away. My heart aches with the thought that my daughter'll be glad to move on, that we'll part company and she'll forget how close we were, like sisters. I drive into the darkness, my thoughts and the radio and the swerving beams of headlights buzzing in my head.

We travel in silence for two, almost three hours. It's almost nine o'clock. The petrol gauge is running low. It occurs to me that we should hang on to Bonnie's money and my cash and use my card to fill up the tank. If Adie is somehow able to check on me, which wouldn't surprise me at all with some of his dodgy contacts, I'd need to be somewhere obscure, and we're still north of Liverpool so he won't suspect we're going to Brighton.

I swerve off the motorway and follow a sign for Orton and Ravenstonedale, down a narrow country road. It won't be too far. The satnav tells me I'm going the wrong way, but I ignore it. It's only a short drive to a service station and I'll soon be back on the motorway. My brain's fizzing with tiredness and my arms and legs are numb from being in one position for so long. I glance through the rear-view mirror. Nan's fallen asleep already, her head on Bonnie's shoulder.

Jade is texting, her thumbs moving furiously. 'What's happening now?'

'I'm getting petrol, Jade.'

'What's wrong with the motorway services?'

'I want my card to register the name of somewhere Adie won't have heard of.'

'Oh, for God's sake . . .'

I sigh. 'We'll all be in bed in an hour.'

'Not if we spend all this time bumbling down back roads in the middle of nowhere.'

'Jade . . .'

'What?'

'I'm sorry we couldn't take you straight to Brighton to be with Luis. I know you must be unhappy.'

'Unhappy?' She puts on the tone I remember so well from when she was a teenager: sarcasm, outrage and injustice. 'Too right I'm unhappy. And frustrated. And bored. And annoyed.'

There's a shriek from the back of the car. It's Bonnie's terrified voice. My heart speeds up and so do my reactions. A car's coming straight towards us, its lights on main beam. I'm dazzled. I swerve to the left and slam my foot on the brake. The car lurches; we bump something. When I open my eyes, the X5 is in a hedge. I turn to look at Jade, then back at Bonnie: they're wide-eyed, shocked. Nanny's indignant.

'Can't you drive more carefully, Georgina? We're stuck in the shrubs now.'

'It's nothing much, just a knock. Let's get going.'

Jade is furious. 'What a nutter to drive so fast.'

Bonnie's voice is a whisper. 'Do you think it was Adie's Boxster?'

Jade shakes her head. 'No, it wasn't. You couldn't see what sort of car it was. It was just some ignorant motorist; these lanes are so narrow. They'll be miles away by now.'

The X5 is leaning over to one side. I sit still for a moment and consider what to do, then I decide to inspect the car for any damage before I start the engine. I switch on the emergency hazard lights, grab a torch from the glovebox and ease myself out through the door, moving softly to the other side and into the darkness to check the car. The ground is soft under my feet, and damp. It's been raining. The sky is as dark as a woollen blanket overhead; no glimmering stars.

I shine the torch on the left-hand side of the bonnet. There are scratches on the side from the branches. The front end of the car is in the hedge. If I just reverse, I'll be able to drive out. I go round the back and squeeze forwards as far as I can. I can see the twist of the wheel, the shadow of the tyre. I crouch down, direct the beam at the huge wheel, illuminating the front tyre on the left, and follow the beam to the gravel. The tyre's flat at the bottom, completely deflated. I stare at it for a few moments and scratch my head. The X5 has the biggest puncture I've ever seen.

Chapter Nine

'Oh, for goodness' sake, Mum. It's only a puncture. I can fix that.'

'Jade . . .?'

'Remember Lee Kassiri, the bloke I went out with three years ago who had half a dozen cars? The petrolhead? I learned all sorts . . .'

'Jade . . .'

She can't open her door because it's embedded in the hedge, so she swings her body across my seat and follows me out of the driver's door. Although it's dark, I know she's frowning.

'Where's the spare in this one, Mum?'

'That's the point. There isn't one.'

'So how do you fix a puncture without a spare tyre?'

'There's a tube of squirty glue to inflate a tyre in the glovebox.'

'Well, pass it over.'

'It's for nail holes, little punctures. We must have hit a pothole. The tyre's completely flat.'

'So call out breakdown.'

'I don't have any breakdown cover, Jade. It lapsed.

I didn't think I'd need it. I only use the car in town.'

Jade clambers back in and collapses in her seat with a huff. 'What are we going to do now, then?'

Nanny's voice comes from the back seat. 'Are we stuck here? What about something to eat?'

Bonnie sniffs. 'I want to go home.'

I climb into the car. 'Don't be daft, Bonnie.' I'm not proud of the irritation in my voice.

'Come on, then, Mum. What are we going to do?'

I breathe out. 'Get on your phone and research local garages, Jade. Find someone who'll come out and fix it.'

'At this time of night?'

I shrug. 'Best I can suggest.'

Jade grunts. 'We could get out and walk to the nearest pub.'

'With my hip? Don't even think about it, Georgina,' Nan says.

I check the satnav. We're in the middle of nowhere, on the edge of the Yorkshire Dales National Park, up a hill.

Jade explores something on her phone for several minutes. It's quiet inside the car, except for her tutting. Finally, she turns to me.

'Right. There's Nateby Motors. They open at nine o'clock tomorrow, Thursday morning. There's another, Thomas Blake and Son, near Tebay. Open at nine. And one more. ABC Tyres at Orton – eight thirty tomorrow. That's it.'

Bonnie taps my shoulder. 'What shall we do, Georgie?'

'Georgina, I'm thirsty. My backside's stiff from all this sitting. And I'm so hungry I could eat a bear.' Nan pokes me in the back. 'What are you going to do about it?'

'We'll just have to sleep here until morning, Nan.'

Bonnie sounds tearful. 'I need the wipes from my bag to cleanse my face. And I need my special night cream.'

She thinks for a moment. 'What if Adie finds out where we are?'

'He won't, Bon.' I can feel my heart beating faster; it's making a pulse jump in my neck. This wasn't how I saw our journey to Brighton unravelling. It was going to be so easy: a small diversion to Edinburgh, a soft bed, laughter and bonding, all of us happy together. My idea of all going on the run together meant I could keep an eye on Jade once she was with her new boyfriend, but now she doesn't want anything but to be as far away from me as possible.

Jade squeezes her phone. 'I'm going to ring Luis.'

I grin at her. 'All right, love.'

'No,' Jade's arm is on mine. 'I meant get out of the way, Mum. I'm not staying in the car. I need privacy. This isn't a bloody circus.'

She crawls across me and pushes the door open, slipping into shadows.

I can hear her voice outside, the lilting softness of her words of love to Luis, rising to outrage for a moment and then becoming gentle again, infused with affection. I suddenly feel completely alone and my throat constricts. Tears prick my eyes. Soon, she'll be living with Luis and I'd hoped our journey together would be about the cementing of our adult friendship, mother and daughter, forever close. I'd hoped she'd want me near her and I could make sure she was all right, not by herself, investing in a relationship that might break her heart. But I'm failing.

Nan's voice is a whisper from the back seat. 'I need to pee soon, Georgina. And my leg's gone stiff.'

I take a deep breath and make my voice light. 'All right, Nanny. When Jade's finished, why don't we all get out and stretch our legs? I'll find Bonnie's cosmetics bag in the back. Then you can sit in the front with Jade. There's more room. Then we'll settle down for a sleep and we can sort out the puncture in the morning.'

'Sleep in this car?' Nan's horrified. 'My backside's already numb. I'll wake up dead.'

I check the time: it's past eleven. There's little chance of seeing any vehicles up this desolate hill at this time of night, but I decide that if someone passes, I'll leap out of the car and try to flag them down and ask for help. Or maybe it's better to leave it until morning. Who knows what type of person might be travelling this way so late at night? The image of Adie following us in the Boxster flits into my mind but I push the thoughts away.

Jade slips back into the car next to me. 'Right. You can all be grateful. I've phoned Thomas Blake and Sons, the garage people. They're coming out to pick us up now. It won't be cheap though. You have some money, Aunty Bonnie?'

Bonnie nods from the back. Jade hasn't finished.

'And there's a B & B near their garage. They gave me the number and I've spoken to a nice lady. She'll have a double and two single rooms ready for us. So, thank goodness for me.'

Half an hour later, my car's safely in the garage in Tebay and we slump over a hot cup of tea in the lounge. Jade and Bonnie decide that they'll have the single rooms and I'll sleep with Nan. Jade's happy. Luis has phoned her, and she makes sure we all know that he said he can't wait until she's in his arms again and tomorrow is only a few hours away, then they'll have forever together. I notice the dreamy look on her face. She catches my eye and glares back.

Bonnie's cheered up. She's going to lard half a ton of expensive age-defying cream on her face and have a good night's sleep. Despite being tired out, her eyes are brighter. She grins and hugs me, then we all embrace each other. I feel a surge of warmth: this is the beginning of the new Bonnie. It's how it should be, all of us together, embarking on an adventure, bonding.

I'm about to suggest that we go up to our rooms, when Bonnie turns, her eyes full of tears, and she sighs.

'You've all been so lovely today. I know we've done the right thing, running away. But I hope Adie's all right.'

'He's not worth the dirt from your shoes, Bonnie. Did you bring any Guinness, Georgina? This tea is weak.' That's from Nan, who's unwrapping a bar of chocolate.

'What made you pick him, Aunty Bonnie? I mean, you and he are so different.' Jade's genuinely interested.

'Opposites attract, Jade. I fell in love with him. He had everything I was looking for. Good looks, confidence, a nice car, and he said he loved me more than anything in the world.'

Nanny guffaws. 'He was a con artist even then. He conned you into thinking he was a decent man . . .'

'How did you meet?' Jade stretches her legs, leans back into the armchair.

Bonnie sighs from somewhere deep. 'I first met him when I was at work. He was a friend and a client of the manager. I was working in a hotel, in reception. But I wanted something else. I wanted to have a better life, really be somebody, and Adie made me feel good about myself. I thought he was someone special.'

Nanny mutters something that sounds like 'special, my arse' and I hear her snap off more chocolate. Then she says, 'Terry Wood was a nice fella, though. I liked him.' Silence hangs in the air like a damp blanket. 'He thought the world of you, Georgina.' A very damp blanket.

Jade helps me out. 'He's a great dad. He comes up to see me every few weeks . . .' She pauses. 'I'll be closer to where he lives when I'm in Brighton.'

I want to say: he lives in Ealing. Where the comedies come from. My stock reply, laughing it all off, hoping everyone'll think that I don't care any more. But I don't say anything. I look at the décor in the lounge, the creamy wood chip walls, and bite my lip. Jade has an afterthought.

'I don't much care for Alison, though. We still haven't really got used to each other. I've always thought her a bit pretentious. Not like Dad. He's been great. He started everything off for me, took me down the gym, out for a run.'

Bonnie leans forwards towards Jade. 'What's it like being a personal trainer, Jade?'

Jade's tone is full of enthusiasm. 'I love it. You meet interesting clients, people who want to stay fit or get fit or get thinner, but they're all interested in being the best they can be. I love the job. It's good to be able to help others work out and to stay on top of the game myself. I'm doing this research at the moment into veganism and bodybuilding. I think the vegan diet's going to be really big, the next healthy way forwards. Luis and I are considering . . .'

'It must be tiring, though, all that training and running and working out.'

'I love it, Aunty Bonnie. It keeps me fit.'

'And will you be able to be a personal trainer in Brighton or London?'

'Oh, yes. Luis says he's spoken to someone at the club and they might be able to help me find some work.'

'I'd have loved a job like that.' Nanny wriggles in the armchair, moving from one aching hip to the other. 'Or a glamorous job like an air hostess.'

I chuckle. 'I can't imagine you as a trolley dolly, Nan.'

Bonnie grins. 'You'd get to wear one of those nice pillbox hats, with your hair done up and perfect make-up. I like the Emirates flight attendants, the red hats that match their lipstick and the little white veils. I'd love that.'

Jade snorts softly. 'It's hard work. You have to serve all the food and drink and keep the customers in their seats, on your feet all day, managing any crisis while you're up in the air. I wouldn't fancy it.'

'It would've been better than working in Bryant's factory, Jade. Or being a dinner lady. I did both those jobs and they were tough. I mean, it must be exciting being up in the clouds' – Nanny fiddles with her door key, twisting it in stiff fingers – 'but serving food to kids who're pushing and shoving and starving, grabbing extras while you're looking away, dealing with nasty supervisors, being paid the lowest possible wage. It was horrible. Nobody got on with the boss – it was continuous dysentery.'

I shake my head. 'Dissent, Nan.'

'Give me an air hostess job any day. It'd be so nice, up in the clouds, everyone being nice to you. I'd feel really special.' We think about that for a moment, then Nanny adds, 'I can't grumble, though. My Wilf made me feel really special.'

After a pause, Jade sighs. 'Luis makes me feel special.'

I count up to five in my head. My timing is perfect, as Bonnie's voice takes on a brittle murmur.

'Adie said I was special, too. I miss him.'

I have nothing to add. Nanny's tucked up in bed with me ten minutes later. I let my eyelids close and try to relax. Nanny mutters something under her breath about all men who cheat on their wives having their genitals removed and I slip into the sleep of the exhausted.

We wake at eight, aching and stiff. Nanny threatens to faint unless she eats something soon. In the breakfast room downstairs, we sit and inhale the smell of coffee and toast.

After breakfast, at eleven, a young lad called Derek

Thomas arrives with a new tyre and Bonnie pays both him and the B & B owner, a lovely lady in her seventies called Joan, with Adie's money. I notice Bonnie's smile, the flourish of independence as she hands over her cash. It's the first time she's paid for anything by herself and I smile, flushed with success: this is the beginning of the new Bonnie without Adie, and it suits her well.

By midday we're packed, sitting in a car with a brand-new tyre, and we're on our way. I breathe out and look at the scenery flying past through the window: green fields, trees with new buds, stray waving daffodils. My thoughts rattle: I miss my home and I'm worried about my business. I resolve to ring Amanda later. But at least we're leaving Adie behind us, and we're going to be far from Beddowes and his threats. We're on our way to Brighton.

Chapter Ten

I can hardly keep my eyes open. The road blurs and cars snarl by, overtaking us. I can't stop yawning and my jaw hurts.

'Shall I drive for a bit, Mum?'

I wriggle the aches from my shoulders. It's not yet four o'clock and the motorway's busy. A huge lorry shudders past, then another. My eyelids are heavy.

'I'm fine. I'm used to this car. I'd rather drive, if it's okay with you, Jade.'

Jade snorts. 'You're so possessive of this banger. It's not as if the car is even new. And you scuffed the paintwork last night.'

Bonnie calls from the back, 'I don't want to drive. This one's too big. I hate driving other people's cars. They make me nervous. Are we in Brighton yet?'

'We're near Birmingham.' My legs on the pedals are cramped and numbing. A hazy mist floats across my vision and I take a deep breath. 'We'll stop near Northampton, shall we? Find a B & B. Have an early night.'

'I have money. I can pay.' Bonnie's little voice is all enthusiasm.

'Can't we just go straight to Brighton, Mum?'

'I'm really tired, Jade. It's just one overnight stop, to catch up on sleep. Yesterday's left me exhausted. I can hardly concentrate on the road.'

She folds her arms. 'Really? Another night? I don't believe it! I'll never get to Brighton at this rate.'

Bonnie calls from the back, 'How far to Northampton?'

'An hour, maybe a bit more.' I sigh and it reaches down to my belly. 'I'll be okay. Once we're there, I can have a rest and then we'll be in Brighton tomorrow.'

Thoughts drift: I imagine a quiet evening, all of us together, a pleasant meal out, sharing laughs and a drink or two. Jade folds her arms next to me. She's sulking.

A voice booms from the back seat. 'I need a pee.' Nanny's completely alert. 'Now. Can we stop, Georgina?'

'I'll find a motorway services, Nan. The next one can't be too far.'

'No. Right now. Stop here, by the side of the road.'

I stifle a smile. 'I can't stop on the motorway.'

'Find a lay-by. This minute!'

'There *are* no lay-bys, Nan.'

A mile flashes by, two.

'I need a piddle now, and I mean now,' Nan shrieks from behind me and my foot presses harder on the pedal in panic.

I drive for half a mile, hoping there'll be an exit. She yells again and I pull onto the hard shoulder and flash the hazard lights. I hope the police don't spot us.

Nanny's surprisingly sprightly, slipping out of the BMW despite the mordant arthritis in her hip. Her feet patter behind the car and I follow her, slamming the door. She crouches on gravel, adjusts her underwear and a trickle becomes a gush.

'You okay, Nan?'

'I'm pissing like a horse. Wait till you're old and your bladder's gone.'

I hear Jade snorting from inside the car, trying not to laugh. I wrap my coat tightly, pulling it round my body. The wind cuts through the material.

'Are you done, Nan?'

A car whizzes past and the horn blares, an intermittent bold tooting. Jade guffaws out loud and I can hear Bonnie snigger. Nanny jerks her head up, totters. I grab her shoulder to stop her from falling. She pulls up her pants, staring after the distant sound, long gone.

'Cheeky bastards.'

I take her arm, tug her towards the car and bundle her in. Jade has tears in her eyes and Bonnie's face is creased with laughter. I press my lips together and splutter. Bonnie pulls Nan inside and fastens her seat belt. She sighs with satisfaction, looping her arm through Bonnie's.

'Thanks, love. My days, that feels better.'

Jade is hooting, in hysterics, and Bonnie's eyes are watering. Nan stares, her face indignant.

'What's the matter? Never seen an emergency toilet stop before?'

I look at Nan, her face contorted in exasperation, and a howl bursts from my lips. Then we're rocking in our seats, tears running down our faces: me, Bonnie and Jade, out of control.

Nan raises her eyebrows. 'A woman has to do what a woman has to do.'

She winks and then suddenly all four of us are screaming and clutching at each other, doubled over and snorting.

I start the car. 'Are you cold, Nan? Do you need to stop for a cup of tea?'

She chuckles. 'Don't be daft. I'll just want to pee again.'

Bonnie splutters and the laughter starts again. It feels

lovely, all sharing the moment. I wipe my eyes and think about the four of us together: Jade's relaxed, Bonnie's happier than I've seen her in ages. But Nan's the most changed: she's revelling in the company. Despite the difficulties she has with mobility and in spite of her heart condition, she's developed a new energy, an enthusiasm. Her eyes are bright behind her glasses and she's bubbly, energetic, one of the girls, no longer enclosed within the claustrophobic walls of a cold house. I allow myself a moment's glow of pleasure. This is all my idea and it's working: we're bonding.

I move the car forwards and then join the stream of traffic. The sky is dappled, pink and blue, merging into a mottled mauve. I turn the radio up and fix my mind on a soft bed somewhere in Northamptonshire.

We stop at The Four Cedars. The owner, Mrs Bolt, is sharp-featured, in her forties and very neat. Her dark hair is cut short and she wears a black skirt and blouse. She looks like a governess in an old-fashioned girls' school. It's almost six o'clock. I ask for two rooms for the night and tell her I've been driving a long time and that we're all very tired. My eyes are heavy and my shoulders feel like concrete.

We sign in as the Jackson four – Sue, Mary, Donna and Lilly – with an invented address in Kendal, and Mrs Bolt gives me two keys for two rooms. There's a smile on my face: we're four women on the run, in our own road movie, and we're independent, enjoying it as much as I'd hoped, on our way to Brighton. A thrilling sense of fun, the open road and the power of mischief bubbles in my veins.

Nanny pipes up, 'Don't get a room on the top floor. My knees are playing me up, Georgina.'

I smile, pretend I haven't heard and pay the deposit in cash. While the others are waiting in the lobby, I call Amanda. I've been so busy with our road trip, I've forgotten to phone her.

She picks up straight away. 'Georgie? Where are you? What's going on?'

'Ah. You'd better take a seat, Amanda. I'm going to need your help.'

I know she's smiling. 'Tell me it's man trouble.'

'Not the sort you'd want. Look, I need a favour.' I'd been thinking about how to tell her, exactly how honest to be.

She makes an *mmm* sound. 'Ask away, Georgie.'

'Bonnie's split up with Adie. He's taken it badly. She's not feeling great either, so I've taken her away for a few days, spontaneously.' I breathe in – it's sort of the truth.

'And Jade?'

'With Luis. Can you hold the fort in the salon?'

I hear her gulp. 'We have a lot of clients booked in . . .'

'I know. You'll need to shift a few regulars round, apologise to a few more. But can you phone the two women we were going to interview tomorrow? Lexi and Ella-Louise. Take them on, a week's trial. If they're any good, keep them both on.'

She sniffs suspiciously. 'How long are you going to be away?'

'Two weeks, maybe more. I'm not sure.'

'Georgie, I—'

'I need your help, Amanda. Please. Pay yourself a manager's salary. Anything. We'll check how it goes this week and I'll ring you in a few days.'

I know she's thinking. She pauses a moment, then her voice is light.

'I've always wanted to be a manager.'

I breathe a sigh of relief. 'Thanks, Amanda. I'm so sorry to do this. I mean, I could be back at the end of next week, who knows?'

'Don't rush. I might like running a salon with three of us and you away.' She giggles.

'I'm at the end of the phone, all the time.'

'Georgie?' I hear her voice, full of interest. 'Where exactly are you?'

'Tenerife.' It comes out before I can stop it. And it's best that she doesn't know, not yet, because Adie'll prise it out of her if he comes round. I'll explain later and apologise. 'A ten-day break – with the option of staying longer . . .'

'Lovely,' she coos.

'You gave me the idea. You said I needed a holiday.' I'm in full liar swing now. 'Oh, Amanda – one thing . . .'

'Anything.'

'If Adie calls, you know nothing.'

'What shall I say?'

'Say I've gone to Iceland with Jade for a fortnight. You arranged the cover with me a week ago. You haven't seen Bonnie at all. Okay?'

'So basically you want me to tell him a pack of whoppers?'

I don't hesitate. 'Basically, yes.'

'Fine.' Amanda's voice is firm. 'That shouldn't be too hard. I never liked him anyway. He's always seemed shifty.'

I nod, even though she's on the other end of the phone. 'I know. Thanks, Amanda.'

I gaze out of the window. Here we are, in a little town in Northamptonshire, miles from Adie, on the way to Brighton, and my business is in safe hands. I feel the load loosen from my shoulders and sail into the air. It's a sense of freedom I haven't had in ages. I'm with the three women I love most and I'm ready for the adventure.

*

95

We're on the second floor. I've hauled Nan's luggage and my own upstairs: her legs ache, and I'm so tired I've bashed a case against the wall and ripped out a chunk of the magnolia woodchip. I stand in the doorway of number five, which Nan'll share with Bonnie, who's in the lobby on the phone to Demi.

It's a neat twin room, flowery drapes in orange, matching duvets, the walls a deep golden yellow. A modern wardrobe with sliding doors and large mirrors makes the space look unpretentious and clean. At the end of the room, the door is ajar to the en suite: a gleaming white basin, toilet and frosted glass-surround shower.

Nanny turns to me. 'I bet people in prison get rooms like this. I've seen them in television on *Cell Block H*.' She sits on one of the beds and bounces up and down. 'It's too soft. I'll get backache.'

I put the case down and turn to go. Her voice hits me in the back like a sharp stone.

'No Guinness, Georgina? I can't manage in this place without a drink.'

I grin at her: some things never change.

'It's six o'clock, Nan. Just have a snooze then we'll go out for dinner.'

She yells, 'And another thing – I've never had a shower in my life. I don't intend to have one now. I'd die in a shower. They say you can drown in two inches of water. It's not right, all that water falling on your head. It'd damage your brain . . .'

I close the door crisply, then wait a moment and put my ear against the wood. She's chattering to herself about whether or not she can take the free shampoo and soap home. I wonder for a few seconds when we'll be able to go back to Liverpool, then I move on to room number six. Jade is installed in the armchair already, arms folded and frowning. There's a double bed, the pillows and covers in the same flowery orange. I shrug. At least we have a bath in our en suite and I plan to take a long soak later.

She takes out her phone. I'm desperate for a nap, so I pull off my outer clothes and roll under the duvet. I close my eyes. Sleep seeps like warm milk into my brain in seconds.

I open my eyes and the room's in darkness. It's eight o'clock. The curtains are closed and, for a moment, I can't remember where I am. I'm in a space without thoughts, floating, then suddenly I crash into reality, remember where we are, blink and roll over. Jade's next to me, her back rounded and warm, and I listen to her breathing. For a moment, I think she's asleep, then I see the sharp light of her phone screen and I can see she's texting. I reach for my own phone. My stomach feels shrunken and empty.

'Are you okay, Jade?'

She doesn't move. 'Mum, what the hell are we doing?'

'I thought we'd stay here tonight then take off after breakfast tomorrow.'

'For Brighton, I hope?'

'Yes.'

'We're not going via the Outer Hebrides?'

I ignore her. She touches my arm.

'Mum, I'm going to Brighton to be with Luis. Why exactly are you going? I mean, I know Uncle Adie cheated on Aunty Bonnie and did some dodgy deal, but it's not your—'

'It's serious, Jade.'

'Then let the police arrest Uncle Adie. Problem solved. Totally. Go home. Go back to Liverpool.'

I sigh. 'There's something else. I think Bonnie could be in some kind of trouble.'

'From Uncle Adie?' Her tone is sarcastic, loaded with disrespect.

'He's had threatening texts. A man he's done a deal with. Duncan Beddowes. Something went wrong. I think he was after Adie that night in their house. Bonnie's best out of the way for a while.'

She's silent a moment, then her tone is full of irritation. 'Anything else I should know?'

'The man Beddowes has a photo of us, Bonnie and me.'

'Oh, for God's sake.'

'We'll be okay in Brighton.'

'Have you thought about how this'll affect me?'

'Brighton's a big place. No one'll find us.'

'Luis lives outside Brighton. In a luxury block of flats by the sea. Luis is a celebrity and he's my boyfriend. I can't have all this baggage . . .'

It's as if she's slapped me. I catch my breath.

'We're baggage? We're just taking a break from Adie, Jade.'

She rolls over and glares. 'Luis is important to me. I don't want to arrive there to live with him and have you three watching me all the time, not to mention Uncle Adie and his dodgy friends . . .'

Suddenly I feel sad, my emotions as soggy as the mattress I'm lying on. There's a rap at the door.

Jade murmurs, 'I'll talk to you about this later,' as if I'm a naughty child.

Then Bonnie's in the doorway in tight jeans and a low-necked flouncy blouse, crimson lipstick, rattling the charm bracelet, my coat wrapped round her shoulders. Nanny's behind her, wearing a dress that looks like it was fashionable in the Sixties. It's A-line, with wide black and white hoops. It stops just above her knees, and she has red tights, kitten heels and Bonnie's lipstick. Her hair's sticking up in the air, tied in a purple scarf.

Bonnie says, 'Let's go out and eat. A change of scenery will do us good.'

Nanny pushes into the room. 'It's like a morgue in here. Open the curtains. You're not even ready, Georgina. Come on. There's a curry restaurant on the corner and Bonnie's booked us a table. It's only five minutes away and I'll be all right walking between you two if we take it slowly. I've never tried a tandy doori, but I could eat a house and wash it down with a beer or two.' She glares as I sit up in bed. 'Are you coming or not?'

I think about the hot bath I'd looked forward to and reach for my stale clothes.

Chapter Eleven

Nanny's having a whale of a time: she's discovered Indian lager. She has, in fact, discovered two pints of it and she's shovelling tikka masala into her mouth, slurping Kingfisher, her lipstick smudged.

Bonnie's pushing king prawns around her plate and nibbling a grain of rice at a time, grumbling, 'I swear my tummy's shrunk.'

Nan looks at the seafood on her plate.

'I don't like the look of prawns, Bonnie. It can't be good for you, eating those crushed Asians.'

Jade's eyebrows shoot up and she stares, appalled.

'Mum, for goodness' sake – she can't say that. Do something.'

I mutter, 'Crustaceans, Nan,' and roll my eyes, embarrassed and helpless.

Jade changes the subject, loudly extolling the benefits of protein to boost performance.

Nanny chuckles. 'Does it work on the football field or in the bedroom, Jade?'

She raises her eyebrows. 'Both.'

'I'd better have some protein in this curry then.' Her

voice is too loud and she lubricates it with more Kingfisher. 'I like the look of the waiter over there. The young one with the tight trousers.'

Jade's mortified and I wave the tight-trousered young man over. 'Could we have the bill, please?'

Bonnie pulls out her credit card and offers it, arm outstretched. 'I'll get this.'

'No way.' My voice is too sharp and she blinks as if I've hurt her feelings. I try again. 'Bonnie, we'd be trace-able. Isn't that the card for your joint account with Adie? Don't you remember, we went to Edinburgh to put him off the scent? So he'd think you were in Scotland.'

She bites her lip. 'I forgot about that. Oh, I think I've done something really stupid.'

I'm about to tell her that it's not a problem, I can pay with cash, but she pouts and tears fill her eyes.

'I went to the cash machine earlier, the one next to the B & B. I wanted to buy a few things.'

I breathe out. 'Don't worry, Bon. We'll be off tomorrow morning. He won't trace us from here.'

Bonnie brightens. 'Ah! I forgot to tell you. He texted me earlier, then he phoned me.'

'You spoke to him?'

'I didn't mean to pick up. Then I said I wasn't going to speak to him until I knew what was going on. He wants to talk to me in person. He says he'll explain everything and it'll all be all right.'

Nanny's glass is empty. 'Tell him to go to hell.'

'I told him I was in Las Palmeras, like you told me to, and I'd be there for two weeks. I said when I came back I'd meet him.'

'What did he say?'

'It's bad news.' She sighs. Tears fill her brown eyes and make them shine.

'What did he say, Bonnie?'

'My passport was in the drawer at home. He knows I'm in the UK. He said he'll find me and . . .'

'And what?'

Nanny tips over a bottle of Kingfisher and lager soaks into the pristine linen cloth. She mutters, 'Oh crap,' and salvages the bottle, upending it and swigging the dregs.

Bonnie dabs her eyes. 'He said he needs to find me before Duncan Beddowes does. He says I need him to help me. Beddowes has threatened to do something terrible and we need to run away together.'

Jade rolls her eyes. 'What a mess.'

A single tear streaks Bonnie's cheek. 'He made me feel really scared.'

Nanny shakes her head. 'If anyone tries to hurt you, Bonnie, they'll have me to deal with.' She brandishes the empty bottle of Kingfisher, then bats her eyelashes at the waiter who arrives with four glasses of complimentary sambuca.

Nanny knocks two of them back without pausing for breath. I shrug my shoulders: she's drinking too much again. Jade, who has a glass of sparkling water, notices my helplessness, gives Nanny a look then takes the other glasses of spirit, one in each hand, and downs them like an expert.

I pay the bill with cash.

'Let's go back to the B & B and sleep on it. After breakfast tomorrow, we'll sort it all out. To be honest, I'm too tired to think about anything at the moment.'

Jade scowls. 'Well don't start snoring again, Mum. I'm up early for a run tomorrow morning and I need my sleep. I've told Luis I'll see him in the afternoon. I'll be staying in his flat overlooking the beach. I don't know where you three will be going.'

Bonnie's eyes fill again.

Nanny's grinning, her lips parted like a hooked fish's. As she stands, her knees give way.

She giggles. 'I'll have another two of those free sam pukers, waiter, please. They were nice.'

I hold her up and heave her towards the door. She mutters about taking the bottle home to bed – or the waiter – and I thrust us both into the cold night air. Tomorrow will bring answers. Right now, I need sleep.

But I can't fall asleep. Jade has an hour-long call with Luis in the en suite, slips under the covers and is immediately snuffling like a baby. I'm wide awake. I think about her, how keen she is to be with Luis, and how I wanted the chance to make sure she's all right. I'm not sure it hasn't pushed us further apart. Perhaps it'll change when we arrive at Luis'. But I've no idea where we'll stay.

My mind runs over the events: Bonnie's escape from the house, Adie's desperate pleading with her to run away with him, and I'm not sure it all adds up. Is this Beddowes character really dangerous or is Adie just exaggerating to persuade Bonnie to go back with him? Whatever he is, and despite the incidents with other women, Adie does care for her. Bonnie's his prize possession.

I press my lips together and vow to stay single forever. It won't be difficult. I think Bonnie's best by herself, too; she's certainly not safe while there's a money row going on between Adie and Beddowes. I snort and roll over, pulling the duvet with me. Jade gives a similar sound and tugs it back. I sigh. Adie must owe Beddowes some money or he's reneged on a deal. Goodness knows what kind of deal. Money – a lot of it – no doubt.

I remind myself that Bonnie and I should lie low for a while, in case he traces her transactions at the cash machine. We can turn our road trip into a kind of mini-break, a fun one, one that keeps Bonnie and her credit card away from the expensive boutiques. I sigh and close my eyes. Jade's exhaling, a soft, contented purring sound.

When I wake, it's half past eight and Jade's side of the bed is empty. I look longingly at the bath and decide to go down to breakfast first. When I knock at room number five, there's no answer.

Downstairs, the little breakfast room with its four tables and clean net curtains is empty except for my family. Jade's in running gear, munching toast. Bonnie's sitting next to her clutching a black coffee; she looks like she hasn't slept. Nanny's eating a fry-up. The green woolly hat is pulled down over wet hair and she's found herself a long cable-knit sweater in green and well-worn stretchy black trousers. I sit in the spare chair with a thud and nod at Mrs Bolt, who pours coffee.

Mrs Bolt says, 'I've just been having an interesting chat with your aunt Anne about the town and how it was years ago. I didn't know she'd lived in Brackley.'

'Anne?' I rub my eyes and slurp black coffee, then reach for toast. 'Oh, Anne. Yes, of course.'

She's in the visitors' book as Mary Jackson and she's never been to Brackley in her life. I resolve to find some tactful way to ask Nan to keep her mouth shut. We're on the run, for God's sake.

Nanny's grinning, waving her hand about. 'I do love this place. It reminds me of when I was young. I came to school here years ago. The grammar school. That would be in the 1940s. We passed the school yesterday on the way to the curry restaurant. Magdalen, it's called.'

Mrs Bolt is refilling Jade's cup: she pauses mid-pour. 'Mag-dalen? Oh, we pronounce it *Maudlin* here. Like the Oxford College. Magdalen College was a prestigious grammar school in those days.'

Jade flashes me a warning look, the *do something before it's too late, Mum*, look. But Nanny's in full swing.

'I know – I went there. Yes. It was a good school. Oh yes. I've such wonderful memories.'

She's pronouncing *yes* as *yeyyss* and I cringe. Bonnie stares out of the window, completely distracted. Her eyes are tired; the skin below is tinged with blue and pale brown. I reach out and pat her hand and she offers me a weak smile.

Mrs Bolt clears away Nanny's empty plate and fills her coffee.

'My grandfather went there. Archie Beldover. Did you know him?'

'Oh, *yeysss*. Archibold. We were acquaintances.'

'Mmm.' Mrs Bolt hesitates. 'The thing is, Magdalen was – right up until the school became comprehensive, I think – a boys' grammar school.'

Nanny gives her the sweetest smile. She doesn't miss a beat.

'I know. All those boys. And me, the only girl. I was so lucky to win that scholarship.'

Mrs Bolt moves away. She comes back with more toast, scrambled eggs, and puts it in front of me without a word.

Nanny waves her hand again. 'Oh, Mrs Bolt?'

The owner turns, frowning, tray poised.

'I wonder, could I have some more coffee? And I'd like a couple of poached eggs. Poached eggs are my favourite.'

To my knowledge, Nanny's never eaten a poached egg in her life. I feel my shoulders climbing towards my neck. Jade gives me an irritated look. Bonnie turns to me and raises her eyebrows as if she's missed something, then lifts the cup of cold coffee, sips and pulls a face.

Mrs Bolt nods but she's not pleased. 'Poached eggs? Of course.'

'Oh, I do like this place,' Nanny says, entirely for the benefit of Mrs Bolt, who's smiling at two new guests, a young couple who've just taken the table by the window. 'The bedroom's splendid. I did so enjoy my half an hahr in the pahr shahr.'

My eyebrows shoot up and Bonnie comes to life, leans over the table and grabs my hand.

'I had to drag her out. She was sitting on the floor singing "Raindrops Keep Falling on My Head". Next time, I'm sharing with Jade.'

I press my lips together to prevent a giggle. Jade jerks her head up, her violet eyes furious.

'There won't be a next time.'

We finish breakfast in silence. Nanny digs in when the two poached eggs arrive.

'Oh, Mrs Bolt, what sheer eggstaaasy.'

Bonnie looks horrified. Nan has yolk round her mouth. Mrs Bolt's back is hunched in irritation. My shoulders start to shake and I cover my face to camouflage a snort. Bonnie begins to snigger. We're both giggling into our hands.

Jade's livid. She folds her arms and leans forwards. It's an announcement.

'Right. When we get to Luis' village outside Brighton, I've found you somewhere to stop for a few weeks. You can all be grateful to me. But then, once we're there, stay out of my life. Got it?'

Chapter Twelve

Trees loom through the car windows on all sides and I'm driving slowly, searching for the turn to Rottingdean. The satnav has a reassuring female voice telling me to turn left after 300 metres, but Jade's screeching is louder.

'Watch out, Mum. That was a squirrel. You nearly hit it. No, not this left turn – *that* left turn. Now we've got to turn round and go all the way back again.'

The March sky dims and there are no houses, no lights except for the car's beam. I can't tell where the road ends and the grass verges begin. It's evening; trees rustle, shadows shift in every hedge and gateway. I try to concentrate on the road in front of me: I don't want the car to end up in a hedge again.

A fox runs out and its eyes gleam, luminous in the headlights. I slow to a jerky stop. Jade's texting furiously, frowning, no doubt telling Luis she's alive and well but only just, thanks to my erratic driving. Bonnie's asleep in the back seat, her head lolling on Nanny's shoulder.

I have time to look in the mirror at Nan, to take in her face, which is a mask of surprise. Her eyes shine behind her glasses, searching through the window; she's out of her comfort zone. She cranes her neck towards the dense forests and silent roads with no houses in sight. When she sees the fox loiter in front of us, she murmurs, 'Well, would you believe it?'

I shuffle the car forwards as it slinks away and wonder how long it is since Nanny's been outside her home city. She's a Liverpool girl who never strayed. There were a few holidays in Wales, at a favourite caravan site, but I'm not sure she's travelled beyond her street since Uncle Wilf died, five years ago.

I glance through the driver's mirror at Nan's startled eyes and I start to worry how she'll cope with living here.

'Nearly there.' Jade's voice is bright again. 'Luis says there are garages behind the flats at the top of the hill, where you can put the car. Once we're at his place – our place – I'll show you where you can stay. It's one of the flats in the block. Not on our floor. And you can't stay for too long.'

I stop at a crossroads and glance into the shadows, then shuffle the car forwards.

'How long?' I ask.

'Till Easter – twenty-first of April. Then he's back so he'll want his flat again.'

'Who?'

'Roque.'

I give up expecting a logical answer and make a left turn down a hill. I wonder how far it is to the sea.

Another mile later, we're driving through a village, along a high street past a Tudor-fronted building.

Nan leans forwards and mutters to herself, 'Well this is a small place. A bit poky. I hope we don't have to stay here.'

'Just keep driving, then up the hill onto the cliffs. The road will be a bit narrower but it's easy to get to the top.'

Jade's an expert on driving in Sussex now. 'There's a path straight there via the beach, but cars go up this steep hill. We're about five minutes from Luis' flat.'

Then the sea is on our left-hand side and we climb upwards. Huge pale cliffs glimmer in front of us. Even though it's dark, I can see the stark chalky-pale shapes in the headlights, giant rocks clad in shadow.

Jade squeals and points a finger. 'There it is.'

And we all crane our necks forwards and gasp at a building set back from the edge of a cliff, overlooking the sea, with steps down to the beach. Little lights glimmer from a white building, a luxury block of flats, square lines and all glass, huge front balconies. A few panoramic windows shine orange and amber; others are dark, or illuminated by a glimmer.

'How many people live here, Jade?'

'There are nine flats. We're on the third floor. You're one floor below.'

Bonnie wakes up. 'It's lovely. I can see why your Luis wanted to live here rather than London.'

Jade turns her head and her face shines with happiness. 'He's not a city boy. He was born several miles outside Barcelona, brought up in a small fishing village. He didn't want the bustle of Central London. And he loves the sea.'

We reach the top of the hill, pull onto the cliff. At the back of the building, a garage door is open and we park inside. I decide the car will stay here until we leave. I don't want Adie to trace us.

We struggle with our bags to the front entrance. The sea whispers down below and Nanny crooks her elbow through mine.

'I don't want to fall over the edge, Georgina.'

It's so dark now, rain drizzling. Nanny leans on my arm, frail, her eyes troubled. Bonnie's clinging to her luggage, including her credit card purchases from yesterday, and Jade has three cases and a handbag. I drag my single case and Nan's old battered one, heaving them by my feet, and I wrap an arm round Nanny. Her eyes search everywhere; her mouth is slack and she looks confused.

Jade enters a code on a keypad at the door and we're in, looking up at a vast marble staircase, black-and-white walls. We take the lift.

Inside Luis' third-floor flat is all white: the walls, the sofa, the curtains, the coffee table, the rug. Everything apart from the huge television on the wall. The windows are vast on two sides, showing picture-perfect views over the beach and across the water. I gasp at the twinkling coastline, the sprawl of the shadowy sea beneath a black sky. I imagine how beautiful it'll be from the balcony in the daytime or when the sun sets.

Luis comes over and hugs Jade. He's not tall: Jade is three inches taller in her heels as she hugs him and they kiss. The three of us watch, waiting. His hair is silky, a deep ebony and, without the headband, it flops over his face and almost covers his dark, dancing eyes. His smile is huge as he grins at us. He's compact, muscular in a blue T-shirt, designer jeans and flip-flops. He turns to Bonnie and beams.

'You're Jade's mother. Of course. It's good to meet you.' He kisses her on each cheek and she's so stunned she can't move. He notices me for the first time. 'You're the aunt?' And he takes Nan's hands in his. 'You're Jade's *abuelita*? So nice to have a big pleasure. Welcome. Welcome to you all.'

Jade links her arm through Luis' and indicates me with a quick nod of her head. 'My mother, Georgie Turner.' He stares at me, unblinking. 'And this is Aunty Bonnie Carrick and this is my great-aunt, Nanny Basham.'

Nanny hurls her arms round him and hugs him. He's even more surprised. She kisses his cheeks.

'I've seen you on television. Oh, I think you're just wonderful, Louise. The goal last week, the overhead scissors kick, was brilliant. My Wilf would've loved you. He liked football . . . mind you, he wasn't a fan of the London teams, oh, no way. Liverpool through and through. Cut him open and he'd have Anfield stamped on his heart, you know, like the Blackpool rock.'

Luis stares for a minute then grins, his face confused, and says, 'That is very good. You want a cup of tea or coffee? I can make.'

Jade takes over and I immediately notice by the way his eyes become misty that he's besotted with her.

'Luis, *querido*, shall we show them Roque's flat, then we can spend some quality time together?'

It takes him a minute to register her meaning. He stands, hands in his pockets, his mouth open, and she puts an arm around his neck. He belongs to her. He fishes two keys on a ring from his pocket.

'Roque say me it is all fine. He is in America, where they open his knee to make better. He is the big defender here and he jumps for the ball and his knee hits the ground and—'

'And *olé*! – smash! I can imagine, Louise . . .' Nanny is all eyes behind her glasses.

Jade folds her arms. 'He's recuperating in the USA until after Easter, so Luis phoned him and asked and it's all right for you to stay. Make sure it's kept nice and clean, though. He's from Madrid. Roque is Luis' best friend. He's very particular about his flat.'

Bonnie nods and I suddenly feel anxious. Jade expects us to be untidy.

We go down one floor in the lift and into Roque's flat,

which is exactly the same inside as Luis' but without the sauna. The views are vast on two sides, and I open the sliding door and stand on the balcony, leaning forwards and narrowing my eyes to see the movement of the ocean. The waves whisper below as the rain falls in small pools at my feet and thuds on glass overhead. I feel safe here.

Nanny turns in a circle, making small whooping sounds. I join her as she leans against the glass of the panoramic window, pressing her nose against it.

'Oh my, Georgina. It's like living in the clouds. Like being an angel up in Heaven.' Bonnie flops in the white sofa and folds her arms.

There are two enormous bedrooms, the walls painted cream. Nanny decides she'll have the smaller one with its own bathroom, and Bonnie and I will share the king-sized bed, the en suite Jacuzzi bath.

I go to the window and stare out at the skyline, at glittering waves, the shimmering inky ocean, the shadowy cliffs stretching like watching giants into the distance. I breathe out. Adie won't find us here. It filters into my thoughts that we can stay until Easter. That's perfect. Hopefully, Adie will have sorted his money problems out by then.

I consider phoning Amanda – she thinks I'm in Tenerife and I ought to apologise. I turn back and notice Bonnie, staring around like a lost puppy; Nanny, grinning like a fish at Luis, who still has his hands in his pockets, and Jade who's clearly ready to go up to Luis' flat for quality time.

I take a breath. 'Right. We'll catch up tomorrow, shall we, Jade? Let's order in some food and have a meeting. We girls need to make some plans. We have to work out what to do next. It's time for action.'

*

I decide to ring Amanda before I order pizza. I dial and wait for several seconds then she picks up.

'Georgie, thank goodness. I didn't ring you because you're on holiday but there's been a funny client in the salon today. And that's not all.' Her voice is breathy and she's whispering. Something's wrong.

I squeeze my eyes closed. 'Amanda, are you all right?'

She laughs, a high, nervous screech. 'Oh, I'm fine. I'm the manager and it's going well. The two girls we took on are little treasures. Lexi and Ella-Louise. The clients are delighted with what they're doing. But he's here, Georgie. Adie Carrick. I mean, he's actually come here to my house – Rhys is out, on the late shift. Adie's in my living room, demanding to know where you are and where Bonnie is.'

I exhale. 'Okay, Amanda, I'll sort him out in a minute. Where are you now?'

'Outside. I saw your name come up on the screen, so I told him I was going to call the cat in. I'll have to be quick.'

'Right.' My mind is whirling. 'You said there's been a funny client.'

'Yes, a strange man, said he wanted an appointment for a manicure but he'd only see you. He was a bit shifty.'

Beddowes' face flashes into my mind.

'Reddish hair? Pretends to be suave, about sixty-ish? Scottish?'

'How did you know?'

My heart thumps. I can hear a scuffle, Amanda's indignant tones, and then he's on the phone, his voice low and somehow squeezed in his throat.

'Georgie? It's Adie.'

'Hello,' I say brightly.

'Where's my wife?'

I answer straight away.

'You tell me, Adie. What's going on? I want to know all of it. I know you've done something stupid but there's no way Bonnie'll have anything to do with you or come back home while it's not safe.'

He's still threatening.

'I know she's in Northamptonshire. My bank—'

'Come on, Adie. What have you done?'

His tone changes. He's wheedling.

'She might not be safe, Georgie. Someone's after me and they are after her, too.'

'So why are you still in Liverpool?'

'I'm about to leave. But I want her with me.' He pauses for a moment. 'It's dangerous.'

'Why don't you go to the police?'

'Oh, for God's sake, Georgie. You know why.'

'I want to know what's happened, Adie. Everything. Is it to do with Duncan Beddowes?'

He's quiet for a moment and then his voice seeps like oil.

'A deal went wrong. Badly wrong. I owe him a lot of money. He wants it now and I can't give it to him. I'm worried about Bonnie. Please, Georgie. I need to know. Where is she?'

'I'll think about what I'm prepared to tell you and maybe I'll talk to you later, Adie. I'm not sure yet. Put Amanda back on the phone.'

'Georgie, I need to talk to Bonnie. I have to—'

'Later, Adie. Bonnie's safe.' I roll my eyes. 'Give the phone to Amanda. And leave her alone. She knows nothing so it's pointless you even asking—'

There's a thud, then a different voice.

'Georgie? It's Amanda.'

My heart's still pounding.

114

'Has he gone?'

'Yes, he's in his car, driving away.'

'Look, I'm sorry for all this grief. I'll make sure he doesn't bother you again. Are you all right?'

'I'm fine, but what's going on?'

'The less you know the better, Amanda.' I stifle a giggle. I sound like a spy. 'I'm not in Tenerife but I may be away for a few weeks. Are you all right with that?'

'Yes, fine, but are you sure?'

'I'll get back to you and keep you up to date. It's difficult right now. Adie's up to his neck in trouble and Bonnie's safest with me. Give me a ring, though, if the Scottish man comes back again.'

'Okay. Georgie?'

'Mmm?'

'Be careful. Please.'

I nod although she can't see me. 'I'll do my best.'

I end the call and dial another number.

'Hello? Can you deliver to Cliff Top? Flat 201. I'll have a mushroom and pepper, a Hawaiian with extra pineapple and a tuna Niçoise, please, and two orders of skinny fries. Thanks . . .'

Chapter Thirteen

Nanny takes off her glasses, rubs her eyes and reaches for Bonnie's uneaten pizza, swigging Roque's brandy that she found in a cupboard. She's polished off most of the skinny fries, and she has smears round her mouth and down her cardigan, Uncle Wilf's old green one. Her woolly hat has slipped to one side and she pushes it back over her hair.

'I like this pizza. I wondered what all the fuss was about when I saw it advertised all the time on telly. It's really tasty, isn't it? And I like this place. It's like being on holiday.'

Bonnie chews her lip. That's all she seems to be eating.

'It's not a holiday, Nan. You heard what Georgie said. Adie's in trouble. He said I could be in danger, too.'

I don't miss a beat. 'He's exaggerating, to get you back, Bon.'

I help myself to the brandy by prising the bottle from Nanny's fist. She takes it back and refills her own glass. I lean back against the sofa; I'm sprawled on the floor, worried about my tomato-covered fingers against the white fabric. A sigh leaks from my lungs. 'We'll be fine here. No one'll find us.'

'Adie's looking for me, though.' Bonnie's eyes are wide. 'I wonder exactly what he's done this time.'

Nanny laughs, a short grunt. 'Something he shouldn't have. But don't you worry, Bonnie. We'll be all right here.'

I think how lovely it would be to go out every day, to take in the wonderful local scenery, but I say, 'We may have to be careful for a bit, though. Stay close to the flats.' My shoulders sag with the thought of bumping into Adie on the beach.

Nanny glares and helps herself to more brandy. 'I'm used to staying indoors. No problem. As long as I have food and a couple of drinks and the television, I'm all right.'

Bonnie kicks off her shoes. 'My feet ache. And my head aches.' She stands up and reaches for the bottle, pours herself a shot of brandy and shuffles softly towards the door. 'I'm going for a bath.'

We're quiet for a few moments. I look at Nanny Basham, her legs pushed out in front of her as she lies back in the armchair, tomato lipstick on her mouth. Her eyes are glittering and I can see she's somewhere else, thinking about something.

I make my voice soft. 'You okay, Nan?'

She raises her eyebrows. 'Hmm?'

'Are you missing home?'

She shrugs. 'It's warmer here. My house is always cold. I have to put the heating on low. And I'm not so lonely here.'

'Are you sure? I mean, we've dragged you away from Liverpool. How are you feeling?'

She shudders a moment and brings the brandy glass to her mouth. 'Tired, to be honest, Georgina. My bones ache a lot nowadays. I'm eighty-eight you know. And my hips are stiff. And my knees.' She shoots me a look, waving the glass. 'I find this helps.'

I push away feelings of guilt. Perhaps I should have done more for Nan, visited more and been better company.

'Are you supposed to drink with your medication?' I ask.

'The heart tablets?' She laughs and wipes her mouth with her hand. 'The doctor said one or the other would take me off. The weak heart or the strong drink. I know which way I'd rather go.'

I'm quiet for a moment, feeling responsible, and the only sound is her slurping.

'Will you be all right, staying here for a few weeks?'

She glares. 'It's about Bonnie being all right, not me. I have to go wherever you go. I can't look after myself now. I'm not good on my legs for too long. But don't worry about me, Georgina. I'll be just dandy here.'

'Okay, Nan.'

Her glass is empty and she stares at the wall. 'The worst thing isn't the aching bones, though. When you get to my age . . .'

I wait but she says nothing, so I lean forwards.

'What's the worst thing?'

'It's the waiting.'

I raise my eyebrows. 'For people to come round to visit?'

'For death.'

I wriggle and don't know what to say, then I make my voice sound jolly. 'You'll outlive us all, Nan.'

Her eyes shine. She's talking to herself.

'That's what's so annoying about the young. They think they have time. They think they're so clever and they're so sure of themselves. They never think tomorrow might be their last day. But each morning when I wake up, I say, "Well, maybe it's today, Wilfie. Perhaps it's time we got together again." But I know he's gone for good – I don't believe in Heaven.'

I swallow brandy and tears prickle in my eyes. 'Do you miss him, Nan?'

'He was with me every day and then suddenly he wasn't. And when he stopped, something else stopped. Each day I woke up, it didn't mean the same any more. I don't mean the loneliness – yes, I was by myself, there was no Wilf, I'd never get him back. But a huge part of me had gone. The heart beating, the way I'd feel all warm when I was with him. It went empty. And cold. Just a hole in my chest where the warm love had been for so long. It was gone. And it just stayed like that, every day. Empty.'

I'm lost for words, so I say, 'Oh, Nan.'

She realises I'm in the room and frowns. 'At least I had him for nearly sixty years. At least I knew what it was to love someone every day. You have nobody at all.'

I shake my head, but she's right.

'You know that big clock on my mantelpiece, the loud one that keeps ticking away all the time, tick-tock? You don't expect it to stop, do you, Georgina? But one day it will tick and then it won't tock. Or it'll tock and then it won't tick again. That'll be it.' She sniffs. 'Gone. At least I had my Wilfie for a while.'

My glass is empty and so is Nan's. I offer the brandy in Roque's bottle. She shakes her head and looks away. The room is silent, except for the sound of our breathing.

Bonnie comes in, swathed in a man's cream dressing gown, an enormous towel round her head.

'You don't think Roque'll mind that I've borrowed his robe? The bath was lovely – a really powerful Jacuzzi. And I just rang Adie.' She swipes my glass and fills it to the top with Roque's liquor. 'We had a long chat. Now I know what's happened.' Her eyes meet mine. 'It's his fault. He's a stupid, stupid man.'

Nanny stretches her aching legs and stares into the

empty glass. Bonnie plonks herself next to me, grabbing my hand, and the towel falls from her damp hair.

'Adie made a business deal with Beddowes and now he can't pay him. Or he won't. He's up to something. He says he's got money hidden away and Beddowes is on to him. That's why he's threatening him, because Adie won't tell him where the money is. Adie owes him that money, but he's trying to sneak off with it all himself.'

'Why doesn't he just go away?'

'He wants me to go with him. He says we can take the money together and go abroad. He won't go without me.'

'He should just pay Beddowes what he owes him.'

Bonnie's damp hair falls across her face, but not before her mouth opens, astonished. 'Beddowes is a crook.'

Nanny wakes up for a moment. 'Adie's a crook.'

Bonnie thinks for a moment. 'It's about laundering money and Adie's lost a lot recently through a bad deal. That's why he's so afraid of the police.'

I remember the short stop Adie and I made in Norris Green, Adie's black case and his hurried exit. I recall the young man at the door in camouflage trousers; it was the same house on TV, where the suspect was arrested by the police. My heart starts to thump. We're being pulled into Adie's nefarious world and it can only mean trouble. It dawns on me that, until now, I'd not allowed myself to believe how serious it could become. Not to mention crazy: a month or two ago, my life had been routine but comfortable. I had my daughter at home; my business was running smoothly, I was making ends meet. Now, I'm in a luxury flat near Brighton, my daughter living upstairs with a Spanish striker, and I've no idea what's about to unfold in my life.

Bonnie's hand reaches for the towel and folds it carefully. 'Adie asked me where we are.'

'You didn't tell him?'

'He said had I been to Northamptonshire and was I with you, and I said yes, but I didn't tell him where I was. He knows Jade's with us.'

'Does he know about Luis?'

'Oh yes, I told him ages ago that she had a new boyfriend and he played for a team in London.'

'Well, that's fine, Bon. He probably thinks we're in London. He won't find us.'

Bonnie sighs and shudders and she puts a hand to her face. Without make-up, her skin is delicate and pale.

'I said I'd consider it for a day or two and ring him back. I said I might meet him. Perhaps we could get the money and divide it up. I mean, we might even go separate ways. I don't know.'

'Bonnie, surely you don't want to go back to Adie? For goodness' sake . . .'

'I don't think so, Georgie. It's just – I don't know what else I'd do. He asked me twice about this.' She waves the charm bracelet. 'If I still had it on, if it was safe. Like it's a big deal to him. He gave it to me as a present, but he thinks he still owns it.' She presses her lips together. 'Like he thinks he still owns me.'

'The man's a conniving bastard.' Nanny's voice is firm. 'You should dump him and say good riddance.'

I recall Nan's words about swapping partners 'like a bloody barn dance' and I chuckle.

'He's not coming in here, that's for certain.' My hands are suddenly fists. 'If Adie finds us, Beddowes might follow him. It's too risky, Bonnie.'

Her face is passive, almost dreamlike. 'I'll ring Demi now. I don't want her to know what's going on. I want her to believe everything's fine. Then I'm going to bed. I need to sleep. Adie can wait for a day or two. My head's a real mess right now.'

Nanny wriggles to the end of her seat, hauls herself to a standing position. 'I'll turn in now, too. Give me an arm, will you, Georgina? Help me get to that lovely little room with the white covers. I need to get my head down.'

When I tuck Nanny up, her eyelids close straight away. Her lips pucker and she whispers, 'Night night, love.'

I'm not sure who she's talking to, but I kiss her soft cheek. I tidy the lounge and notice a tomato fingerprint on the white chair arm where Nanny was sitting. I find a chemical spray under the kitchen sink and a soft cloth, then I rub at the fabric until the smudge is pale pink. Jade won't be pleased. I consider texting her, but as soon as I look at my phone, I decide against it. I should go to bed; it's past eleven, but I can hear Bonnie's voice from the bedroom, her tone soft with affection, talking to Demi.

'It sounds lovely . . . the beaches must be really nice . . .'

I go back into the lounge, wishing that Jade and I spoke to each other with the same intimacy and trust. I screw the top on the brandy bottle and move to the window. Down below, the coast is in darkness. Lights flicker and glimmering colours reflect in the sea. I yearn for the cool air on my skin. Tomorrow will be an interesting day: I have no idea what it'll bring.

The next day, it's raining heavily and the sky and ocean merge into a blur, grey as tinfoil. I text Jade a cheery *good morning* and she simply replies *Luis is training and I'm busy*. We mooch round the flat, listless and bored, watching television, saying little. It occurs to me that we should all go out. Adie doesn't know where we are, unless Bonnie's told him everything. It wouldn't surprise me if he's managed to wheedle everything out of her.

In the late afternoon, Nan asks for another takeaway meal and I decide that we need fresh food. I leave Bonnie and Nan watching television and go to the panoramic window. The view is as beautiful in daylight as I thought it would be: chalky cliffs, sheer drops down to a pebble beach and a huge stretch of grey ocean. The rain has blown away and sunlight plays on the waves, light winking and shifting. I reach for my pink woollen coat and my handbag, and pick up the door keys.

The walk down the steps from the clifftop takes a few minutes, then I'm on the beach with the breeze in my face. I push my hands deep in my pockets and put my head down, moving briskly. There are steps up onto a pathway and I take it and walk down the hill into the village. A few people pass me, some shuffling, some hurrying and some loitering. A heavy man jogs past: headphones plug his ears and his face is expressionless against the sharp breeze. I stop to gaze at the skyline, the wriggling reflections of colour against the sea, and I feel anonymous and safe. It's as if I'm breathing fresh air, the calm secret of so many unknown people, a tangle of passers-by who'll never know each other and will never think to look into someone's eyes or pry into their lives.

I turn into a side street, where dim yellow lights glow inside a pub. A wiry man stumbles out into the cold and places a cigarette between his lips. I pass the black-and-white Tudor building and terraced shops with brick fronts. It is just after five. I pause outside a café and gaze through the window: painted wooden chairs on tables, diners with their heads close, talking; a man at the counter, busy frothing coffee from a machine. I read the menu: dish of the day, drinks – hot chocolate – and it occurs to me that perhaps we might all be able to slip out for lunch, or elevenses.

I'm not sure about Nanny, about her ability to stray far from the flat: the uphill walk back home would be difficult, not to mention the cold, the strain on her heart or her limbs, although she might manage it via the beach. But it would be good to be outside. I'm lost in thought as I wander along the road. I pass a launderette, a Polski Sklep. I recall the shops in my road at home and wonder when I'll go back. I feel like a lost soul, roaming far from my centre, out of kilter, directionless, alone.

There's a supermarket: it's small, with a single door. I step inside, with no idea what I'll buy. The idea of taking a few bottles of Guinness home for Nan makes me smile, although I'll need to monitor her alcohol consumption carefully. She's overdone it recently.

I wonder about buying something healthy for breakfast. We can't live off takeaway pizza every night. I browse through bags of salad, fresh vegetables, packets of rice and reach for two types of tea, wholemeal bread and some things to spread on toast. On the top shelf are boxes of muesli: organic, full of nuts, healthy – that's tomorrow's breakfast organised. I reach up and teeter, my fingers touching the box, but I can't grasp it. I try again and my nails press against the cardboard and push it further away.

'Damn.'

I'm on my toes again, the cereal still out of reach, and there's someone beside me, appearing from nowhere. He lifts an arm, grasps the muesli and offers it to me.

'Is this the one you wanted?'

There's a tattoo on the inside of his wrist, a snake shape.

'Yes, thanks.'

I stare at the man. He's dark, tall – of course, taller than me – sinewy, broad-shouldered. He's my age, I suppose. His hair is curly, black, threaded with silver strands, and his eyes are deep blue, the piercing blue of the ocean. He's wearing jeans, a light jacket and a T-shirt. I stare at him. Our eyes are locked together and I can't drag mine away. He doesn't seem to want to look away either. But the connection is – what is it? Not attraction, surely, not at my age? I'm past all that now. But I'm still staring at his face, his open, friendly smile. I force a wide grin to stop myself looking so flabbergasted.

'Thanks.'

'You're welcome.'

He turns away and I grip the muesli. His voice is soft: I try to analyse the traces of an accent. English – beyond that, I'm not sure. I wonder if he noticed my accent, from the one word I spoke to him, and wondered what I'm doing in Sussex. He's gone but I'm still standing by the shelf, thinking about him: his face, the intense eyes, the warm smile.

I pay for the groceries and walk back to the flat, deep in thought as the lift whizzes me to the second floor. I can't understand what passed between the man and me. Probably, it was simply a tall person handing a shorter person an item she couldn't reach. That's all. An act of kindness. Perhaps I should've asked – *Is this your local supermarket?* It would've started a conversation. But what would we have said to each other in the grocery aisle? *They do nice muesli here. Yes, have you tried the new washing-up liquid?*

Back at the flat, we eat, watch television and decide we all need an early night. I lock the door, pack away the food in the kitchen and turn off the lights. Bonnie's already asleep in the king-sized bed, so I clean my teeth in the dark, pull off my clothes, wriggle on an oversized T-shirt and slip under the covers. The bed is warm; Bonnie's breathing is light. I roll away from her and close my eyes.

The man's face comes back to me. The dark-haired, soft-voiced muesli hero. I wonder if I'll bump into him again. I laugh quietly to myself. I'm in a village near

125

Brighton. I've only been here for a day and I'm already fantasising about the locals.

I roll on my back, thinking. What if we met again and began a conversation? What could I say? I could ask him about the area. *I'm new here. From Liverpool. Can't you tell? Where's a good place to eat out?* And he might say to me, *I know a nice little place, great atmosphere, soft lighting. Why don't we go there?* And I'd smile and say, *Oh, I'm sorry, I hope I wasn't being forward*, and he'd offer that gentle smile, the level gaze would meet mine.

I wrench my body over. What am I doing, dreaming about a man I've barely even met? An ordinary stranger in a T-shirt and jeans. He probably lives in a bedsit with a young hippy woman, slim, long hair, a flowing dress; they're probably burning joss sticks together this minute. Now I'm really cross with myself: I'm being ridiculous. I don't want a relationship anyway. All the poor man did was hand me a box of cereal and suddenly I'm ready to change my life forever. That's not going to happen, not ever. I grind my teeth, roll over and try to sleep.

Chapter Fourteen

The next week passes slowly. I check Jade's post in the hallway on the ground floor, hoping there's anything that makes me remember normal life outside – a leaflet advertising takeaway pizza or double glazing. Nanny tells me she doesn't like the supermarket muesli – it sticks in her teeth and tastes of straw – but she's developed a taste for Marmite, smothering it on slices of toast every morning.

Bonnie hasn't been out, even though I suggest she accompanies me to the shops or on the beach for a walk. She says she feels too nervous. I buy her prawn salads and Ryvita at the supermarket. I've called in most days, but there's been no sign of the stranger with the tattoo on the inside of his wrist, the dark-haired hero who plucked the muesli from the shelf in a Sir Galahad style. I'd forgotten how much I dislike not being tall enough to reach top shelves.

I haven't seen Jade at all. She prefers to be by herself when Luis is training, which is every day. She texts me that Luis' club has found her some personal training work and she's gone to Italy with him because his team are playing Roma in a cup game. She promises to 'pop down when she can find the time'.

I spend most days watching television with Nanny or cooking something interesting for dinner. Nan's enjoying trying new foods; she's feeling valued, sharing our life together and being included. I do my best to offer her new tastes. Not meals for one in a box now but something freshly cooked. Nanny likes moussaka, lasagne and spaghetti *alla puttanesca*. She's thriving on three Guinnesses a day and a nightcap before bed. I haven't seen her look so good in a long time. Her skin has developed a healthy sheen whereas before it was papery and dry. She still wears Uncle Wilf's jumpers, but the woollen hat is abandoned in the evening when the flat is warm and now her hair is shiny and cotton soft.

It's Bonnie I worry about. She spends hours each morning dressing and doing her hair, putting on make-up, just to sit in the armchair and leaf through a novel. She picks at the muesli and leaves most of her evening meal, although she's drunk a fair amount of gin and nibbled her way through a bar or two of white chocolate. She's developed an air of bored silence – complete indolence, in fact – not helping with cooking or cleaning, and criticising the meals I make and my unkempt appearance. I'm quite happy slouching round the flat in leggings, a sloppy top and bare feet. Perhaps it's my fault: perhaps I need to be more sympathetic, take time to let her talk about missing Adie. But my mind returns to thoughts of Jade and I long to catch up with her. I text her immediately that I hope all is well and I love her. I know she won't reply for days.

On Wednesday night we watch Luis' team on television. They draw with Roma 2–2 and Luis doesn't score. Nanny says he looks like the edge has been taken off his game and makes various rude references to his bedroom habits with Jade, which troubles me. Jade is someone else now, independent, and I'm glad she has her own life, but I wish I could be part of it. At least, she'll be home the day after tomorrow.

Bonnie has her nose in a romance, *Belinda of the Burning Mist*. She checks her phone frequently, after which she heaves a shuddering sigh; although I don't know if it's prompted by the spellbinding plot, the lack of texts or whether she's desolate without Adie.

At night, I sit up in bed while Bonnie turns restlessly. The curtains are open and I stare at the skyline. I think about the muesli hero with the tattooed wrist. Probably the courteous shopper at the supermarket was just that: polite, helpful and tall, no more. I decide to forget about him.

By Saturday evening, I'm wishing for my own bedroom and the gym back home. Instead, I leave Bonnie languishing on the sofa and Nanny watching television cuddled up in the armchair, and I go for a long walk to buy food for a late meal. It's past eight, almost dark already, the end of a warm spring day. The light fades away in soft brush-strokes and shadows seep into every corner.

I walk along the beach into the village and gaze in all the shops. I have a shopping list. Nanny's asked for the usual – something to whet her whistle. Bonnie wants face cleanser and a specific deodorant that I know will be expensive. I've almost run out of the money from the salon takings and as I walk, I contemplate whether or not to go to an ATM and if it's likely that Adie could trace me. He'd have his ways, but I'll have to take some cash out soon. Bonnie's funds won't last forever.

I'm not keen to go back to the flat. Beautiful as it is, it's claustrophobic, filling instantly with the stale scent of Bonnie's bad moods. Jade'll be back tonight or tomorrow and I've decided to catch up with her in the afternoon – Luis is playing a game in Newcastle today so she's gone there. I envy her the liberty she has to move freely across the country and, for a second, I wonder if Adie could track where she is.

I push the thoughts away and step into the brightly lit supermarket. I shop for ingredients for a meal – it's cheaper if we don't rely on takeaway meals and healthier, too. Tonight, I'll do a Thai green curry. I'll buy extra vegetables – we can have a ratatouille tomorrow.

I pick up my ingredients, snacks, some Prosecco that's on offer. My bags are already too heavy. I look round for the tall muesli man; he could carry my groceries for me. Instantly, I'm furious with myself for moments of weakness, so I haul the two tote bags onto my elbow and march towards the flat.

As people pass by, I examine a few faces. No curly-haired man with piercing blue eyes. I walk back to Cliff Top; the shopping becomes increasingly heavy and the handles dig into my palms. I force a smile: this is the price of independence.

Bonnie's in the Jacuzzi bath again. Nanny hauls herself up from the chair and struggles to the breakfast bar where I'm unloading shopping. She rummages in the bag for a can of beer and fizzes it open, then takes a swig and smacks her lips. Her eyes follow me as I unpack vegetables and suddenly she starts laughing.

'My goodness, Georgina. What's that? The Jolly Green Giant's willy?' She reaches for the courgette and brandishes it in a way that seems improper for a woman of her advanced years. 'Well, I've never seen one of these before. What on earth do you do with it?'

'Cook it, Nan.'

She cackles. 'What does it taste like? A tough cucumber? Or is it just a little marrow.'

'Exactly.'

'And this?' She's laughing again. 'What's this purple thing?'

'Aubergine, Nan.'

'My, my, Georgina. There are some funny vegetables these days.' She reaches for the bag of okra and I wince. 'Oh, look. A lot of little ones. What are these called?'

'Okra. Ladies' fingers, Nan.'

'I suppose they go with the green willy and the purple willy, then?' She leans against the counter, chortling, waving her can of beer. 'It's a funny old life. We never had these erratic vegetables when I was young.'

'Erotic, Nan.'

She's playing with the courgette, banging it against the counter. The deep green colour is reflected in the frames of her glasses and her eyes dance. 'It's a strong vegetable, this. Very robust. What do you make with it?'

'Ratatouille.'

'Ratty tails?' Nan collapses forwards laughing and I worry she'll fall. She hoists herself back upright and sucks on the can. 'I like living here. Fancy food. Fancy vegetables. Good beer.' She finishes the can and tries to crush it between her fingers. It hardly bends. She abandons it where it is and moves steadily back to her chair. 'I'll just see what's on television. I might take a look at the cookery programme. See if you're telling me the truth about these vegetables.' She smirks. 'It would be fun to see Jamie Oliver chop this lot up with his carving knife and make ratty tails.'

'That's right, Nan.'

I concentrate on putting the groceries away and check my phone. There's no message from Jade. It's a good enough reason to visit her when she's back, to check if she's all right. I'll go up tomorrow, to put my mind at rest. First, I set out my ingredients for a Thai green curry.

*

131

It's almost ten o'clock at night and we're watching a film. Nanny's sitting with her feet on a stool, a glass of Prosecco in her hand. She likes it, so much that she's on her third glass. So's Bonnie, who's flicking through her phone, gazing at texts from Adie and Demi, old photographs. Every so often, she gives a deep sigh. The film titles scroll down on the television screen and a familiar song plays: 'Nobody Does it Better'.

Nanny breathes out. 'Oh, I did enjoy that.'

Bonnie raises an eyebrow. '*The Spy Who Loved Me*?'

'No, Bonnie, love. The Tied green curry – I'm developing a taste for this spicy food.' She grins. 'And Prosecco. Very nice.' She holds out the glass and I fill it halfway. She frowns and I fill it up to two thirds.

Bonnie thumbs the screen on her phone again. 'I'm not a Roger Moore fan.'

'He's handsome.' Nanny screws up her face in judgement. 'But I prefer Sean Connery. He had nice manners and a sexy voice. And I like his hairy chest.'

'Daniel Craig would do for me,' Bonnie mutters. 'He looks lovely in a dinner jacket.' She gulps Prosecco. 'Adie looks good in a dinner jacket.'

I grunt but she doesn't notice, so I say, 'I'm not a fan of the Bond films. All the women are purely decorative. Always attractive, vacuous and dispensable – they get shagged and then they're killed off.'

Bonnie looks up, horrified.

Nanny considers for a moment then nods. 'You're right, Georgina. Even the May Day one got blown up in *View to a Kill*. I love the way she grabbed James Bond, though, and threw herself on top of him in the bed.' Nanny sucks the rim of her empty glass. 'I wish I'd been a bit more like that.'

Bonnie sits upright and stares.

I say, 'More like May Day, Nan?'

She shakes her head. 'No, more like – the one to decide things. You know, we left it to the men to make all the important decisions. When to buy a new sofa, when to go on holiday, when to have sex.'

Bonnie sighs. 'I know what you mean. But in some ways, it's nice to have someone else deciding these things for you.'

'No, it isn't.' I pour more Prosecco for myself and immediately Bonnie and Nan shoot their empty glasses towards me. I fill all three. 'We should make our own decisions. Women should want to be more assertive.'

Bonnie's face is almost inside the glass. 'Look where it got you, though, Georgie.'

I make my eyes into tiny missiles. 'Look where you've got us with your passive attitude, Bonnie. On the run and a stupid husband who stole money and got himself into trouble. That's what happens when you let men make decisions.'

Nan nods to herself. 'Assertive. I wish I could've been like that. I'd have preferred it that way. Instead of fish and chips and an early night on a Friday, I could have said, "Wilfie, darling, let's get the bus down to Otterspool Prom and make love under the stars." He'd have gone wild if I'd said that.'

I guffaw. 'You'd have got frostbite. It's freezing on Otterspool Prom.'

Bonnie looks at me sharply. 'How do you know?'

I swig more Prosecco. 'Mickey Maguire, 1982.'

Bonnie sits upright. 'The blond one who worked in the chicken factory?'

'During the summer holidays. He was a student at the university. Tropical diseases.'

We all look at each other and start to giggle. Bonnie stops first, her eyes full of questions.

'Nan, was Uncle Wilf your only one?'

Nanny sits upright. 'Ah, there was no messing round when I was a girl, Bonnie. You were always told never to get yourself into trouble. I was terrified of it, getting myself in the family way, before I was married. I made him wait. Yes, my Wilf was my first. My one and only.'

We sip Prosecco and the room is quiet. I imagine Bonnie's counting her lovers. I am. I'm already up to six.

Nan says, 'The first time was rubbish, though.'

Bonnie agrees. 'I know. And the second.'

'Poor Wilf had no idea,' Nan grumbles. 'We were in our twenties but neither of us knew what we were doing. A quick how's your father and he was done, and I'm lying there in my lacy wedding night negligible wondering, *What was that about? When will I start to feel something happen?*'

I don't crack a smile. 'That's terrible, Nan.'

Bonnie giggles too loudly and drains her glass.

'Adie wasn't much cop in bed after the first few years. I mean, it was all right. Better after a gin or two.' She breathes out. 'He thought he had to say something while we were – you know, doing it – so he'd say "I love you, I love you" and grunt in a deep voice. It was like having sex with Chewbacca.'

I say nothing but I'm thinking of the wonderful years I spent with Terry and how we were totally compatible in bed. It was a shame that we grew apart: somehow, we lost the ability to be on each other's side. It was a pity about all the arguments and how, by the end, we could barely speak to each other without a clumsy row. Then, much later, when Jade was taking GCSEs, Alison came on the scene. I remember him coming home from work during that time, a new smile on his face, and how he started to buy me little gifts, which I thought meant that he was

134

trying to be romantic and make me love him again. I loved him already, despite the silences and the screaming rows.

Of course, the presents came because he was as guilty as sin. He'd been flirting with her in the office; there were shared drinks, romantic meals, and then of course he shared himself with her so much that she persuaded him that he'd be happier with her forever after. And that was it.

I remember when he told me he was leaving me: Jade was out with friends. I'd made us a special dinner and he came home late. He stood, his hands clasped in front of him, and said, 'I'm sorry, Georgie. I've met someone else.' Unoriginal. The most painful words I'd ever heard. They'd exploded in my ears like bombs. I threw the tepid teriyaki at his face then I threw him out. I couldn't speak to him after that.

Stupidly, I'd hoped things were getting better between us. We'd been married for long enough – I'd just assumed it was a tough patch and we'd get through it. Terry was in his late forties and I suppose he was susceptible. Weak. Alison, all clinging dresses, cute dimples and big teeth. She was twenty-eight years old and ambitious; she turned his head. I felt a fool. He looked one, teriyaki sauce darkening his hair and clinging to his white shirt. I don't think I'd ever felt anger, hatred, bitterness as such a physical pain.

I met her, three times. She called round to see me: they'd been together for a month and she asked if we could make peace. I gave her a piece of my mind. After that, I could hardly talk to Terry, even on the phone. I found the best solicitor I could and demanded a clean-break settlement. I never wanted to see him again. Then, after the divorce, I glimpsed them together in a supermarket, holding hands. She was pregnant. I backed away and dived down the frozen food aisle shivering until they'd gone.

He was Jade's Sunday dad for a while: she'd greet him on the doorstep and he'd drop her off there after he'd taken her out for the day. I couldn't speak to him. If the truth were known, it would've broken my heart to look at his face. He was mine and then he was someone else's. He became someone else. After baby Arran came along, whining Alison begged Terry to get a job down south, so they moved to Ealing. Where the comedies come from. Jade sees him from time to time, but says nothing of it to me now. I notice my glass is empty and someone's talking to me.

'Georgie?'

'Um?' I stare at Bonnie and she's gawping back, her mouth open. Nanny's eyes glitter. 'Sorry. Did you say something?'

'You were away with the fairies.' Bonnie shakes her glossy hair. 'I just asked you if you could ever see yourself with another man? I mean, after . . .'

I bray loudly, then giggle like fairy Tinker Bell and roll my eyes.

'I'm fine by myself, to be honest, Bon. Men only bring trouble. As you very well know.' I shake my head. 'Anyway, no one would be interested in me now. Why would they? There are so many younger women looking for an older man, one who's set up, with a good income.'

My mind replays images for a moment. I've had two dates since Terry left me. One date with a man called Derek who said he was fifty-two in our online chat. We met for coffee and he was five feet tall, sparse teeth, at least seventy. Then there was a Chinese meal with Kevin, the lonely musician from Fazakerley, who talked non-stop about his ex-wife then, at the end of the evening, tried to kiss me with lips like soggy chips. I shake my head to loosen the memories.

'No, I'm independent, Bon. I have my own life. Why would I want to change?' I stand up and stretch, yawn. 'I'll wash up the dishes tomorrow. I'll have a bath and turn in – I'm shattered. All this cooking and chatting and drinking have got to me. See you both tomorrow. G'night.'

I'm better off single, investing nothing, hoping for nothing. I stumble towards the door on flat feet. I've drunk far more Prosecco than I thought and my head's started to whirl. As I twist the handle and step into the corridor, I hear Nanny's voice, confiding and low.

'He's a lot to answer for, that Terry Wood. He broke her heart. She'll never be the same, poor thing.'

I close the door behind me with a crisp click, put my head down and lurch towards the bedroom feeling miserable.

Chapter Fifteen

Even in my sleep, my dreams are invaded by anxiety: I'm ridiculously jittery about calling on Jade later. I wake feeling washed out. Bonnie's still asleep, so I dress quietly, pull on my coat and go for a walk. The path down from the cliff to the beach funnels the wind against my face and blows away my crowded thoughts. I walk along the shingle, picking my way across the expanse of pebbles and up to the path. There's a lone dog walker and a bouncing spaniel coming towards me, an elderly couple holding hands. Jade and Luis could have arrived back late last night, so perhaps an early Sunday morning visit won't be welcome. I hate the thought of seeing her face at the door, disappointed to see me, hoping I'll have a quick cup of tea and go away. The sea hushes my worries like an old friend.

I check my purse – I have fifty pounds and some coins. I turn the windy corner into a side street where there's a little brightly lit café and order a coffee and a croissant. Djimi's Café is warm and welcoming: a man in his fifties with a smooth head and a voice of cinder toffee, crackly and sweet, puts a cappuccino in front of me in a white cup and makes a comment about the weather being mild. I assume he's Djimi.

I watch him swaying round the wooden bar as jazz singer Ella Fitzgerald's smoky voice rises from the speakers; he's lithe and brisk and his jeans are tight across the backside. There are other people in the café: an elderly snow-haired man reading a newspaper, his half-moon glasses perched on the end of his nose. He wears a heavy sweater, the cable-knit sort in cream, which gives him the air of a fisherman, or a professor. Djimi presents him with a huge egg roll on a plate and the old man nods without taking his eyes from the paper. There's a young woman and a man with a toddler in a high chair. The man's chatting, waving his hands, while the woman pushes spoonful after spoonful of food into the child's mouth, laughing and cooing as the baby giggles uncontrollably. I haven't heard a child laugh like that in so many years. It takes me back and I want to cry.

Djimi places a newspaper on my table, a broadsheet, and I scour it for news of home. As I turn to each page, I expect something about Adie, an arrest perhaps after the Norris Green heist. I wonder if it's all blown over, if Beddoves has gone back to Scotland and given up the chase. I wonder how I'd find out. It occurs to me that I ought to go to the police, but a recent newspaper story jumps into my head, the terrible headline: Stitches for Snitches. The woman who told the police about her wayward son: the man who grassed on someone else in a gang and the dreadful photos in the paper of their scarred faces. The cuts were livid and indelible. Someone's always ready to pay them back, to dole out punishment for the dreadful sin of telling tales to the authorities. I decide it's best to stay quiet, at least for the time being.

In the paper, there's a lot of celebrity news, scandal,

139

some politics, but the only update from Liverpool is a story about a hit-and-run accident, in which a teenage boy was killed, and an interview with someone who works in the prison about the difficult conditions. I sigh: all bad publicity for my hometown. My heart aches for the vibrant city where I grew up and lived every day, where I feel I belong with all my fibre. It knows me and I know it, completely. Sussex is still just somewhere I'm staying for a while. I've no idea how long.

Of course, Brighton may be Jade's home now. Then where: Spain, beyond? Will she go where Luis goes? Will their relationship last?

Djimi, the shaven-headed café owner, pulls me from my thoughts, refilling my cup.

'Hello, dreamer,' he says.

'Oh, I'm sorry.'

'More coffee? Can I get you a croissant to go with it? Another one?'

I smile: he's an expert businessman. 'Just coffee. That would be lovely.'

He grins. '*Luvvly.*' He's imitating my accent. 'You're not from round here, are you, dreamer?'

I hesitate for a second and wonder if he knows Adie. Or Beddowes. I'm being silly.

I smile and say, 'I'm from Liverpool.'

'I thought it was somewhere up north.' His laugh is a light gurgle, a drainpipe emptying. 'Do you live here or just visiting?'

I shrug. My instincts tell me to be evasive with everybody. 'Somewhere between the two.'

He nods. 'Come here again. I'll get you a loyalty card.'

'That'd be great.'

'*Greattt.*' He imitates me and winks. 'Nice to meet you, dreamer.'

I sip coffee and close my eyes. It's half ten. If I walk for an hour, maybe I could go straight up and see Jade when I'm back. My feelings swing from the excitement of seeing my daughter to the expectation of her disapproval, maybe worse.

By the time I walk the scenic route back to Cliff Top, it's almost midday. I've bought Jade a cheap gift: a leafy plant in a pot, wrapped in bright paper. I'm used to the outside door keypad now, and taking the swanky lift with the big mirror is second nature, but instead of pressing the button for the second floor, I press the third. My reflection shows a woman huddled in a soft pink coat, her head a blonde thatch-like bobble on the top. I can see root growth: I need to find a hairdresser.

I glide out of the lift like I live here. I'm still incredulous that I do: I'm a resident on the second floor, at least for another few weeks, until Roque's back from his knee surgery and convalescence in the USA. I remind myself to buy a different type of stain remover. Nanny's added Guinness and Thai green curry to the pizza stains on the white armchair and Roque's spray-on product just spreads it around. I walk through the hallway on the marble flagstones, knock on Luis' door, wait a minute and ring his bell.

Luis comes to the door, hair over his eyes, wearing a smart shirt and designer jeans. He stares like he doesn't know me. I wait. He continues frowning: I help him out.

'Hi, Luis. It's me. Georgie.' He's still looking confused. 'Jade's mum?'

He clearly doesn't know what to say, so I smile at him. He calls 'Jade . . .' I don't recognise my daughter's name in his mouth for a split second, then she's next to him, gaping at me.

'Bloody hell. Mother!'

She never calls me mother, but I grin.

'Yes, it's the bloody-hell mother. Can I come in?' I show her the potted plant. She hesitates, blocking the space in front of me: we're standing in the doorway. 'Mum, maybe you could come back later. I mean, now's not really convenient.'

I glance at her and at Luis, who looks awkward and runs a hand through his floppy hair. They're both dressed: it's convenient enough. I shrug.

'I'll just stay for a minute then.' I barge in and give them a smile. 'Perhaps a quick cuppa? I don't want to hold you up.'

They're both in a queue behind me.

Then I'm in the white lounge, standing absolutely still, holding my breath. I can't move: I'm frozen in the moment. There are three figures sitting on the white sofa: one tall, one medium and one small. They're staring, their mouths open. I hear Jade behind me, her voice soft.

'Mum . . .'

Then there's the drowning sound of my heart thumping.

Luis touches my shoulder. 'We are now caught with the pants down. Maybe you want tea? Coffee?'

Terry stands up, embarrassed; his face is red and painful, like he's been hit with a cricket bat. He gapes and says, 'Hello, Georgie.'

Alison pauses for a minute, then leaps up and rushes towards me, pecking the air close to my cheek.

'Well, we didn't expect to see you here.'

She smells of frantic flowers, petals desperate to release as strong a stench as possible. I take a whiff and pull a face. She has a tight cream woollen dress on: she's put on weight, but she looks good. I huddle inside the pink coat, with no make-up, conscious of the reek of my own perspiration and the noticeable two inches of root growth, and I feel myself shrinking.

Terry hasn't moved. He has on a dismal red sweater and jeans, which are too loose in the leg. His hair is shorter than when I . . . I swallow. He looks like a married man. Stifled, bored, with no personality. I remember him younger, leaner, sexy in a leather jacket, his hair fair not a dull steel grey, but fashionable, layered, short on top, longer over the ears. His grin has disappeared. Now, he has a sad mouth with vertical lines either side.

I glance at their child, Arran, who has his mother's large eyes and dimples. He's cute, wearing a football shirt, the colours of Luis' team, and when he twists round, the name Delgado is on the back. I wonder if it's a gift from Jade.

Too much time has passed; too much silence and it's awkward, so I say, 'Hello. Well, this is a surprise.'

Terry mumbles, 'You're looking well, Georgie,' and Alison shoots him an unimpressed look.

She turns a dimpled smile on me. 'You don't know Arran, do you, Georgie? He's nearly four now. Say hello, Arran.'

Arran puts his head down, then looks at Terry and says, 'Who's the strange lady?'

Alison butts in. 'She's a visitor, darling. She's Jade's mummy, just like I'm your mummy.'

Arran makes a face and picks his nose. I turn my back on them completely and beam at Jade, then at Luis.

'I just popped up to say hello. I won't stay. I bought you a plant.' I shove the offensive leafy package at Luis, who looks confused.

Jade has her hands on her hips. 'Dad came round because we're going out for Sunday lunch. It's been arranged all week.'

I stop myself from saying the first thing that pops into my head, which is that I hope they all choke on their food because Jade hasn't contacted me for days and I haven't been invited anywhere. Of course, I'm overreacting, stunned, caught like an animal in headlights. I smooth my face with a smile so I don't look like the uninvited wicked witch at Sleeping Beauty's christening, and I turn back to Terry and his family.

'That's lovely. I can recommend Djimi's Café. It's only ten minutes away. I had a bite there this morning.'

Luis offers his best grin. 'We go now to Embers in Brighton. Many people go there. The food is good. You must come with us one day.'

I smile at him like the queen. 'Thanks, Luis, that's so kind.' Sitting across the table from Terry and his perfect family would give me acid reflux. 'Well, I'd better be going. Busy day ahead.'

Jade has her anxious look, a frown between her brows. 'Shall I text you, Mum?'

'That'd be nice. When you can. I'm sure you're both busy.' I almost add 'and we're downstairs, bored witless.' The smile smeared across my cheeks is beginning to hurt. 'Well, enjoy your lunch, everyone. And –' I look directly at Terry, desperately ignoring Alison '– have a safe journey back to Ealing. It's so nice to see you.'

I turn and whirl towards the door. Jade's behind me as I reach for the latch.

'Mum, I'm sorry. I didn't think you'd come up here when Dad . . . I mean, I never bother you with details about when I see him . . .'

'Don't worry, Jade.' I kiss her cheek. 'Bumping into your father is one of those hazards we risk in life. I mean, he's like carbon monoxide, isn't he? Even though he's not always visible, there's always a risk he's around, lurking in a dark corner somewhere being perpetually noxious.'

She shakes her head. 'Mum . . .'

'Text me, Jade. Have a good time at the restaurant.' I

throw one last beam of my pearly smile at her. 'Enjoy the potted plant.' Then I hurl myself outside the door and walk away down the corridor.

When I turn the corner, I'm shaking. I lean back against the wall and my breath comes in gulps. I'm angry with myself that I was petulant, sarcastic, undignified; that I still allow him to have this effect on me. I push myself up to standing and make myself tall to gain some self-respect. A deep inhalation and I'm on my way.

I decide to go to the beach and take the stairs. The staircase has a shiny cubist theme in black and white: on every floor, there's a matching black-and-white framed picture. On the second floor it's a print of a horse in the countryside. On the first, it's a seascape, a boat tossing on the waves at night, with a huge moon in the sky. I push my hands in my pockets and trot down to the ground floor, through the exit, and then I walk down the path to the sea.

I let the wind take my hair, slap it across my face. I hope it'll make me see sense, blow away the awkwardness, the embarrassment of seeing Terry with smiling Alison in Jade's flat. Of course, I know Jade sees her father regularly, but I try never to think about it.

I walk over the pebbles, picking my way to where the stones are smaller and the ground becomes softer shingle. The sun glints on the waves, making the surface of the water shift and glitter like silver. For a moment I'm hypnotised, gulping sea air into my lungs, filling myself with the calm that comes with the cold breeze. A shiver shakes me and I turn to go back.

He's running towards me, in grey shorts and a T-shirt, but I recognise the dark hair. He's jogging, his legs lean and muscular, listening to music through little earphones. I watch him approach. As we're almost level, he turns his gaze on me. Intense blue eyes, that moment of recognition again, our stare holding for seconds too long. He says, 'Hello,' his voice soft but distinct, and carries on running, jogging into the distance, athletic as a Greek god. He doesn't look back.

I'm shaking my head, wondering if he lives nearby. Where did he come from? He looked sinewy, fit. I frown and recall his expression as our eyes met, about the single word, *hello*. Was it politeness at seeing another person on the beach, because I stood back to let him jog past? Or was it recognition, because he remembered the incident, when he reached up in the supermarket and handed me the muesli? Did he remember me? I stare at the ocean for a moment and the wind blows my hair. A little shiver of excitement trickles down my spine as I make my way back up the white stone steps to the clifftop flat.

Chapter Sixteen

Back in the flat, everything is silent. I walk into the lounge, over to the kitchen area, and stare at the empty glasses and unwashed dishes. I'm lost in thought, still thinking about the jogging muesli man, the intense meeting of his eyes with mine.

I wash the plates and dry them, imagining Terry and Alison and Arran sitting in Embers in Brighton, opposite Jade and Luis. I can almost hear the conversation: *Your mum looked well, Jade.* That's from Terry. *I thought she looked a bit tired, to be honest.* That's Alison. *I don't really know her well, not as well as I know you all,* Luis admits, smiling at Jade. Arran is picking his nose. Jade is telling everyone about the benefits of healthy food: she's forgotten about me, and then Terry says, *Oh, by the way, what was your mum doing here? She's a long way from home,* and Jade laughs, *Ha, ha. You'd never believe it, Dad. She's on the run from Uncle Adie, who's upset a gangster friend in a dodgy deal.* Then Alison mutters, *Oh dear. I'm so glad we moved away from all that, Terry. What a family – I know she's your mother, Jade, but I'd never expose Arran to such risk . . .* I shake my head and force away the image of them having a wonderful, happy family time.

Then he's back in my mind, the mystery man jogging on the shingle: a local man living an ordinary life while I hide here from Adie. Perhaps that's it. I envy his normal routine, shopping in a supermarket, going for a run, while my life is so uncertain. I worry about Jade and hope her uncle's nefarious business won't affect her. At least I can keep an eye out for her.

There's no one around. I knock on the door of the small bedroom.

'Nan?'

She mumbles back from inside the room.

'Georgina, my knees are terrible this morning. Come and help me out of bed.'

I push the door and rush in. She's sitting up with a glass of beer, so her knees have probably already propelled her as far as the kitchen and back. She adjusts the spectacles on her nose, blinking.

'Have you had breakfast?'

She waves the glass. 'I had to do this myself. You weren't here.'

'Where's Bonnie?'

She shrugs. 'No idea. I fancy eggs this morning, Georgina. Two, just fried in butter, on toast. Or poached, like in that nice place we stayed with that posh Mrs Bolt. If you pass me my clothes, I'll be all right from here. You can go and cook me something to eat. And a cup of sweet tea.'

I check inside my bedroom as I go back to the kitchen. Bonnie's not there and the duvet cover is perfectly smooth: she's particular about her side of the bed. I wonder if she's popped out for a walk or to look for me. I don't know why, but a feeling of anxiety rises in my chest and squats on my shoulders. I'll text my sister after I've fed Nanny.

An hour later, there's no response from Bonnie to my messages and, of course, there's nothing from Jade. Why would there be? She's having a lovely family lunch in Embers.

It's three o'clock by the time I've tidied away, washed some clothes in Roque's hi-tech machine and hoovered the floor. Nanny's instructed me on the art of laundry.

'Don't let my smalls dry out as rough as cardboard. Dry them flat. If they're lumpy, it makes the skin on my bum raw.'

There are still no messages on my phone. I sit in front of Nanny by her feet as she lolls in the armchair watching a comedian from the 1960s chase women in swimsuits round a forest before he gurns into the camera. I notice smears of egg yolk on Roque's chair arm. I breathe out deeply.

'I hope Bonnie's okay.'

Nanny ruffles my hair. 'Your roots need doing. I can see the grey.'

'I know, Nan.'

'Are you worried about her?'

'Bonnie? Always.'

It's true. I remember when we were teenagers, when too-trusting Bonnie dated all the wrong boys – I've always felt responsible. It's been up to me to look out for her.

'Or are you worried about Jade, all loved up with Louise?'

'That too.'

She pats me. 'It's tough being a mum.'

I nod. 'You didn't want kids, Nan?'

She says nothing. Then she pats me again. I feel the hard bones in her fingers rap against my neck.

'Another cup of tea would be nice.'

I wriggle and turn to her. 'Okay.'

'Four sugars.'

'Right.'

I go over to the kitchen, put two sugars in a cup and put the kettle on. I wonder whether to tell her about Terry and his family. Then I think about the man jogging on the beach and who he might be. I stir the tea loudly, to make believe it's sweet.

'Here's your tea, Nanny.'

'What's worrying you, love? It's not just Bonnie, is it?' Her knobbly hand finds the side of my hip and she taps it. 'Sit down with me. We can sort it all out.'

I take a deep breath. I want to tell her about Terry, sitting on the sofa upstairs with my daughter and his wife and son, one big happy family, all smiles, and Luis taking them all out to Sunday lunch, while I hide down here, irrelevant and forgotten. I want to tell her about the strange man running by the sea, meeting him in the supermarket, passing me muesli, his piercing blue eyes searching my face. I wonder if he's a local; if I'll bump into him again.

In the end, I say, 'There's a café in the village, Nan, Djimi's. Does great coffee. We must go down there. We should have a break from these four walls.'

She gives me a long, hard look, then nods her head. 'That might be nice, Georgina. I like the look of those crumbly croissants.' She pronounces it *cross-ants*, but I'm in no mood to smile. 'Is it nearby? I can't walk for too long nowadays.'

'About ten minutes from here. All downhill. You could manage it with Bonnie and me, and we'll get a taxi back to avoid the steps up to here. It might be good exercise.'

She puts her hand on my arm. 'Tell me something, love. I'm in the dark a bit. I know Adie's been a fool and this Beddowes is after him and Bonnie. How safe are we here, really? What happens if he finds us? And when can we go back home?' She tips her head to one side and grins. 'Not that I'm in a rush. I like it here. The place is always warm and having company is nice. But I was just wondering at night, you know. We're two floors up, so I hope there's no likelihood of me waking up and finding a very bad man with a shotgun at the bottom of my bed.'

'I think we're all right, Nan.' I check her expression and she seems happy. 'Give me a couple of days. I'll have a better idea of how things are. I mean, Bonnie said Adie probably knows we're with Jade and he thinks she's in London. We'll be okay. In an ideal world, we're all right here and we can just enjoy ourselves until Easter. By then, Adie should've sorted his problems out and it'll be safe enough to go home.'

I think for a moment, wondering if I'll have enough time to develop a better relationship with Jade before we go back to Liverpool. Nanny's eyes burrow into mine, luminous behind the glasses.

'Shouldn't we just tell the police about Adie?'

'Who knows exactly what's going on? Let's just stay well back . . .'

' . . . in case it all blows up in our faces? All right. But, Georgina . . .'

'Nan?'

'Don't keep it all to yourself. Talk to me. We're both trying to look after Bonnie.' She taps my wrist. 'We're on the same side, you and me. And we're both a couple of hard-boiled women. Not soft and sweet like your sister.'

'That's what worries me.' I sigh, struggle to my feet and move towards the kitchen area. 'Shall we discuss what to cook tonight?'

Nanny giggles. 'Why don't we whip those courgettes out and make some ratty tails? I'm looking forward to trying it out.'

151

'Maybe with a bit of crusty bread to soak up the juices.'

'And a beer or two.' Nanny wriggles in her seat. 'I'm getting used to the high life now.'

There's a knock at the door and I stand absolutely still and listen, my heart thumping. Nanny turns her head to stare at me and I put a finger over my lips.

There's another rap, louder, and I hold my breath. Nanny raises her eyebrows and I shrug. Time hangs, frozen, and I slowly breathe out. Silence stretches. I move on my toes to the door and peep through the spyhole. There's no one there.

I creak the door open. There's a bouquet of flowers outside, on the floor, roses: typically Adie's style. I bend down and pick them up as if there's a time bomb lurking in the blooms. My eyes roam to find details of the sender and my fingers pluck a card: *Love from Jade and Luis.*

I call back to Nanny, 'It's Jade. She's sent flowers.'

I hear the pounding of feet and Luis appears around the corner, now in a tracksuit top and shorts, grinning.

'I hear your voice, Georgie. I bring you the flowers from Jade and me.'

I invite him in, close the door quickly, and smell the flowers as a gesture of thanks.

'There're lovely, Luis. You didn't need to . . .'

'Jade and me, we feel so bad. We say sorry. We don't expect you to come up to the flat, but Jade says of course you can come up. It was not lucky that Terry is there and also Alison and Arran.'

Nanny's eyebrows shoot up: triumph that she's found me out and pity that I've had to hide the truth.

I shrug. 'It doesn't matter, Luis; Terry is Jade's dad. I know they see each other all the time. It's only fair.'

Luis grins, easy-going and happy to agree with me. 'Jade feels bad so I bring to you the flowers.'

Nanny eases herself to a standing position and walks over, inspecting the roses with unbending fingers. I hand them to her.

'Lovely, aren't they, Nan?'

She beams at Luis. 'It's been a while since a handsome man brought me flowers.'

I stifle a smile. 'Thanks, Luis. Say thanks to Jade. That's so thoughtful.'

The grin breaks across his face. 'Jade's out shopping after the lunch. She is back soon. I bring the flowers to say to you that we have a free evening on Thursday and maybe we take you all out to Embers in Brighton to make things equal. A dinner together, all five people, a nice time?'

Nanny grabs his hand. 'That'd be lovely, Louise.'

He gazes at her and his eyes are soft. He takes her hand in both of his. I understand why Jade is so keen on this good-natured young man.

'I order a table and a taxi, too. It will be a good evening all together. Jade enjoys the meal with her father but she says me she thinks Alison can be the right fucking bitch.'

He grins hopefully and I realise he has no idea what he's just said. I press my lips together to stifle a smile.

'Thanks, Luis. We'll see you on Thursday, then. And the flowers are lovely. We'll put them in water.'

I take the bouquet from Nanny and place them on a small table.

He blinks slowly, then repeats our arrangements to be sure.

'Okay, so now I go and we meet on Thursday. You will like Embers. It is a good place with nice people there.'

He kisses my cheek and then Nan's.

Her hand hovers and she pats his shoulder. 'I look forward to it.'

He's at the door, saying goodbye, and I hear the clatter

of heels. The scent of expensive perfume hits me before Bonnie sails round the corner, her arms full of shopping. Luis greets her with, 'Hello, Aunty Bonnie,' and he's gone. I stare at the bags marked Iggi, Noa Noa and Lulu Rose. She has a wide smile on her face as she rushes into the flat and places her purchases on the coffee table next to the roses.

Nanny says, 'The flowers are from Jade. We're all going out for a big dinner with them.'

Bonnie flops onto the sofa, kicking off her shoes.

'Brighton's great. It was only a quick taxi ride there and back. I'm exhausted. Georgie, you wouldn't put the kettle on, would you? I'm desperate for a cup of tea.'

I'm about to move then I check myself. 'Bonnie, what's all this shopping?'

'I treated myself . . . And you. And Nan.'

'How did you pay for it all?'

'I didn't. Adie did. His credit card. I thought I deserved it. We all do. I mean, I couldn't stand being stuck in here any longer and I thought, I'd do a bit of pampering—'

'Bonnie, are you mad? Adie can trace where we are—'

She leans back, lifts her feet in the air and wiggles freshly scarlet toenails. 'Oh, don't worry about that.'

'Are you kidding? We're safe here as long as—'

'I just spoke to Adie on the phone when I was in the taxi coming back here. I told him we're in Brighton.'

My mouth drops open. 'You did *what*?'

'I spoke to him earlier. He said he was on his way to London to do some final business and then he's leaving the country. So I said to him, well that's a coincidence because we're not far away. Adie has a plan. He knows how to get rid of Beddowes for good and pick up enough money to allow us to live a life of luxury. He was very positive about it.'

'I bet he was.'

'Oh yes, Adie said it's all sorted. Everything's going to be all right.'

Nanny's scowling. I'm furious.

'Bonnie, we can't let him come here.'

She laughs, a light trill, and gives me her sweetest smile.

'Do you think I'm crazy? I wouldn't invite him to this flat. No, I've said we'll talk next week, when I've had time to decide. On the phone.'

'Don't invite him here, whatever you do.' I can hear the anxiety strangling my voice.

'He's in London for a week or so. Something to do with his business deal. I know how to play Adie. I'll keep him hanging on a bit.'

'Then what?'

'Maybe I'll meet him in London. See what he has to say. Maybe we'll get back together. Maybe we won't.'

She gives a shrug, pretending she doesn't care, but her face is shining. I shake my head and wonder if all my efforts have been futile.

Chapter Seventeen

'What shall I do, Georgie?' Bonnie paces up and down in the flat. She slumps in the chair and folds her arms. 'I could meet him, stay in a nice hotel in London with a spa.'

I pull a face. 'I know what I'd do.'

'Oh, I don't know what to think.' She stares at the phone in her hand, the one she's just used to call him again.

Two days have gone by. It's the third conversation they've had. He's begging her to meet him. I'm glad Nan isn't here to pass comment. She's in her bedroom, bustling about and singing, which is probably why Bonnie's taken the opportunity to ring him again. I force myself to grin so hard that my cheeks ache, to prevent myself from telling Bonnie to tell Adie to go to hell.

'Make him wait. Give yourself more time. You might still decide to go back to him.' I cross my fingers behind my back, like I did when we were kids and I told lies. 'The important thing is that you get to decide. And don't rush into things.'

'He asked me about the charm bracelet again.'

'Perhaps he wants it back. Perhaps he needs the money and he's thinking of pawning it.'

'He says it's a symbol of our love.'

I groan. 'Used, worn out, seen better days?'

'He says we could start again. He used my pet name.'

I roll my eyes. 'Bon-Bon.'

'He loves me. He misses me.'

'Our mum used to say you'd miss a wart if you had one long enough. Have something to eat.'

'I should go and see him. Talk it out. I said I might. Face-to-face.'

'I'm surprised you want to see his face ever again, Bon.'

'Should I go to London? Just one last meeting so that he can explain everything?'

'I wouldn't trust anything Adie says, Bonnie. Just get over him, move on.'

She shrugs, annoyed. It's not the answer she wants. I start to bustle in the kitchen area, bending over the fridge, boiling a kettle. Bonnie's voice is petulant.

'I don't want dinner. I'm not hungry.' She inspects her phone again, slumping on the sofa. 'Well, maybe a Ryvita and a glass of wine.'

I find a prawn salad and tip it onto a plate then put the frying pan on to make Nanny an omelette. I make two coffees and a strong tea. Cooking smells hover round us and Bonnie swallows as if she's going to be sick. Three plates of food are ready.

There's a shuffling of feet from the small bedroom and Nanny appears. She's wearing one of Bonnie's dresses. It's a dazzling silver sequined number with a plunge neckline, which has no sleeves. It hangs off her shoulders and stops just above her knees. Nanny's little limbs protrude like four milk straws. Her knees point inwards. She has Uncle Wilf's green woollen hat on again and her hair sticks out

157

in wisps. Her eyes shine behind thick spectacles as she does her best to waltz into the room, her feet shambling, her falsetto voice straining to sing the lyrics of *Pretty Woman*.

She smiles at Bonnie. 'What do you think?'

I don't blink. 'Looking good, Nan.'

'It'd look nice with one of those boa constrictors.'

'Feather boas, Nan.' I stifle a smile.

Bonnie's mouth is open. 'That's my brand-new dress . . .'

Nanny poses, hand on hip. She has crimson lipstick on.

'I was just wondering if this would be a good outfit for me to wear for dinner with Louise and Jade on Thursday night.'

'You'd look a million dollars, Nan.'

I remember Bonnie dressing up in our mum's clothes when she was six or seven, her hopeful eyes seeking approval. Nanny's expression reminds me so much of those happy times.

'She can't wear that.' Bonnie wrinkles her nose and folds her arms.

Nan's face freezes, unsure. I stare at Bonnie: she's behaving like a diva. I take a breath.

'We can find you something glamorous to wear, Nan. Bonnie or I will have something nice that'll be perfect for you. Or we can buy you something special.'

'Well, she certainly can't wear that.'

'And why not, Bonnie?'

'She'd look ridiculous.'

I clamp my lips together. Nan glances from me to Bonnie and back to me like she's watching ping-pong. Her lip trembles and I'm suddenly furious with my insensitive sister. I clench my fists, then the words splutter out.

'You're ridiculous.'

Bonnie is up, her face flushed. 'At least I have a man

who finds me attractive. At least I have someone who values me. Not like you. You're . . .'

'I'm what, Bonnie?' I stride over to the sofa: we're face-to-face.

Her eyes flash. 'You're a dried-up old husk who nobody fancies any more.'

Something snaps and I can't stop myself.

'At least I'm not a stupid pouting bitch whose husband takes off with any tart he can find in order to relieve the boredom between dodgy deals.'

She screams and launches herself at me; her nails are curled claws aimed at my face. I grasp her wrist and shake her hard. She lashes out with a booted foot and catches me on the shin. I yelp and glare at her for two seconds, then shake her, twist her arms – I'm stronger and she topples back into the sofa. I fling myself at her and push her back into the cushions, leap on top of her and wedge my knees either side of her body. For a moment, she can't move, so I glare at her and she shrieks like the possessed. She wriggles, grabs my hair, two hands full, and pulls. I grasp her wrist and wrench it hard with one hand then lift the other, ready to slap her face. The moment stands still. Her bracelet falls, slithering to the floor, and my voice comes out, quiet as fear.

'Bonnie . . .'

She pouts. 'Georgie. I'm sorry.'

'What are we doing? This is stupid. We shouldn't be fighting each other.'

'I know.' She falls back against the chair, snivelling. 'I've been so silly. Oh, I'm just so mixed up. All this stuff with Adie. I don't know what to do.'

I bend down and pick up the bracelet, placing it in her palm. She wails even louder.

'He said this bracelet was precious. Now it's broken, like Adie and me.'

'Oh, Bonnie. I'm sorry. Come here.'

I wrap an arm round her, hug her to me, and she sobs in big gulps. I turn my head to look at Nanny. She's sitting in her armchair in the silver dress, hugging herself, her little legs splayed. Her lipstick is smudged and a tear trickles down her face. She's shivering. Her mouth moves and I hear the murmur, soft as air.

'I look ridiculous.'

'Come here, Nan.'

I haul Bonnie over to Nanny and we throw our arms round each other. Before we've had time to think about it, we're all clinging to each other's necks, crying and howling together.

Chapter Eighteen

The next day, we tiptoe round each other so politely that we barely breathe the same air. Bonnie's perpetually hunched over, ashamed. I'm afraid to speak, in case I say the wrong thing. Nan's eyes are soulful behind the glasses, hurt, and she'll only speak in monosyllables, which is unlike her. Bonnie's bracelet lies on the bedside table, the clasp broken. Then, on Thursday, the day of our meal at Embers, I decide that we need to cheer ourselves up, so I whisper to Bonnie that we should take Nan shopping to London. Bonnie doesn't need to be asked twice, but Nan makes us ask nicely five times before we persuade her to venture out.

'I don't like those London taxis, Georgina. All sorts of people sit in those seats. They smoke and have bad breath and they pass wind. You don't know who's sat on the seat and then you put your bottom on it. It's not healthy. I have to be careful at my age. They might have germs.'

We take a fast train and arrive in the city centre by eleven o'clock. We clamber out of the taxi and Nanny gazes around her at the people moving in all directions. She stares up at the top of a building and then looks to me aghast, her glasses reflecting the lights in the shop windows. Bonnie pays the driver and Nan clutches my arm.

'He was a nice man, that taxi driver. Very friendly. But it was a lot of money to pay, ten pounds. We might have been better going on the tubes.'

'We'll be fine, Nan.'

She gasps and her grip tightens. 'Oh, Georgina, look at all these people. Look at the crowds. There's not enough space for everyone. No wonder they make people pay all that Digestion Charge. It's too full up.'

'Have you heard that on TV? We'll be great, Nan.'

I steer her towards Selfridges and into the revolving doors.

When we emerge, she grabs my wrist.

'I didn't like that. It was like being in a sputnik. Why can't they have a proper door that opens and closes, not these funny whirligig things. They make me dizzy.'

We arrive at an escalator and she hesitates. I urge her forwards.

'Now, Nan. Now.' I grab her arm. 'Now. Now, Nanny, jump.'

She leaps on and pulls at my coat sleeve, beaming.

'This is good, Georgina. I can climb the stairs with no effort. I'll have to tell the landlord to put one of these in at home for me.' She peers at me slyly. 'Can we have a cup of tea? And a cross-ant or a cake.'

'All right, Nan, when we've finished shopping. Let's buy you something to wear for Embers.'

We climb off the escalator on the first floor and Nanny gapes at the array of dresses. Bonnie's face has taken on a soft sheen, eyes glazed. Adie's credit card is in her bag. I've been craning my neck since we arrived in London, hoping we don't bump into Bonnie's ex. She's been looking in all directions too, probably hoping to catch a glimpse of him.

My instincts tell me that she's decided to meet him on Saturday. I've heard her whispering into the phone on the balcony and I'm sure it was to him. I recognised the acquiescent titter she does when he makes jokes. I realise I'm chewing my lip with annoyance. My sister has started to flourish, become more confident since she left him; she can't go back now.

Bonnie suggests a soft red dress for Nanny, long-sleeved and calf-length, and some court shoes in a deep crimson. But Nanny's hanging back, her neck craned, looking for a sparkly frock that'll dazzle Luis.

I find one in pale grey with cap sleeves and sequins at the bodice and a long filmy skirt. I place my thumb over the price tag and when Nan's inspecting something else, I buy it and some shiny slip-on shoes. When I hand her the bag, she grabs my arm and gazes at me like I'm the good fairy in *Cinderella*.

We leap into another taxi, which takes us to the appointments I've made at a salon recommended by Jade. While Bonnie has a manicure and pedicure, Nanny and I are booked in with Gretchen and Seok, whom I've told to make us both look a million dollars.

Seok begins to massage Nanny's head with his fingertips. She stares at his black hair tipped with electric blue, then her eyes close behind the glasses. We sit next to each other and they bring us a complimentary beverage. The cappuccino is for me and Nan has a hot chocolate with whipped cream. She sits up to drink it and there's a dot of froth on her nose. She raises her eyebrows when Seok begins to mix colours in a bowl, but then she relaxes in her seat and closes her eyes.

Over an hour later, I meet Bonnie at the till, and she

shows me her perfect pink nails and says she's already paid the bill with Adie's card. I feel much better now, with sleek hair just below my jaw, properly coloured and nicely styled. Nanny stands next to me and runs fingers through her new style. It's shiny, soft and silver in a cute pixie cut, but Seok has added a streak of electric blue through the fringe, suggesting that, 'Nan likes a little mischief.' Her smile is wider than I've ever seen it.

We haul our shopping outside and hail a taxi. It's a bright day, the sky cloudless, and the wind ruffles our perfect hair. Nanny threads an arm through mine as I ask the driver to take us to the station. Nan wants to go to Djimi's Café for late afternoon tea. I grin at her and she raises her eyebrows.

'Can we do this again, Georgina? I'd like to go again. I'll even put up with the crowds and the revolting doors.'

'Revolving, Nan.'

'I'd like to go up the London Eye next time. To see all the sights. And ride on one of those topless buses.'

I smile and promise myself I'll make up for all the time she spent stuck indoors when we were in Liverpool. I'd never realised her capacity for fun, or her need for it.

'We'll make time, Nan.'

She clutches her shopping and snuggles behind the safety belt, gazing out of the window. Bonnie gives me a look and I wink. I stare at the shops as the taxi cruises by and imagine taking Nanny to see the sights one weekend, perhaps before we return home and start preparing for summer. It'll be busy in the salon now; it always is in spring. There will be the April Shower offers of luxury treatments at Beauty Within and the proprietor isn't even there to make sure everything is shipshape.

The train has us back in Sussex by five thirty and we

stop at Djimi's Café at Nan's request. Djimi's pleased to see us. He comes over straight away, his head newly shaven, sporting a neat goatee beard and tight black jeans.

'Hello again, dreamer. I see you've brought your sisters with you.' He looks at Bonnie. 'Oh, no, this must be your daughter. Pleased to meet you, gorgeous.'

Nan and Bonnie are flattered; I'm not. He beams at Bonnie and she giggles, thrusting out her newly manicured hand.

'I'm a happily married woman.'

I almost groan. He hasn't taken his eyes off her.

'And what does the old man do for a living? He must be something special, to afford a looker like you.'

I'm about to ask what decade he thinks we live in, and to tell him in no uncertain terms that the times when women were judged purely by their appearance should have long gone.

Bonnie smiles. 'Thank you. He's an entrepreneur.'

Nanny's wriggling in her seat. She waves a hand. 'Hurry up, Djimi, please. We'll have Capuchins all around. Don't keep a woman waiting.'

Djimi turns his smile on her. 'Of course, my darling. Can I recommend some pastries? I have some nice brownies, cream horns.'

Nanny gives him a sharp look. 'I'll have one of each.'

I put my hand on Djimi's arm. 'Bring the coffees and one cake. We're off out later.'

He's back in moments with coffees on a tray and a cream pastry. Nanny's eyes shine. Djimi turns to go, then he catches my glance and grins.

'It's good to see you again. I wondered whether you'd gone back to the frozen north.'

'Not yet,' I tell him.

'We like it here. We've been to London shopping,' Nanny adds, chomping on the cream horn.

The cream shoots out and lands on her lap. She scoops it up and shovels it back in her mouth.

He moves his gaze to Bonnie. 'Where are you staying?'

'At Cliff Top. We have a flat there.'

'Very nice,' Djimi grins. 'I look forward to an invite.'

He moves away and I glare at Bonnie. She shrugs, an exaggerated movement of her shoulders.

'What? What? A café owner's hardly going to tell anyone.'

'Best to say nothing to anyone, Bonnie. Seriously.'

She sulks and looks at Nanny, who has cream where lipstick should be. I roll my eyes.

It's past six o'clock and our table is booked for eight thirty. Nanny's tired after an exciting day. She and Bonnie go to their rooms, Nan for a nap and Bonnie to begin the two hours it'll take her to get ready.

I go out for a walk. I miss regular exercise. I miss my own four walls and my own space in bed. I miss my old life, but it's been a real joy spending time with Nan and Bonnie. It occurs to me that we're all happier for it, somehow energised.

I walk down to the beach, across the pebbles and gaze out at the horizon. It's dark, but the lights from the flats shift and glimmer orange on the waves. A winking glow from a ship is in the distance, stuck on the horizon. The sky above is a dark belly of clouds, the ocean below the rough darkness of bark.

I push my hands into my pockets and walk briskly. My mind moves with the pace of my feet. I want to go back home, to my own house. I'm ready to leave. I worry that Bonnie'll probably decide to go away with

Adie. Worry and guilt sit heavily on my shoulders. Bonnie and Adie going abroad would leave me free to live my own life, but the idea of releasing her into his clutches without me nearby to fight her battles would be like dropping a soft rabbit into the snap of an open trap. I don't know what to do. Going back to Liverpool also means leaving Jade. I know she wants her independence, but the sudden separation will slice me open like a blade.

I pull out my phone and call Amanda. I hear the friendly crackle of her voice and, almost immediately, I know I'll return, whatever happens. I'm whisked back to my home across the ether when she says, 'Hi, you dirty stop-out.'

'How's tricks, Amanda?'

'We could do with you here, Georgie. Lexi's opened up the reception area – it's a full-time nail salon now. She's a wizard. And the customers love Ella-Louise; she has a really lovely way with people. We're booked all day. We work late nights now on Thursdays and Fridays to fit everyone in. Business is booming. We need you back just for a break.'

'I'm working on it.'

'A man's been in asking for you.'

'Adie?'

'No.'

I suddenly feel cold. 'Who's been in the salon?'

'Your Scottish friend. A couple of hours ago. He says he's an associate of yours. He must be – he showed me a picture of you and him and Bonnie on his phone.'

My body prickles. The hand holding my phone is a hard fist. 'Duncan Beddowes? What did he say?'

'He said you'd contacted him with a business proposition. He said he needed an address, to get hold of you urgently. I told him you were abroad and he said no, you were definitely in Brighton.'

My breath stops in my lungs like I've been punched. I stand still and gasp for a few seconds.

'How does he know that?'

'I didn't tell him. I said you'd gone somewhere sunny.'

'What did he say then?'

'He stared at me then he laughed as if I'd made a joke. Then he made one back.'

'What sort of joke?'

'That you'd certainly feel the heat when he caught up with you. I didn't think it was a nice thing to say. Then he left.'

I turn immediately, look over my shoulder and head back up the steps towards Cliff Top. My eyes search the beach and the road above for Adie or even Beddowes and secretly, despite everything else going on, for the mystery man jogging on the beach. I've no idea what draws me to him. Perhaps he represents normality, running along the shingle like it's the most ordinary thing to do. I remember our eyes meeting and him saying hello, as if we spoke every day. He certainly makes me imagine he has a life that isn't crazy, spinning out of control like mine. He seems trustworthy, safe, and again an image of him seeps into my mind. Again, I'm hoping we'll bump into each other by chance.

It's quiet on top of the cliffs. Seagulls squawk and squabble over scraps of litter then lift themselves heavily into the air and are flung away by the wind. I'm cold now. A sudden sensation of vulnerability seizes my heart and shakes it. I move quickly, breathing into the top of my lungs, shivering. I want to get back to the flat and lock the door. My brows knit and I wonder how our simple life in Liverpool became an unpredictable soap opera, a whirlwind of potential trouble. It's all Adie's doing. Now, the idea of going out this evening with Jade and Luis worries me. I don't feel so safe here. I wonder if we're safe anywhere at all.

Chapter Nineteen

I push my fears to the back of my mind and put on my sassiest party dress and my broadest smile. A couple of hours later, we stroll towards Embers like we're superstars. Luis is smart in a dark jacket and jeans, his hair floppy and sleek. Jade has her arm through his and she's wearing a strappy black dress, short beneath the long cream coat. Her violet eyes shine and her lips are deep crimson.

Bonnie's in one of her new acquisitions, a knee-length cream dress with layers of lace on the skirt. But Nanny has the knock-em-dead look, with her new silver hair and the streak of blue, and the grey sparkling dress and soft shoes. She's borrowed Jade's orange faux-fur coat and she looks every bit the zany film star.

She totters from the taxi to the restaurant, one elbow crooked through mine and one through Bonnie's, and gazes up at the neon sign with 'Embers' in lights, shining red coals underneath and little flames emerging from the top. I hardly recognise her nowadays, compared to the person she was in Liverpool, wrapped in Wilf's old cardigan, sitting in the armchair and grumbling about Sunday lunch. A grin breaks on her face.

'This is swanky, Georgina.'

A man steps out from the darkness and a flash bulb pops. I hear the words 'Mr Delgado, Luis – over here.' Someone's taking his photo and Jade smiles into the camera like a professional. I grin, disbelieving for moment, reminding myself that he's a sports star and she's a WAG. I secretly hope that Bonnie and I aren't in the photo. We'd be easily identified if it ends up online and Adie's sure to find out. He'd recognise Jade, too. A shiver of fear wriggles through me and I feel exposed, vulnerable. I force the worries away. Nothing will spoil our night out.

Inside, a waiter greets us, a dapper penguin in a tight suit.

'Señor Delgado, *bienvenido*. Welcome to you and your party. Your table is ready, by the window, as usual. Please, come this way. I'll take your coats.'

Nanny beams as he holds out her chair for her and then, when she's seated, it's gently pushed forwards. Her glass is filled with water and she taps the waiter with her finger and says, 'I'll have wine.'

Jade nods to the waiter. 'Two bottles of our usual, please.'

'The Rioja, madam. Of course.'

'And sparkling water for Luis – he has a game the day after tomorrow.' She turns to me. 'We don't usually dine out on a Thursday. Luis trains so hard and watches what he eats. He rarely drinks alcohol.'

The waiter smiles briefly, then he's gone.

Bonnie, Nanny and I sit with our backs to the window. I've already seen the spectacular view of Brighton, little lights twinkling against a soft black sky. Drinks are poured and we pick up glossy menus. The penguin waiter is poised by Luis' elbow, waiting for our order. Jade and Luis are opposite, discussing the nutritional composition of the

171

menu. Apparently, they always choose the same dish. Nanny has trouble making her mind up.

'Well, I'm not having pigeon. You never know where it came from. Perhaps it was just wandering by outside and the chef thought, "Ooohh, I'll have that on a plate for tonight".'

'Unlikely, Nan.'

I decide on a quinoa and edamame salad. Bonnie says she'll have the same. Nan frowns, her eyes straining behind her glasses.

'What's fillet wellington? It sounds very tough, like rubber boots.'

'Beef in pastry, Nan.'

'Like a pie? I'll have that then.'

Jade pipes up, 'What about the Irish lamb stew, Nan?'

'Oh no. I'm not eating lamb. It hasn't had a life, has it? I'll have the beef pasty, please. And another glass of that red.'

Luis and Jade order the vegetable tagine and Nanny helps herself to the Rioja. We lose ourselves in conversation and wine under the soft flicker of yellow lights from the dangling chandeliers.

The food arrives and it's delicious: even Bonnie manages to eat most of the salad.

She leans forwards. 'What's it like being a high-profile girlfriend, Jade? I've always wanted to be in the limelight.'

I press my lips together, preventing myself from making a sarcastic comment about Adie's nefarious antics and the sort of limelight we're in now. Tonight, he's best forgotten.

Jade's laughter tinkles. 'Luis and I don't consider ourselves public figures. It's just how life is. Luis and I are a partnership.'

Luis nods. 'We are so happy, like how a foot fits in a boot.'

I pour more wine and Nanny grabs the bottle from me.

'Luis and I expect to be together beyond his time as a top striker. Luis and I are for keeps.'

She turns shining eyes on him and he kisses the tip of her nose. It seems like she's no longer my child. She's a young woman who's morphed into the hybrid character called *LuisandI*. I'm still worried about her, though. I hope she'll be all right. I don't want her hopes raised, her heart broken. I know only too well how that feels.

I poke at my salad and notice everyone else has finished their meal, even Bonnie. Nan's plate is clean apart from a smear of gravy. She dabs her finger in it and sucks loudly. The penguin waiter arrives with the dessert list.

'Afters? Oh, I couldn't,' groans Bonnie.

Jade has made up her mind. 'I'll just have a coffee.'

'Same for me,' Luis nods.

Nan has a savage look on her face. 'What's a profitty roll?'

'Choux pastry filled with cream, covered in chocolate,' the waiter explains.

Bonnie perks up. 'I might manage one of those . . .'

I pour a little more wine in our glasses, swallow the richness of Rioja and watch Nan. She's enjoying herself, regaling Luis about all the fun you can have on a caravan holiday.

'Wilf's sister, Josie, and her husband, Ken, and my Wilfie and me . . . oh! we did have such good times. It was a lovely place, Rhyl. We'd have such larks together, go on long walks and laugh all day.'

She notices me staring, my mind in a haze, and she says, 'They were my best times. But today comes close: a posh dinner here with you all and having fun shopping in London with my girls.' She pecks Bonnie on the cheek. 'They spoilt me rotten today. I felt like a queen. It was lovely.'

I grin. 'You look like a queen, Nan.'

'What do you think to my new outfit, Louise?' Nan preens across the table.

'*Muy guapa*,' he says and Jade translates, 'Very pretty.'

Nan pushes knobbly fingers through the silver-and-blue fringe, sitting up as tall as she can in the soft sequined dress. I gaze at Jade and Luis, happy together, and my thoughts drift to the gallant muesli man who jogs on the beach. I wonder if he ever dines at Embers.

'You okay, Mum?' Jade frowns and I shrug.

'Fine, love. I was just thinking how kind of you it is to bring us here.'

'It's nothing,' Jade giggles and Luis says, '*De nada*.'

Bonnie sips her wine and Nan starts to tell everyone about the hairdresser she met in London today, Seok, and how talented and friendly he was.

'I've no idea what it cost to have my hair done by such an expert. It was like being a film star. And we had free drinks: hot chocolate with cream and bits on top. It was a real treat.'

We're chatting, our heads bent forwards, laughing about a story Jade and Luis are telling about one of the coaches at his daily training session, when my eyes are drawn towards the entrance. There's a kerfuffle in the doorway. The waiter's talking to someone, a burly man in an overcoat, who raises his voice, demanding a table despite not having booked. I know who he is immediately and I fight the urge to run. My mind wrestles with how he'll have found us: how he knows we're here. I'm sure it's no coincidence. A Scottish voice, resonating, lifted in indignation.

I lean over towards Jade. 'That's him. Beddowes.'

Jade frowns. 'What's he doing here?'

I shrug.

She grabs my hand. 'Get Aunty Bonnie and Nanny out

of here, Mum. He doesn't know me. I'm with Luis. We'll be fine.'

He's still there, metres away, arguing. I hope he hasn't seen us. I catch my breath and stand up, force my best smile.

'Time for a quick toilet visit before pudding. Come on, Nan. You've had plenty of wine – you must need the loo. Bonnie, here, give me a hand.'

Nanny nods. 'Ooh, you're right. Good idea, Georgina.'

Bonnie pushes back her chair; she and I take Nanny's elbows and we guide her to the ladies', shove the door open and step inside.

'My goodness, the floor's all glittery gold and spangles.' Nanny stands in the middle of the ladies' loo and gazes round her. 'It's like a big stage – with shiny gold mirrors everywhere. You'd expect Michael Jackson to come down from the ceiling in a chariot and start singing "Thriller".' She scoots into a cubicle.

Bonnie checks her make-up in the mirror, arranges her hair. I grab Bonnie's arm and lower my voice.

'Don't tell Nan. Beddowes is out there. I'm sure it's him. I don't know why or what's going on. It might be nothing. Can you stay here with Nan and I'll creep out and have a look?'

'What's happening? Georgie, is everything all right?'

Her eyes are wide with panic. I pat her shoulder. 'Just wait here. I'll be two minutes.'

She turns back to her reflection and starts to spray perfume from her handbag. I can hear Nanny shuffling in the toilet, lifting her dress.

I sidle out of the ladies' and close the heavy door behind me. Ducking behind a pillar in the restaurant, I peer at Jade and Luis, at their backs, their heads leaning together. I'm about to cross the room to them, when I see the

175

towering bulk of a man approaching their table. The swagger, the red hair, the overcoat: I recognise him immediately.

Beddowes offers his hand to Luis, who shakes it, and then Beddowes turns to Jade and she says something to him, moving her head. I'm frozen, not knowing whether to run to my daughter or stay hidden. I watch, huddled behind the pillar, and suddenly I sense Bonnie standing next to me. I put an arm out to hold her back. Nanny's with her and they hide behind me. I lean close and we form a sandwich with our bodies.

I whisper, 'I told you to stay . . .'

'I didn't think he'd really be here. What shall we do?' Bonnie is pale behind her fresh make-up.

Nanny grabs my wrist and I keep my voice low. 'I don't know. Wait until he's gone.'

I watch his every move for a sign of what's happening. He's laughing, but the shift of his body, the way he leans forwards, tells me he's not being friendly.

Luis turns to Jade, his face confused. He's unsure of this intrusion, but Jade has the measure of Beddowes. She throws back her head, laughs and talks to Luis, shutting Beddowes out.

The burly man leans forwards on the table, threatening. Then a hand touches my shoulder and there's a low voice in my ear.

'Is there a problem, madam?'

My heart leaps and I swirl round. It is the penguin waiter, who's clearly noticed three women hiding suspiciously behind a pillar.

'That man, talking to my daughter and Luis. We need to avoid him. Can you – can you show me another way out?'

He puts a finger on his lips. 'I understand, madam. He

176

was very insistent at the door. I had a feeling he had a motive other than merely to dine here. Leave it with me. I'll lead you out the back way. Do you want me to call the police?'

I shake my head. 'Not unless he's aggressive towards my daughter. Just tell him to go.'

'Very well, madam. There's a taxi rank not far from here. Follow me, if you will.'

I frown and Bonnie shakes her head, her eyes bulging. We trail after the waiter into the kitchen area, where he hands us our coats.

'I completely understand the situation, madam. As soon as you're on your way, I'll ask the uninvited guest to move away from Señor Delgado's table. You have no need to worry.'

We're cocooned in our coats: we follow the waiter through the kitchens. There's a lot of commotion, steam, stainless steel surfaces and white-coated chefs bustling about.

Nanny touches the waiter's arm. 'What about my pudding? I haven't had it yet.'

He smirks, a thin moon curve of his lips. He murmurs something to a woman in a white apron and cap, who leaves and returns moments later with a perfectly sealed cardboard carton.

'There are the desserts, madam. It was a real pleasure having you here at Embers. I do hope you'll come again. And I apologise that your evening was curtailed.'

I turn back to the waiter. 'Thanks for being so understanding . . .'

'Sadly, I, too, appreciate how it feels to have unwanted attention from an ex-partner.' The waiter offers me his small smile. 'It's best just to get safely home for tonight. I wish you a pleasant journey, madam. Goodnight.'

I decide it's best not to tell him the truth; it's easier if he believes Beddowes is my persistent ex, although the thought makes me shudder.

We arrive at the back door, the wind blowing in our faces, and the waiter points to the corner, which leads to the front of the restaurant and the main road. Night-time Brighton is alive, people celebrating in colourful clothes, squealing with laughter. I wrap my arms round Bonnie and Nan.

We clamber into an idling taxi five minutes later, by which time my heart is clattering in my chest. Bonnie helps Nanny through the door and we huddle together.

The taxi driver says very little, but he weaves through traffic, out of town and onto the dark, desolate road home. I'm lost in my thoughts, wondering what's just happened. Bonnie is staring through the windows. Nanny has the dessert box open; she's started to attack a profiterole, holding it between her thumb and fingers. She makes soft sounds of contentment.

I pull out my phone to text Jade and I realise I have no idea what to say. I thumb a message: *Hope all OK. We're on our way to the flat.*

A message pings almost immediately. I see Jade's reply. *No worries. All fine here. Speak soon.* I wonder if Beddowes is still there, but then I remember the waiter promising to remove him and to phone the police if he becomes difficult. My head is crammed with thoughts: How did he know where we'd be? Does he know where we live?

The taxi turns in towards Cliff Top and slows down. I pay the driver and we move away from the cab like shadows. The sea breathes, makes a hushing sound like a warning. We stand in swimming darkness and I try to make sense of what's happened this evening, and how Beddowes has arrived here.

At the door, I press the keypad and usher Bonnie and Nanny safely inside. It's past ten o'clock and they want to go straight to bed. I decide to stay outside, have some time and space to think about everything that's happened this evening. The fresh air clears my head.

I stroll down the steps towards the beach, picking my way carefully over the pebbles in the darkness, and let the ocean wind buffet my face. I close my eyes and huddle inside my coat. The skyline is indigo velvet, almost black now, tinged with a thin line of lollipop orange and sharp blue, reflected from the flats behind me. Little lights illuminate the coastline: Brighton sprawls in the distance and I worry about Jade there, at Embers. I breathe in the cold night air and wonder what to do about the mess we're in. I had no idea how serious this was going to become and now I've no idea how to fix it.

Someone's behind me, a light movement, and a hand touches my wrist, gentle fingers. I gasp, turn and look up into intense eyes, a serious gaze, curly black hair threaded with grey. I catch my breath, fear mixed with something else.

He says, 'Hello. Are you all right?'

I nod. The muesli man is still staring at me, so I say, 'I've just had a difficult evening.'

'You must be cold out here.' He's wearing a light jacket. The wind blows his curls from his face. He suddenly smiles. 'Would you like something to drink? A coffee, perhaps. There's a bar just down the road. It doesn't close for another hour.'

I look at his serious expression, the expressive eyes, the handsome face, and I grin. He seems normal, safe. Lovely.

'Why not?'

I'll text Jade when I get there, tell her I'm at Djimi's. I can explain properly later.

I walk across the dark beach next to the tall stranger with the snake tattoo on his wrist and I wonder what on earth I'm doing.

Chapter Twenty

We stroll down the beach and into the village. He leads the way down a narrow street towards a dimly lit pub on the corner. I'm suddenly nervous, although I'm not sure whether it's his presence or the silence of the street in darkness. I'm on my own in a strange place with a strange man and suddenly I'm alert to the excitement of it all. I chatter non-stop about how nice Brighton is, how I've recently dined at Embers, how I love the area and how amazing the view is from Cliff Top. He says very little. Perhaps he can't get a word in.

We go in to The Two Chairmen, which he tells me is an eighteenth-century pub with a fascinating history. Inside, the bar is all dark wood, dangling opaque globe lights. There are a few people in there: two men on stools drinking from full glasses, a couple whispering together. He ushers me to a table, his hand lightly on my back, and I ask for a coffee.

As he moves to the bar, I wonder what I'm doing. What if he thinks I'm a lady of the night and he's tried to pick me up? Or worse, what if he's a dangerous criminal, a friend of Beddowes, even? But he has a warm smile and

I decide to trust my instincts. I'm in a public place, just a few minutes from Cliff Top: I can bolt if I have to.

I text Jade that I'm having a coffee and she replies that she and Luis are fine. They've decided to stay behind at Embers for a while and will be back before midnight. Jade says this is a one-off late night; his coach expects him in training early tomorrow but he'll sleep in the car. I smile. Ideal timing.

He sits, places a cup of coffee in front of me and holds an orange juice in a tall glass. I study his face for a moment. Deep-set eyes, strong blue, his face framed with dark curls, strands of silver grey. I guess that he's probably my age. He has deep laughter lines around his eyes. He's obviously laughed a lot. His face is unshaven, dark stubble on his cheeks that I didn't notice before. I realise I'm staring at him and I look away, take a gulp of coffee and say, 'Thanks.'

'I'm Marcus Hart.'

'Georgie Turner.' I hold out a hand and he squeezes it gently.

'Are you feeling warmer now?' he asks and I nod.

Marcus puts both hands on the table and I glance at the snake tattoo on his wrist under the cuff of his jacket. His face is serious.

'To be honest, I was a bit worried about you.'

I beam at him, mainly to alleviate his concern. 'Really?'

'I often go for a walk or a run on the beach below the cliffs. I love being by the sea. It's where I go to think about my work, to get inspiration. But I saw you staring into the water and I just wondered, well, if everything was all right. You were on your own and it was late. I thought there might be a problem.'

'Oh.'

It occurs to me that Marcus has asked me for a drink

because he feels sorry for me, or just to stop me from leaping into the sea. He doesn't like me at all: he's not attracted to me. He's just being kind. Suddenly, I feel awkward and I don't know what to say.

I mumble, 'Thanks, yes. I'm fine.'

For a moment I wonder if I should tell him about my problems, one called Beddowes who was in Embers this evening, but where would I start? It's better to say nothing, just in case.

Marcus meets my gaze. 'You're new to the area, aren't you?'

'Is it the accent?' I giggle and I'm immediately annoyed with myself. He'll think I'm flirting.

'It's a bit of a giveaway.' He grins and I notice the easy smile, great teeth. 'Do you live in the flats at Cliff Top?'

I opt for the truth, almost. 'Yes, I'm staying in a friend's flat for a week or two.'

'Are you on holiday? A lot of people come to the Brighton area at this time of year. It's lovely in the spring.' Marcus shrugs. 'I live here, so I tend to forget all the things tourists get to enjoy.'

'Oh.' I drink my coffee and wonder what to say. For some reason, I'm yo-yoing between chattering too much and sitting in embarrassing silence. I take a breath. 'Do you work here, then? I thought I'd seen you here before.'

'I work mostly from home. I'm a journalist – well, sort of. The office is in London, but generally I'm here. I go up for meetings. In addition to the day job, there's some stuff I'm trying to get off the ground, a play about politics, a short story about a pianist. What about you? What do you do when you're not being a tourist?'

I titter. 'Apart from shopping for muesli and bumping into strange men when they're out jogging?'

I hear my too-cheerful voice and know I sound silly. I'm

out of practice with dating, if this is a date. I'm probably boring him, babbling again. I put on a serious face and try to regain some dignity.

'I have my own business. I'm a beauty therapist.'

I wonder how he'll react. After all, he's a journalist and a writer. Why would he be interested in someone who paints nails and waxes pubic hair for a living? He's probably not interested in me at all, now he's discovered he doesn't need to save my life, now I'm not going to hurl myself in the ocean.

He grins. 'Sounds like you're a busy person. I've seen you in the area a couple of times.' His gaze is level. 'So, are you staying here by yourself?'

'With my sister and my aunt – three women together. It's a long story.'

'Well, if you need someone to show you round . . .' He shrugs. 'I'm local and my time is flexible. While you're here, I'd be happy to help.'

'I'd be delighted, Marcus.'

It sounds strange saying his name. I want to ask him more about his situation, if he's married, if he has a girl-friend, or a boyfriend. He might simply be a nice person. I decide whatever he's offering, I'll be glad of a friendly face. A friendly, handsome face. And he has a nice physique. I sit up straight and try to control my eyeline, which has been examining the arc of his body, the way his T-shirt clings to his chest beneath his jacket, the visible curve of his collarbone.

'What do you recommend?'

He sips orange juice and his eyes twinkle with an idea. 'Do you like old films?'

I know very little about old films. But I've seen *Breakfast at Tiffany's* and *Gone with the Wind,* so I nod. 'I love them.'

'*A Night at the Opera* is on at The Carlton down the road. We could go and see it.'

I smile, but I'm puzzled. I'm pretty sure I have *A Night at the Opera* in my CD collection at home – it's an album by Queen. So I say, 'Brilliant.'

'The Marx Brothers' films are so underrated. We could go this week, if you're free?'

For a moment, I don't know how to reply. I hold out my phone.

'Put your number in here. I'll have to check my diary when I get back. I'll text you.'

He looks at me steadily for a moment and then he takes my phone. I wonder if I'm being too coy now, too cool. He types in his number and hands me my mobile, then takes another mouthful of orange juice. I look at my watch and swallow the last of the coffee. Marcus notices that I'm ready to leave and pushes his glass away.

He smiles. 'Shall we go now?'

We walk up the street, past the tiny terraces. The wind blows his jacket open. It feels good to be walking next to a handsome man. I gaze up at him and smile.

'It's a nice pub, full of atmosphere. Is it your local?'

He nods, turns to me. 'I used to come in here a lot. Mostly, I stay at home and work now. It's nice to have a reason to go out and get away from the computer.'

'You must work hard.'

'There's the day job and the projects I'm working on. It'll be good to drag myself away and see the film. It's on for a few days this week. I'd like to see it again.'

'Oh, definitely.' I offer him my most positive face.

We stop by a fence and I look over a small hedge towards a green painted door, number 22.

He shrugs. 'Well, this is me – this is where I live. I can walk back with you to Cliff Top, though . . .'

I stand still and turn to face him. 'No, it's only a few minutes away.'

'All right, if you're sure.'

A silence settles between us. I'm secretly pleased that he doesn't insist. He clearly recognises my need for independence.

'Well, send me a text, Georgie. Let me know when you're free.'

'I will.' I wonder if he'll hug me, even try to kiss me. I stare into the penetrating gaze; in the dark, his eyes shine and I can't look away. Neither of us moves, so I say, 'Thanks for the drink, Marcus.'

He breaks into an easy smile. 'It was good to meet you.'

I turn and start to walk away, resisting the inclination to swivel back.

'Goodnight, Georgie.'

I reach the end of the street, turning into the wind towards the main road. Cliff Top is a ten-minute walk via the beach on the other side.

I have the offer of a date. It feels strange, unreal, after all this time. I wonder whether or not I should text him a thank you for coffee. I certainly don't know the rules of dating any more. I glance at my phone with his number in it, under the name Marcus Hart, and I smile: he seems nice. I check the time. It's past eleven. Jade'll be home soon – perhaps she's already back.

I decide not to mention Marcus to Bonnie or Nanny for a while. I don't want to keep secrets, but what can I say? He's not even a friend yet. He's just someone I might go to the pictures with. I'm suddenly chuckling. He'd make a nice friend, a companion to show me the sights of the Sussex area. I recall his handsome face, the roughness of the stubble on his chin, the deepness of his voice. I imagine how it might feel, him whispering my name in the darkness. I recall things I've missed over the last few years, since Terry left: things I haven't allowed myself to think about. How it feels to be close to a man, to enjoy the sensation of another person breathing, another body held close. Marcus, tall, muscular, that scent of masculinity, the hardness of an embrace.

I'm getting carried away with the idea of him being a lover. I decide to stop immediately. I'll go to the pictures with him, once. Familiarity will change this silly feeling of having a crush on him. After all, I know nothing about him.

I cross the road quickly and head towards the beach, surrounded by the whispers of the waves in darkness as I walk towards Cliff Top.

Back in Roque's flat, I bolt the door and swish the big curtains together, blocking out the vast dark sky, the twinkling lights and the coastal curve of Brighton. Bonnie's in her pyjamas, flicking through a magazine. Nanny's in the armchair, finishing the creamy puddings with sticky fingers. Chocolate and pastry smears now accompany the fingermarks on the chair arms. I put on my best innocent face.

'I thought you were both going to bed?'

'I'm too tense to sleep.' Bonnie throws down her magazine.

Nan yawns, as if reminded. 'You've been out a long time. I'm parched. You're looking red in the face.'

'I had a long walk, Nan. Cleared my head.'

I pull off my shoes, throw my jacket on the sofa and put the kettle on. It's gone half past eleven.

'You need to be careful out there. Cocoa please, Georgina.' Nan twists round and yawns. 'It'll help me sleep. It's been a busy day. Lovely though.'

I close my eyes, grateful that she doesn't seem too worried by the events of the evening. I hand Bonnie a cup of chamomile tea. She pulls a face.

'This won't calm me down. Not after tonight. Nothing will. I won't sleep. I need Mogadon.'

I join her on the sofa. 'I wish I knew what to do.'

Bonnie's mouth is open. 'Whatever happened in the restaurant?'

'Beddowes spoke to Jade and Luis. No idea what he said, but you can bet it was trouble.'

'About Adie?'

Nanny slurps cocoa. 'I thought we'd heard the last of Adie Carrick.'

Bonnie says nothing. The silence hangs in the room like sadness. I need to hear a voice, even if it's my own, so I say, 'I just don't get it. Why did Beddowes make an appearance? How does he know we're in Brighton?'

Nanny wipes her mouth and the cardboard container drops on the floor. 'It's a good job you saw Beddowes before he saw us, Georgina.'

I pick up the empty cardboard carton. 'I just don't get it.'

There's a sharp rap on the door and we all stiffen. No one moves: we just breathe. I imagine the seconds ticking, each one a boom. Then Jade's voice calls from outside.

'Mum. It's me. And Luis.'

Chapter Twenty-One

I let them in and Jade marches across the room and sits on the sofa, still in her coat. Luis stands behind her, leaning on the back of the furniture. He looks tired. Nanny gazes at him, grins and adjusts the silver dress. Bonnie picks at her newly manicured nails.

Jade is clearly angry. 'We had to wind down after that man spoke to us. He threatened us. He's a weirdo. He asked where Adie was, where you were, Mum, and Aunty Bonnie. I said I'd no idea.' She turns on my sister. 'Aunty Bonnie, this is terrible. What's Uncle Adie going to do about it?'

I butt in. 'How did he threaten you?'

Luis sighs. 'We are stuck between rocks and hard places. He say he can make my career short. He say he hope I don't break a leg in the next match.'

Jade huffs. 'I said if anyone harmed Luis I'd break their bloody neck. He told me to pass that comment on to Uncle Adie, because he might find his neck was on the line next. Or . . .' She looks at Bonnie and clamps her lips together.

'He knows where we are, then?' Bonnie murmurs.

'Not necessarily.' I change the subject as Jade shoots me a look. 'We're safe here, aren't we? I mean, no one knows we're living here.'

'Where can I buy a dirty big knife?' Nanny sits upright. 'One of those massive Kalashnikovs.' I try not to grin at her mistake: even I know it's a rifle, but Nan is serious. 'You can get those anywhere on the black market, can't you? If he came in here, I'd cut his—'

'Adie says he's got money in a secret place in London.' Bonnie wriggles in her seat.

Jade snaps, 'Then why doesn't he just pay Beddowes what he owes him and we can all live quietly?'

Bonnie shakes her head. 'He says Beddowes is a crook.'

I stop myself from bursting out laughing. She glances round the room, ready to make an announcement.

'So, I've decided. I'm going to see Adie on Saturday and we'll get the money and go away. Beddowes won't find us. Adie's smart. You'll all be all right then, once we've gone.' She pouts and shows me sad eyes.

'You must be out of your mind.' Jade folds her arms. 'Uncle Adie must owe him loads – Beddowes means business. He won't let you get away with the money. He thinks it's his.'

'We can go abroad.'

I stare at Bonnie and breathe in sharply. It's typical of my sister's good nature. She'd let Adie drag her away overseas just to resolve the problem; she's ready to trust him again. It takes me a second to decide that I won't let her do that. Nanny has the same thought. She pokes Bonnie with a long finger.

'Running away is no good, Bonnie. We need to do what everyone should do with bullies.'

'Take them on and fight them.' Jade's face is tight: she means business.

Nan murmurs in agreement.

'We can tell the police.'

Luis has a point. I nod.

Bonnie's voice is quiet. 'I'll see Adie on Saturday afternoon. He's arranged it. We'll go away together. Give us a day, Georgie, to go somewhere miles away and then you'll have to tell the police.'

'I agree that it's time to ask for help,' I say, looking at their worried faces. 'It's too dangerous not to tell them. They'll give us protection, arrest Beddowes. Maybe then we can go home.'

'Maybe Luis and I can live here in peace.' Jade turns to Luis and he kisses her lips.

'Maybe I can just play the football games and not worry about some bad man in the crowd.' Luis looks troubled. 'I am too tired tonight.'

Bonnie's resigned, her face sad. 'Maybe Adie and I'll be all right together.'

'Maybe you won't.' I play my trump card. 'You'll be stuck with Mr Play-Away Adie and Beddowes will still be after us all.'

Nanny makes her hand into a fist. 'I agree – I still say I should find someone who'll sell me a big Kalashnikov.'

I change the subject. I need to bring the conversation to an end on a lighter note then send Jade and Luis off for some all-important sleep.

'Anyone know anything about the Marx Brothers?'

Bonnie blinks. 'Richard Marx, the singer? He has a lovely voice. Why?'

I shrug. 'I saw something about them earlier and I couldn't remember any film titles except *A Night at the Opera*.'

Jade rolls her eyes. 'I covered it in film studies at A level. Comic performers from the 1930s. *Duck Soup* and *A Day at the Races*.'

I remember. 'Oh yes, *those* Marx Brothers. Groucho and Harpo and . . .'

'I used to love them.' Nanny leans forward. 'Why? Are they on the telly?'

'Cinema,' I grunt.

'Ooh, I'd love to see them. Shall we go to the pictures then, Georgina?'

I close my eyes and imagine being in the cinema watching the film. The Marx Brothers are clowning around on the big screen, Harpo playing a beautiful tune on the strings, Groucho wiggling his cigar and his eyebrows. We're in the stalls: Marcus has his arm round me. My head is on his shoulder. Nanny's head is on his other shoulder, her fingers weaving through a huge bag of popcorn. I almost laugh out loud at the idea.

Jade stands up. 'It's past midnight. Bedtime.' Nanny raises her eyebrows and Jade grins. 'We need to sleep. Luis has a lunchtime game on Saturday. A home game, but we'll be up early to get to London. We have to leave at seven.'

'Important game for points,' Luis explains. 'If we win, we go second.'

Nanny hauls herself up and hugs him. 'Score one for me, Louise. I'm sure you'll win. You're a great player. I love the way you run so fast the defenders can't keep up with you. And I like the back pass and the overhead scissors kick.'

Luis smiles, but his face is anxious, strained. 'I do my best score one for you, *mi corazon*,' he says, and Nanny's eyes gleam.

Jade and Luis leave together. I glance up and down the hallway and watch them go before locking the door and pulling the chain across.

'Bedtime for me too,' I say.

Nanny hugs herself. 'I don't want to take this dress off.

I'm having such a good time. It's not every night I go out looking glamorous with a top football star, eat luxury food and then sneak home in a taxi.'

Bonnie sighs. 'Big day for us on Saturday.'

'It is.' Nanny eases herself up. 'Louise has to win the match or they won't get second place.'

'I mean Adie and me,' Bonnie mutters and puts her hand to her head, closes her eyes. 'I'm meeting him in London. Then we're going off together.'

'I'm coming to the meeting,' I say suddenly.

'He said you mustn't come, Georgie. He said just me and him. He's booked a place to meet and a train ticket for me.'

Nanny folds her arms. 'Balls to what he says. You go, Georgina. I've never trusted that Adie Carrick. His eyes are too close together.'

Bonnie breathes out again, her little face holding so much stress and anxiety, so I squeeze her hand. 'Where are you meeting him?'

'The Ritz in London. For afternoon tea. It's booked. Palm Court. Half five.'

'How about I come with you, stay out of sight? At a distance, keeping an eye.'

Nanny chuckles. 'You could have a newspaper. *The Telegraph*. With the eyeholes cut out. Sit behind and watch them, like a spy.'

'I'm serious, Nan. Someone needs to make sure you're all right, Bonnie.'

She nods then wrinkles her nose. 'You'd better wear something smart, though. They won't let you into The Ritz in jeans.'

It's Saturday, almost lunchtime. Nanny's snuggled in the armchair with a sandwich and a Guinness, her aching legs

193

stretched out in front of her. The game starts in five minutes. Our train leaves in two hours. Bonnie's still in the bathroom. Her preparations for tea at The Ritz require time and concentration. I bring coffee and sit at Nanny's feet. She takes a bite of sandwich.

'They are kicking off soon. Look, Georgina – it's the preview, where they guess the results of each game. And this is the chart, the top ten goal scorers. There's Louise. I do like the way he ties his long fringe back in a little knot on his head.'

'I expect it helps him to see the ball, Nan.'

The game starts. Luis, in blue, intercepts the ball almost immediately and runs towards goal. A tall player in red tackles him and Luis is felled. Nanny grips her glass.

'Foul, ref. Book him. Hands off my little Louise – I don't want him injured.'

Luis clambers to his feet and a referee, the man in black, blows his whistle for a free kick. Luis stands back, runs at the ball and sends it soaring into the crowd. Nanny tuts.

'You're not on your game, son. You can't kick the ball up there. Aim for the net.'

Half an hour passes, and no one has scored. Luis has lost the ball on three occasions and missed an open goal. The commentator repeatedly disapproves.

'Delgado isn't sharp today. It's not like him to give the ball away.'

By half-time, all the TV pundits agree that the game is sluggish. It appears that Luis 'hasn't turned up', that he 'hasn't got his scoring legs on today'. One pundit even suggests that he isn't as good as everyone had thought, that he's been 'wrongly *levitated* to one of the best strikers in the world'. I snigger, but Nan is furious.

'He'll come back second half. You watch him. That'll shut you up, you thick twit.'

I'm not sure if she's shouting at the pundit, the screen, the referee or me.

The second half starts and Luis miskicks the ball to a stocky player in the other team, who promptly aims it at the net and scores. Luis puts his head in his hands or his fingers in his ears. The crowd groan and the commentator says, 'Delgado's aura of invincibility has gone.' It's nil one. The camera is close-up on Luis, who looks strained and tired. He moves slowly, his eyes glazed like a zombie's.

'This is terrible.' Nanny's face is distraught. 'How come he's playing so badly? Maybe it was the food at Embers. He should've had the wellington, like I did.'

I shake my head. 'Maybe it's because of what happened with Beddowes. I hope he's all right.'

I've chosen to wear a simple black dress with my pink coat and ankle boots to The Ritz. That should be smart enough, but also anonymous enough to blend in. I wonder how close to Bonnie I'll be able to be once she's with Adie, but one thing is for sure: Adie won't take her away without going through me.

The taxi is late and Bonnie's still in the bathroom. I almost text Marcus and suggest going to the cinema early next week, but then I lose my nerve. I deliberate whether to text, and then the taxi beeps from below and Bonnie dashes into the bedroom in a panic for her coat. In a flurry of indecision, I rush to the loo and text him from there, just three hurried words: *I'm free tomorrow*. He replies almost instantly. I have a date at the cinema. I push feelings of nervousness away and follow Bonnie downstairs to the idling taxi.

We're quiet on the train, Bonnie checking her face in the mirror and adding more powder. She's already corpse-pale. I gaze out of the window at hedgerows flashing past, and then the scenery becomes greyer and more industrial, with factories and little rows of houses.

My phone rings. It's Jade.

'Mum, I'm coming back to collect my stuff and then we're off to Spain.'

'Hi, Jade.'

'Luis just couldn't play today. He's exhausted.'

'Was that because of the Beddowes incident? I saw some of the game. He didn't look great.'

'Well, he wouldn't be, would he, Mum? Not after what happened to us on the way to the match.'

I pause to take in what she's said. 'What happened?'

'It was really frightening. Luis and I went by car to the football ground first thing. Our driver was amazing – if he hadn't broken the speed limit, we'd probably have been killed.'

'Oh, Jade. What—'

'We were on the motorway, just past Crawley. A Jaguar overtook us, slowed down and then tried to run us off the road. Of course, it was that man from Thursday night, Beddowes. I saw a red-haired figure in the passenger seat of the car as it tried to bash us. He was on his phone, laughing. So Luis can't play under this strain – he's been given a week to train somewhere warm and I'm going with him to lie on the beach. Then when we're back, he'll have to be back on his game and really deliver. So make sure it's all sorted out. We can't go on like this.'

'Oh, Jade, I'm sorry.'

'Just go to the police, tell them to arrest Beddowes, Mum. I don't want Luis involved in all this. What about his career?'

I take a deep breath. 'I'll try.'

Then it arrives, the famous Jade tirade; she's been performing these regularly since her adolescence: they became worse after Terry left. I hear her breathe in, in preparation.

'You'll have to do better than try, Mum. It's your fault. I didn't want you here in Sussex. You followed me. You couldn't keep away; you couldn't stay out of my business. Now you've brought all this trouble here, and Luis and I are suffering because of it.'

I know she has a point, but I say, 'That's not entirely fair.'

'It's not fair you being in Sussex, Mum. It's not fair to interfere, to be in my life. I don't even know why you don't all go back to Liverpool. Take all your trouble back there and just leave me alone.'

My head is telling me that leaving would be a noble thing to do, a wise move. But my mouth takes over.

'Don't be ungrateful, Jade. We came down here because I need to look after Bonnie. And I need to look after you.'

Her breathing is heavy on the other end of the line. 'Look after? Snoop into my life, you mean. Interfere. Get in the way.'

'I couldn't see you give up everything for a man you hardly know, who might let you down—'

'How dare you, Mum!'

'Jade, everything I've ever done has been for your sake. I've always put you first.'

'Oh, don't give me all that "you're my world and I can't live without you" crap. I'm twenty-four.'

I can't stop myself. Anxiety pushes words into my mouth before I think them through.

'You'll change your mind when it all goes wrong, wait and see.'

'Mum, just go back to Liverpool; take Aunty Bonnie and Nan and all the trouble Uncle Adie's caused with you. You've been nothing but a pain since we left home, sticking

197

your nose in my life. I don't want you here interfering in everything we do, getting in the way. I've tried to put up with you but I've had enough now. I don't need you any more.'

I swallow air and suddenly I can't breathe.

'Jade?'

'I'll be back in a week. Sort out this mess then get out of my life and go home. And after that, do what you like – I really don't care.'

I turn to Bonnie in the seat next to me. She's staring at me, her face filled with pity. And then Jade's gone and I'm holding my breath, squeezing the phone in my fist.

Chapter Twenty-Two

London is alive and pumping with energy, but I feel deflated; I can't think of anything but my daughter. I'm worried that she hates me now. My body is hunched, like I'm carrying cement on my shoulders: I feel worn down. The weather is surprisingly warm for early April and there are sales everywhere. Shoppers are out in force, bustling across the road, dodging through traffic. Almost everyone in London is inadvertently celebrating spring, wearing flowery prints, light jackets, pastel shades, but I still feel sad. Suddenly, the sun comes out and the buildings seem to light up, welcoming pinky-greys and warm reds.

Bonnie and I are in the same taxi, although she's ignoring me. She wants to meet Adie alone and I'm sticking to her like an irrefutable stench. She's dressed to kill in a pale peach tailored suit and a dark coat. Her hair is pinned up high in a chocolate icing swirl and her tiny gold earrings shine. It's all done to impress Adie. In comparison, I feel like Cinderella's sister in my pink woollen coat and dowdy black dress. But I need to be here. I won't let her throw her life away for a cream tea in china cups. Bonnie's voice pulls me out of my thoughts: she's in full swing.

'Drop us as close as you can to The Ritz, driver. I don't want to be late.'

We're early and I can tell Bonnie's edgy. She sidles out and I push two notes into the taxi driver's tray by the Perspex window and tell him to keep the change. He notices me for the first time.

'Thanks, darling.'

We stand in front of The Ritz and I gawp up at huge arches, the high, glitzy signs, the stone Greek-style head looking down in judgement.

Bonnie smiles. 'I deserve a bit of luxury after the stress of the last week or so.'

I shrug and drag my feet behind her. She doesn't turn to speak to me: she's nervous about meeting Adie. I'm nervous too, but it's because he'll persuade her to go away with him.

A doorman approaches us, stiff in a black top hat and a dark coat, brass buttons shining. His eyes connect with Bonnie's and his voice is authoritative.

'Good afternoon, madam. How may I help?'

Bonnie's jittery, trying hard to be in control.

'Good afternoon. I have an appointment for afternoon tea. Would you mind conducting me to the tea rooms?'

He assesses her for a moment, looking down the length of his nose, which wrinkles slightly. I wonder if he's marking her accent as two out of ten. I'm bursting with protective feelings, as if she's walking into a trap and I can't help.

I follow, invisible, as the doorman leads Bonnie into the huge hallway, carpeted in plush red and gold, through enormous archways and under shimmering chandeliers. I imagine this is how the Taj Mahal must look inside. Lavish, expensive and gaudy. The doorman turns to her, expressionless.

'Afternoon tea is served in Palm Court, madam.'

She steps into an enormous room, all gilt and cream, huge high mirrors reflecting white light, pristine linen and flowers in long glass pots, lush green leaves and golden statues of fat frolicking cherubs. Adie's at a table in the middle of the room, thumbing through his phone. Bonnie smiles and her voice is all breath.

'I'll take it from here, Georgie. Wish me luck.'

I squeeze her hand. In the background somewhere, a pianist in a dinner jacket is tinkling a pretty tune. I lean back against the wall and wonder what to do with myself.

Bonnie's weaving through tables and I glance towards where Adie is seated. He stands quickly and extends both arms to Bonnie. He has a charcoal grey suit and a black tie. His face is ash grey, pallid. She kisses him.

A sudden thought of panic makes my pulse leap. I wonder if Beddowes is here, if Bonnie's at risk. I peer round the doorway. Adie's face is serious; he's staring into Bonnie's eyes. Bonnie has her back to me. She's taken off the dark coat. Adie pours tea and offers her something from an elegant cake stand. I lean back to make sure Adie's eagle eyes don't catch me watching. I almost wish I'd brought a newspaper with eyeholes as Nanny suggested. But Adie won't see me: his eyes are glued to Bonnie's face. He's smiling, simpering, touching her cheek with his fingertips, and she'll be about to fall for his new set of lies.

My eyes search the tea room for Beddowes, but there's no sign of him. I check over my shoulder, glance as the lift doors glide open and shut – a young woman comes out with a case – and then back to the people drinking tea: two businessmen; a family with prim children, teenagers so well behaved I wonder if they breathe. A couple in love are sharing a sandwich, bite for bite; three women, all young, blonde shining tresses, their heads close together, are laughing. A group of six men in smart suits chatter in Chinese. An American man sits alone; I can hear his Texan voice ordering Earl Grey Imperial, his stomach resting on his knees and cake in his mouth.

Then Adie leans forwards and grabs Bonnie's wrist. He's frowning and I know immediately something is wrong. Bonnie's body is angled to one side, awkward, troubled. She waves an arm and then Adie stands up, shouts something. The Chinese meeting stops and all six heads turn in unison. Bonnie freezes; her back is rigid inside the peach suit.

Adie pushes his chair away angrily, strides towards the entrance, towards me, and I duck out of sight, moving round the corner, in front of the huge lift, turning my back. I hear him walk past and, when I take a peek, I see his grey suited frame hurry away down the carpet, the tiny thin patch on the back of his head a small white dot disappearing out of view.

Inside Palm Court, Bonnie has her back to me. She's slumped forwards over the china teacup. I rush over to her table. Adie's food is unfinished; his teacup half full. Bonnie looks up at me, her eyes huge, brimming with globes of tears.

'He's gone – that's it – he's left.'

'I hope he's paid the bill first,' I grumble. 'Sixty quid each and you've eaten nothing.' I reach out for a napkin and bundle a couple of slices of cake into the folds. 'At least Nanny will appreciate these.' Bonnie slumps across the table, her head in her hands, sobbing. 'Let's get out of here, Bonnie, and go back to the flat. We'll be safer. You can tell me all about it there.' I grab her arm, the napkin full of sandwiches and cake, and we bustle towards the door.

*

She sniffs and gulps on the train all the way back to the flat. In the taxi, she snuffles into her hanky and, by the time we're at Cliff Top, in the lift, she's crying again. In the flat, Nanny's curled in the armchair, her feet tucked under her, watching television. It's almost nine o'clock and she hasn't moved all the time we've been away. Her beer glass has made a brown ring on the arm of Roque's chair. She tilts her head.

'So, how was Adie and that posh tea?'

I hand her the napkin, hoping that the food is still fresh. She unfolds it with a smile and starts on the sandwiches straight away, chewing with enthusiasm.

'Mmm. Funny bread but very tasty. Nice. Oh, what a lovely piece of cake. Proper raspberry jam.'

I sit Bonnie down on the sofa and grab her hands. 'Explain again exactly what happened.'

She shakes her head. 'It was going so well then he found out I wasn't wearing the charm bracelet. He was angry.'

'You're still not making any sense, Bonnie.'

She wipes her eyes; two hours of careful make-up smudged in seconds.

'He was being really romantic. He said I looked a million dollars. He had tickets for us, for a plane out of Heathrow first thing tomorrow to somewhere fabulous in the Caribbean. He made it sound so perfect. But then he grabbed my wrist and said, "Hang on, where's the bloody charm bracelet?" And I told him the clasp had broken and it was here at the flat.'

'So then what happened?'

'He said to me that I was wasting his time. He called me a stupid bitch.'

Nanny turns sharply, her mouth full of crumbs. 'The cheeky bastard.' Bits of sponge cake fly in all directions.

I squeeze Bonnie's hand. 'So what was that all about?'

'He said I had to go back and get the bracelet and meet him at his hotel. He said he'd be in the bar until midnight.'

'I don't understand, Bonnie.'

'I should go back now. I'll just make it.'

'Rubbish. Ignore him. Stay here.' Nanny's mouth is full of sponge and spittle.

'But . . . I could get a taxi. Perhaps I should speak to him first.'

Bonnie stands and pulls out her phone. I place my hand over hers.

'Think about this carefully, Bon.'

She shakes her head. 'If I don't find him tonight, I've lost him forever.'

'Don't even think about ringing him, let alone trying to see him. It's not safe.' I tug her chin to make her look at me. 'Beddowes wants Adie, not you. Let him go, then we can all go home. Seriously, Bonnie – you're not safe with him. Being with Adie is the most dangerous place imaginable now.'

Her brow is creased with worry. Nanny picks up the last piece of cake.

'You should tell the police, Georgina. We agreed that.'

Bonnie's miserable. 'All right, then I won't call him. But let him get away, Georgie. Just give him tonight. Let him get as far as a plane will take him, out of the country. Then we'll call the police.' Her brows come together and I worry that she might cry again. 'But why did he want the bracelet so much? Why did he say that if I didn't bring it, he didn't want me either?'

'I've no idea.' I stare from Bonnie to Nanny. 'Maybe the police will know. But for now, we keep our heads down and wait until he's gone. And that means you staying here, Bonnie. When the time is right, I'll give them a call and you can tell them all about it. Maybe then someone will explain what on earth is going on.'

She's snivelling again and I wrap my arms round her while she sobs into my shoulder. Nanny smacks her lips and stares at the comedy film on the television. My head is stuffed full of things I can't understand: my row with Jade, who's ignoring my texts, on her way to Spain. Beddowes' threats, his appearance out of the blue at Embers. The all-important charm bracelet and why it's such a big deal. Adie rushing off from The Ritz in a temper. Adie asking Bonnie to meet him at his hotel in London so they can escape to the romantic Caribbean and yet during their tea together, he was calling her rude names.

I force myself to think about the date at the cinema tomorrow. At least it'll take my mind off this madness. Marcus has texted me again, telling me he's looking forward to seeing the film – and me. I'm feeling ridiculously nervous. I know I need some kind of normality in my life at the moment. But I've forgotten how to date, how to behave when I'm with a man. Should I be coy, amusing, distant, keen or cool? It's been so long since I've had a proper date. My life has become so crazy – the situation with Adie and Beddowes is so bizarre and so suddenly potentially serious. I can't wait to meet Marcus tomorrow and to feel like any other ordinary person. I hug my sobbing sister and wonder if my life will ever be normal again.

Chapter Twenty-Three

I stare at the billboards outside The Carlton, a tiny fleapit cinema fifteen minutes' walk from the flat. I've told the others I'm going for a walk and not to wait up. Bonnie wanted to come, but changed her mind when I said I intended to stroll along the beach and into the village for a few miles to clear my head.

It's a chilly evening. I've worn jeans, a jacket and a simple top, because I didn't want Nanny to ask why I was going for a walk all dolled up. I stare at the image of mischievous cartoon faces, the Marx Brothers peeping out from a long orange theatre curtain. I'm five minutes early but I've decided if Marcus doesn't turn up, I'll go in and watch it by myself. There are black-and-white photos: Groucho wheedling around a woman in a silk dress, Harpo in a tuxedo waving a trombone. I think of Nanny, how she'd have enjoyed the film, and I feel guilty.

There's a light touch on my wrist and I turn to look at Marcus. His dark curls are perfect, the sort of curls many women would envy, shiny and soft. His eyes gleam and he's wearing a dark jacket over a T-shirt and jeans. Casual but gorgeous. The stubble is still there. I want to kiss his cheek, but I decide it's best to play it safe. If he's gay or married or just being friendly, then I don't want to make a fool of myself. But then he grins and I feel a tiny tremor between us, which suggests that he's looking forward to this date as much as I am.

The Carlton is almost empty and smells of dust. The seats are red velvet, the material threadbare and worn. We sit near the front and he takes out some spectacles, thin-rimmed, intellectual-looking things, and puts them on. On screen, the Marx Brothers begin clowning at a frantic pace and I study his handsome profile as the light flickers across his cheek and reflects on the glasses. He smiles and I want to put my head on his shoulder, or at least slide my arm through the crook of his, but I don't. I'm not sure of the rules. I used to go to the cinema with boyfriends, sit in the back row necking and miss the entire film. But I was in my teens then. Terry and I used to sit on the front row with our bodies close. I'd lift my legs and put them across his thighs and he'd rub my feet. We were familiar, at ease with each other, but tonight's date is with a complete stranger. I have no idea how to behave – I don't know Marcus at all.

We sit close, warmth and a kind of expectation pulsing between us, and we both fix our eyes on the film. For a moment, my mind is elsewhere. Perhaps he'll invite me back to his home. It would be warm, a log fire, a bottle of wine. I imagine us both on a fluffy rug, the red glow flickering across our flesh as we lie together in the ecstasy of passion. I glance at him and wonder if he's thinking the same thing. No, he's not; it's just me, imagining all sorts of foolish thoughts. He's watching the film intently, his lips curved in amusement. I want to reach up and touch them. I'm being ridiculous. It seeps into my mind that I'm feeling all this desire because I'm a rejected woman in my mid-fifties whom nobody has wanted for years. I could just be making a big mistake with my feelings for this man. Feelings that are probably entirely about passion and lust after a long time of being alone.

As the credits roll, I glance at the wall clock. It's after ten. I should be back at the flat before too long: the old Cinderella story. As we leave the cinema, he takes my hand in his. His palm is dry and hard and my own hand feels smaller than it is. I smile to myself and enjoy the dreamy feeling as he squeezes my fingers gently.

'Did you enjoy it?'

'The film?' I come down to earth quickly. 'I loved it. I adore Harpo. He's my favourite.'

He grins. 'Me too. Such a talent, both comic and musical.'

'I read somewhere that the Marx Brothers were from an immigrant family; they had French and German parents.' I look up at him. 'They were Jewish, weren't they?'

Marcus grins. 'Exactly.' He's quiet for a moment then says, 'Like me.'

I'm about to tell him I've never been out with a Jewish man before, but I search for a more sensible comment. 'So, are you Orthodox?'

'My parents are modern Orthodox. I keep kosher when I'm with them.'

My mind races to all the wrong, mischievous things. I want to ask him if he's allowed to consort with a crazy Liverpool woman, one who's been married and abandoned, one who's currently hiding from criminals. I stare straight into his eyes and hope he can't read my thoughts.

To fill the silence, I say, 'That's really interesting.'

We're on the main road, walking towards where the hill rises towards the Cliff Top flats. Cars flash past, a bus containing only two people, a taxi with its orange-red light on. Marcus wraps his arm round me.

'Georgie, I can walk you back to your flat. Or you could come back to my house in Rowan Terrace and have a coffee.'

I slow my pace. I'd love to go back to his house for a coffee, whatever he means by that: a hot drink, some kissing. Maybe it would all end in passionate sex. I feel a shudder of warmth go through my body. It's been such a long time and I'd given up even thinking about it. I imagine lying in bed with him, his arms and legs draped across mine, and I'd be relaxed, laughing, and I'd tell him about Adie and Beddowes, the scenes at Embers and The Ritz. I'd love to explain everything while I lie in the warmth of his arms, and then he'd kiss me and all the stress and worry would drift away and we'd be lost in a whirlwind of passion again. I exhale, turn to him and make a snap decision. I'm not ready yet for any of this.

'I'd love a coffee. Really I would. But maybe another time, Marcus. The film was great. We must do this again sometime.'

I wake remembering our goodnight kiss last night, briefly shared warmth on our lips, and my promise to text Marcus today. It's past nine and I'm bleary-eyed. There's a leaflet in Roque's postbox advertising a man with a van. I make tea and toast, Nanny huddles in the armchair watching breakfast television and Bonnie searches her phone for texts from Adie. I hand Nanny a toasted sandwich and she grunts muffled thanks as she wolfs it down. Bonnie turns her nose up at the slice of wholemeal toast. I leave it on the chair arm and put a muffin in the toaster, hand out a sweet tea to Nanny and a milky Earl Grey to Bonnie. She looks up, pale, her eyes tired.

'Nothing from Adie.'

I shrug. 'Perhaps he'll send us a postcard from Bermuda.' Bonnie's face crumples and immediately I want to make things better. 'He stands more chance of being safe from Beddowes if he's out of the country.'

'I should've gone with him.' Her chin trembles. 'I've forsaken him.'

I stop myself from snorting and wrap my arms round her. She's hurting so I'm hurting, too.

'Maybe he'll find somewhere nice to live and get in touch.' I'm being dishonest for her sake. Liar, liar, pants on fire. I hope we never see him again. 'Hang in there, Bonnie. We'll be all right.'

'She'll be better off away from that mean Adie Carrick and his wandering willy.' Nanny's eyes are on the television.

Bonnie buries her head in her arms and I offer her my breakfast, tea in one hand and a toasted muffin in the other. She turns away and Nan holds out her hand.

'Georgina, why didn't I get a muffin?'

'Have mine, Nan. I'll get another.'

She grimaces, steals my breakfast and I go back to the toaster. There are two muffins left and two slices of bread. I'll need to go out for provisions.

There's a knock at the door. Crisp, once, then again. Bonnie's eyes are huge. Nanny glances at the door and back to me. I sidle softly over to the spyhole and put my eye against the opening. I can see two of them. The woman has blonde hair, short, tucked behind her ears. I can't see the man's hair; his hat is pulled down low. They both have the same chequered band around the brim, the same silver badge. I can read the printed letters on the front of their jackets: POLICE. I open the door quietly and raise my eyebrows as the man's eyes meet mine.

'Bonnie Carrick?'

'No.' I look from him to her. He shows me a plastic identification card. They have name badges. 'What do you want?'

'We have reason to believe that a Mrs Bonnie Carrick is staying here.' That's from the woman.

I close my eyes. This can only be trouble. I hear Nanny's voice call from behind me.

'Who is it, Georgina?'

'The police, Nan.'

'Well, for goodness' sake, let them in. We need to talk to them, don't we? It's about bloody time.'

I open the door and they walk in, standing together, their shoulders inches apart. The man is tall, thickset, ruddy-faced, and the woman is slim, high cheekbones. They notice Bonnie and the policewoman says 'I'm DC Charlotte Howes and this is DC Brian Daly. Are you Bonnie Carrick?' She nods at them, her face white. 'We'd like to ask you to come down to the station with us.'

Nanny swivels towards them. 'She's done nothing.'

The man speaks in a kind voice, his tone hushed. 'You're not under arrest, Mrs Carrick. We'd like you to help us with some enquiries.'

Nanny leans forwards. 'That Beddowes is a crook. You should arrest him. And Adie Carrick, if we're going to be honest – he should be behind bars.'

The two police officers exchange glances. Bonnie slides slowly from her seat and sighs. 'I'll get my coat.'

'I'm coming with you.'

DC Howes raises her eyebrows. 'And you are?'

'Georgie Turner. Bonnie's sister.'

She nods. 'Yes, it would be a good idea if you came along, too.'

I turn to Nanny. She's finished her muffin.

'Will you be all right, Nan?'

211

'As long as you're back by lunchtime.'

DC Howes says, 'We can't predict how long this'll take.'

'Don't worry, Nan.' I'm at the toaster, buttering the last two muffins. I pop them on her plate. 'I'll be back in time for your next meal.'

Bonnie and I take our first ride in a police car. It's parked outside the entrance to the flats and a young couple with a pushchair and a child with white candyfloss hair are about to go in. They stare at us with interest as we're ushered into the vehicle.

The journey to the police station takes thirty minutes as we weave swiftly through Brighton traffic. DC Howes drives but neither officer talks during the journey, except to answer a crackling message that clatters through the car radio.

At the station, we're escorted into a small white walled room with a table and three chairs but no window. DC Howes tells us someone'll come to see us shortly. Bonnie and I have barely time to raise our eyebrows and put our heads together to whisper 'What the hell is this all about?' when a woman comes in. She has a dark suit, a white shirt, and her manner is brisk and efficient. Her hair is deep chestnut, tied back in a sort of neat bun; her fringe is glossy. She must be in her forties, with well-defined cheekbones and thin lips. Her body is lean, the body of a runner. She gazes from me to Bonnie.

'I'm DI Jessica Fuller. Thank you for coming in.'

I want to tell her we had no choice, but instead, I say, 'I'm glad we're here. You know we've been targeted by Duncan Beddowes? He's a dangerous man. Do you—'

She speaks directly to Bonnie. 'Mrs Carrick, can you tell me when you last saw Adrian Carrick, your husband?'

'How did you know where we were living?' I say.

I don't care that I've interrupted her. I press my hands together and my palms are damp.

DI Fuller glances at me briefly. 'We have several officers on surveillance.' She turns back to Bonnie, who's started to tremble. 'Mrs Carrick. Can you tell me when you last saw Adrian Carrick?'

I breathe out. He's got away, although I don't know why I should feel relief. It would be better if he'd been apprehended. Bonnie's voice wavers.

'Saturday evening. In London. We had tea at The Ritz.'

DI Fuller leans forwards. 'Yes, we know. I'd like to know the exact reason for your meeting please, Mrs Carrick, and the circumstances under which Mr Carrick left you.'

'He argued with me. He wanted me to go away with him on holiday. Then he got up and left and that was it. He told me to meet him later, but I didn't go. I wish I had. I haven't heard from him since.' Bonnie is completely trusting, her little voice hushed and sad.

I frown. DI Fuller takes a deep breath.

'Mrs Carrick, we're looking for your husband in connection with a serious crime. We need to talk to him with some urgency. He's been doing business with a dangerous known criminal. The man in question has a lot of contacts in this area, people who're willing to break the law, hide him and help him to cover his tracks.'

Bonnie doesn't take this in. Her mouth hangs open and she doesn't move. I grab her hand.

She murmurs, 'I don't understand.'

DI Fuller nods. 'We need to bring him in, Mrs Carrick. He can help us with our enquiries. He's made an enemy with his recent business transactions and we have reason to believe that his life is in danger.'

My sister is shaking, her breath coming in little gasps. I put my arms round her and suddenly she blurts out, 'I don't know where Adie is. He's gone. I love him and I wouldn't tell you where he was even if I knew where he was. Which I don't.' She starts to sniff and I rock her towards me.

DI Fuller nods, scribbles something down on paper and says, 'All right, you're free to go.'

We stumble outside and I flag down a taxi. Bonnie trembles, staring with wide eyes.

'He's in trouble, Georgie. Now we're all in trouble. What shall I do?'

We clamber inside the cab and I tell the driver our address. Bonnie's phone buzzes and she checks her messages, then her face pales; she's trembling and breathless.

'It's Adie.'

She reads the text once and then a second time. Her eyes fill with tears.

'Oh, Georgie . . .'

She passes me the phone, her hand shaking. It takes me seconds to check the message:

> Don't try to find me, Bonnie. I'm far away now. It's a new start for me. I won't be back. Forget me. It won't be too hard for me to forget you. Move on.

I grasp her hand. For a moment, relief floods through me. He's gone. But Bonnie's face is frozen, a mask: her chin quivers and she starts to cry. Then it hits me that, although Adie's safe now, we certainly aren't. Adie was the target; he was the one Beddowes wanted. With him out of the frame, Beddowes might turn his attention to us.

Chapter Twenty-Four

April showers hammer on the windows and the sea is metal grey outside. Bonnie spends the next five days in bed, moping. DC Howes and DC Daly arrive and I tell them Bonnie's asleep.

They visit again and I say that she's been awake for fourteen hours and has just dozed off. It's all true. They've had a statement from her but they want to ask her even more questions, so I wake her and she talks to them, whey-faced, her hair unwashed. She hasn't said anything about Adie's final text, but she mentions Beddowes, his conversation in Adie's office, and her escape from the house.

I say my piece, ask them what they know about Beddowes and insist that he should've been arrested, but the answer is always the same: 'He's on our radar. It's just a matter of time now before we bring him in.'

It falls to me to ring Demi. I phone in the evening and speak to Kyle in Krabi, to tell him that his father-in-law has done a runner. He replies in an anxious voice that he'll speak to Demi. He asks if they should come back to England immediately and I suggest that the Easter weekend might be a better time to be with Bonnie. I don't want to lure them into any potential danger here. Kyle agrees that they'll come back for a week at Easter and then resume their honeymoon plans by jetting off to Sydney.

Bonnie receives a text from Peter Redmayne, Adie's solicitor, saying that Adie's contacted him to sort out his affairs as he's started a new life abroad. Mr Redmayne isn't at liberty to reveal any details of Adie's whereabouts but he has arranged to provide for his family. A sum of money and the house in Frodsham will be signed over to his wife if she's prepared to allow Adie to walk away from the marriage and to ask no questions.

Bonnie is in a sort of limbo, eyes glazed, dishevelled, still in pyjamas. Nanny sits by her bed, stroking her hair and making soft clucking noises, pushing teaspoons of tomato soup into the corner of her mouth, telling her to forget Adie. I rush out in the rain for provisions. Bonnie wakes crying during the night, calling for Adie, and I hug her and rock her until she falls back to sleep.

Marcus has texted me twice, thanking me for the date and asking if we could meet again. I'm surprised at myself: I've thought about him fleetingly but my head has been full of Jade and Bonnie. I text Marcus and explain we've had a family problem. He replies almost immediately and invites me round his house for a meal on Wednesday evening.

My mind buzzes, thinking of the excuse I'll need to make to Nan and Bonnie in order to sneak out. I feel like a teenager again and, to be honest, it feels good, newly exciting. I ask myself if I should tell them I have a date, but I decide against it. They'd swoop on me like vultures of gossip. I wonder whether I'll want to stay the night and how I'd resolve that problem. Despite everything, I

216

find myself smiling and slipping into warm thoughts that encase me like scented bathwater.

Then, late on Wednesday afternoon, Jade arrives with Luis. I worry that she'll still be angry with me, especially because the problem with Beddowes hasn't been resolved. But she's tanned and smiling, carrying presents from Spain. She hugs me. There's no mention of our argument or her refusal to reply to my texts.

I usher them inside the flat quietly: Bonnie's lying down in our room and Nan's looking after her. Jade's brought wine, a variety of T-shirts with slogans in Spanish. She and Luis sit on the sofa, holding hands, as I tell her the news, and she frowns a moment, nods then says, 'It's no surprise, Mum. She's better off without him.'

I squeeze my eyes closed. 'The police have been here twice and they say that Beddowes will be arrested soon, but we can't go home yet. Bonnie's not in a good place.' I hear my voice take on a wheedling tone. 'I hate what happened to you and Luis. But it'll soon be all over now.'

Jade hugs me and I look over her shoulder and see Luis smiling. He's a good influence on her bad temper.

Nanny creeps through the door from our room and puts a long finger to her lips.

'She's had some of the tomato soup and gone back to sleep like a tot. Poor thing. She's exhausted.'

Nanny pulls the new T-shirt on over her blouse, smiling at the purple slogan: *Buena Onda*. It means cool, apparently, and she struts around, thinking she looks the business.

Luis leans forwards. 'I have a game in Turkey later this week. Jade and I, we go away tomorrow for five days. Then when we come back, maybe this is all finished with Beddowes.'

'So I'm not so worried now, Mum. We're back in less

than a week. It'll be the run up to Easter and Luis won't have a game then until Easter Saturday, so we can ride this out together. The police will arrest Beddowes and you can go home.' She looks at me meaningfully.

I nod, realising how terrifying it must be for them both, especially with such a public life.

'I'm sorry this has happened, Luis. It must be really difficult for you, too.'

He pats my hand. 'Jade's family so you, too, are family. We are snuggled bugs in rugs. We take care of each other. It is fine – I am rested now and in Spain I train hard every day.'

Nan shrugs. 'I was hoping we could go down to Djimi's. It would be nice to have a stroll on the beach when the weather perks up, get some fresh air. But the policewoman suggested we stay indoors.'

I pull a face. 'I'll go out if I want. After all, we're not prisoners and I'm not being housebound because of Beddowes. I might even have another long walk later. I'm going to do a bit more walking, you know – a few miles every evening. I miss the exercise at home. And I love the beach at night. I enjoy the darkness of it.'

Nanny's staring. Of course, I'm thinking of meeting Marcus. I'll tell everyone about him later, perhaps, if the date goes well. I remember Nan's comments about Terry breaking my heart. I'm not letting on about Marcus, not yet.

An hour later, Jade and Luis hug me and say rushed goodbyes. Luis is off to train in London first thing in the morning and Jade says she has a hundred things to do.

I open the door to our bedroom: Bonnie's sleeping, curled on her side, breathing lightly, so I go back into the sitting room and peck Nan's cheek. I brush my hair and put on some lipstick. I look tired but when I practise a bright smile, I'm passable.

'I'll be out for a while, Nan. I'm going to take a long walk. Don't wait up.'

The sky is darkening outside and the wind is cuttingly cold, but I set off with a spring in my step.

I find the little terrace of cottages easily – I remember the way to the pub on the corner. Marcus meets me at the door, warm light shining behind him, and he smiles, ushering me inside. His home is lovely. I was right about the log fire, almost: flames leap in a wood-burning stove, set into a huge fireplace with a wooden beam. There are more dark beams in the ceiling, and the whole place is open-plan and simply decorated. Bookshelves are everywhere, books crammed into every corner, and there's a soft pale green sofa and a huge Persian rug. His computer and desk are against a brick wall painted white. Behind the sofa is a wooden table with four chairs and, behind that, a kitchen with an Aga. Saucepans hang from a rack and there are baskets of vegetables and fruits. The question screaming in my head slips out of my mouth.

'Do you live here by yourself, Marcus?'

I take a seat on the sofa and moments later, he moves from the kitchen and sits beside me, handing me a glass of red wine. He has a cream shirt on, open at the neck, revealing curling chest hair; he's wearing dark skinny jeans and his feet are bare. He drapes an arm behind me and stretches out his feet.

'Mostly. My son comes home for holidays sometimes, the odd weekend. Zach is a music student in Manchester. At the moment he's in Berlin for a month, playing the violin in an orchestra.'

I wait for more information, but he says nothing. I start to gabble.

'Your son must be very talented. It's not easy, is it,

playing a violin? It must take years of practice. My daughter lives in the flats near to me at the moment. She's going out with Luis Delgado, the footballer. Do you like football, Marcus?'

I clamp a hand over my mouth: I sound like I'm bragging and Marcus is so modest.

He shakes his dark curls. 'I've never really been one for team sports. I go running, and to the gym sometimes, but I don't keep up with much sport or television. Perhaps I should. I'd be interested to hear all about it. What about you? What do you do?'

'I have a gym in the basement of my house where I run my business. I'm lucky really. It's taken me ages to get a good reputation, regular clients.'

I suddenly miss my home and wonder how Amanda's managing. But I'll be back soon, in a few weeks. I peer at Marcus and wonder if I'll miss him. At the moment, I know so little about him. Without thinking, I splutter out the words that have been buzzing like a fly in my mind since I arrived. I need to swat it dead.

'So, where's Zach's mother? I mean, are you married?' Again, I've blurted everything out at once. Clearly, I have no idea how to behave on a date.

Marcus laughs. 'Not any more.' He rubs a hand through his curls. 'Once in my twenties. Leah. She was remarkable. Talented. Ambitious. Left me for a rich banker.' He grins. He's obviously not upset. 'Then in my thirties I met Chloe. She was a free spirit. We had Zach. She left when he was fifteen, five years ago. She went abroad – she sees him twice a year. It was quite a difficult time for him; his life was all exams and adolescent angst.' He makes a mischievous face. 'I did the best job I could of being a single parent, taking him to rock concerts, on holiday, trekking through Peru. I promised him we'd be fine, the two of us.

It was tough for him at first, but he seems happy enough now he's at uni.'

'And what about you? Have there been many women since then?' I roll my eyes: I'm not being very subtle.

Marcus smiles. 'Not while there was just Zach and me. There was one long-distance relationship a year ago that I couldn't sustain.' He notices my face change: I realise how far Liverpool is from here. He adds, 'Budapest.' I notice the wine glass in my hand for the first time and take a sip. He leans towards me, smoothing my hair with his fingers. 'What about you, Georgie?'

'Terry. Jade's dad. We lasted over twenty years. I suppose I took him for granted a bit. He went off with a woman called Alison. We don't really speak much now.'

Marcus smiles and takes my hand. 'Are you ready to eat?'

We sit at the scrubbed wooden table and he serves up a simple meal of spicy lentils in some sort of vegetable casserole with rice. It's delicious. We talk about ourselves: he's fifty-four. His father, Jakob, was two years old when he came over from Germany to England. His mother is called Miriam, born in London, and his parents are in their late seventies. He tells me that he loves cooking.

I lean forwards. 'My family have a great recipe for Scouse, handed down over generations. Have you ever eaten Scouse?'

'I haven't. I'm clearly missing out.' His face breaks out in a grin. 'What is it?'

'Stew. Beef or lamb, onions, carrots. But the secret is in the cooking.'

'You'll have to give me the recipe. Would it work with seitan or beans instead of meat, perhaps?'

I beam at him. 'That would be an interesting Scouse.

My current meat-free specialities are chowder and rata-touille.'

'Sounds delicious. I look forward to sampling them.'

'Ah . . .' I shrug, 'I'd have to come here and cook, though.' I imagine Nan and Bonnie on the sofa, Marcus sandwiched between them, asking him too many questions while I make onions sizzle in a pan. 'There wouldn't be much room in the flat . . .'

'You'd be welcome here. There's plenty of space. And I'm always on my own. Working from home tends to make me a bit solitary, so I'd be glad of the company.' He takes my hand across the table. 'And you are lovely company, Georgie. Warm and funny. It's great having you over.'

He pours coffee and we move closer to the fire on the squashy sofa. When I check the time, it's almost nine. He wraps an arm round me.

'Georgie, you've never really told me what you're doing in the Brighton area. I mean, is it somewhere you might choose to stay?'

I lean against his shoulder and rest my head, then I snuggle down. That way, he can't see my eyes: I don't want to tell him everything, not yet.

'We're having a bit of trouble with my sister's husband. It's difficult. She needed some time away from him. So we came here – Jade moving in with Luis gave me the idea – and we brought my aunt Nan with us because she lives alone and needs some care during the day.'

'Perhaps I could take you all out sometime, show you the village and the countryside.' He sits up, stretches his arms. 'Would your sister and aunt enjoy that? I mean, if your sister's had a tough time . . .?'

'Marcus, that's really kind.'

'And perhaps you and I could go out into Brighton, to the theatre or dinner.'

222

'I'd like that.'

My eyes meet his gaze, deep blue as the ocean, serious and still, and before I know what I'm doing, we start kissing. I put the coffee cup down and he does the same then we kiss some more, sprawling over the sofa so that our bodies press together. His hands are in my hair and we're kissing and kissing and I haven't opened my eyes yet. I breathe him in and we're two creatures bound by the sense of smell, touch, taste. It's so nice I don't want it to stop. I'm still kissing him despite my head telling me to put a halt to it, but I need to listen to my head, so to dampen my passion, I recall the image of Beddowes in Embers trying to intimidate Jade. I pull away suddenly and his hand caresses my face.

'Everything all right, Georgie?'

Of course it's all right. It's too all right. It's better than that. But the clock is ticking and Nanny's home with Bonnie – the thought of Beddowes knocking on their door has started to leak panic in my imagination.

'I'd better go home and check on Nan.'

'I haven't offended you?' His eyebrows shoot up.

I put my hand out and ruffle the soft curls. 'Not at all. I've had a great time. We must meet again.' My voice is hopeful. 'Maybe I can stay longer next time.'

I stand up and he's next to me. We kiss again and I realise how easy it would be to be with him for another hour, two, ten . . . He reaches for my coat and I slide it on.

'Oh, Georgie, I nearly forgot. I found this when I was in the office the other day.'

'Office?'

'I go to London from time to time. I work for a famous news and current affairs magazine I know you'll have heard of. I'm a satirist.'

An image of a satyr – a creature half-man, half-goat

223

– with Marcus' curly hair leaps into my mind. I giggle and the image bounces away.

'Oh, you write satire?'

'Political stuff, current affairs usually. Anyway, when I was in the office I came across this old tabloid. I thought you'd want to see it. It seems you're a bit of a superstar.'

A warning feeling creeps over me. I look up and offer him a smile. He shows me the newspaper and I examine the picture on the second page of a tabloid daily I've never read. The paper is creased, out of date. There are stains around the curling edges, but the photo's clear and I remember it being taken.

Jade and Luis are stepping out, looking smart, on their way to Embers, and next to them is Bonnie, smiling directly at the camera, Nanny in her filmy dress grinning with pride and me, looking at the ground, at my boots. But we're all recognisable. The headline reads: 'DELGADO BURNS THE CANDLE AT BOTH ENDS', and beneath is the question: 'IS PARTYING WITH HIS NEW GIRLFRIEND SPOILING LUIS' GAME AS HE PLAYS A SHOCKER?'

I shake my head and feel immediately sorry for Luis; I remember the meal at Embers, Beddowes' unpleasant threats and then the incident in their car. I worry that this is damaging Luis' good reputation, taking the edge off his sharp skills. Then I wonder if I'm dragging Marcus into the melee with Beddowes, too, and if I'm being entirely fair having a relationship with him. Disappointment seeps into my skin as I stand.

'Time to go home, I think. I'll walk by myself.'

Marcus wraps me in his arms, kisses me and whispers, 'Text me, soon.'

I'm sauntering along the beach towards our beautiful white glass-fronted clifftop flat twenty minutes later. A cool breeze hovers in and the waves whisper. I decide I've done the right thing, walking away from Marcus Hart. I don't want to get serious about a man, certainly not with so much craziness crowding my life. I'm too old, too cynical, too hard-boiled. Besides, I'll be going home soon. I smile to myself: he's a pleasant diversion, though. I check my lips for signs of excessive kissing. I feel like a teenager: I even have my route worked out in case I'm asked where I've been walking.

It's quiet on the stairs to the second floor. I open the door to the flat, about to offer a line about the lovely walk I've had, and gape at the two police officers standing in the lounge, talking to Bonnie, whose face is frozen in alarm. I recognise the slim, fair-haired policewoman, DC Charlotte Howes, and I say, 'Hello. What's going on?'

Bonnie stands up and waves a piece of paper. I take it from her and read the print – a round, unassuming print, simple language, but it takes my breath away: *Bonnie. It's just a matter of time.*

'What's this?' I look from the police to Nanny then to Bonnie.

She leans back on the sofa. 'It was left downstairs, taped to the lift door, half an hour ago. I found it when I went down to see if you were on your way back. Then I rang the police.'

DC Howes turns to face me. 'We're taking this seriously. I'm arranging for an officer to come here to keep an eye on you.'

I frown. 'I'm assuming it's from Beddowes? So, did he come into Cliff Top to deliver it?'

Bonnie nods. 'I just saw the envelope, sellotaped on the lift doors, with my name on.'

'No address, then? So he knows we're in the block of flats, just not which flat. Yet.'

225

Bonnie's distraught. 'There are only nine to choose from . . .'

DC Howes' expression is unreadable. 'By all accounts, it's his style. He's the sort of character who likes to try to intimidate people, cat and mouse. But he hasn't worked out which floor you're on yet, and that's good. You obviously have something he wants and he's playing a waiting game, trying to frighten you.'

Bonnie's eyes bulge. Beddowes has clearly succeeded. It occurs to me that DC Howes doesn't know about the bracelet. I remember my walk back to the flat. I could have passed Beddowes in his car or on the stairs. My heart's thudding and my blood sings in my ears.

'We'll have an officer here with you first thing tomorrow.'

'One officer? Tomorrow?' I hear the shock in my own voice, louder than I intended.

'He's very good, one of the best. The Met are working closely with us to bring Beddowes in. He's wanted in London. I'll make sure there's all-night surveillance on the flat tonight. You'll be fine.'

I show the police officers to the door and lock it after they've gone. There's only a Yale key and a chain. A hefty person like Beddowes could barge through with his shoulder.

Bonnie huddles in her chair. 'What's going to happen to us?'

I shrug. 'Let's have some of Roque's brandy.'

I find the bottle in a cupboard and pour it into three glasses. Nanny eases herself to a standing position, then moves over to the kitchen area, rifling through a drawer. Bonnie gulps hers down. Her eyes are huge.

'I've been thinking – why is Beddowes so keen to find us?'

Nan's face is angry. 'Revenge, since Adie left him high and dry without his money.'

226

'Maybe,' I shrug. 'What's on your mind, Bonnie?'

'Adie kept on talking about the bracelet – asking did I have it safely, I mustn't lose it. I don't know. It feels like it could be really important.'

'It's worth a bob or two,' Nan suggests.

Bonnie frowns. 'It feels like something else. Not just the cost of it. I keep remembering Adie's eyes every time he mentioned it. He was desperate. What if Beddowes wants the bracelet?'

'We'll put it somewhere safe for now, Bonnie. We'll be best off hiding here with the police bodyguard until they arrest Beddowes. It can't be long.' I give her a wide smile. 'The cops are outside now, so if he comes anywhere near here, they'll pick him up.'

Bonnie is small, sitting on the sofa, shivering. 'I want to go to sleep. I'm tired. But I'm terrified I'll wake up and he'll be standing next to the bed.'

Nanny's still rattling cutlery in a drawer. I pick up my phone.

'Let's have an early night. I'm just going to call Jade and tell her what's happened. She and Luis are off to Turkey tomorrow. Hopefully, she's right: by the time they're back, it'll all be over.'

Bonnie stands and she's shaking. 'That's what I'm afraid of, Georgie. Who knows what he might do to us?' Tears shine in her eyes. 'He knows where we live. He got through the keypad on the door. How long will it be until he knows which floor, which flat? He's more than capable of doing something awful.'

Nanny's voice is low. 'He'll have to get past me first.'

She has a determined look on her face, her brows coming together in a frown and her mouth in a straight line. The green woollen hat is pressed down firmly on her head and she's brandishing a carving knife like she's the grim reaper.

Chapter Twenty-Five

When I wake the next morning, Nanny's gone. Bonnie's still asleep, I'm in my pyjamas, someone's rapping on the door and Nanny isn't in her room or in the kitchen. The safety chain on the door has been undone. I rush to the spyhole, hoping it's her and that she's locked herself out. But it's a big police officer, close-cropped hair, dark craggy face, limpid brown eyes and broad shoulders. He holds an identity card up and his voice rumbles like a passing lorry.

'Femi Princewill. Close Protection Unit, Metropolitan Police. You're expecting me.'

I fling the door open. He's well over six feet tall, chest like a barrel beneath his stab vest. I feel safer already.

'Yes. Come in, please.'

He smiles, his face full of warmth and humour.

I grab his cuff. 'My aunt, Anne Basham. She's gone. Please help.'

Femi Princewill breathes out softly. 'When did you last see her?'

'Last night. We went to bed around eleven. I just got up, checked her room. She's gone.'

He smiles, shows perfect teeth. 'Are you Mrs Carrick?'

'I'm her sister, Georgie Turner.'

He puts an arm on my sleeve. 'Nice accent. Liverpool, isn't it? You're a long way from home.' He grins. 'Could you make me a coffee? No milk, two sugars. I'll contact my Sussex colleagues and they'll have a car out to look for her right away. Do you have a photo? Brief description? What she was wearing?'

I realise he's practised at calming people who are panicking. 'Glasses, green woollen hat. Black coat, maybe. She's tiny, five feet tall, in her late eighties. White hair, little streak of blue in the fringe. She's not very mobile – I mean – she can get about but she can't walk for long. She has arthritis in her hip and a heart condition.'

He nods. 'I'm on it.'

I busy myself with a coffee for Femi. I hear him talking in a hushed voice, calmly repeating my description of Nan, and a voice on the radio crackling an answer. When he's finished his call, he goes over to the door and inspects the lock. I put the mug of coffee in his hand.

'Thanks. I'm going to have your security system upgraded here. Make it a bit safer. Where's Mrs Carrick?'

'Still asleep.' My eyes flick to the wall clock. It's half eight.

'Right, I'll have my coffee then maybe we can wake her up and I'll go through what's happening here. My job is to provide close protection and I'll give you both some clarity about how that works.'

He has an infectious grin. He must be in his late forties, early fifties. He's built like a boxer and has the same rugged toughness, but with a sparkle in his eyes and mischief in his grin.

I clatter round in the kitchen and think about Nan. It's not like her to wander. I call across to Femi.

229

'I'm really worried. My aunt doesn't go off by herself.'

His back is to me. 'I'm sure there's a simple explanation.'

He's talking on the radio again. I wait until he's finished.

'You don't think Duncan Beddowes would have . . .'

He comes over to me, tower tall, and leans on the granite work surface.

'I can't say for sure. There's no sign of a scuffle. If he'd got in here and intended harm, why would he choose to take your aunt? But leave it up to our team.'

I remember last night, the carving knife, Nan waving it from the kitchen.

'She wouldn't have gone without a fight, that's for sure.'

Bonnie emerges from the bedroom, bleary-eyed.

'Georgie, can I smell coffee?' She notices Femi in his uniform and tight belt, broad-shouldered and smiling. She smooths her hair. 'Hello.'

'I'm Femi Princewill. You must be Mrs Carrick.'

'Please, call me Bonnie.'

He takes her outstretched hand. 'I'm so sorry to hear about your husband.'

She blinks at him. 'Adie meant the world to me. But he was involved up to his neck in criminal activities. I suppose it was inevitable that he'd leave.' Her lower lip trembles. 'It's broken my heart, though.'

He guides her to the sofa and she sits down. I hand her a cup of coffee.

'Nan's missing, Bonnie.'

Her face is distraught. 'Oh no!'

Femi folds his arms. 'There's nothing to worry about yet. There's an alert out and I'm sure we can find her.'

Bonnie puts her hands to her lips. 'If anything happened to Nanny . . . How long has she been missing, Georgie?'

'Hard to say. I've been here for half an hour, so it's longer than that.'

'Has she gone up to see Jade?'

I shake my head. 'Jade and Luis'll be on their way to the airport. Nan's coat and her woolly hat aren't here, so perhaps she's stepped out somewhere.' I briefly consider texting Marcus to ask for help but I push the thought away.

Femi breathes out. 'Does she have money? The means to travel somewhere.'

'I don't think so.' I grab my handbag. My purse is still there with several twenty-pound notes folded inside and my bank cards. 'I can't imagine where she could be.'

Femi frowns. 'Has she done this before?'

'Never.' Bonnie looks at me. 'We've been out to a restaurant and shopping but usually she walks between us, so we can support her when she gets tired.'

'How far would she get by herself?'

I shrug. 'Metres, not miles.'

It's gone nine already. I pass Bonnie a slice of toast with butter. She gasps at the plate.

'Georgie, I couldn't.'

'It might be best to eat something, Bonnie.'

Femi smiles at her and she nibbles the corner of the toast. He sits next to her and glances from her to me and back to Bonnie again.

'Okay, I need you both to understand exactly why I'm here. I work for the Close Protection Unit in the Met, so I'll be here with you while Duncan Beddowes is at large. There is every possibility that he'll be brought in over the next few days. He's a known criminal. We'd also like to talk to Adrian Carrick.'

Bonnie shrugs. 'Adie's overseas. I don't know where he is but he's definitely not coming back.'

Femi looks at Bonnie and she stares down at her fingers, twisting her wedding and engagement rings.

He smiles at her. 'My job is to stay here and make sure you're all right. I'll eat here, sleep here and answer the door to anyone who comes. That way, you'll feel safer until Beddowes is brought in.'

'Thank you, Femi.' Bonnie's voice is a whisper.

'So, all we need to do now is find Nan,' I say and walk over to the window.

Below, the sea is corrugated iron, the wind rippling the surface. There are passers-by on the beach crawling along, bent against the wind. I wonder if Nanny is one of them. The village is minutes away. If Beddowes is out there, Nanny's at risk. Or she could have tumbled, hurt herself. She could be on the beach. The swelling surface of the rolling ocean makes me shiver. I turn to Femi.

'No news of Nan?'

'I'll tell you as soon as there is.' He goes over to the door, moving a chair, and sits down. 'Meanwhile, it would be good for you both to discuss how to pass the time. I'll have provisions brought in. Would you like books, board games? Do you like to watch television?'

Bonnie's eyes open wide. 'How long are we going to have to stay here?'

He chuckles. 'Believe me, I understand how cooped up you must feel. As soon as we have Duncan Beddowes, everything will be back to normal.'

I flop in Nan's armchair and sigh. The white arm is mottled with yellow egg, red wine and ketchup, a smear of grey and brown from all the other food and drink. I miss her.

'Femi, is there no news on your radio? I mean, has anyone seen her?'

He shows me a sombre face. 'I'll let you know as soon as I hear anything.'

Bonnie closes her eyes and I do the same. I imagine the

232

ticking of the clock. Perhaps it's the flicking of the second hand, echoing, an itch inside my head, making each minute slow and crammed with the increasing possibility that something's happened to Nan. I count to a hundred, then back again to zero. Nan would say 'a watched pot never boils'. I open my eyes, push myself up and go over to the sink to wash the mugs.

'Femi, I'll go mad stuck in here worrying. All I can do is cook and watch TV. It's torture.'

'It won't be for long.' Femi's face is concerned. 'I don't want to scare you, but we're so close to arresting Beddowes. He knows we're on his tail, so he'll be at his most dangerous.'

Bonnie sighs. 'Perhaps we can get some DVDs, some films. There's the one about the prime minister who falls for the Cockney girl. I like that one. I miss my television at home.' She curls up tight on the sofa. 'Do you think we'll be home for Easter?'

Femi grunts. 'I hope we all will be.'

She leans forwards. 'My daughter will pop back home for a while. She's on her honeymoon.' He smiles and she tosses her hair. 'What do you do for the Easter weekend, Femi?'

'I'm at work often. I'll go to my mother's for Sunday dinner.'

Bonnie's face is all interest. 'So, tell us all about you. Do you have a family?'

'My son works for a mental health charity. He and his partner have a new baby, so they have their hands full. I try to visit them from time to time, to babysit or give them a hand with doing up their house. They've moved recently. My daughter's younger; she's doing A levels.'

Bonnie doesn't miss a beat. 'And what about your wife?'

I open my eyes wide, surprised by Bonnie's brazen

confidence. She isn't afraid of being direct. I recall my embarrassment, asking Marcus about his marital status. Bonnie meets Femi's eyes and he grins, makes a little laugh.

'We split up two years ago. She has someone else. One of my ex-colleagues, as it happens.'

'I'm sorry.' Bonnie's face is forlorn.

'Oh no, not at all. I'm still great friends with them both. It wasn't working out with Diana and me anyway. We never spent time together except with the children. It was over before it was over.'

'So, do you have another girlfriend?' Bonnie is in full swing; she doesn't notice that I raise my eyebrows.

'I'm too busy. Diana used to say I'm married to my job. That doesn't mean I'll be single forever. When I get round to it, I'll start meeting other ladies.' Femi chuckles. 'I'm still young and available.'

I wait for Bonnie to say 'and attractive', but she just smiles at him.

'I've no idea what I'll do now Adie's gone.' She wells up again. 'How I'll adjust. I mean, Georgie's a professional single, but I'm not sure I'm as tough as she is.'

I imagine Marcus, his expressive blue eyes, and I say, 'When someone special enough comes along, I'll review my single status.' For some reason, Bonnie throws me an evil look. I change the subject. 'Still no news of Nanny?'

It's almost twenty to ten. Nanny's been missing for over an hour, maybe more. I can feel my skin tingle, my breathing tighter: I'm so worried. Bonnie seems more relaxed: she stands and stretches, kicks off her heels. She clearly trusts Femi completely.

'Can I make you another cup of coffee, Femi?'

I stare. It's the first drink she's made for anyone since we arrived.

He nods. 'Yes, please. Black, two sugars.'

Suddenly, I've had enough. I pull my coat on quickly and I'm out of the door, despite Femi calling after me that the police will take care of it and I should stay in the flat and not put myself at risk. It's a bitterly cold day. I rush down the cliff steps, the wind pushing me back.

The first place I check is the beach. Nan isn't there. There are no passing dark-haired joggers, either. I stare out at the shifting ocean for a while, and then I rush down to where the steps lead from beach to the road into the village. I move quickly and stand by the kerb, watching cars lumber past. My eyes scan every pedestrian, looking for a little woman in a green woollen hat, white hair, an electric blue streak, and huge glasses. I can't see her anywhere.

I head towards a pedestrian crossing and wait for the signal to cross. I'll go to Djimi's Café: he might have seen her. Subconsciously, I'm listening for police cars, ambulances. Who knows what might have happened to Nan? I've already wasted too much time.

I jog down the pavement, weaving through pedestrians, almost bumping into a young man who staggers towards me, his breath foul, clearly having had too much to drink already. I stop by the kerb and look around. Across the road on the other side, my eye catches sight of a frail figure with a green woollen hat, standing by a lamp post.

'Nanny!'

She can't hear me but bystanders stare as if I'm deranged. A man in a trilby deliberately looks the other way. I shout again, 'Nan.' She's gripping the lamp post, bewildered. My heart starts to thump. There's a gap in the traffic and I rush into the middle of the road. A sports car heaves past my shoulder, coming the other way, and a horn beeps angrily. A couple more cars speed by and I run again. Nanny's in my arms before she sees me.

'Nanny. Where have you been?'

'To Djimi's Café. I took five pounds from your purse, Georgina – I didn't think you'd mind. I thought I'd be all right on the beach. Then – oh, you'll never guess what happened. I've had such an interesting ride. I've seen the sights! It was such fun. And I've got a present.' She waves an envelope.

I link her arm through mine and help her to walk towards the flat. We'll go the beach way, not up the road, via the hill: Nan'll struggle up the cliff steps, but the rest is flat. She leans against me, taking small, pitching paces.

'Nan, you'd better tell me all about it.'

'A taxi stopped for me. He was a lovely man – not the driver, the assistant in the front. He wouldn't accept any money. And he took me to Djimi's. He was a real gentleman. And I sat in the taxi while he went in and fetched me a coffee and a cross-ant wrapped in tissue paper, then he took me for a ride round Brighton.'

We hobble across the beach towards the flats. My heart has started to thump in my throat.

'Tell me about this man.'

We pause for Nan to rest.

'Oh, he was so kind. We drove for miles and I saw the Royal Pavilion and the Palace Pier. I sat in the back of the taxi. It was a lovely big car. And he said he'd show me the sights, the marina, while I ate my cross-ant in the back seat.' We climb the steps to Cliff Top. Then Nan wheezes, 'He dropped me off and gave me a present.' Her face is damp and pale. She rests against my arm and tries to catch her breath.

We take the lift to the second floor and Nan smiles. 'He had a lovely voice. The same sort of sexy accent as James Bond. But this man had red hair.'

I freeze. 'Nan, what did he say to you?'

'He said Brighton was a bad place for me to stay and now I'd seen it I could go home happy.'

'What was his car like?'

'It was a big black taxi.'

'Did it have a light on the front of the roof?'

Nanny blinks behind the glasses. 'No. He stopped for me by the side of the road just at the top of the hill. I was taking a breather and he said, "Do you need a taxi, madam?" It was as if he knew me.'

Nan steps into the flat and Bonnie squeals with delight. Femi ushers Nan to the sofa and holds her hand like it's made of porcelain. She grins up at him.

'I'd have been back sooner if I'd known they were sending this young man round to look after us.' She turns to me. 'What a busy morning I've had. So many lovely men. I've had such an adventure. I'd love a cup of tea.'

Bonnie flops next to Nan. 'I'm exhausted, Georgie.'

I go to the kitchen area and fill the kettle. 'We've been so worried, Nanny.'

'So I believe. The nice taxi man told me you'd be all hot and bothered.'

I frown at her and pass her cup of tea. She sits down, stretches out aching legs and smiles. Femi moves close to her.

'Would you like to tell me what happened, Mrs Basham?'

She beams. 'I had an adventure.'

'I think she's been with Beddowes, Femi.' He turns his head in my direction. 'He's given her something in an envelope.'

Femi knits his brow. 'Tell me about him, Mrs Basham.'

'Everyone calls me Nan,' she smiles. 'He was so nice. He said he'd love to come up and see me sometime. I told him to bring the cakes and I'd make him a coffee.'

I look from Nan to Femi, whose face is serious. 'Nan, did you give him our address?'

'Oh yes. Floor two, and I told him the flat number and that we'd appreciate visitors. It gets lonely up here.'

'Nanny . . .' I don't know what to say next.

Femi exchanges looks with me and I know what he's thinking. He takes the envelope.

'This could be important, Nan. May I open this?'

She nods and we all watch. He pulls out something small.

'It's a rail ticket. First class, to Liverpool, for tomorrow morning. One way.'

I crouch next to her. 'What did he say to you when he gave you this, Nan?'

'That I reminded him of his mother.' She smiles, remembering. 'She's eighty-six and lives in Edinburgh. I told him we went to a cash point there to avoid being followed. He seemed very interested. Then he said I should take care of myself. He said Brighton wasn't a good place for old ladies to be.' She pulls a face. 'I wasn't so keen on him when he said that.'

Femi shakes his head. 'This is his style, from what I've seen of his files. He likes to intimidate people.'

'Beddowes?' Nan grits her teeth and puts her hands on her hips. Her face is suddenly furious. 'Was that him? Then he can stick his rail ticket where the sun don't shine. I'm staying here – with my girls.'

Chapter Twenty-Six

It's almost ten thirty at night. I've texted Marcus three times, told him that I feel stifled in the flat and wish I could accept his latest invitation to dinner. He's sent a photo of a stew he's made, his own version of Scouse, practising for when I'm free to come round. He's also sent a second picture, a bottle of red wine, Madiran, which he says he can't wait to share.

Femi's had nothing to drink apart from Vimto, which he's apparently partial to, but Nanny, Bonnie and I have almost polished off two bottles of Prosecco and Nanny wants to open a third. Bonnie's eaten most of her takeaway chow mein. Nanny's demolished a pile of sweet and sour, rice, spring rolls and seaweed.

I'm the only one who isn't hungry, but Femi finished off my food after he'd eaten his own. He's chatting away happily, as if our situation is completely normal, and his confidence is contagious.

'We've known you were staying here for some time now. We have close links with the Merseyside and the Sussex police, where Beddowes is wanted for various incidents. We're working together to bring him in.'

'So why the hell haven't you arrested Beddowes yet? He came into the flats and left Bonnie a note!' I say. My voice is tinged with irritation.

Bonnie is wide-eyed, reaching for her glass.

Femi grunts softly, 'We're close, Georgie. Any day now.'

'And what about when Beddowes threatened my daughter and Luis? Where were you then?'

Femi's brow is a tramline of wrinkles. 'Trust me. We'll get him. And soon.'

I stand up, staring at all three of them.

'Beddowes knows where we are. He could be outside the door right now.'

Bonnie's and Nan's eyes move to the door. Femi reaches out, puts a hand on my arm.

'I'm here. There's constant vigilance. You'll be fine. Seriously, Georgie. Try to relax.'

I mutter, 'It's easy for you to say,' and sink back into the sofa.

Bonnie links an arm through mine. 'I'm not going to think about Beddowes. I'm just looking forward to Easter, and Demi and Kyle being home for a few days.' Bonnie sits upright. 'I might sell the house once it's all over. Move away.'

'I'm not sure I want to go home.' Nan looks genuinely upset. 'I mean, I'm having a great time here. Apart from being threatened every day with danger and death.'

Bonnie pushes herself upright. 'I'll open another bottle. Do you want another Vimto, Femi?'

'I'll do it.'

He's on his feet like a well-oiled spring, pouring drinks. Nan has her arm outstretched, glass ready. He brings the bottle over and sits on the carpet, near Bonnie's feet. I sigh without meaning to and suddenly my bones ache with a tiredness that's beyond a fraught day.

'I'll just drink this and then I'll be off to bed.'

Bonnie reaches out an arm and squeezes my shoulder. 'Have you heard from Jade?'

'She and Luis are in Turkey. She's been souvenir shopping today while he was training.'

'She'll be fine. But you never stop worrying about kids, do you? I miss my daughter so much.' Bonnie stares across at Femi. 'More than I miss Adie, really. I mean, since she got married and went to Thailand, all I want to do is pick up the phone and chat to her, tell her about what's gone on here. But I don't want to spoil her honeymoon and I don't want to worry her.'

Nan gulps her Prosecco. 'You have us, Bonnie. We'll look after you.'

Bonnie shakes her head. 'Thanks, Nan. But it's different – it's a special sort of relationship when you have your own baby.'

Femi chuckles. 'My son isn't a problem. He has his family. But I do worry about my daughter. She takes her work so seriously, four A levels, and she doesn't always eat properly. You know how it is, the kids' faddy diets and wanting to be thin. And she's up all night studying. I only get to see her in fits and starts because of my work. Sometimes I don't feel I'm the best father.'

Bonnie pats his huge arm. 'What's her name?'

'Loveth.' Femi's eyes are round with pride. 'Loveth Grace.'

'What a beautiful name. Demi is Demi Adrienne.'

'I like the name Demi.' He chuckles softly. 'It sort of rhymes with Femi.'

Bonnie's laughter tinkles. For a moment it's like they're the only two people in the room. Then Bonnie breathes out.

'Jade's just Jade, isn't she? No middle name.'

241

I remember being pregnant, tucked up in bed, Terry's face serious, wanting to call her Jade Amber. I told him with a kiss what a silly name that would be, two gemstones together, and he put his arms round me, caressing my swollen nine-month belly, saying that I was more precious than gold and he'd love me forever. Now, he has Alison and Arran to love.

'She's just Jade,' I whisper.

'You're so close, though,' Bonnie says into her glass. 'Like sisters. We're so lucky to have our girls.'

Femi presses his lips together. 'Loveth stays with me some weekends, holidays. It's like a breeze has blown in, fresh air and flowers. She's just so happy and cheerful'

'I know what you mean.' Bonnie's face falls. 'Demi and I used to go shopping together. We have the same taste in shoes. I do hope she'll have time to stay for a while, so that we can catch up. She'll be broken-hearted about her dad.'

'Kids are a worry. I'm going to get Loveth something special for her eighteenth birthday next month. She wants driving lessons but of course I'm concerned, with her out on the busy roads.'

'I fret about Demi all the time. I phone her every other day now,' Bonnie breathes softly. 'I so want to see her. I can't wait till Easter.'

I snort. 'It's childbirth that does it to you. Once you've given birth, you'll always be vulnerable. Makes you a sucker forever.'

'Childbirth was horrible.' Bonnie seems to find this funny. 'I had two days of hard labour and a forceps delivery with Demi.'

I chuckle. 'Caesarean section trumps that every time. Epidural. A row of stitches. I couldn't laugh for a week.'

'I laughed the first time Demi pooed,' Bonnie shrieks, her eyes watering. 'It was like green jelly.'

I remember and giggle. 'It was madness. Constant feeding and Jade non-stop screaming. All those sleepless nights.'

'Leaky nipples.'

'A belly slack as an old plastic bag.'

I chortle and look across at Nan, her legs stiff, stretched out as she leans forward in the armchair. Her Prosecco glass is still full and her hand is gripping the stem, shaking. A tear slithers on her cheek.

'Nan?' She's crying. 'Sorry, we didn't mean to upset you.'

She takes off her glasses, rubs her eyes and puts then back on. 'How would you know about him?' She gulps from her glass. 'He was called Steven.'

Bonnie looks at me and shrugs. My skin goes cold. Nan swallows more wine.

'I never loved anyone more. More even than I loved Wilf. Although he was just like Wilfie. The same eyes. Steven Christopher Basham, that was his name. He'd be nearly sixty years old now.'

Bonnie's face is blank, confused. Femi's eyes are on Nan. She swigs again.

'I can hardly bring myself to talk about it, not even after all these years. I treasured him. Not a day goes by that I'm not grateful for him, the warm bundle in my arms. He had a smile, like the sunshine had come out. He'd look at me, up into my eyes, and his little face would beam, so happy. I'd dress him up lovely. I was so proud. Too proud. It broke my heart.'

I slide over to sit at her feet. 'What happened, Nan?'

'It was all a long time ago. I woke up early one morning and thought, he's slept through. Wilf and I had never had a whole night's sleep since he was born. I'd be up a couple of times at least, feeding him. I didn't mind. I'd just hold him, look at his little face and watch his eyelashes rest on his cheek as he'd drift off. I loved to listen to the sound of his snuffling.

'But that morning, he'd not woken us. I said to Wilf, something's wrong, I just knew it. I rushed over to the cot in our room and there he was. Cold. Not breathing. Still, like a silent angel. He'd gone. Just like that.' Her voice fades.

Bonnie leans forwards. 'I'm so sorry, Nan.'

'He was only a little scrap. Tiny, from the day he was born. He was four months old. The doctor didn't know why he'd died. Perhaps there were too many covers on the cot, or he'd rolled over and suffocated. He was perfect. Little face so sweet, rosebud mouth, his eyes closed. But he'd gone, my little boy. And that was it.'

I grab her hand. 'Oh, Nan. I didn't know.'

'We didn't talk about it. Wilf and I asked the family to let him rest in peace, our little Steven. And I wouldn't have any more. I couldn't risk losing . . .'

She swallows more wine and I look at Bonnie, who has tears in her eyes. She wipes them with her knuckle and sighs.

'Nan, I feel so bad, talking about Demi and not knowing . . .'

Nan finishes the dregs in her glass. 'It's done now. And I'm still here. Sometimes I wonder if they're together, Wilf and my little Steven, waiting for me. But I know it's more likely that they're just gone and then I'll be gone, too.'

I tell myself that I'll never grumble again about Nan's drinking or her criticism or her obstinate ways. All I feel at the moment is heart-breaking pity. She sits upright.

'Ah, listen to the wine talking. I haven't shared this story with anyone in nearly sixty years. Well, we mustn't get morbid, must we, girls? Not while there's more

Prosecco.' She presses her lips together and cradles her glass. 'Femi, I'm not ready for bed yet. Let's have some loud music, shall we?'

He's already on his feet. 'What do you like, Nan?'

She forces a smile. 'Something I can dance to, have a good bop, you and me. What about some Rolling Stones?'

Femi is over by Roque's speakers, pressing buttons, and suddenly the opening chords of 'Jumping Jack Flash' fill the room. He holds out his hand. Nanny drags herself into his arms and they're fast waltzing. I pull Bonnie to her feet.

'Are you serious, Georgie?'

'If Nan wants to party, then we party.'

I bend my knees, flail my arms, put on my serious groove face with the sticking-out chin, which probably makes me look like a constipated chimpanzee, and I start to dance. Bonnie joins me, moving slowly, a sexy sway. Nanny leans against Femi, her eyes closed, mouthing the words and jiggling one leg. I wonder if her hip will ache tomorrow.

Then another song comes on. It's Jose Feliciano, 'Light My Fire'. Nanny moves to me, takes my hands in hers and waves both of our arms in the air, like kids doing 'Oranges and Lemons'. I copy her movements and she smiles into my face. Bonnie's in Femi's arms, a polite waltz, their bodies respectably distant, but their eyes are locked.

Nanny winks. 'He's a nice man.'

I visualise Marcus and wonder how it would be to dance with him. I imagine the smell of him, the heat from his body. Femi grins like a conspirator. He's put on some music from the Sixties and Seventies that Nan can dance to, and her smile is wide and brave. Her story has made my heart ache for her. I'm determined we'll dance ourselves back into a good mood.

The music plays on and the four of us are linked together in a can-can line, bopping to Free, joining in raucously with the chorus, 'All Right Now', at the top of our voices. Nan's face is shining again and even Bonnie looks less tired, a smile on her lips.

Energy takes over and my legs are suddenly light. I'm off on my own, soaring like a newly blown bubble, dancing and twirling, my arms punching the air, singing 'All Right Now'. Nan attempts to clamber onto Roque's armchair, wobbling and joining in, and Bonnie's voice soars, louder than I've ever heard her sing. 'We're all right . . .'

There's a thump, a bang and the door shakes. We all stand still. Femi springs to the music and turns it off in an instant. He looks at us, wide-eyed, a finger across his lips, and gestures to us all to crouch down away from the door.

I move to Nan and Bonnie and wrap an arm round each. Femi takes the telescopic baton from the pouch attached to his stab vest, moves softly behind the door. We wait, no sound but our breathing and our hearts thudding in our ears.

There's another knock, a double rap, insistent.

I mouth, 'It can't be Jade.'

Femi waits, then makes his voice level.

'Who's there?'

We wait in silence, nothing moving, our minds racing. Seconds tick, a minute . . .

I meet Femi's wide eyes and then I stare at the door, pad silently to the spyhole and peep out, then catch my breath. One cold blue eye is looking back, the light blue of arctic ice, framed with sparse red lashes. I turn to Femi and he moves me behind him. My heart bangs so hard I can't breathe. Bonnie's little face is screwed in a tight ball and she puts her head down, her hair falling over her eyes. She's expecting the worst. Nan gapes, her glasses shining. She's confused.

Then something slips under the door. It's a note, an envelope. Femi slithers it towards him, peers through the spyhole and turns to me. His voice is almost inaudible.

'I think he's gone.'

He's talking into his radio, giving directions, then he moves to where Bonnie and Nan are sitting and I join him. He tears open the envelope, unfolding a message, scrawled in capitals. We lean over his shoulder and read it together: ADIE OWES ME. BONNIE WILL PAY.

Femi's eyes narrow, serious, concerned. He turns his back and speaks into the radio again. I move away, taking a moment to stop shaking, to clear my mind. In a second, everything has changed. I'd thought Beddowes was annoyed with Adie, difficult, even dangerous; I'd used his and Adie's falling out as an excuse to run away with Jade and persuade Bonnie to leave her philandering husband. But I'd always assumed that Adie or the police would sort everything out, that we'd have a nice minibreak for a few weeks in Brighton, bond like sisters, and then somehow we'd all magically be happy and go home again.

I catch my breath. My heart thuds with realisation. This is really serious now. Duncan Beddowes knows where we are: he was behind the door, so close to coming into the flat. Our world has become wild, life-threatening, spinning dangerously out of control. I glance at my sister, tears brimming in her eyes, and put my arms round her and hug her hard. Nan moves to join us and the three of us bind our arms together tightly. We're in this deep, up to our necks.

Chapter Twenty-Seven

More police officers arrive and I make cups of coffee. Apparently, there's no sign of Beddowes outside. DC Charlotte Howes asks a brisk flurry of questions and she offers Nan refuge in a care home for a while to feel safer. I tell her crossly that we were supposed to be safe in Roque's flat. Bonnie's almost hysterical and Nan's face has become a mask, harrowed and tired. I suggest we leave Femi to it and go to bed. DC Howes agrees with me and the three of us slink away to our rooms. It's past one o'clock.

In the warmth of our double bed, I wrap my arms round Bonnie, who soaks my shoulder with tears and says that the end has come. I rock her gently; remind her about the words Femi repeated three times after the police had arrived: 'We know where Beddowes is. He'll be under arrest soon and you'll be able to go home. Trust me.'

We do trust Femi, but of course we don't trust Beddowes, who's closing in on us. He knows exactly where we are. Bonnie's breathing is interspersed with an occasional shaking sob, like a hiccup, even though she's asleep. It's like being children again, Bonnie waking with nightmares and me hugging her, telling her she'll be fine. Now, I'm wide awake. I can't shake off the image of a single pale blue eye staring, emotionless, through the spyhole.

Finally, I fall asleep, and when I open my eyes and reach for my phone, it's almost midday. I consider texting Marcus. I wonder when I'll see him again. Last night's scare has filled my head with worries about my relationship with him. I probably shouldn't even consider a romance while Bonnie's life is threatened. I barely know him. I don't even know how he feels about me; although so far the signs have been very positive.

Yet, I'm drawn to him. He's warm, natural and easy to be with. There's a sort of equality between us. I don't have to try to be interesting or attractive; I don't feel judged. Conversation flows between us and I like him. Besides, he's good-looking. I can't stop myself from laughing out loud. Good looks, conversation, respect. What more could I want in a man? But then the sinking feeling comes back in the shape of Beddowes and I know I shouldn't risk a relationship with Marcus with danger lurking behind every corner.

I pad to the lounge in my pyjamas. The room is empty and quiet, as if nothing happened last night. Nanny and Bonnie are awake, both in dressing gowns, eating croissants and drinking coffee, which Femi has supplied.

There's another officer who introduces herself as Holly Wickson. She has a Tyneside accent and a matter-of-fact handshake. She can't be much older than Jade. She's red-haired, a sleek bob, and slim inside her stab vest, with sharp blue eyes. She tells us crisply that she's our second protection officer. Her eyes glint, determined. Femi must notice my perplexed face, because he squeezes my arm and makes his voice low.

'She's mustard, this one. We're lucky to have her on board.'

Holly's quick as lightning. 'After last night, security has been increased. Beddowes' arrest is a priority.'

Bonnie's tired and sulky. 'I thought it was a priority already.'

I turn to Femi. 'Beddowes knows where we are. He'll come again. We're sitting ducks, aren't we?' I think for a moment. 'Or is that the idea? Maybe we're bait, to lure him in?'

Holly folds her arms. 'That's why I'm here now. He won't get past Femi and me. But in case you're worried, there's backup all the time just moments away. We have a van of officers watching the flats.'

Femi breathes out. 'Now Adie's left the country, it seems Beddowes has turned his attention to Bonnie.'

Bonnie whispers in my ear. 'It must be the bracelet. Why else would Adie have kept on talking about it?'

I pat her hand. 'Where is it?'

'In our room.'

Bonnie pushes herself upright and walks towards the bedroom like a ghost. I follow her, leaving Nan to eat the last pastry. When I open the door, she's sitting on the bed, the gold bracelet dangling from her fingers.

'Here.'

I turn it over in my hand, shake it. 'It looks normal enough.' I make a small humming sound. 'Perhaps the charms have some sort of significance?'

'It's possible.' Bonnie shrugs.

'So, from the clasp: a pound sign, a crown, a crucifix, a . . . what's this figure?'

Bonnie takes it from me and holds it up. 'Looks like a knight in armour.'

'A knight. Then a ladder, a flower and some numbers.'

'Okay.' Bonnie hovers over the bracelet. 'So let's see what we can come up with. The pound sign must mean where the money is. Then a crown. That's the queen.'

'Or a king.'

'Palace.' Bonnie again.

'Royalty? Riches?'

'Princess?' Bonnie's thinking of her daughter and, of course, I'm thinking of mine.

I sigh. 'And the next one. A crucifix.'

'God,' says Bonnie.

'Jesus? Religion?Christianity.'

'A cross. King's Cross, in London. He said the money was in London,' Bonnie suggests and I breathe out.

'King's Cross? Do you think that's where Adie's money is?'

Bonnie's eyes are large circles. 'So the knight. St Pancras, perhaps. That's near King's Cross. Or maybe it's a church.'

I stare at the charms. 'What about the rest? A box. A bunch of flowers, a ladder, the numbers. A phone number. It's five digits.'

'The flowers might be a clue. Someone's name. The name of a house.'

'What sort of flowers are they?' I ask.

'Begonia, perhaps.'

'It's telling us to be-gone-here, then.' I burst out laughing: I sound hysterical. I put a hand to my head. It's started to ache. 'Bonnie, we should show this to the police, tell them.'

'Won't they want to keep the bracelet? It's all I have of him.'

She looks like she's about to cry. I slip an arm round her.

'Let's say nothing about it for the time being, shall we?

It won't hurt. The bracelet isn't what they want. All they really want is Beddowes.'

The day disintegrates. It's after five and conversation is dwindling. Marcus texts to ask how I'm feeling and my reply is terse: *all fine, thanks*. I don't want him to worry or to come here. An officer arrives with a bag of provisions and he huddles in the corner talking to Holly and Femi in a low voice.

We're waiting for seven o'clock, for the football match, when Luis' team will play the Turkish opposition. Nan and Femi are in front of the television already, watching the sports channel, listening to the pundits' excited voices making predictions. I hear Luis' name mangled when a commentator suggests he's on a run of poor form after his last game. Bonnie's dozing on the sofa, her mouth open a little. Holly's helping me to make a hotpot. I can't stand the idea of takeaway food or to be sitting here doing nothing. While the casserole is in the oven, I walk over to the panoramic windows and press my nose against the glass. I feel like a fish encased in a tiny tank of water. Even my mouth is open, gulping air.

Then we sit down in front of the game. Nan holds a glass of Guinness and I notice a new brown ring on the arm of Roque's chair, blending in with the smudges of tomato, wine, beer and gravy from days before. The screen flickers with interviews: both teams' managers and the captain of the Turkish team, Beşiktaş.

Bonnie looks bored, forking food and replacing it on her plate, and Holly has taken up a position by the door on a chair, eating slowly, a book on her knee. Femi's sitting on the sofa next to Bonnie, looking uncomfortable in the confined space, leaning forwards, watching the game. I feel safest on the floor. If anybody charges in, I don't have far to fall. I don't want to drink wine tonight. The Prosecco we binged on last night has put me off alcohol – I need a clear head in case we have unwanted visitors. I count on my fingers. It's the thirteenth of April. Jade'll be back in four days. My heart thumps faster than it should. I hope this mess will be over by then.

On the screen, Luis runs onto the pitch, his long fringe pulled back in a little knot on his head. He leaps up and down, warming up, and his face is focused and confident.

The game kicks off. Nanny's shouting at the television as soon as the Turkish boys take the ball and within five minutes they've scored. Nanny's accusing the referee of inherited illegitimacy, and Femi chuckles and agrees with her. Bonnie's eyes are closed now, although I know she's not asleep, she's thinking. Nanny sups more brown ale from her pint glass and I glance across at Holly, who's reading. Every so often, her keen eyes swivel round the room before she goes back to the novel. I assume it's a crime thriller.

I ease myself from the chair, collect the plates and wash them like a zombie. From somewhere in the room, I hear cheering. It must be a goal – Luis' team are level. My mind flicks back to last night, the early hours of this morning. Beddowes is close now.

I move to the huge window and gaze down at the cliff path and the stretch of beach two floors below. I can make out shadows, lumbering cliffs. The television rattles behind me, dull voices percolating, almost muffled. The sea is motionless, a smooth battleship grey. The coastline of houses leading to Brighton is barely visible, a dark sketching with irregular tiny lights, pencilled against an indigo sky.

I breathe out and imagine the cold wind against my face, snuggled inside a warm coat, walking with Marcus along the beach, the water streaked crimson from the sinking sun. We could stop for a coffee at Djimi's Café, or find a quiet pub, be anonymous among normal people as they laugh and joke about the weather, football, politics. I recall my home, my own house, my own bed . . . I place both hands against the window and imagine the glass falling out and me tipping forwards, flying in an arc through the open frame and down, down, crashing against the cliffs, a slumped body lifeless on the shingle beach. At least I'd be free, outside, not cooped up, waiting to be killed. But I'm not so desperate. Just desperate to go outside and breathe fresh air. I turn back to the game.

'How's it going, Nan?'

'One all. Louise is wonderful. He's running rings round the Turkeys. He made the goal – kicked it straight onto the head of the number five. Come and watch.'

Nanny and Femi are straining forwards, urging the game on. Bonnie's fast asleep now. Weariness has come over me, settled into my bones, making them ache, setting them as stiff as setting cement. I close my eyes and a pulse twitches behind them. My head has started to feel heavy, too weighty for my shoulders, and there's a stabbing pain over my left eye.

'Goal!' Nan screams. 'Well done, Louise, you little beauty – two one.' Her face brightens. 'He's unstoppable, Georgina. You should see him dodging and diving. He's a little wizard.'

I force a smile and feel weak. 'I'm all done, Nan. I'm off to bed. Are you going to be all right?'

Her eyebrows shoot up above the glasses. 'But it's not half-time yet.'

I shrug. 'Night, Nan.'

Femi winks at me and I catch Holly's eye. She smiles and returns to her book.

254

In the bedroom, I don't turn the lights on. I clean my teeth at the basin in the en suite, wash my face then smear a little cream across my cheeks and brow. Slithering between cold sheets, I wonder if Beddowes'll come again tonight. If he does, perhaps I'll sleep through it. Perhaps I'll be dead by the morning, but I'll know nothing about it.

I curl into a ball and wrap my arms round myself. For a moment, I imagine that my arms are not my own, they're male and muscular. Marcus is next to me; I'm safe in his embrace, warm and relaxed. I smile at the thought and remind myself that I'm fine, I don't need a man, but the comfort of another body would help the tension to soak away. Jade has Luis now and suddenly I feel alone. Soon, when all this is over, I'll have to say goodbye to my daughter. She'll be fine – Luis makes her happy – but I'll be on my own. Of course, I don't need a relationship; I'm used to being independent. But Marcus is lovely, good company, and I imagine how nice it might feel now to be in his arms. My lids become heavy and then the world drifts and swirls like warm liquid.

Chapter Twenty-Eight

I wake at eight o'clock. Bonnie's asleep, as usual, and when I peep in at her door, Nan's still in bed. In the living room, Femi and Holly are drinking coffee, bleary-eyed; they tell me they dozed in turns throughout the night while the other kept watch. I pace around like a caged animal, go to the window and stare out. It's a cold spring day; everything seems new, tinged with blue, ice clear. Smudges of orange sun stain a pale sky and blur the edges of the sea. I feel trapped behind the thick glass of the window, staring at white chalk cliffs and the pale shingle beach. Everything out there is alive, moving and shifting, and my life is suspended indoors. It's hard to breathe.

My phone buzzes and I lift it to my ear. A soft male voice, husky and secretive, whispers, 'Are you awake?'

I reply a coy, 'Yes, only just.'

He pauses and then murmurs, 'Can you go out onto your balcony? Can you see the ocean?'

I look across at Femi, who meets my eyes and raises his eyebrows in concern. I wave the phone and mouth 'just a friend' at him. He nods, so I step out onto the balcony. Cold air rushes into my face and I gulp in the sensation of sudden independence.

'Marcus?'

I hear the humour in his voice. 'Step forwards. Look over the edge.'

Down below, the clifftop gleams in the bright spring light and I shield my eyes. He waves. He's wearing a dark coat, standing next to a red car, which is some sort of rugged 4 x 4, a Suzuki Jimny. I hold the phone next to my mouth, wave back and grin.

'Hi, Marcus.'

'Come down.'

'It's all a bit busy here.'

'It would be lovely to see you. I've brought breakfast.'

I breathe in. 'I'll try.'

Back in the living room, I'm suddenly filled with excitement and energy. An idea flashes into my mind. I reach for my coat. Holly and Femi are watching me. I make a quick decision about which of them is most likely to fall for my story. I turn to Femi and wave my hand frantically in front of my face, stick my tongue out and pant ridiculously.

'I need fresh air.'

'What's the matter, Georgie?' I notice the concern in his eyes.

'I'm having a hot flush. I feel dizzy.'

He frowns and looks to Holly for help. She obviously has no idea what I'm experiencing – she's twenty-five years younger than me. I make a little groan, just subtle enough to be credible.

'Femi, I have to pop out to the chemists. It's urgent.'

'Georgie, you can't . . .'

'I need medication. It's the menopause. It's really bad.' I groan again and clutch my stomach and then my head.

Holly pats my arm. 'Tell us what you need. I'll radio someone and get it brought in.'

I double over and pant like a bloodhound, then wave my hands again. The truth is, I have no idea what pains of the menopause feel like. I've never had a single symptom in my life and my play-acting is based purely on horror stories that customers have told me in the salon. I try to make myself flush and look warm. The coat helps, along with the central heating, which Nan's turned up to full.

'Are you all right?' Femi's expression tells me that he's out of his comfort zone, so I play my trump card.

'I have to pop to the chemists in person. They'll find out what strength medication I need. They'll have to phone my doctor in Liverpool. It's special stuff.' Holly's unsure, so I say, 'If I don't go, my entire immune system will collapse.' Femi looks horrified, so I add, 'And so will I.'

Holly grabs my arm. 'I'll come with you.'

'No.' I move away from her. 'I'd be much happier if you stayed here with Nan and Bonnie.'

'Can you be really quick?' Femi asks.

'Quick as I can. I'll go via the beach.'

And then I'm down the stairs, outside and in Marcus' arms. His mouth is against my ear.

'It's been too long, Georgie. I wanted to see you.'

'I can't stay.'

He indicates the car. 'A drive. An hour? I brought breakfast.'

I'm in the car before I can change my mind and I duck down when we pass a blue transit van parked just around the corner. I'm guessing it's the police on their watch. We're speeding down the hill, through the village and away. After five minutes, we reach a road with trees on either side, like a shaded canopy. I can hardly see the sky.

He smiles. 'How did you manage to get away?'

'I said I had a medical emergency. I'm off to the chemists for some magic pills.' I pull a face: I shouldn't have lied, but at least I'm outside. 'I can't stay away long.'

'So why do the police want you to stay indoors? Is your sister's husband being a nuisance?'

'It's complicated.'

The road cuts through fields, rolling green on one side, dimpled with little yellow flowers and then lighter grass, pale gold in the distance. It's as if the countryside has opened its arms and welcomed us, there's so much space. The road veers downhill towards the deep blue line of the ocean. We turn another corner, down a bumpy lane and into an open space big enough for just two cars. We stop; Marcus opens the back of the Jimny, pulls out a basket and a rug, and takes my hand.

We stroll to the edge of a field, where the land falls away and I can see the turquoise sea. The sparkling water merges with the jagged white teeth of cliffs and the expanse of sky above. There's a little brown path, a light scar across the grass, which wriggles down to the water below. I wish we had time to go down there.

Marcus lays out a checked rug, a flask and lunch boxes. He flops down, grins and begins to pour coffee into cups.

'Have you eaten?'

I shake my head and he opens the box and offers me a bagel, filled with salad and something creamy.

'Tuna?'

'Chickpeas, mashed avocado and mayonnaise,' he tells me. 'I baked the bagels specially this morning.'

I stare at him but he's not joking. I wonder if there's anything this man can't do. The air is biting cold. The coffee burns my fingers and, eaten in the fresh air, it's the most delicious breakfast I've ever had.

He rolls over onto his stomach and points to the clump of trees.

'If we had time, we could go down there and watch the deer.'

'There are deer around here?'

He nods. 'They're beautiful. I remember one day, two years ago, I was coming back from London. I'd been into the office and we were launching a new spoof column. I'd had meetings all day; it had been a long day. It was summertime, quite late but it was still light, and I had the radio on to keep myself alert. I wasn't far from here, when I turned a corner and had to slam my feet on the brakes. I stopped just in front of the most incredible deer, just standing in the middle of the road.'

'What did you do?'

'I waited. She took her time, watched me for a moment. I thought about lifting my phone and taking her picture but I didn't want to alarm her. Then she just sauntered towards the side of the road and was gone. It was a privilege to see her.'

'Do you think there will be deer on the way home?'

'Perhaps.' He takes my hand and I notice the dark ink of the tattoo on his wrist. 'I wish we could get out to the countryside. There are some fantastic walks through the woods and down to the sea.'

I nod: I wish we could spend more time together, too. A gust of wind grips my shoulders and makes me shiver. He shuffles forwards, puts his arms round me and I'm instantly warmer. Then we're kissing, lying on the rug amid the toppled flask, empty cups and the sandwich boxes, our bodies close, and I wish we had all day to be together. His face is next to mine. I stare into the blue of his eyes, flick my gaze to the roughness of the stubble on his cheeks, touch the dark curls with silver strands, run my finger over the curve of his lips. I can feel his breath on my face and then I make myself wriggle away.

'Marcus . . .' It occurs to me how exposed we are, out in the countryside, and the sense of us being in danger hits me like a cold wind. I'd been enjoying myself too much, the freedom of being outdoors, his company. I wasn't thinking of how much at risk we could both be. 'We should go back.'

'I know.' He gives a lopsided grin. 'We need to rush you back from the chemists with your emergency medication.'

'I'll have to say I took it on the way home. Or the chemist had run out. I have nothing to show them.'

We're in the car. He starts the engine.

'We must do this again. There are so many lovely places.'

'It's been wonderful. I know it's only been an hour, but it feels like a lifesaver.'

He kisses me. 'Can you make it to my house for dinner again?'

'I'd love to, but . . .' I take a breath. 'Marcus, I haven't explained properly why we're not allowed to leave the flat.'

'Something to do with your sister's husband. They've split up and it's acrimonious.'

'It's more serious than that.' I take a deep breath. 'Adie's disappeared – owes money to a man, a wanted criminal, who's threatened Bonnie. He tried to break into our flat. The police will catch him soon, but until he's behind bars, we're not safe.'

Marcus' face is anxious. 'Then we're not safe out here, are we? I should get you back to Cliff Top.'

I nod my head. I'm surprised he's not angry; I've put him in danger: he has a son – who knows what Beddowes might do? I offer a hopeful smile. 'They're close to catching him.'

There are fields on either side, tall trees, dark shadows. Marcus takes my hand briefly.

'Please let me know as soon as they find him. And stay safe.'

'It can't be long now.'

I rest my head on his shoulder for a few seconds and we drive in silence; from Marcus' frown, I'm sure he's contemplating the threat which hangs all around us. I wish I'd spoken to him about it earlier: I'd just hoped it would go away. We're three miles from the village, in the narrow road with pointed trees that stretch to the skies. I'm looking either side of me, into the dense darkness of the forests, my eyes searching for the russet flash of a running deer.

It's strange to be driven. When Terry and I were together, it was usually me who drove, first the battered old Mini then the Polo. The image comes back to me: Terry, not like he was when I last saw him with Alison, faded and sad, but lithe and full of energy. Terry and I were always joking. Together, from our early twenties until it all went wrong, we knew everything about each other.

I glance at Marcus and he senses my movement and smiles at me. I wonder if things could become the same with us, in tune with each other, a natural affinity. It occurs to me that my feelings for him are developing more quickly than I'd like. He seems to feel the same: he's concerned about me, attentive and caring.

Through the windows, I notice the signs of warming spring. There's a flurry of birds in the trees; little flowers poke their heads through the earth. I roll the window down a little and a sweet smell floats towards my nostrils, the scent of grass and buds in the warmth of the sunshine. Perhaps that's why I feel a sudden surging of happiness: Marcus and I are having a spring romance. Perhaps it'll blossom into something special, sweet as nectar. Or perhaps the rains will come down and drown it, a brief promise of buds and then nothing more. I have no idea what to do about him, but for now he's as refreshing as the breeze that sifts through the open window.

I notice that Marcus is driving faster. His face clouds.

'That's funny.'

'What?'

He frowns. 'There's a car right on our bumper. It's been following us for a while. Whatever speed I do, it's still there.'

I peep over my shoulder. The black Jaguar is dangerously close. Suddenly, the lights behind us begin to flash and then the car roars forwards, level with us. Beddowes turns his head and looks straight at me, his eyes narrowing. Marcus accelerates and we're ahead, then the Jaguar slides beside us again. Beddowes points a finger at us. He's keeping pace. Marcus urges the Jimny forwards and I hope we're going to leave Beddowes behind, then the black car glides into view and is parallel again. Beddowes smiles and turns to his driver. I think he's going to ram us, just as he did with Jade.

A car appears in the distance, coming this way on the other side of the road: two cars, one behind each other, on course for Beddowes' Jaguar. He's in their way. The car at the front blares its horn. Marcus brakes heavily. I jolt forwards. The Jaguar rushes past us, accelerating away, and I breathe out.

Marcus turns anxious eyes in my direction. 'Was that him?'

I nod.

'Let's get you back. I'm sorry, Georgie. I shouldn't have brought you out.'

I make a joke. 'It was worth it. To see you and have chickpea bagels.'

He offers an encouraging grin, but we're both shaken.

He drives back at a pace and my eyes are constantly searching the verges and side roads for a lurking black Jaguar. Marcus drops me off at the entrance to the flats at Cliff Top, kisses me once and makes me promise to message him that I'm safe.

I rush upstairs, knowing that I can't tell Femi that I've seen Beddowes. I ought to say something. It would help the police to catch him if they knew where he'd been spotted. But then I'd have to admit I wasn't at the chemists. I'd have to tell everyone I was having a secret picnic with Marcus. I decide to keep it to myself for now. My mind is a whirl of confusion: what if Beddowes was watching us eat breakfast? What if he has the details of Marcus' number plate? I ought to tell the police everything and come clean. I've put him at risk now too, and I feel overwhelmed with guilt.

Inside the flat, Nan's eating toast, watching television. Holly's talking to someone on the radio and Femi's listening to Bonnie chatting about Demi's honeymoon in Phuket. I take off my coat and mutter something about feeling a bit better now.

Bonnie swivels her eyes in my direction. 'I didn't know you had menopause problems, Georgie. I texted Jade when I heard and she said you'd never complained to her about it before.'

I shrug. 'It only comes on when I'm under stress.'

I take a deep breath and wonder if I should tell all, explain where I've been and let them have the important information they need about Beddowes. It might help the police find him. I cough, hesitate: I'm about to admit the truth about where I've been. Then Holly interrupts me.

'I've just spoken to someone at HQ. Beddowes has been sighted in the area earlier this morning.'

Nan doesn't take her eye off the screen. 'I hope they've arrested him, the pig.'

I agree energetically and decide I don't need to spill the beans about the picnic, not yet. Hopefully, Beddowes will be behind bars at any moment now.

'Have they got a car registration number for him? Some identification?' My face must be red with guilt. At least it backs up my menopause excuse.

'He owns a fleet of Jaguars, all black. He must have several different drivers.' Femi frowns.

Holly looks at me directly. 'He was spotted half an hour ago, driving behind a jeep. We had an unmarked car coming in the other direction. We have the vehicle registration. We'll arrest him today.'

I close my eyes and wonder for a second if I've been identified, if the police have traced Marcus. Hopefully, they are spending their energies trailing Beddowes and my secret liaison is still safe.

Femi's brows come together. 'You can't go out again, Georgie. Whatever the crisis. He may know that we're close to catching him now and it'll make him react like a trapped rat. It's much too dangerous. He's likely to strike at any point. This is it.'

Chapter Twenty-Nine

Three days drag by. Nothing happens, although Bonnie and I are on edge all the time. Every creak of the door, every unexpected sound, and we're jumpy. It's the seventeenth of April: Jade's due back with Luis, who's being hailed a champion by the press after scoring a hat-trick against Beşiktaş, his team beating them 4–1.

Femi brings daily papers for us to read. They're full of the joys of Easter: grinning pictures of models in bikinis holding up strategically placed Easter eggs or seasonal stories about chickens running amok on the motorway. A political commentator has released an angry letter about the need for food banks and shelter for the homeless. I stare at his photograph below the headlines: he looks about fourteen years old. There's no mention of Beddowes, no hint that he may be in the area. I wonder if he's disappeared or if we'll ever truly be safe.

I ask Femi: 'Has anybody seen him?'

Femi breathes out heavily. 'We're close to catching him.' He forces a smile in my direction. 'Our guys know where he is. We're just waiting for the right moment, so we can bag him and a haul of money which we believe he will lead us to.'

I groan. 'Perhaps he's gone back to Scotland to see his mother for his Easter eggs.'

Bonnie's genuinely terrified and I press my lips together: anything I say about Beddowes might upset her now. Nan's at the breakfast bar, chopping vegetables for a stew for supper. I'm amazed at her new independence, at the interest she's taking in cooking, at her enthusiasm. She waves a courgette at me.

'He won't come in here. I'll have him if he does.'

Holly's voice is hushed. 'He's certainly gone quiet. He could be lying low, waiting for his moment. We'll flush him out soon, though.'

'Like a rat down the toilet,' Nanny adds cheerfully.

I smile.

Jade and Luis arrive at half past one in a police car. An officer steps out and shepherds them upstairs, waiting outside the door. They'll be under close protection all the time now, and Jade has lost the privacy she values so much. She is furious as she throws herself on the sofa next to Bonnie, her arms full of Turkish souvenirs. She glares at Femi.

'You haven't caught him yet?'

'He's still in the West Sussex area.' Femi folds his arms.

'You have his vehicle registration. Just go and get him.'

I remember with a twinge of embarrassment that I've withheld information about Marcus, about being a passenger in the Jimny. I don't know whether to mention it now but it occurs to me that I've left it too late.

Holly steps in. 'We're biding our time. We have a plan in place; you know we're waiting for his next move. The rest is classified.'

I know I should leave it, but I'm still visualising Beddowes' car crawling alongside us, and how he did the same to Jade and Luis in the taxi. Now they are back, I'm worried about their safety again, even with the bodyguards lurking outside the door. I clench my teeth, stressed and ashamed of my dishonesty, especially since Femi has been so kind. But instead of being grateful, I blurt out the first stroppy words that come into my head.

'And I suppose when all of us have been murdered in our beds, that will be classified information, too.'

Holly puts on a soothing voice. 'I know how you must feel.'

'You have no idea.'

She shrugs. 'You're in good hands, Georgie.'

I don't miss a breath. 'Like the other night when Beddowes was behind our door?' I'm still remembering Beddowes trying to ram us. The police clearly don't know I was in the Jimny or that Marcus has any link to me: they would certainly have mentioned it by now. But I don't feel safe at all. Guilt gnaws away at me. I should tell them about Marcus, about Beddows pursuing us in the Jaguar, about being the passenger. I pull out my phone and text Marcus to check he's all right. A cheery text comes straight back and I exhale relief.

Femi pats my arm. 'Try not to worry, Georgie. We have a van of officers on surveillance outside and close protection inside.'

I notice Bonnie's troubled eyes – Jade and Luis are now back in the firing line again. I glance at Nan's anxious face. All the people I love are at risk, and I'm not helping by withholding information. I'm furious with myself. But instead of admitting my part in the Beddowes sighting, I grumble. 'How can I not worry, when I'm cooped up in here waiting for a crazy criminal to break the door down and threaten us all?'

Bonnie starts to sob. I've said too much. Jade stands next to me.

'Mum's right. You promised it would be sorted out by now. And the officer has just told me that Luis and I are going to have a police guard day and night. What about our quality time?'

Femi looks sad. His eyes have taken on a wounded-puppy look.

'You have my word. We're almost there with Beddowes.'

Bonnie mumbles 'Thanks, Femi.'

Holly adds, 'He'll be in custody soon.'

'And we're the bait to lure him here?'

My breathing is ragged and my heart thuds in my chest. I'm flustered, guilt-ridden and scared. Jade and Luis are staring at me.

Nan's bored. She shuffles from the kitchen area and over to the sofa, diving into Jade's holiday shopping and pulling out a sequined bra top in turquoise with gold tassels. She holds it against her chest and does a little wiggle. The tassels spiral where nipples are supposed to be.

'Ooh, a belly dancer's outfit. Is this for me? I've always wanted one.'

Luis shuffles his feet and says something to Jade in Spanish. She grins.

'I've got something for you, Nan. Here.'

She pulls out a tissue parcel and hands it to Nanny, who rips the paper apart, her face shining. She produces a packet, full of nutty cakes.

'What's this?'

'It's baklava, Nan,' Jade beams. 'Honey and pistachios.'

Nan's disappointed. 'They'll stick to my teeth.' She frowns. 'I'd rather have the belly dancing outfit. Or couldn't you have got me one of those hash pipes?'

Jade meets Luis' eye and they both smile.

Luis says, 'We bring lunch on the way here.'

'You haven't eaten yet, have you?' Jade asks as she unloads cartons from a shopping bag.

I must look disappointed because Jade hugs me.

'We brought falafels, dolma, flatbreads. A really nice spread for us all to share. I thought you'd enjoy some healthy Middle Eastern dips.'

Before long, we've spread the food on a cloth on the floor and sit around, pulling bread apart and dipping it in hummus. Jade's opened a bottle of red wine, but I say no: I need to be alert, to keep my wits sharp. Everyone's mood has lifted. Nan has a glass of wine in her fist and is complimenting Luis on his hat-trick and winning the game. Even Bonnie seems happier. The wine is relaxing her sip by sip.

Suddenly, she sits up and leans close to my ear. 'Georgie, shall we have another look at the charms on the bracelet?'

I stand up and nod towards Jade meaningfully. 'We'll go in my room, shall we? Try on the T-shirts and maybe even the belly dancing outfit. Are you coming, Nan?'

Bonnie stares for a moment, then my meaning sinks in and she pulls herself to her feet. 'Good idea.'

I turn to a bewildered Luis. 'You can come, too.'

His face takes on an even more confused expression, but the five of us troop off in a line, leaving the police officers guarding the door. Nan sits on the bed.

'What's this all about?'

Luis frowns and puts our presents down on the bed.

'I bring the clothes for you to try. I think you forget them.'

Bonnie shakes her head. 'We need to talk about the bracelet Adie gave me. We haven't mentioned it to Femi

270

yet. I believe the charms are clues and it explains where the money is. It's probably somewhere in King's Cross.'

I watch Bonnie's face. A cloud passes across it. I know she must be thinking about Adie.

Jade is suddenly interested. 'Let's have a look, Aunty Bonnie.'

Bonnie slides her hand into her jeans pocket, where she's kept the bracelet for the last few days. A reminder, a keepsake. It occurs to me that it would be a nice gesture for me to offer to have the clasp fixed – if I'm ever allowed to leave the flat again.

Jade picks it up and scrutinises the charms. 'Shouldn't we tell the police about it?'

I shake my head. 'They'll confiscate the bracelet and Bonnie wants to keep it.'

'Adie's last present.' Bonnie sniffs and brings the bracelet to her lips.

She's tearful again, so I say, 'It can't do any harm if the police don't know about it. Why don't we look at it again? If we have to hand it over, we'll just say we didn't know it was important. It can't hurt to hang on to it.'

Jade fingers the charms. 'I get it! Money – the pound sign. King – the crown. Cross – the crucifix. What about the knight?'

'St Pancras?' I have no idea.

Luis peers over her shoulder. 'He has only one eye.'

Jade sits upright. 'It's King Harold, isn't it?'

Bonnie leans forwards. 'King Harold?'

'Battle of Hastings.' Jade holds up the bracelet. 'And look.'

'A book? A box?' I ask.

'A square,' Jade suggests. 'Hastings Square – it's just outside King's Cross station.'

Nanny's wriggling on the bed, bored, holding up the belly dancer's top.

'What about the flowers, the ladder, the separate numbers?' Bonnie asks. 'There are five of them.'

Jade's brow creases. 'The numbers could be a combination code to a safe. The flowers are puzzling.'

The conversation bubbles about the flowers: is it a begonia, a rose, a carnation? I sigh too loudly. We've been sharing lunch, laughing, handing out souvenirs as if we're a normal family, solving riddles as if we're part of a spiffing fun adventure: Enid Blyton's *Famous Five*. Everyone seems to be missing the point. Beddowes is still out there; he's a constant threat to our safety and everyone's giggling over the charms on a silly bracelet. I'm suddenly claustrophobic. It'd be nice to see Marcus, to breathe some fresh air. I feel penned in. I need to be outside.

For a while I'm thoughtful, then a plan fits together in my head. I turn away, drift back into the living room, smile at Femi and Holly, and then I text Marcus and ask him if he can meet me at the bottom of the cliff path, just to say hello. He replies immediately, asking if it's safe for him to venture to Cliff Top and if so, he'll be there in twenty minutes. I text that there's a police van watching the area round the flats, but we should be quite safe meeting discreetly on the beach below, and he replies that he's looking forward to seeing me.

Then time passes and we're all sitting in the living room. Nan's still dipping her finger in the pot of hummus. The clock reads half past four. Marcus'll be outside now, on the path, waiting. I stand up, brush the crumbs from my clothes and reach for my pink woollen coat, making my face as casual as possible.

Jade is first to notice. 'Where are you going, Mum?'

Femi looks across at me. 'You know you can't go outside, Georgie.'

I smile. 'I'm going to pop down to the ground floor for Jade's post. I won't be a minute.' My smile grows wider. 'I need the exercise.' They're staring. 'I really need to stretch my legs.'

Holly moves to get up. 'I'll come with you.'

I shake my head at her. 'I'll be seconds.' My voice is too high.

Before she can follow me, I grab my phone and I'm outside the door, in the hallway, breathing different air. I run down two flights of stairs, then I go outside into the fresh breeze. Relief seeps into my skin like new life.

Behind the building, I see the stationary van again. I guess it's the police watching the area around the flats, parked up on the top of the hill by the side of the road: a dark blue Transit. I look the other way and stroll towards the cliff path as if it's the most normal thing in the world. I know it'll take them a few minutes until they realise I'm gone, so I text Jade: *Popped out for a breath of fresh air on the beach. Back in two minutes.* That might buy me time to talk to Marcus.

My legs move freely down the steps. The breeze chills my cheeks, bites through my clothes. I breathe in deeply and can't believe how good it feels to be outside, to inhale fresh salty air. For the first time in ages I feel alive again.

Marcus is watching the clouds blow by, the sunshine melting orange light into the waves. His back is turned to me; he's wearing a dark jacket and jeans, his curls blown by the breeze. My heart begins flapping and I take a deep breath, then go up behind him, put my arms round him and lean my face against his back. He turns and a wide smile breaks across his face.

'Georgie.'

We hug and he kisses me. I feel warm in his arms. His brow creases with concern.

'Is everything all right?'

I look into the intense blue eyes. He seems to be able to read my thoughts.

'Can we take a stroll by the sea? I need to talk.'

'Of course.'

He takes my hand in his and our arms touch, side by side, as we walk. I breathe out, a big shuddering sigh, and realise I have no idea what to say or where to start. We're quiet for a while. It's wonderful to be with him, our feet on shingle, the sun sharp and bright, reflecting tangerine light onto the waves. Marcus' voice is low.

'Are you okay after what happened on the road? That man, Beddowes. Have they caught him?'

I swallow a hard lump of sadness in my throat.

'Is everything all right, Georgie?'

We find a low rock and sit down. He takes both my hands and I notice his troubled expression. I have no idea how to begin to explain, so I blurt out the first words in my head.

'How much did I tell you about Bonnie's husband, Adie?'

He squeezes my hand. 'He has money problems, debt, some dodgy friends.'

'It's become really serious. He's left the country. You know we have a guard, close protection. Beddowes has been to the flat; it's like he's playing with us, like we're bait: the police think it'll all blow up soon.'

'Georgie, this is crazy.' He brings my fingers to his lips, kisses them. 'Why is he after your sister?'

'Basically, since Adie's disappeared, Bonnie's his target. It's Beddowes' payback for Adie, to harm the person closest to him. That's his sort of warped morality. We're all sticking together to look after her.'

'That explains why he was following us.'

He closes his eyes and when he opens them, we're staring at each other, neither of us able to say a word.

Then I blurt it out before I know what I've said. The thought had been fizzing in my mind, troubling me for a while and, suddenly, it's out of my mouth.

'So, it's probably best if we don't see each other again.'

I hadn't planned to say it, but immediately it makes absolute sense.

He frowns, shakes his head. 'But—'

'Marcus, it's been so good being with you. I mean, in other circumstances, I . . .'

I stop. His eyes are wide. He looks stunned. But I know I'm doing the right thing, for both our sakes. It's clear that it's the right time to finish it now, to put our relationship behind me. I can't see any other way. Not with Beddowes following us at every step. I have to manage the situation by myself – Marcus is a distraction I can't deal with now, and he could be at risk if he's seen with me. He's already been at risk. Beddowes tried to attack us in the car after the picnic. I can't take chances with his safety.

He's still holding my hand. I gaze over his shoulder at the ocean. The water is indigo, dark inky depths. The sky is crammed with clouds; there's a scrap of creamy grey at the edge of the horizon, the line of buildings, Brighton in bright sunshine.

We're silent for a while, then he whispers my name. I lean forwards and we kiss. His lips are warm despite the cold. When I open my eyes, he looks sad. I pull my hands away from him and make them into tight balls.

'You're a lovely man, Marcus. I wish . . .' I'm surprised at the constriction in my throat, the way I can't say the words. Instantly, I take a breath, pull myself together. 'I wish you all the best, really I do.' I stand and he does the same. 'Thanks for being so great. I'm sorry. Truly I am. Right person, wrong time. That's how it is.'

'Georgie, this dilemma you're in will soon be over. You said so yourself. I'll wait.'

'I've put you in enough danger, Marcus. Beddowes tried to ram us and it's my entire fault. I put you at risk and I felt awful – that was stupid and selfish of me.'

He sighs and puts his arms around me. 'I'm not afraid. We can weather it out together. I'm here now.'

I swallow sadness and shake my head. 'Marcus, you have a son.' I shrug his arms from my shoulders. 'And you shouldn't be involved in this.' I take a step backwards; push my hands into my pockets. 'Take care of yourself.'

I turn and walk away. I don't look back, but something tells me he's watching me go. I head away from him, away from the cliff path, towards the village. I know I should go straight back to the flat, to Femi and Holly guarding the door, to Bonnie and Nan, but I can't, not yet.

Tears are blurring my eyes and I have to keep walking. I've no idea where to go, but my legs take me to the steps from the beach, across the road. On the pavement, I turn towards Djimi's Café. He'll offer me a smiling face, a kind word. I have loose change in my pocket; I can buy a coffee there. And I can buy myself time to recover.

Chapter Thirty

Djimi's Café is still open. It's half past five and the place is empty. I go in and the door shuts with a click. Djimi doesn't notice me – he has his back turned; he's busy with something. I sit at a table near the window, take out my phone and ring Jade.

'Mum, where are you? I'm still at your flat, waiting.'

'Are the police looking for me yet?'

'Femi is just about to send a search party. Are you all right?'

'Yes. No.' I breathe out. 'I'm fine. Jade, I'll be back soon. I need a bit of time for myself. Can you talk without being overheard?'

I swallow hard. This is the first time the pressure has affected me in this way. Too much has happened in such a short time. A tear slides down my cheek, another . . .

'I'm on the balcony. Has something happened, Mum?'

I gulp and force my voice to be level.

'I'm all right. It has nothing to do with Beddowes. I just need you to buy me a bit of time. Can you do that for me, love?'

'Only if you tell me what's going on.'

I smile at the speed of her response and the irony of the situation: our roles are reversed – now, she's the anxious one.

'Can I explain properly later?'

'You're worrying me.' Jade's voice is breathless at the other end of the phone. 'Are you sure it's not Beddowes?'

'No, it's . . . okay, it's a man, Jade. Someone I've met.'

'Not Djimi from the café?'

'No. Not him.'

She whispers, 'Was that what the menopause thing was all about?'

'Yes. Can I explain later? Can you find a way to let me have an hour? I mean, I don't like asking you to tell a lie but—'

'Okay, Mum. I understand. Hang on. I'll tell the others . . .' She raises her voice and I know it's for the benefit of everyone in the room. 'You were so lucky to get a special appointment this late in the day. I hope she can sort the menopause crisis out.'

I almost laugh. Jade's brilliant.

'When you've seen the doctor, come straight back here.'

'Thanks, love. I appreciate it.'

Her voice is loud. She's still acting.

'Okay, Mum. Thanks for letting us know. I expect it'll take you an hour or so. Make sure you take a taxi back, for safety. I'll speak to Femi. I mean, he'll understand that it was an emergency health thing. And you won't be long.'

I force a weak smile. She's strong, resilient, plucky: so much like I was at her age. I don't feel so resilient now.

'No, I won't be long, Jade. Thanks.'

I know she's smiling at the other end as she whispers, 'And you can tell me all about it when you're back, okay?' She raises her voice again. 'Oh, Femi wants a word.'

His gravelly voice is in my ear. 'I'm not happy about this, Georgie. Where exactly are you going?'

'Health Centre in town. Last minute appointment. Dr . . . Payne.'

I stifle a grin. In the middle of my sadness, I force a gritty smile at my choice of surname and hope that Femi doesn't check. Then guilt floods through me that I'm telling lies to such a good man. Before I can speak again, Jade is back on the line.

'All right. Femi says be as quick as you can. Bye for now, Mum.'

I put my phone in my pocket. The smile is still on my face, shining with love for my sharp-witted and loyal daughter. But inside I feel confused, anxious, troubled: a melting pot of emotions. I look up and see Djimi's brown eyes, his creased forehead. He's nervous.

'Hello, dreamer. I didn't expect to see you. I was just closing up.'

'Is there time for a coffee, Djimi?'

He studies my face for a moment. 'I suppose so. Of course. No problem.' He straightens, smiles at me. 'How's your charming sister? And your lovely aunt?'

'Fine, thanks.' I breathe out. My mind is too full for chit-chat.

Djimi seems to understand. 'I'll get you that coffee.'

My thoughts brim with worry. I stare at my hands. A few minutes ago, my fingers were linked in Marcus'. My mind shifts to Bonnie's bracelet, whether we could use it as a bargain with Beddowes. The note he left to Bonnie held a definite threat. But our problem is more than money. It's about Beddowes wanting to pay Adie back. Adie's gone – he's run away, leaving his wife and the rest of us to deal with the trouble he's caused. I'm momentarily furious: Adie's spineless, a coward.

The anger dissolves. I'm too sad, too hollowed out. I remember the warmth of the cinema, the curve of Marcus' lips, smiling at the film. I remember his home, how welcoming he was, how interesting and attentive. I recall the thrill of kissing him, our bodies close. Despite only having three dates with Marcus, he's become important to me. I tell myself it's because I'm flattered, I like the attention, but that's not true. It's more than that.

Marcus is different: it's an old cliché, I know, but I've started to care. I told myself it was just lust. Perhaps it was, at first, but it could've been something special. Tears come again, frustration and disappointment, but I refuse to allow them to take over. I fight back, swallow hard and clench my fists. I can do this – I can sort out all the problems we have surrounding us here and then we can go home. Perhaps I'll even have time to say goodbye properly to Marcus. Femi and his friends will catch Beddowes soon and it'll be over by Easter. I'll have my old life, my routine, my business, and I'll move forwards: Liverpool is hours away from Sussex. I'm an independent woman who can manage by herself. I tell myself I'll be fine; I'll go back home and forget about Marcus Hart.

The door opens and closes; I'm aware of it vaguely but I'm buried in my thoughts. If there was a way I could hold on to Marcus, I probably would, but I need to be tough now – I can't allow myself these weak thoughts. I picture his face, the intelligent eyes, the corkscrew curl of his hair, and I smile. Someone sits down heavily opposite me and a strongly accented voice whips me back to reality.

'Penny for them, Georgie.'

I meet a pair of ice-blue eyes, orange lashes, a hard craggy face, and catch my breath. Beddowes turns, stares towards a movement over his shoulder.

'Just disappear for a moment, Djimi. I have some business to tend to.'

Djimi's poised with my mug of coffee in his hand. His face is strained and his eyes bulging.

'Yes, Mr Beddowes,' he says, his voice toneless, and he puts the coffee on the counter and scuttles towards the café kitchen.

'You know Djimi?' My mouth suddenly has a bad taste in it. I meet Beddowes' glare.

'We were here with your aunt Anne recently. Delightful lady. She has a sweet tooth. Good company, though, and very accommodating with information.' I don't look away. 'I hope she's done the sensible thing and used the rail ticket I gave her. I'd hate for anything to happen to such a nice woman. And at her age, too.'

I say the only thing I can to keep Nanny safe. 'She's gone back to Liverpool.'

'Good, good. So that just leaves you and the delightful Mrs Carrick in the luxury flat at Cliff Top.'

I glower at him. 'And local cops and the Met.'

'They haven't found me yet and they won't.'

My hands shake. I clasp them hard under the table.

'It's not just Bonnie you're after, is it? You want something else.'

'Indeed I do. I believe you know what it is. Do you have the bracelet here, Georgie? Can you give it to me?' His eyes narrow.

My mind is racing and suddenly I'm blabbing without thinking. 'That's what it's about, isn't it? The charms are clues. They show where the money is.'

He smiles, his lips a tight line. 'You're a bright one, aren't you? So you'd better let me have it before anyone else in your family gets their little fingers on it.'

'So why did Adie give it to Bonnie?' I need answers. 'Couldn't he remember the clues himself?'

'It was supposed to come to me.'

I'm curious. 'So what happened?'

Beddowes leans forwards. I can see the pockmarks in his skin.

'We were about to pull off something big together, Adie and I. I didn't know him, but he was recommended to me as a useful partner in a one-off deal. He'd done a few minor things in the past, flip a few houses illegally, move some money, but nothing as huge as I offered him. He was very keen, of course. This one was a big deal that would make us both a tidy sum. I put a lot of money in and I expected him to do the same. But Adie lost his deposit, when one of his contacts was arrested in Liverpool; he was unable to come up with his portion of the investment, so he borrowed it from me.

'The deal came good: we made a tidy profit. The money was put in a safe place in London and, of course, because the initial outlay was mine, I expected the lion's share.' His eyes narrow. 'But Adie was broke and he thought he'd try to pocket it all. The bracelet was sent from a third party in London, to tell me where the money had been placed, but Adie thought he was being clever, meeting the contact first and intercepting it. I saw that he'd put the bracelet round his wife's wrist for safekeeping. He thought he could use the clues and steal my money. But he underestimated me. So, yes, I need the bracelet. Can you give it to me?'

'If I do, will you go away and leave us alone?'

I'm trying to strike a bargain, but even as I speak, I realise how futile it is. I'm clutching at straws.

He chuckles and it's the most heart-stopping sound I've ever heard. He shows me a cruel, hard face, narrowed eyes, and I realise instantly that he's capable of murder.

'I can't do that. Adie owes me and someone has to pay for what he's done.'

'Adie's gone.'

He glares at me. 'And so Bonnie takes his place. You, too, perhaps. But if you give me the bracelet I'll let your daughter go. And her boyfriend. They aren't important. But I want the bracelet.'

'How can I trust you?'

He smiles. 'Do you have any other choice?'

I squeeze my eyes closed at the mention of Jade. I have to make sure she's safe. My thoughts race. Perhaps she and Luis could find somewhere other than the flat upstairs to stay for a while. My mouth is spurting words before I've had time to think it all out.

'I haven't got it. But I've solved the clues, Mr Beddowes. I know where the place is, where the money is. I can tell you.' I'm babbling. My heart's pounding so hard the blood is singing in my ears.

'Where?'

My thoughts gallop. 'London, but you know that. The first clue is a teddy bear, the second a train. Paddington station. The next is a number, four. Then a bridge. Number four, Bridge Road.'

I'm making it up; my mouth and my mind are running a race to keep up with each other. It takes all of my self-control to breathe.

He leans forwards. 'Are you sure that's correct?'

I nod. My voice has become strangled in my throat. Beddowes watches me and I try to glower back, but I'm staring into the face of a killer.

'I want that bracelet, Georgie. I want to see it for myself. Bring it here for me. I'll give you until tomorrow – eleven o'clock. That should be enough time.'

I glance around for Djimi. He's probably still hiding in the kitchen. I don't know what to say, but it occurs to me that Beddowes probably won't kill me now, not here in the café. I breathe in deeply.

283

'If I bring the bracelet tomorrow, how will you know when I'm here?'

He laughs. 'How do you think I knew you were here now?'

I shake my head. I'm not sure. Perhaps Beddowes was watching the flats and followed me. After all, he knows the address. But the blue Transit was parked nearby, full of surveillance officers. And then I realise with sadness that Djimi must have phoned him. Beddowes obviously frightens Djimi and has an influence over him. I look into his eyes, force myself to drill my gaze into his, like animals squaring up. He murmurs 'How do you think I knew where you and your boyfriend were the other day? I keep tabs on what's happening everywhere. And I need to get my hands on that bracelet. It would be very stupid to refuse me.'

'I'll bring it. But I want a guarantee that you'll leave us all alone, that you'll go away and stay out of our lives.'

'You have my word.'

His smirk makes me shiver. 'I want more than that.' My mind is in turmoil. 'I won't give you the bracelet unless you can convince me you won't harm any of us.'

He pitches forwards and grabs my wrist, leans across the table and puts his face next to mine. His breath is bitter, a mixture of coffee and cigarettes. I can see his pitted skin, the lines round his mouth, the discoloured teeth. His grip on my wrist is too tight. His voice is an acid whisper.

'I won't be messed with, Georgie.' There's spittle on his lips. 'I promise you this. Unless I get the bracelet, your sister's days are numbered. She won't see the other side of the weekend. And then there's you . . . I haven't made my mind up what I'll do to you . . . and Jade . . .'

I glower at him. 'You dare touch my daughter!'

His grip is steel but I won't flinch. He holds my stare. 'You'll do as you're told . . .'

Something in my spirit – fast-pumping adrenalin, boiling anger railing against the crippling injustice, the desire to survive now I'm faced with the threat of a towering bully – flares inside me and words I can't control fly out of my mouth.

'I'm not scared of you, Beddowes.'

He wrenches my wrist and I let out a yelp. The seconds stand still, then his voice is low, grating.

'Get me the bracelet. Your sister's dead already, but I promise you . . .'

The door clicks open behind Beddowes and my eyes widen. Marcus is standing in the doorway, his face serious with concern.

'Georgie?'

Beddowes lets go of my wrist and whirls round. His shoulders are mountains in front of me. He stares at Marcus. Then his chair scrapes and he stands, lurches towards the door. I wonder if he'll hit Marcus, or if he has a gun. Marcus doesn't move. Beddowes whirls back to me.

'I'll see you here tomorrow, eleven o'clock.'

His eyes move to where Marcus is standing. He pauses, snorts and tugs open the door. Then he's gone.

Marcus is next to me and I stand. His arms are around me, his voice soft in my ear.

'Are you all right?'

I nod in answer, pull back, gaze up into his face and then we hug again. He holds me tight and I whisper, 'Can we go?'

Marcus takes my hand. As we move towards the door, Djimi's behind us.

'Georgie, I'm sorry.'

I look at him, curl my lip. 'Why didn't you ring the police, Djimi?'

He rubs a hand over his smooth head: he can't meet my eyes.

'He was in here the other day. He had your aunt outside in his car. He threatened my business, he threatened my family. There was nothing I could do.'

Marcus' face is concerned. 'I'll walk you back to the flat, Georgie. The police need to know.'

We're outside in the darkness. I gaze up and down the street and wonder if Beddowes is in his Jaguar, watching us. I lean closer to Marcus.

'Would you mind if we went to your house? Just for a few minutes, a coffee or something. I need to . . . I need to get my thoughts together.'

His grip on my shoulder is warm, comforting.

He glances over his shoulder. He's checking for Beddowes: the street is empty. 'Of course. There's a short cut from here, a path behind the houses. We won't be followed.'

We walk in step together, turning the corner into a biting wind, and I realise my whole body is trembling.

Chapter Thirty-One

Once inside Marcus' house, I close the front door and it's as if all the tension is locked outside. I'm suddenly warm and safe. I hadn't thought how I'd react but relief floods through me like electricity. I fall into his arms and we share mouthfuls of kisses. The memory of our conversation earlier flits through my mind: our relationship is supposed to be over and I don't know whether to pull him closer or push him away, so I kiss him some more. Then I surface for breath and his eyes meet mine.

'What went on before I came? He was intimidating you, Georgie. I could sense the atmosphere as soon as I came into the café.'

'How did you know I was there?'

He runs a hand through his curls. 'When you left me on the beach, I was bewildered. I wasn't completely sure what had happened between us. I mean, you said it was over between us, but I thought you were upset. And I was worried about you.' His eyes gleam steadily. 'I couldn't leave you like that. I saw you wander towards the village and cross the road so I followed you. I lost sight of you at the point where you turned into the street that led to

287

the café but I kept following. Then I looked in the window and saw you with the big man in the overcoat, and he seemed to be harassing you, so I came in.'

I inspect my wrist and breathe out. The bone is achingly sore. I'm suddenly tired.

'I have to go back, Marcus. I can't stay long.' I push my hair out of my eyes and feel my heart thudding in my chest. The mess with Beddowes is mine to sort out and I have to keep Marcus separate and safe. 'It's better if we don't . . . I'm still in shock.'

He reaches out, touches my shoulder. 'I understand. Shall I run you a bath? It'll give you time to relax, and then I'll make you something to drink. Can you stay for half an hour?'

I remember my phone call to Jade. Back at the flat, everyone thinks I'm at an appointment with a doctor. I have time. I nod. 'That would be lovely.'

I'm lying in lavender-scented water gazing up at black beams five minutes later, tiny white lights like stars set into the ceiling. It's a beautiful bathroom: wooden floors, gold taps, a white wicker chair and the stand-alone antique bath I'm luxuriating in. There's a candle in a jar flickering in the window, a strong smell of jasmine or musk, and two white fluffy towels hang on a wooden rail. A white bathrobe hangs behind the door; there are a few items in a wicker rack: shampoo, conditioner, a soap scented with olives and a small bottle of aftershave. I close my eyes, inhale the sweet scent and relax. My body is warm; I breathe out and a sense of calm washes over me. I feel my muscles loosen and tension seems to seep away into the water.

My thoughts drift to Marcus. I imagine him quietly pushing the door open and coming in, slipping off his shirt and jeans and slithering into the soapy water opposite me.

For a moment, I'm thinking about his body. Naked, he would be lithe and muscular: in my mind, I'm running my fingers over the slant of his collarbone, touching the rough tangle of his chest hair.

I open my eyes, smile briefly and push the thoughts away. No more soft thoughts; no more investing in the relationship and definitely no more kissing. Marcus and I are in the past. It certainly isn't possible in the present and I can't plan for the future.

I need to concentrate on Beddowes. I told him about the bracelet, faked an interpretation of the charms. I lied. I worry that I've put Jade even more at risk. I need to focus my mind, to decide what to do. A thought seizes my heart with an iron grip. What if Beddowes followed us here? What if he's downstairs? What if Marcus is being held at gunpoint, or worse? I tell myself to breathe, to be calm, to control my imagination.

I stand up and arc a leg out of the bath, covering the wooden floor with a splatter of bathwater, then reach for a soft towel. It envelops me completely. I pull the plug, grab my clothes from the floor and pad onto the landing.

His bedroom door is open and I go in. I've no idea why I'm snooping in his room. It's a beautiful space: dark wooden floors, a pale rug. The bed is made of metal, covered with a heavy white duvet cover and plump pillows. The ceiling has two black beams and there's an open fireplace, an oak wardrobe, drawers. By the side of his bed are several books, a spectacle case and three photos.

I pick up the first one. It's a dark-haired young man, about eighteen years old. It's not Marcus. He has straight hair, a long fringe, hazel eyes, a tentative smile; his mouth is almost too wide for his face. It must be his son, Zach. The second picture is smaller and older, in a black frame. A grey-haired man, bearded, with brown eyes crinkled at the corners and bushy brows, and a woman with shoulder-length curly hair and a pale dress smile into the camera. Between them is a boy, probably just a teenager, with the same intense eyes and dark curls as the woman. It's Marcus: I recognise the grin. Both father and son wear yarmulkes and the family stand close together.

I pick up the third photo of a young woman. She has one of those mysterious half-smiles, like the *Mona Lisa*. Cascading black hair; the sort of deep-set eyes that make a face look intelligent and beautiful at the same time. It could be Marcus' first wife, Leah, the one he said was remarkable. Or Chloe, Zach's mother, who left her son with Marcus and walked away. It's hard to tell how old the picture is, but it's not as modern as the photo of Zach. I wonder why he keeps it next to his bed and if he's still in love with her.

There are two other rooms. One is probably Zach's bedroom, a double bed, a brightly coloured duvet cover; there are several violins, a guitar and a cello, cream painted brick walls, posters of rock bands. The other room has a hush, a stillness about it, which draws me in. There's an upright piano, quite old, stain marks on the brown polish, sheet music, slightly yellow. Beethoven's *Moonlight Sonata*. There are wall-to-wall bookshelves, more books, a small desk. I go into the room, lift the lid on the piano and press some of the yellowing keys. The sound is a soft, tentative tinkling.

I can hear music downstairs. It's a CD of classical music, rousing piano-playing, dramatic chords. I discard the damp towel in the bathroom, pull on my clothes, carry my shoes and patter downstairs. A fire glows in the hearth and Marcus is by the cooker. I move a safe distance away.

'Lovely music. What is it?'

'Rachmaninov. Piano Concerto.'

'I'm more of an Aerosmith girl myself.' I play-punch his arm, determined to create a light mood.

He grins. 'I like both.'

He puts a bowl of soup into my hands, thick liquid, and we sit in front of the blazing fire. I'm not hungry. I push my bare feet towards the flames and wriggle my toes. I swallow two comforting mouthfuls of soup and he watches me carefully.

'Do you play the piano?'

He shakes his curls. 'I dabble a bit, for fun. I'm not very good.'

I recall the rooms upstairs, the piano in the spare bedroom, the stillness and serenity in the house, and I'm pulled back to my own home in Albert Drive, the modern decor, the rooms always full of bustle and laughter.

'We're so different. Our lives are poles apart. I've no idea why you like me, Marcus.'

He moves closer to me on the sofa. 'Does it matter? I mean, if we like each other, difference isn't important. What's important is empathy, understanding, sharing together. Difference can be a beautiful thing.'

'But I'm a Liverpool girl with wild habits and a tendency to find herself in trouble. And you're sophisticated and intelligent and nice.'

That grin again. 'You're sophisticated and intelligent and nice.'

I rub my face against him like a friendly cat, just for one second. The stubble prickles my cheek and I laugh.

'So, why do you like me?'

'Because you're lovely. You're funny and witty and smart and great to be with. I've never met anyone like you before. You're a breath of fresh air. You make me happy.' He shrugs. 'And I know it's the wrong time and the wrong place to say this, and I don't want to mess with your mind

291

when you have so many other things crowding your life, but I've started to care about you.'

He offers me his hand. I take it and examine the snake tattoo on his wrist.

'What's this?'

His eyes glow as they meet mine. 'It's a letter S for Sarah.'

I run my finger over the embellished S. I can see it's not a snake now.

He shrugs. 'She was the better part of me.'

I'm about to ask him about her; she was clearly important, an ex-girlfriend, when he puts his arms round me, kisses the top of my head. A moment of sadness passes between us and hangs on the air. I stare at him for a moment. Then I move away, filled with the feeling of foreboding, the dragging sensation of a storm approaching, that the thunder and lightning and wrath of Duncan Beddowes is on the horizon. It suffocates me and I feel sad.

'I'm sorry – I need to go soon.'

'I hope I've helped a bit. Did the bath make you feel better?'

I nod. 'A lot. It was lovely. Thanks.' I balance the bowl on my knee. The soup is cool now. 'But I should head back. I need to give the police an update. Beddowes could be watching all the time. And I've told him a lie. He's looking for Adie's money and I told him the wrong place. Of course, he doesn't trust me. He's given me until eleven tomorrow to get the bracelet to him, the one with the charms, which are clues about the money. I don't know what to do. He's threatened Jade.'

He frowns for a moment, puzzling out what I've said and filling in the details he doesn't know using the information I've given him. His voice is low.

'May I walk back with you to Cliff Top?'

I nod, hearing my voice rise. The panic is still very much with me.

'The police'll have to sort it. Time's running out.' I meet his eyes. 'He's threatened to kill Bonnie – me, too. We have two close protection officers at the flat. They're both really good. Jade's flat is being watched, too. It's all such a mess.'

He frowns. 'You must be terrified, Georgie. I have no idea how difficult this must be.'

I chew my lip. 'What if I've led him to your house, Marcus? What if he followed me back here?'

'Let's get you back to your flat. The sooner the police arrest Beddowes, the better.'

'Beddowes believes the best way to cancel out Adie's debt is to harm his wife. Some sense of equality, a sort of payback. Plus, Bonnie's an easy target. She's sweet-natured and easily scared, and Beddowes is the kind of perverted person who gets a kick out of frightening people. I stood up to him at Djimi's Café. That's why he was trying to intimidate me.'

Marcus pulls himself from the sofa and holds out my coat.

'Come on. We should head back. You need to talk to the police. They can keep you safe. I can't, not here.'

He takes my hand and I leave it in his, for now. We head back along the beach towards Cliff Top, avoiding the police Transit. I text Jade that I'm on my way. We walk quietly, both thinking, listening to the soft tread of our footsteps on the shingle. My hand is warm in his and, occasionally, he squeezes my fingers gently. I consider asking him about Sarah, about the tattoo on his wrist and if she's the girl in the photograph by his bed, the one with the mysterious smile. But it's easier to stay quiet, both of us lost in separate thoughts. I shiver. The desperate desire to go home tugs at me. I long to be back in my own city, in my own house, in my old life. I don't belong here in Sussex and I am ready to leave.

Soon, we're standing together at the bottom of the cliff, staring out at the twinkling lights on the curve of the coastline, the murmuring ocean filling our ears. It whispers a warning. The sea is dull grey, the surface ruffled into waves, wrinkled by a stiff breeze, masking the unhidden depths below. I glance at Marcus and wonder if it'll be the last time I see him. He pulls me to him, reading my thoughts.

'I understand now why you wanted our relationship to be on hold. I respect that. I don't want to lose you though, Georgie.'

His words echo in my ears and I close my eyes. I can't think about him, not at the moment.

'Perhaps we can talk about us when this business is over.'

'Thanks for understanding.' I reach up on tiptoes, hug him for the last time and force a laugh, too loud. 'When you met me in the supermarket at the muesli shelf, you didn't know that you'd find yourself in this ridiculous situation . . .'

My attempt at a joke falls flat. He takes both of my hands and his face is contorted with concern.

'Eleven o'clock? Is that what he said?'

The icy wind makes me shiver. I pull away.

'Something'll happen by then, I guess.'

'I know you can't focus on us, Georgie. Not at the moment. But could I ask . . .'

'Marcus?'

'Will you text me tomorrow? I mean every few hours during the day, whenever you can. So I know you're all right.'

A sudden gust takes his curls and blows them around his head. I glance up at the Cliff Top flats, three floors, nine dwellings. Lights are on in a few windows, a television flickering. People living their lives; ordinary people oblivious of the terror that lurks somewhere for Bonnie and me.

'Yes, of course I'll text you.'

'I'll come here from time to time, when I'm out for a jog – I'll look up at your window. I know you're on the second floor.'

'Yes, but don't come up to the flat. The police are guarding the door.' I make my voice hopeful, to convince us both. 'We're in good hands.'

'Promise you'll text me, let me know you're all right. And I'll reply. We'll keep in touch. I need to know nothing's happened . . .'

'I promise.' I force a smile, turn and start to walk away as quickly as I can.

'Georgie?'

I look back. He's silhouetted against the pale gloom of the horizon. Behind him the water is as smooth as oil, dark as ink. He extends his arms.

'I'll see you really soon. Then we can talk. We can make up for lost time.'

I shrug. 'I'll go up to the flats by myself. The police have a surveillance van on the clifftop, just around the corner. You'd better go, Marcus. Someone might be watching the beach . . .'

Imagining Beddowes' eyes on us, or the police inspecting our every move through binoculars, I turn my back, walk up the steps to the top of the cliff, pressing the keypad to let me into the flats, making myself focus forwards, away from Marcus. He's a nice man. I might never see him again, but I can't let those thoughts seep back into my head, not now.

As my feet pound on the stairs up to the second floor, I wonder what's going to happen next. I can't imagine what's coming – I have until eleven o'clock tomorrow. But I won't meet Beddowes. Then what? It's inconceivable. A thought repeats itself in my head: this thing is unavoidable and there's nothing I can do now but face it head-on. Yes, I'm afraid. Terrified. But I promise . . .

Suddenly, I'm speaking aloud, my voice strong, the words echoing like a chant, a mantra, bouncing off the glossy white walls. I hope he's listening somewhere. I hope he can hear me. I shout as loud as my voice will let me: 'I promise you, Beddowes – whatever happens tomorrow, I won't let you hurt my family.'

Chapter Thirty-Two

I knock on the door of Roque's flat and a different officer lets me in. He's tall, in his thirties, with thin fair hair, pale-skinned, as if he never goes outside. He introduces himself as Tim Bartlett and tells me he's a senior officer; he's here to discuss an update on Beddowes with Femi.

I remember my excuse and wait for Tim or Femi to admonish me, to tell me I shouldn't have been to the doctors, but they just smile politely and carry on talking with Holly, their heads close together. Nanny rushes to meet me, as fast as she can move with her sore hip, which she reminds me has been playing her up something wicked. She asks me how the visit to the GP went and hugs me. Jade and Luis have gone back upstairs to their flat.

Bonnie hurls her arms round me and we all clutch each other in a scrum. It feels so good to be held by them both, their bodies warm and alive, that tears fill my eyes.

I murmur, 'I saw Beddowes.'

We put our heads together, three conspirators, and whisper to each other.

'I thought you'd been to the doctor?' Bonnie's eyes are wide with fear.

'I saw Beddowes afterwards.' I say the lie quickly and hope it's not too large a fib.

Nan sits me on the sofa, pulls herself next to me and leans against me like one of those oversized soppy dogs. Bonnie presses a cup of tea into my hands. She's made it herself. It's lukewarm, but the cup gleams in my grasp and I'm smiling. Nanny grabs my spare palm and rubs it between her fingers.

'So, what happened?'

Bonnie bumps up on the other side of me, almost spilling the tea, and rests her head on my shoulder. 'We need to tell Femi. We have to let the police know everything.'

I close my eyes and remember Beddowes' face inches from mine, the spittle, the bitter stench of his breath in my face.

'He threatened me.'

Femi's watching, listening. He and Tim move towards me and he says, 'Where did you see Beddowes?'

'At Djimi's Café. After I got back from the doctor. I'm sorry. I know I should've rushed back . . .'

Holly's on her radio.

'I'll send an officer to the café. Maybe Djimi will be able to tell us something useful.'

Nan's eyes are shining behind her glasses. 'Is he a friend of Beddowes? The rat.'

'I think Beddowes has bullied him. He went in there when you were in his car, Nan – remember?'

I shrug and my mind is filled with the image of Marcus. I wonder if he's still outside or if he's taken himself home, back to the lovely warm cottage. I'll text him soon, as I promised I would. I sigh. Femi touches my arm.

'So, tell me about your brush with Beddowes, Georgie.'

'He was obnoxious. He said he'd harm Jade. Femi, we need that man arrested.'

'You shouldn't have been out there,' he says.

I shrug. He pats my shoulder.

Tim says, 'We're on to him. We're close.'

'He threatened me.'

Bonnie grabs my hand. Holly's on her radio still. Femi's looking out of the window, guarding the door, chatting to Tim, who's just leaving. Bonnie's voice is low.

'The bracelet – we just worked it all out, Nan and I. We know where Adie's money is.'

'I told Beddowes it was in Paddington station. He said he wanted to see it himself and that I had to bring him the bracelet by tomorrow. But if I did go, what then?'

I glance at the police officers, who are deep in conversation. Femi's eyes flick to me and I wonder if he is suspicious. I put my finger to my lips. Bonnie whispers, 'Don't go near Beddowes – he can't be trusted not to hurt you. While you were both gone, Nan and I looked at a street map and searched for the clues on the bracelet. We've solved it. The clues make total sense now. Money, crown, crucifix: it's at King's Cross. King Harold, box shape: Hastings Square. Flower, ladder: there's a flat above Poppy's flower shop. I googled it. It's real. The five numbers are separate, in sequence, like a safe combination.'

'Beddowes told me what happened.' I lean close to Bonnie. 'Adie kept the bracelet so that he could steal Beddowes' money. He's furious. He can't get his hands on the cash without it.'

Nan whispers, too loud. 'Should we tell Femi?'

'The police'll want the bracelet if we tell them.'

'Oh no.' Bonnie's horrified. 'I won't part with it.'

'Then we won't tell them yet. Maybe not at all – unless we really have to.'

Femi glances over from the doorway, raises an eyebrow.

'Tell Femi what?'

I don't even pause for breath.

'We've just voted you the sexiest police officer we've ever met.'

Femi chuckles. 'I'll gladly take that.'

Tim makes a mock-disappointed face, then the two men laugh together. I wink at Bonnie and Nan. Tim says goodbye and the door is secured. Holly takes up her position on a chair, winks and opens her book. I smile as brightly as I can.

'Femi, what's the news on Beddowes from Tim?'

He grins. 'Today is the day, everyone thinks so. There'll be a swoop on several places. One of his henchmen has been spotted near Paddington station within the last hour.'

My heart skips. I sit up. 'So, we'll be home for Easter?'

He nods. 'Hopefully.'

His radio rattles and he mutters a quick reply.

Suddenly, I'm excited. My thoughts turn to Liverpool: vivid images of home illuminate my mind. I can't wait to go back, see how the business is doing, chat to Amanda and sleep in my own bed. My thoughts drift back to Marcus and if I'll see him again.

Femi's talking, animated. ' . . . they've arrested Djimi Bâ from the café. He has information about Beddowes.'

'What a pig.' Nan's furious.

I frown. 'No, he was threatened, forced to help him. I felt sorry for him. He was scared of Beddowes.'

Nan hugs me on one side and Bonnie on the other.

Nan says, 'I hope they get Beddowes and lock him up, throw away the key.'

'You've been so brave, Georgie.' Bonnie links her arm through mine.

'I didn't feel brave at the time.' I'm tearful for a moment. 'The man's deranged.'

300

I notice my hand shaking and it occurs to me that I have to be strong, for Bonnie's sake. I'm worried about my daughter, recalling Beddowes mentioning her name, the hatred like acid in his mouth. I know the police are looking after her. But that doesn't seem to be enough. Tears prick my eyes.

'I'll be all right soon.'

Nan and Bonnie are staring at me. I glance at the clock, then at Femi.

'Can I go and see Jade?'

His voice is hushed. 'So, today's the seventeenth. She and Luis are out; he's training with the football club until late, then tomorrow he's training and afterwards, he has a charity event. We have an undercover officer with them now. I'll make sure you have the chance to meet up with her, although it won't be until the day after tomorrow. There'll be a police presence with them both at all times. Try not to worry.'

I'm impressed with how well Femi knows my daughter's schedule and secretly glad Jade will be away tomorrow. At least the police will take care of her. I struggle to my feet.

'It's past eight. Shall I make us a cup of tea? Have you all eaten? I can't sit here all evening with nothing to do.'

Holly glances up from her book. 'I'll give you a hand.'

Nan joins us. 'Any of those big courgettes? I like them fried in garlic.'

Holly's eyes are bright. 'Do you like courgette spaghetti?'

'What's that like? Is it like bolognese?'

Bonnie pipes up, 'I'd do them spiralised in fresh lemon juice, black pepper and a little sea salt.'

I'm leaning on the counter, pulling out ingredients. 'We don't have much fresh stuff.'

'I'll radio some provisions in,' Holly suggests. 'And ask

301

for a spiraliser. Then we can spiralise carrots, even potatoes.'

Nan laughs. 'We can turn the courgettes into wiggles?
Whatever for?'

'So we can eat something a bit more interesting and
nutritious than the same old toasted sandwiches.' I sound
just like Jade.

Bonnie's voice comes from the sofa, where she's stretched
out her legs.

'Spiralised potatoes might make great baked chips, too.'

Just over an hour later we're all munching spaghetti made
from spiralised courgettes. Nan's had a whale of a time
with the orange plastic spiraliser with its inserted metal
cutter. She waves it round at the dinner table, her eyes
shining. It's her new favourite toy.

'It's like a giant pencil sharpener, Georgina.'

Then we sit in silence, drink tea and watch the second
hand of the wall clock jump then jump again. It's quarter
to twelve and I count the hours until my time is up with
Beddowes. I have eleven hours, just a little more. Perhaps
I should just take the bracelet, meet him and hand it over.
But my gut instinct tells me he'd still kill me. Then he'd
go after Bonnie. At least he believes Nan's gone back home
to Liverpool with his first-class train ticket in her hand.

I text Marcus, three simple words: *All fine here.*

He replies straight away that he's thinking of me. My
heartbeat quickens but it's not excitement: it's pure fear.

We wake at eight and my heart plummets like a sinking
stone. Today is the day it'll end, one way or another. We
mope about the flat, tired, moving slowly. Femi and Holly
are more watchful than ever. No one speaks. Tension is
as taut as wire. I text Jade three times. She tells me Luis

is training then signing shirts at a children's hospital. She promises me that there are plain-clothes officers with them, but I know her well and I can sense the fear in her words.

The clock ticks slowly. We play cards, watch television and pretend to read books. I stare at the clock at a quarter to ten and my heart's in my mouth. Bonnie's eyes are saucer-huge. Nan looks tired. I text Marcus that all is fine. He replies that he's been jogging outside, on the beach, looking up at the cliffs. Now, he's at home working, writing an article. He misses me. He hopes he'll see me soon.

By ten o'clock, I need to sit down: my legs are like jelly and I can hardly move. My heart thuds in my throat. It's as if we're on death row, waiting. By eleven, I'm convinced Beddowes will throw open the door at any moment. The seconds drag and I can't take my eyes from the clock.

To keep myself busy, I text Marcus, telling him again that nothing has happened yet. He replies that he's at his desk, trying to write something witty about an American president, but I'm in his thoughts all the time. I send him a ridiculous gif of a politician gurning and he replies with another. I text that I'd love to be on the beach instead of cooped up in here and he sends me a beautiful photo of the Sussex coast-line at sunset and the words: *soon, you and I could be here together*. I reply *that would be nice*, add a smiley face. We're behaving like teenagers and I know it's because we are trying our best to relieve the cord-tight tension.

Time continues to tick after eleven o'clock comes round. I watch, terrified, as the second hand moves from one number to the next. Then it's noon, and to take my mind away from the fact that Beddowes might burst in at any moment, that he's an hour overdue, I show Nan how to use the spiraliser again. She howls with laughter, tears in her eyes as she shreds courgettes through the orange plastic-and-metal device, pushing the vegetables in at one

303

end and watching the green and white flesh wriggle out at the other.

Time plods slowly through the afternoon. My eyes ache from watching the second hand move, tick-tock. It seems to be slowing. There's no sign of Beddowes. Femi and Holly have their heads together, whispering. Holly radios her boss frequently and I hear Beddowes' name mentioned, but there's no word on his arrest.

I phone Jade, who tells me she won't be home until midnight. We'll catch up first thing tomorrow. I text Marcus again. I can sense the relief in his replies. He writes positive messages: he hopes Beddowes has disappeared, that it was just an empty threat, that he's backed down, changed his mind, been arrested. I'm more cynical, but I'm glad of the contact with Marcus, with the outside world. My thoughts are stifled inside the four walls of the flat: I can hardly breathe. I'm still waiting.

In the evening, we eat a quiche with spiralised courgettes, carrots and beetroot. I'm not hungry, just exhausted. The clock continues to tick inside my head, even when I'm not watching it. I wash the dishes and the muscles in my legs ache. My wrist has started to hurt, a pulse thudding below the skin: although it's only lightly bruised, it's a constant reminder of Beddowes' grip on me, the heavy weight of his hold on us all.

By nine o'clock, I'm tired out, resigned, ready for bed. If Beddowes comes, he can kill me while I sleep. I'm not waiting any more. I breathe out.

'Does anyone mind if I turn in? I'm shattered.'

I slope off to the bedroom and pull off my clothes. I'd love a bath, but the idea of being caught at gunpoint when I'm naked in the water scares me and I quickly forget the welcoming thought of relaxing in warm steam. I'll bath tomorrow. If I'm still alive . . .

I slip on pyjamas. In bed, my feet and toes are cold, so I tuck them beneath me and close my eyes. The sheet is like smooth ice, the bed is roomy, too big, and I roll over and clutch a pillow, pulling it to my body. I imagine Marcus is with me, feeling the contact of a warm human body, of safety and heat, the touch, the scent of bare skin. I feel guilty when I realise that I'm smiling.

'Georgie?'

Bonnie's standing by the bed in her nightie and I shake myself awake.

'Bon?'

'Do you want to move over?'

I pull myself and the pillow from the middle of the bed to the edge. She curls in next to me. I close my eyes and start to drift.

'Georgie?' I open one eye. Her face is inches from mine. 'Can I have a cuddle?'

I ease myself over and slide my right arm under her neck. She rolls onto my shoulder and I can feel the warmth of her breath against my face. She's quiet, but I know she's thinking.

'You know, I miss Adie most at night. When I'm on my own. I just miss being with – you know – somebody.'

I grunt. 'I know what you mean.'

'It was awful what happened to you, Georgie. Beddowes scares me.'

'I'm here now. It'll be all right, Bon.'

'I miss Demi. I spoke to her on the phone today, but I had to pretend everything was normal. It only made her feel so far away.'

I say nothing. I'd love to talk to Jade. It must be so much worse, Bonnie's daughter being in another country. She makes a little noise, like a mewing kitten.

'Do you think Beddowes will come tonight?'

'If he does, it'll be fine, Bonnie. Femi and Holly will sort him out . . .'

Bonnie breathes out and I close my eyes. Sleep settles across my body like a warm blanket and I sink into relaxation. For a moment, I'm locked in the warmth of Marcus' arms. Our limbs are entangled, skin against skin. He kisses my lips, murmurs into my ear. 'Georgie . . .' I ought to let these thoughts go, but I'm peaceful now, drifting off. I sigh. Then his voice again, higher, more persistent. 'Georgina?' It's not him. It's someone else.

I drag myself from the hammock of sleep.

'Georgina.'

'Nan?'

I blink and she's there in the darkness, in her blue winceyette nightie, the woollen hat over her head. I can see the silver white outline of her hair, the dark shadow of a vibrant streak of blue.

'Nanny?'

'I can't stand here in the cold all bloody night. Will you let me in?'

I budge over and she slides in next to me, flopping across my painful wrist.

'I'm not sleeping by myself, Georgina. Not with that man Beddowes out there. I can't stand the idea of him coming into my room with his machete out and there's me all tucked up in bed by myself.'

I hug her and she rolls close. My arm is already starting to go numb.

'Go to sleep, Nan.'

She mumbles in my ear, her voice too loud.

'If he's going to kill us, he may as well shoot the bloody lot of us together while we're all asleep in the same bed.'

Her logic confuses me. I breathe out, push the thought away and drift into slumber.

Chapter Thirty-Three

I sleep deeply for a long time, like I'm in the grave, then I wake. Bonnie's snuffling to my right. Nan's to my left: she's managed to occupy half of the bed. Her legs are spreadeagled across my hips and her arm rests on my face, squashing the length of my nose. She's rattling like a chainsaw, her snores far too loud for such a tiny bird-like woman. I wriggle, a determined shimmy, until I roll over towards Bonnie. She mumbles something in her sleep and waves an elbow, which connects with my cheekbone. The muscles in my legs are fizzing, going numb. I sigh.

I move my left arm over Bonnie, to pick up my phone from the bedside table so I can text Marcus. My wrist hurts. I squirm closer, shuffling Bonnie forwards, and my fingers touch the phone. I edge it towards me, just with my nails. I lift it and manage to slip my fingers beneath it and then it's in my palm. I raise my arm as Bonnie rolls over towards me, and her elbow flies up and catches me on the other cheekbone. I yelp and drop the phone. Bonnie cries out as it falls on her forehead.

Then Nanny grunts. She's wide awake.

'What time is it?'

I scrabble for the phone. It's on Bonnie's chest. She makes a sharp noise of annoyance and I say, 'Half five, Nan.'

I roll on my back. Nan does the same on my left side. Bonnie throws herself over on my right. We're all staring into the darkness in the direction of the ceiling. We're quiet for a while and then Nanny's voice is a quiet croaking.

'She was the best of women, your mam. She was always like a proper sister to me, never just a sister-in-law.'

Bonnie and I think about our mother for a moment.

I say, 'She was great. And Dad, too.'

Bonnie makes a scoffing noise. 'You were always Daddy's girl, Georgie. You could twist him round your finger.'

Nan sighs. 'He was a decent bloke, Kenny Turner. He thought the world of your mam. We all did. She was good to us, every one of us.'

For a while, memories of my mum flood back. Then I turn to Nan. 'Isn't that how you met Wilf? Through our mother.'

'It was 1950. I was nineteen. Josie Basham was only sixteen, but she was a real character, and we were working in the same factory, Bryant's in Garston. We were friends straight away. Then she invited me to her house one Saturday evening. They were very firm people, her parents, especially her mother. I never saw that woman smile. She had a mouth on her, though. All the old Scouse sayings, she had one for every occasion. And Josie had to be so proper at the table. "This is my friend Anne, Mam," she said and her mother replied straight away, "Come on then, girl, eat up or you'll waste away to a warehouse." So we picked at the bread and ham and then Wilf came in from work. He worked on the railway then. Josie's mother took one look at him looking at me and said, "You should see your face, Wilfie. You'd scare a police horse," and he blushed so much his ears went red. I was embarrassed, too.'

Bonnie chuckles. I recall those old Scouse sayings. I think about Nan and Wilf all those years ago, how they must have loved each other. Nan hasn't finished her story.

'We went out together for six months, the pictures or just walking. Then Wilf asked me to marry him. To tell you the truth, it was getting passionate and I had to keep fighting him off, poor fella. So we went to my house and he asked my dad, you know, for my hand in marriage. My mam said nothing. She just stood at the sink peeling potatoes. And my dad said, "All right, lad," just like that. Then we went to tell his parents. Wilf was twenty-three but he was so nervous. Mrs Basham just said, "Who knitted your face and dropped a stitch, our Wilf?" and he said, "We're getting married, Mam." His dad offered us a drink of whisky each. It was so strong. They were good people, though. Proper Scouse people.'

'Those were the days, Nan.' I realise I have no idea what the world was like back then. 'What did Mum's parents think of my dad?'

Nanny chuckles. 'He had a good job, Kenny Turner. A trade. He was an engineer. Wilf's mam said, "You'll be all right with that one. He's got more money than soft Joe." And he was so in love with Josie. You should see the engagement ring he bought her.'

I smile in the darkness. 'I remember my grandma Basham. She had a saying for everything. I remember her being very old but feisty as hell.'

Nan breathes out. 'That's where you get it from, Georgina. You're just like Wilf's mother.'

I'm not sure that's a compliment.

Bonnie whispers, 'Which one am I like, Nan?'

'Like my Wilfie. He was the nicest man. Good-natured,

sweet, so full of love. You remind me of him every time I look at you, Bonnie.'

I remember Uncle Wilf, memories from when I was a child. He was stout, balding on top. He never looked anything like Bonnie. I just thought he was really old. My mother passed away before Jade was born. It makes me so sad that my daughter never met her gran.

Nan's still reminiscing.

'You had good parents. They thought the world of you.'

'Of Bonnie?' I ask.

'Of both of you. They were so proud of the pair of you.'

I shake my head. 'My mother hated me. I was such a bad kid. Always in trouble at school. Then later, when we were teenagers, she was always accusing me, saying I led Bonnie astray. She had a saying for me as well. "Use your loaf, even if it's only half-baked," she used to say.'

Nan giggled. 'I heard her own mother say that to her all the time.' Nan muses for a moment. 'Josie adored you, Georgina.'

'She didn't, Nan. Bonnie was her favourite.'

Nan's voice becomes louder. 'No, she loved you both, equally. You gave her a lot of trouble, that's true, but she admired your pluck. It was Bonnie she was worried about.'

Bonnie's little voice cracks with emotion, remembering about our parents.

'Why?'

'She thought you were easily led, too kind. Then when you met Adie Carrick, she was terrified he'd bring trouble. Josie never liked him, Bonnie. He used to come round to your house in his flash car, wearing a suit and tie. She'd say to me, "That Adie Carrick wouldn't be out of place in the dock. He looks like the accused."'

'She was right. Sorry, Bon.'

Bonnie sniffs, takes a deep breath. 'Remember when we were locked out of our own house and we had to go to Nanny's, Georgie? And Uncle Wilf and Nan came downstairs and caught us breaking in.'

I grin. 'We'd been out at a party. You were going out with Carl.'

'Don't remind me, Georgie. I thought I loved him. He dumped me. Went off with Barbara Duff. I cried my eyes out for two weeks.'

'You had terrible taste.'

Bonnie howls with laughter. '*I* did? What about you? With your punk rockers and drummers and that blond bloke who worked in a chicken factory in the holidays.'

'Mickey Maguire. The one who studied tropical diseases. He followed me like a sheep. I broke his heart in the end. Went off with his lecturer at a party.'

'Georgie, you were so naughty!' Bonnie sounds happier already. 'But do you remember when we climbed through Nan's kitchen window because we had nowhere to go? Mum had bolted the door.'

Nanny chortles. 'I remember you two, the pair of you standing in my sink with your big boots on looking guilty as sin.'

'If it hadn't been for Dad, Mum would've come down on you a lot harder. I always thought it was funny, how she'd blame you and never me, because I was the youngest, and then Dad would argue with her and get you off the hook.'

'I was a bad influence, Bonnie.'

'Not at all.' Nanny's tone is firm. 'Do you know, Josie said to me, "Our Georgina is gold dust. I'd trust her with Bonnie anywhere. She has a good head on her shoulders and she can stand up for herself."'

I breathe sharply. 'She never told me that.'

'Of course not,' Nan chuckles. 'Parents didn't do all that lovey stuff they do now. You had to be tough with your kids. It was for the best. A firm hand at all times, that's what it was about in those days.'

I protest. 'She never told me she loved me. Ever.'

'She died too young, Josie did . . .' Nanny's thinking aloud. 'You know, I'm not sure Wilf ever said that to me, that he loved me.'

'What?' Bonnie's aghast. 'Adie used to say it all the time. That he loved me with all his heart. That I was his treasure.'

'That says it all then.' Nan's tone is grim. 'He adored me, Wilfie. And as for Adie, well, it has to be said, Bonnie: he didn't have a heart. Or a conscience.'

I glance at my phone. 'It's gone six. What's it to be: sleep or more stories?'

'We could have an early breakfast,' Nan suggests. 'Then come back to bed and sleep all day.'

'It's the nineteenth – Good Friday in two days' time,' Bonnie says and suddenly we're all wondering if we'll really be home for Easter.

No sighting of Beddowes, so far.

My heart thuds harder than it should and to calm myself, Marcus fills my thoughts. My conscience prickles like a hair shirt and, before I can stop myself, I blurt out loud, 'Nan, Bonnie – I owe you an apology. I've told you both a bit of a lie.'

'What have you done now, Georgina?'

Her crumpled face turns to me, smiling, all interest.

I take a breath. 'I've met a man. Here, in the village.'

I want to avoid the details, keep the conversation simple. It's too new, too private, too sad, and I don't really know what to say.

'Spill the beans,' Bonnie giggles. 'Is that where you were

312

when you were supposed to be at the doctor? With this new man.'

'Sort of, yes. Before I bumped into Beddowes. We were outside on the beach, talking.'

Nanny chuckles. 'So, all these late-night walks you've been going on have been an excuse to meet up with this fella?'

I nod, but she can't see me so I murmur, 'His name's Marcus.'

'What's he like, Georgie?'

'He's nice. I like him, Bon. He's . . .' I can't find words. Bonnie helps me out.

'Is he good-looking? How old is he? Where did you meet him?'

'My age, roughly. I met him buying muesli in the supermarket.'

Bonnie sniggers and I remember the first time we met, the dates we shared, his smile.

'We've been to the cinema together, I've had dinner at his house and we sneaked out for a picnic. Yes, he's good-looking. Or at least I think so.'

'Did he deduce you?'

'Seduce, Nan.'

'Well, you know what I mean, Georgina. Did you get any sex? Goodness only knows, it's been long enough. I've been waiting for you to get off your backside and find a man since you split up with that lovely Terry.'

'It's probably over with Marcus, Nan. I mean, with the Beddowes thing going on, I can't really concentrate on anything else. And then we'll be going back to Liverpool. There's no way I can run a relationship from home, given the distance.'

Nan chuckles. 'Where there's a will, there's a way. Or where there's a willy . . .'

313

I hug her. 'You're a very bad woman, Anne Basham.'

'I'd be a damned sight worse if I were your age and found myself with a gorgeous man like your Marcus. Ooh, just the thought of it.' She rubs her knees in an inappropriate simulation of passion.

The duvet falls from my shoulders. But I'm quiet, considering how a relationship with Marcus would be lovely if I lived in Sussex. But I don't and I never will. I text Marcus and tell him I'm okay. I assume he'll be asleep, but a text pings back after two minutes and it says simply: *I'm thinking of you.* Bonnie's breathing is steady on my right-hand side. She's asleep. I wrap my arms round Nan.

'You know Uncle Wilf loved you, Nan, even if he didn't tell you so.'

'Oh yes. I loved him, too. I loved him so much.'

'And I love you, Nanny. You're one of the best women in the whole wide world.' I kiss her cheek and it's like sinking my face into marshmallow.

She gives me a throaty chortle. 'You're not so bad yourself, Georgina.'

I close my eyes and breathe in. Warmth and tiredness overwhelm me. I float, feeling purely happy. Even if Beddowes shot us all dead now, I would've been blessed to have shared this journey with these lovely women, and with my beloved daughter. I breathe out a fat sigh of contentment and drift into the softness of sleep.

Chapter Thirty-Four

I wake because someone next to me is moving. It's Bonnie. She's out of bed, then wriggling into clothes. I stare at the pale skin of her back, her bra strap as she pulls on a light jumper.

'Georgie, have you any idea what the time is?'

I shake my head. My hair's sticking up and my cheek aches where Nanny's elbow had been resting. I roll over and pick up my phone.

'It's nearly ten.'

Nanny's asleep, curled like a child, her thumb in her mouth. I slip out of the bed on Bonnie's side, cover Nan gently with the duvet and find some clothes to pull on. I'll have a bath later this afternoon or this evening and maybe put all of our bedding in the washing machine.

I stroll over to the window, pull back the curtains and stare out at a shining April day. The sky is bright blue over the beach and clouds stretch like an unfolding roll of cotton wool. The sea is dark and smooth, tinged with ice grey. I stare out across the sweeping coast, the lines of tiny houses, and think of Marcus. I imagine him jogging down on the shingle, by the heaving waves, strong legs

moving easily. I send him a quick text: *Lovely morning.*
All is well. Bonnie comes over to stand next to me. I slip
my arm round her waist and we gaze out at the sea.

Bonnie follows me into the en suite. I wash my face,
put on a dab of cream, comb my hair. She picks up her
mascara then throws it down again and laughs, 'Hell, I'm
going nowhere,' then brushes her hair.

She looks fresh-faced and bright-eyed. She hugs me.

'I've never said it properly, Georgie, but thanks for being
so understanding. You know, all this mess with Adie.'

I squeeze her against me; she's as slim as bamboo.

'You've done so well, Bonnie. You've had to be really
brave. It was tough. One minute he was deceitful, the next
he was showering you with gifts, then he ran away.'

'He dumped me.' Her eyes meet mine.

'You'll bounce back. You can count on my support,
Bon.'

She gazes up, eyes shining, full of bulging tears.

'Adie was Demi's dad. And we were together for so
long – we had good years. I know it all went wrong. He
got too greedy, lost his way. But he did love me once.'

I hug her again and she rests her head against my
shoulder. Then an idea comes to her.

'Shall we bring Nan breakfast in bed?'

'Okay. What shall we make?'

Bonnie frowns. 'Poached eggs. She said she liked those
ones in the B & B we stayed in. Do you know how to
make them?'

I nod. 'Easy. On toast, with a mug of sweet coffee. She'd
love that.'

Bonnie nods steadily. 'I was thinking. The house in
Frodsham is too big for me now. I might sell it, buy somewhere smaller. I'm going to have to learn all the difficult
things. Using a mower. Putting out the bins. Managing

316

finances.' She sees me grin and a smile breaks out on her face. 'Poaching eggs.'

I wrap an arm round her. 'You have your family here, Bon. You could always come and work with me. Do facials. You could do that.'

'I could.' She smiles. 'Come on, Georgie, I'm dying for a cup of coffee.'

We walk to the door and I glance back at Nan sleeping. She's curled on her side, her back to me, a small mound under a white duvet. I can see the top of her head, the green wool of her hat.

Bonnie says, 'She's loved it here, Georgie. She's had the time of her life, going out to glamorous places, meeting football stars, painting the town. How will she go back to living alone in that poky place?'

'We'll come up with something. We'll make sure she's okay.'

Bonnie sighs. 'Funny, isn't it? Since we've been here, I've got to know her so much better. You, too. We've had so much trouble, so much to be scared about, and yet we've grown closer.'

'We'll have the best Easter at home,' I promise and think of Jade.

I can't wait to see her and I resolve to text her, or maybe go upstairs before breakfast and call on her and Luis.

Bonnie and I grin at each other, rush down the hallway and step out into the lounge. We stand still, leaving the door wide open behind us. For a moment, I can't make out what's happening.

I see Jade first, sitting on the floor, facing me, her face pale beneath her tan. Luis is next to her, his hand clutching hers. The room is silent, the atmosphere ice-cold. My mind races: where's Femi? He's next to Luis, sitting on the floor, a huge cut on his face, his eyes widening as he sees us come

317

in. Holly? I look for her. She's by the door, slumped against the wall. Blood is all over her hair, making it deep crimson. Her eyes are half-open. She's not dead – I hear her groan.

Bonnie catches my arm. I'm confused. My eyes meet my daughter's gaze.

'Jade, what the hell . . .?'

He's in the armchair, the one Nan sits in, with his back to me. I can see the top of his head, reddish curling hair, thinning at the crown.

He calls out, 'Are we quorum?'

I have no idea what he means. He glances over his shoulder.

'Georgie, Bonnie. Come and sit down here.'

He waves something towards Jade, Luis and Femi. It's a gun. I can see the metal of it gripped in his fist.

'Sit!'

Bonnie gasps. I take her hand. We troop round his chair. He's smiling, but his eyes are glinting. He points the gun at the floor. Bonnie sits next to Femi and I move the other side of Jade.

'Mum?'

She stares at me, her forehead puckering. I have no idea how to help her. Beddowes leans forwards.

'And so, to conclude our business.'

I turn and gaze towards Holly. She's conscious but stunned. I hunch my shoulders and wonder if Beddowes will shoot us all, one by one. I glance at Femi, who looks back meaningfully with wide eyes. He doesn't know what to do. My mind lurches, trying to find a way out, but I can't. I can only think of Jade: I've let her down, made the wrong call. I should've told the police everything about the bracelet. My mouth is dry and my mind is a rolling train out of control on a downhill track. I struggle to breathe. He's saying my name and I turn sharply.

'We meet again, Georgie. I must say, you've disappointed me. I thought you'd have more sense than to refuse my little request.'

I shrug, search my brain to say something smart and then stare at the gun he's waving in my direction.

'I owe you for a couple of things. One, for your failure to keep our rendezvous. And two, for the wild goose chase you sent my man on to Paddington station.' He's not smiling.

I reach behind me and touch Jade's jumper, place my hand against her back. Comforting my child is uppermost on my mind. Beddowes' eyes flash.

'I'll make you suffer, though. You can watch me kill your daughter before I deal with you.'

I open my mouth to scream at him but it's useless. His eyes fall on Jade, a lingering appraisal.

'It was good of you to drop in to see your mother, Jade. You timed it perfectly, just after I'd made myself comfortable here, to wait for your aunty Bonnie to show herself.' He eases himself back in the chair and crosses one leg over the other. 'But now you've given me a tough decision to make. I'm not sure whether to finish off the two officers here first, or whether to break the nation's heart and put paid to one of the best strikers in the footballing world.'

Luis understands quickly, pulls an arm round Jade, his brow furrowed. I grind my teeth and my thoughts strain for an idea, a way out. Nothing comes. Beddowes turns to my sister and his face twists in a cruel smirk.

'Mrs Carrick. Bonnie.' He pauses; his eyes glide over her. 'Bonnie by name and bonnie of face. I was so sorry to hear that Adie had abandoned you. What a great shame.' His voice is sarcastic, bitter. 'I dare say you feel used, having to pay his debt for him now. But that's really all you're good for, being the loyal puppy-dog wife you are.'

Bonnie lowers her head, shaking. A tear plops onto her knee, and another.

'So, you have something I need, Mrs Carrick. The bracelet Adie gave you. Where is it? Do I have to shoot everyone here one by one, or will you let me have it now?' He points the gun in the air, sliding it in a circle, aiming towards me, Luis, Jade then Femi, choosing. 'Where shall I start, Bonnie?'

She's shaking, her fingers fluttering like leaves in a storm. Femi puts a hand on her shoulder. She rummages in her pocket and pulls out the gold charms, the chain, holding it out towards him.

'Come here. Bring it to me.'

Bonnie tries to stand, but her legs give way. She totters and falls back. I reach out my hand.

'Here, Bonnie. I'll give it to him.'

I meet Beddowes' glance and he nods. Femi passes it to me. Bonnie is so pale, I think she might be sick. A tear gleams on Jade's cheek. I put out my hand and wipe it.

'The bracelet.' Beddowes' voice is low, a gravelly command.

I clutch it in my palm so hard that the charms stick into the flesh. I sit up; stare at Beddowes, into the space over his head. Then I notice something moving beyond the open door. Nanny's in the hallway, having emerged from her bedroom; I see her shadow flicker. Then she's gone. I wonder if she's fallen, or dropped to the floor. I'm not sure what she's doing. But I know I have to play for time. I take a breath.

'Mr Beddowes, I want to say I'm sorry about all this. I mean, I'll bring the bracelet now, of course, but could you not see your way to letting us go?'

'The bracelet.'

I'm on my knees, moving a foot to the floor, ready to stand.

'I mean, let Jade go, and Bonnie. Please.'

I stand, my legs shaking. If he shoots now, I'm gone. I'd take the full impact.

'Mr Beddowes, I can understand why you'd want to kill the police officers. I mean, in your line of work . . .' I'm talking for the sake of it.

Nan's on the floor in the hallway, on her knees, crawling into the room. I've no idea what she's doing. She's gone into the little galley kitchen, ducking down behind the worktop and the cupboards. I have to keep on talking.

'But . . . we haven't done anything wrong. Bonnie, Jade – they're completely innocent. It's Adie who swindled you, stopped you from finding the money.'

He points the gun at me. 'Bring it here and shut up.'

I take another step, holding my breath.

'Now.'

'All right. All right. I'm doing it.'

My instincts are shouting that once I've given him the bracelet, he'll grab my arm, pull me in front of him and shoot me in the head. I take a small step forwards, then another. I pause. He could shoot me where I stand. I breathe deeply; try to stall him, to play for time.

'Mr Beddowes, why don't we take a minute, talk things over . . .'

'Give it to me.'

Suddenly, with a speed I didn't know she was capable of, Nanny's behind his chair. She points something at the back of his neck, grasps his collar.

'Right, you bastard.' Her voice sounds like the croak of the possessed. 'I have a gun pointing at your head. One move and you're jam sponge.'

The thought that she's watched too many cop movies crosses my mind, but my heart's thumping too hard for anything else to matter. I have no idea where she's found a gun. I recall her mentioning the black market. Nan is in the zone.

'Throw your weapon down, Beddowes . . .' Behind her glasses, her eyes swivel to me and then Bonnie, then back to Beddowes. 'One move and I'll shoot you in the neck.'

My eyes meet Beddowes' icy stare. For a moment, he's shocked, stunned, then his face calms in resignation. Nanny tightens her hold on his collar and I see her other hand push the weapon harder into the skin of his nape.

'Throw the gun down.'

Beddowes lets the gun slide to the floor. It falls next to me and I stoop and snatch it up, holding it up like an ice-cream cone. Nan's eyes shine behind the glass of her spectacles.

'Now, don't move.'

My heart's in my mouth, leaping into my throat. I clutch metal, point it at Beddowes, but my arm's quivering. Beddowes moves to stand. He clearly thinks we won't shoot. He's calling my bluff. His eyes meet mine, glittering shards of steel.

'Sit!' commands Nan, and she shoves her gun hard into Beddowes' neck.

Then something snaps, a light splitting sound, and Nan holds up her weapon and blinks at it. It's the courgette spiraliser; the orange plastic casing is broken. Beddowes is on his feet. He turns, grabs her arm and throws her to the floor. I hear her yelp.

Then there's a commotion, scuffling and shouting, and someone's flashed past me like a whirlwind.

I drop to the floor and point the gun at Beddowes, but Femi's on top of him. Beddowes is lying on his stomach, his arms wrenched behind his back, and Femi's clipping handcuffs onto his wrist. His voice is muffled now, his face squashed against the floor. Holly has pulled out her radio, called for support, and now she's fallen back against the wall. Bonnie's sobbing.

I slump to my knees; I feel dizzy: I'm going to pass out. I shake myself, make myself crawl to Nan, but my legs won't move: it's like wading through syrup. Femi's radio rattles as he grips Beddowes' shoulders, his face a mask of concentration. Nan's flat on her face, but her arm is twisted beneath her. I touch her hair gently.

'Nan? Nanny? Can you hear me?'

She groans and turns her head, looks up and grins. 'I showed that pig, didn't I, Georgina? I showed the bastard who's boss.'

Chapter Thirty-Five

In seconds, the room is buzzing with police officers: two paramedics tend to Holly, who seems to be fine, smiling as her wound is being bandaged. Beddowes is being hauled away by two police officers, his head bowed, silent. A young man comes over to Nan and leans over her, talking loudly.

'Are you all right? Can you tell me where it hurts?'

Nan moves her head. 'I'm not bloody deaf, son.' She groans. 'My arm's terrible. And my hand.'

He gently helps her to a sitting position. A red mark has started to puff up and spread across her cheek. She chuckles softly and winks.

'I bet Bruce Willis couldn't have held them off with a courgette cutter, eh?'

'You're a genius, Nanny. A brave one.'

The paramedic is bandaging her wrist.

She shakes her head. 'Not really, love. I just thought to myself, he's not harming my girls. And anyway, what did I have to lose? I'm eighty-eight.'

I smile. 'You might be eighty-eight, Nan, but you moved

across the room like the SAS. I've never seen you sprint so fast.'

She notices the paramedic. He's in his early twenties, fresh-faced, pale blond hair. She beams.

'How am I doing?'

'A bruised wrist,' he mutters. 'A bump on your cheek. I can take you in for a check over. Does anything else hurt?'

Nanny doesn't stop to think. 'Just here.' She indicates her hip. 'I have chronic arthritis. You couldn't just give it a good massage with some melted lard, could you? Then I'll be fine. I'm not leaving my girls now.'

Smiling, I move away, over to Jade, who's clutching Luis' hand, and Bonnie, who's standing close to Femi. There's a plaster on his face, a bruise blooming below. I grab Jade and she falls into my arms.

I whisper into her glossy hair, 'It's all over now, love.'

She pulls away, her eyes full of tears. She's furious.

'Mum, it was awful. Luis and I came down to see you. I wanted to surprise you because we'd been so busy, and Beddowes opened the door. He forced us to wait for you. He said if we moved he'd shoot us all. He made Femi radio our bodyguard, to say that we were here and all was fine. We couldn't do anything to stop him. I was really scared.'

Luis takes her hand. 'It was very bad. But now, as you say, it is finish.'

'I let him in.' Femi breathes out slowly. 'He was armed. Then he hit me. He smashed Holly over the head.'

I glance over at the paramedics, who are chattering to her. Femi's voice is full of relief.

'We're all right now, though.'

The room's crowded: people in uniforms bustling

around, talking in low voices. They're moving furniture, taking photographs. My eyes come to rest on Roque's armchair, where Beddowes had been sitting, the arm rests covered in stains of ketchup and sauce. I sigh.

'What a mess.'

Femi shrugs. 'These things happen. It'll be sorted out, don't worry. You were very brave, Georgie.'

'We all were.'

Luis grins. 'Roque, he knows nothing about all this. When he returns, he will lose his bloody plot.'

Jade smiles at him. 'I must stop using these expressions, Mum. He's so bright; he picks them up really quickly.'

'Why did Beddowes want the bracelet so badly, Georgie?'

Femi's eyes are round, earnest, and I hate lying but I know how much the bracelet means to Bonnie. I take a breath.

'I've no idea. It's solid gold, worth several thousand pounds. He probably wanted everything he could from Adie, he was so furious with him.'

'I have to admit, I thought we weren't going to make it. Beddowes had the gun trained on us all and I was convinced he'd kill us, one by one.' Femi grins. 'Thank goodness for Nan. And you.'

I shrug. 'I just fell on the floor holding the gun and dithering. I was terrified.' I force a smile on my face. 'Look. Nan has an admirer.'

Bonnie glances across at the paramedic inspecting Nan's knee. She's still in her winceyette nightie, the green bobble hat on her head, smiling at him and pointing to her thigh. I want to hug her.

Bonnie shakes her head. 'She was so brave, Georgie. So were you.'

I force a laugh, but suddenly I'm exhausted.

'Well, we can all go home now. In time for Easter; Good

Friday's the day after tomorrow. Maybe we can get a bit of shopping done first.' I gaze at the flat, at the uniformed officers bustling about, and relief floods through me. 'I can't wait to leave this place and go home.'

Jade makes a sad face. 'Luis has a full day of training tomorrow and then there's the away game on Saturday. We'll be busy here until the end of May, when the football season ends. Then he wants us to spend June at his place on the coast outside Barcelona. I'm going to meet his parents.'

I take a second to register what she's said, then I smile at her so positively I'm almost gurning.

'You two deserve some quality time together. Of course you must go to Barcelona. I'm sure you've seen enough of me to last you over the next few months.'

Jade hugs me. 'You're the best, Mum. We'll meet up in July, shall we? You can come down and visit over the summer.'

Luis agrees. 'One day you, too, must come to meet my family. Then together we are all pigs in the same shit.'

Jade smirks and looks away.

Femi's in conversation with DC Charlotte Howes. Their faces are serious. I hear her say, 'We may never know where the money was hidden.'

Bonnie and I exchange glances. DC Howes comes over. 'How are you feeling?'

Bonnie grins, shakes DC Howes' hand.

'Okay, I think. Thanks for all your help.'

'My pleasure. At least we have Beddowes now.'

'I might be able to help you with the money, too.' Bonnie offers her cheeriest smile. 'I might know where it is.'

I stare at her; I have no idea what she's going to tell the police officer, but her face is calm and confident.

'There's something Adie said to me, a while ago. I'd

forgotten about it but it's just come back to me now. He said to remember an address. It was Hastings Square, in King's Cross. Poppy's flower shop.' She offers her most innocent expression. 'Do you think that could be it? He said some numbers as well, but I can't remember them . . .'

'That'll be the combination of the safe.' DC Howes is delighted. 'I'm sure we're on to it. The safe'll be no problem. Well done, Bonnie.'

I glance at Bonnie, impressed with her quick thinking. She's a sharp one. I raise my eyebrows. She winks back.

'Glad to help. I'm coming down to earth now. But we're fine, thanks to Femi and Holly. And Georgie and Nan.'

'You've all been through a lot.' DC Howes smiles at Bonnie. 'You've done so well. I've been on to HQ and they need you out of this flat for a while. You'll need to spend the night elsewhere. I hope that's okay.'

Nanny joins us, supported by the paramedic, a grin on her face.

'Where do we have to go, Constable?'

Femi grins. 'You were the heroine of the hour, Nan.'

She smiles, pulls off her woollen hat and ruffles her hair. The electric blue streak stands out against the soft white wisps. He puts an arm around her.

DC Howes' expression is businesslike.

'I'm afraid you can't stay here. Obviously, you'll all have to give statements this afternoon. But you'll have to make other arrangements for tonight.' She turns to Jade and Luis. 'That includes you both as well, I'm afraid. We'll need to go through the flat upstairs, too. Routine. Everything'll be back to normal by tomorrow, though.'

Luis nods, holding up his phone. 'I speak about this to Femi already. He tells me a good place. I have booked a hotel in Brighton. It is a big one with a spa.'

'A spa sounds nice,' Jade grins.

'Another thing.' Luis takes Nanny's hand. She stares up at him adoringly. 'I know you go home tomorrow. I have to be training but me and Femi, we think you might like to have a breakfast at the top of The Shard before you go. So that you can see London from a high place, Nan. You would like that?' He looks hopefully at Bonnie and me. 'I arrange a car to take you there tomorrow. You are booked in for breakfast at a quarter to eight so that you can watch the day begin in London. You can get the train back here in plenty of time to drive home.'

Nan almost swoons. 'Breakfast taken up The Shard? How romantic, Louise.'

Jade agrees. 'Breakfast's a great idea. It's a shame you have to be at the club, Luis. I wish you could come with us, *mi alma*.'

Luis shrugs. 'It's important for me to be normal again. Training hard is what I love. And you, too.' He links his fingers in Jade's. 'But you can have a good time with your family, Jade. I see you after.'

Nan waves a hand like the queen. 'But we'll miss you, Louise.'

Femi's eyes meet Bonnie's.

'You've all had a really tough experience. Hopefully, a night in a smart hotel and a good breakfast will help you to come back down to earth, to feel normal again.'

Bonnie gives a little cough and gazes up at him. 'Will you be able to join us for breakfast?'

'Sadly, no. I'll be busy tomorrow. Reports to write . . .'

There's a noise at the doorway and I turn to see a police officer barring the way of a tall man with curly hair. He's looking round the room and his eyes catch mine.

'Georgie.'

'Please, Femi,' I grab his arm. 'Let him in.'

Femi goes over to the doorway and then Marcus is in

the room and next to me in two strides. He hugs me so tightly my feet leave the floor. He whispers in my ear, 'Thank God you're all right.' He links his fingers through mine and I'm staring into anxious ocean-blue eyes. 'I was on the beach. I saw the police arrive in droves. They wouldn't let me in or tell me what had happened.'

I lose myself in his embrace again. I'm coming down to earth, almost normal.

I whisper, 'It was touch-and-go here for a bit.'

I don't say any more, because Marcus' cheek is against mine. I feel the prickle of stubble and then I kiss him so hard, the tension seeps from my body. When I open my eyes, Nan's standing by my shoulder, a smile on her face.

'I suppose this is the man you were telling me about, Georgina.'

'Nan, this is Marcus.'

His puts out a hand and squeezes her fingers gently.

Nan chuckles. 'I thought it was him. You've got a smile on your face like the Egyptian sphincter.'

'Sphynx, Nan.'

I glance at Marcus and his eyes crinkle with amusement. I have that melty feeling all over as he shakes Jade's hand, then Luis'.

Femi and Bonnie move next to us and there are warm words as I introduce Marcus. Jade winks at me, shows me her thumb up, and I wink back. It occurs to me that I'm going to give a statement to the police, stay over in Brighton, zip up to London, then drive us all home. I probably won't see him after today. But he's holding my hand and for now, it feels good.

Bonnie circles her wrist with the bracelet and stretches her arm out to Femi, who dutifully does up the clasp.

She sighs. 'He fixed it for me. And it's all over now, Georgie. We're just ordinary women. We can have an ordinary life. We can go home.' She smiles, a huge grin, and I can't remember when I last saw her look so happy. 'I suppose there'll be more sorting out to do. Getting my life in order. But I'm looking forward to it. I'll be fine.'

I glance at Marcus, who slips an arm round me and asks me if I'm sure I'm all right.

Nan digs me with her elbow. 'He's a good man, that one, Georgina.'

I nod. But everything'll change now. It'll go back to normal. DC Howes suggests that we should pack and leave now, to clear the space for the police. I hug Marcus again and he asks me when I'm next free. I honestly don't know: my mind is still full of the events of the morning. I promise to contact him and he kisses me.

'I'm so glad you're okay.'

I watch him go. He turns back at the door: I take in the intense expression for a moment then I grin and wave. It would've been nice to go with him, to share one last day with him at his home, to sit on the sofa and talk and sip wine. But I need to be with Bonnie and Jade and Nan. I turn to my daughter and my sister and kiss their cheeks. Then I cuddle Nanny.

'We're going home, Nan.'

'I don't want to go home.' Her face takes on a sulky pout. 'Back to that tiny place, with its gas fire on one bar and dry dinners in a box. How can I do that now? Anyway, I've sprained my wrist.' She holds up her bandaged left hand and waves it in my face to make her point. Her eyes are huge behind the glasses. 'I've lived the high life here, drunk champagne, been round Brighton with a gangster in his Jaguar, fought him off with a courgette cutter. You can't expect me to go back to that cold house with the little television and terrible meals for one.'

I see her point. She's standing in front of me in her thin

331

nightgown, her hands on her hips, her wrist lost inside a huge bandage, her little face a picture of stubbornness. I hug her.

'We have a night at a spa hotel to look forward to. And breakfast in The Shard. It'll be spectacular. Shall we go and pack?'

Nan nods, her chin drooping. Bonnie's already in our bedroom, filling her suitcases. Luis and Jade have gone, presumably to do the same.

It's quiet in the bedroom, although Bonnie's humming a little tune. I decide I'll pack my things, then Nan's, because her wrist is too painful to do anything at all but hold a drink, according to her. After we've given statements and arrived at our hotel, I plan on having a long soak in a steamy bath. But first, I'll ring Amanda, tell her I'll be back tomorrow evening, then we can plan for the summer beauty rush. I pull out my phone and a text comes in straight away. It's just a simple message but I read it three times: *Don't leave without saying goodbye.*

My heart is beating double time. It's from Marcus. Of course, he knows what I know, that I'm going home tomorrow, that I'll be miles away from Sussex and that it's over between us.

Chapter Thirty-Six

I can't believe how much better I feel. Being pummelled on the treatment table, receiving a massage rather than giving one, is just the experience my body needs. Nan and I have aromatherapies, as do Jade and Luis. Bonnie has a spray tan, nails and facial: the full body treatment. Nan wants us all to go for a swim in the heated pool, but none of us have costumes: Nan threatens to dive in naked.

Later, we have dinner in the restaurant, too much to drink, our voices far too loud. I can see the grudging tolerance on some of the other guests' faces as they look across at us, their hands covering their mouths. I imagine them saying, 'Oh well, they're from Liverpool. What do you expect?'

During dessert, two young women, one blonde, one brunette, giggling with shyness, come over and ask for selfies with Luis. He stands between them, grinning, while Jade glares from behind a coffee cup. Bonnie eats her whole meal and follows it up with apple pie and cream. Her appetite has returned and doubled. Adie would've disapproved, but she's forgotten his preference for a slender, hungry wife.

We laugh a lot, talk over each other, fill our glasses from newly opened bottles and laugh some more. We're celebrating life, together. If it wasn't for Nan, we wouldn't be here now, and we're bursting with the new joy and freedom of it all.

Then we yawn, take the lift to our rooms, our arms round each other. Bonnie and I have a deluxe suite. A private butler opens the doors for us, shows us the huge television, the coffee machine, and offers to bring us anything we desire. Nan immediately asks for a bottle of champagne and the Chippendales, and the butler politely replies, 'I believe I can accommodate at least one of your requests, madam.'

Sumptuous curtains hang to the floor and when I draw them back, I see the street lamps glowing, soft amber light over the pier. Inside the room, there are enormous sofas and a dining area. Bonnie squeals in delight at the marble bathrooms. She grabs my hand.

'This place is great, Georgie. Luis is lovely, bringing us here.'

Nan claps me on the shoulder with her good hand. 'So, the police know where Adie's money is now. We could have pocketed it and lived happily in luxury forever.'

I glance at Bonnie. She pouts, the memory still raw.

'I did the right thing, telling them where it was, even if I had to tell a fib about how I knew. I don't want Adie's dirty money.' She sniffs and fingers the little charms on the bracelet. 'To be honest, I'm not sure I want anything more to do with Adie at all.'

'Then let's forget him.' I move away. 'I'm shattered. Nan, ask the butler to wake us at six. The car will be here at half six to take us for breakfast at The Shard.'

Hark at me. '*Ask the butler.*' '*The car.*' '*Breakfast at The*

Shard.' I allow myself a giggle. It'll be good to go back home but, before we do, we're going to have some fun together.

The spring sunshine across the cityscape casts light shadows, pink as candyfloss. We sit at a round table, staring through the tall windows at miniature London buses below. We're so high up, everything is small, but the sun hangs in a blue sky, a butter ball, pale yellow at the edges, lighting the whole room a blinding white through the clear glass.

A waiter brings us coffee in little cups, but we hardly notice him. Nan's mouth is open, her jaw slack, staring through the windows. The buildings melt into the horizon in greys and deep blues, overhung by scraggy puffballs of cloud. London is vast. Bigger buildings loom in front of us. I recognise St Paul's in the distance, the Gherkin in front of that. It's beautiful.

Then breakfast arrives and we all start talking at once. The waiter told us we can have whatever we want: Luis has already arranged to pick up the bill. Nan orders a cocktail with gin and limoncello, although she has no idea what limoncello is. Jade asks for one with vodka and crème de banane, so Bonnie orders the same. We're all revelling in the delight of being alive. Nan asks for the Shard Full English and Jade laughs.

'Poor Luis'll be drinking filtered water while we lap this up. I'll have to bring him here as a treat sometime. It's stunning.'

Bonnie sighs. 'We have a long drive home. I bet you're not looking forward to that, Georgie.'

'Let's make it fun.' I put my arm round Nan. 'We'll stop somewhere, find a supermarket and buy all the things we need for a nice Easter weekend together. Chocolate eggs.

Prosecco, a celebration dinner. Then we'll all stay at my house. Spend time together, the three of us. What do you think?'

Bonnie nods. 'Great idea. I don't want to go back to that big place in Frodsham yet.'

Nanny swigs her cocktail and chimes in, 'I don't want to go back to the poky, lonely little hole on the other side of the park, ever.'

'Right. A weekend together, all three of us. Just a nice lazy time. Plenty to drink and eat, plenty of laughs.'

It flashes across my mind that we need some time to relax together and to work out what to do about Nan. I can't let her go back to living alone now. Besides, spending time with Nan and Bonnie will help me to fill the space left by Jade. And Marcus. I haven't texted him back. I don't know what to say and it occurs to me that since I'm leaving, it's probably better to say nothing.

Jade grabs my hand. 'Our flat should be ready later. I'm cooking Luis his first traditional English roast on Sunday. I've bought champagne and he can have a drink after the game on Saturday. It'll be so nice to be a normal couple.'

Nan claps her hands. 'Right, Georgina. We'll be round your house on Saturday. We can watch Louise on your big television.'

'And Demi and Kyle will be coming back in the evening too, just for a week. I'm so excited.' Bonnie grins. 'I'm going to pick them up from the airport.'

'That's settled, then,' Nan says. 'We'll have the best Easter at your house, Georgina.'

'Fine by me.'

I gaze at Nan. A shadow flits across her smile. She doesn't want to go back to her own house. I can see the anxiety settling across her shoulders. I pick up her bandaged hand.

'How is the wrist, Nan?'

Her face is mischievous. 'Oh, it's terrible. I can hardly lift it. I mean, it won't be easy to get dressed or bath or eat . . .'

She's polished off half of her full English breakfast unaided and most of the gin limoncello cocktail has gone. She gazes at me hopefully, huge puppy-dog eyes behind the glasses.

'You've enjoyed yourself here, haven't you, Nan?'

'Oh, yes. I know Beddowes was an evil swine and we could've all been killed, but I wouldn't have missed it for the world.' She clamps her lips together. 'Anything was better than being on my own.'

I rub her fingers, touch the bandage. 'We can work something out, Nan.'

She beams, drains her glass and tucks into a sausage.

By half past ten, Nan and I are packed, standing with Jade in the foyer of The Shard, waiting for the taxi to take us to the train back to the coast. Bonnie's already nipped out to the shops with her credit card and comes back in a flurry of smiles, hauling bags full of essentials, which means perfume and make-up, as well as some gifts for Nan and me. The friendly woman on the reception desk with piles of hair in a dark chignon has ordered a cab for us, which will arrive in five minutes. Jade links her arm in mine.

'Luis is just over the road in Guy's Hospital, signing shirts, but I'll come back with you. We'll say goodbye at Cliff Top, Mum.'

My throat swells and I hope I won't make a fool of myself. I'm going to miss her and it'll be hard to leave her behind, but it's time for me to let go.

Someone arrives at the desk with a huge bouquet and I notice the receptionist point in our direction. Nan nudges me as a young woman in a green uniform approaches. She brandishes a bunch of roses and lilies, all shades of pink and white, wrapped in silky purple.

Nan whispers to me, 'My days, I'll bet they were expensive.'

A voice calls over to us.

'Bonnie Carrick?'

Bonnie's face pales beneath her subtle foundation. I know why at once: bouquets are Adie's trademark, a gesture of apology. A little shiver goes through me. I hope he's not back, now Beddowes has gone.

I call out, 'Over here,' and take the flowers, holding them out. 'Bonnie?'

She shakes her head. 'I can't. You look, Georgie.'

I find the card, gold-edged, the script in purple, and I grin. 'They're from someone called Femi Princewill.'

She giggles, puts her hand to her mouth. 'What does he say?'

I pass the bouquet to her and she holds it against her cheek and flushes.

'He sends you best wishes, Bon. He hopes we're all feeling better. And he wants to stay in touch.' I glance at Nan. 'He's added his phone number.'

Bonnie hugs the flowers. 'I'll definitely call him, after Easter.'

Nan frowns. 'I thought the bouquet was from your Marcus.'

For a moment, I feel a pang of disappointment.

We take a taxi to the station; I clamber out and grab Nan's arm.

'Everyone ready?'

I glance at Jade. Once we're back at the flats, I'll say goodbye. She's on her own now, just Luis and her, and they'll make their own life. I hope I don't cry. But she'll be fine: we all will. Bonnie hesitates a moment, notices something in the distance and squeezes my arm.

'Hang on a minute. There's something I've got to do.' She offloads the bouquet with Nan and grabs my hand. 'Come with me, Georgie.'

She tugs me across the road towards a restaurant. Inside, people are chatting, drinking coffee, and I can smell the warm scents of cooking. There's a woman huddled near the doorway wrapped in a dirty red sleeping bag. Her face is tired, pale, etched with tiny lines, and she has dark hair streaked with grey. A grizzled dog is at her feet and her legs are covered with a tattered rug. She looks up as we arrive. Bonnie grins at her.

'Hello.'

The woman frowns, leans forwards and strokes the dog, some kind of Alsatian. Its tongue hangs out like a floppy sock. The woman's fingers are wrapped in threadbare mittens, riddled with gaping holes. Her ears are covered by a woollen hat, a small dark beanie. She smiles up at us with stained teeth. She must be younger than me.

Bonnie crouches. 'Excuse me. Are you all right?' I wonder if she's about to invite the woman to come back with us. 'I mean, do you have any money, a shelter?'

The woman looks confused, a little cross. I hope she's not insulted. Her voice is heavy with an accent I recognise as Northern Irish.

'I have nothing, nobody, just my dog, Sammy. He's all I need. He's good company, Sammy. We live off what we can. But we'll be all right, the two of us. Tomorrow is just another day.'

'My name's Bonnie.'

The woman extends a gloved hand. 'Annie. Pleased to meet you.'

Bonnie points a finger towards the car. 'My aunt's called Anne. She's over there by the station, waving.'

'That's nice. The lady in the green bobble hat with the

339

bunch of flowers. I can see her.' The woman lifts her hand and waves. 'Hello there, Anne.'

Bonnie fiddles with her wrist. 'I have something for you.' She undoes the bracelet and holds it up, drops it into the woman's gloved palm. 'It's got lots of charms. It'll bring you good luck.'

The woman blinks at Bonnie. 'Sure, it's solid gold, isn't it? And you don't want it?' She closes her fingers over the links before Bonnie changes her mind.

Bonnie stands. 'No, I don't want it, Annie. You have it. Good luck to you.'

Annie cackles, holds the bracelet to her heart. 'God bless you, Bonnie. And good luck to you, too, the both of you. We'll be all right now, won't we, Sammy? God bless you, Bonnie. And your aunty Anne, too.'

Bonnie and I walk arm in arm back towards the taxi.

I whisper, 'I'm proud of you, Bon.'

She smiles back at me. 'We can go home now.'

We're back at the flats at Cliff Top three hours later. My BMW is outside and packed full with our cases, Bonnie's shopping and her huge bouquet. I hope the engine will start after all this time in the garage.

I drag my case in one hand, lugging Nan's with my other arm. My wrist doesn't hurt now: Beddowes won't trouble us again. Jade shuffles her feet as we stand by the car. The sky is deep blue but it's turned cold and a stiff wind funnels across the clifftop and blows our hair in strands over our faces. I shiver.

Jade's hands are in her pockets. 'Time to go, Mum.'

I glance at my daughter and raise my eyebrows. 'Well, this is it.'

Nan's cold, shivering inside my faux-fur coat.

I throw my arms out, hug Jade and whisper, 'Stay safe.'

She mumbles, 'You're the best.'

When we pull apart, our eyes brim. She gulps and we hug again.

'Thanks, Mum. For everything.'

I mutter, 'Love you,' into her glossy burgundy hair and she squeezes me too hard. I swallow tears. 'Bye, my darling girl.'

Jade turns and saunters back to the flat, looks back, blows me a kiss. I feel a lump swelling in my throat and think: this is it, then she's gone.

We scramble into the car and Bonnie helps Nan into the back seat. We strap her in.

'I hate these bloody seat belts. I can't breathe.'

'You have to have it on, Nan.'

'Stupid things. Why can't everyone just drive safely?'

I check the satnav and take a deep breath. 'Are we all ready?'

Bonnie presses her nose against the glass. 'Goodbye, Brighton. Goodbye, Cliff Top. Goodbye, beautiful balcony and beach view. And hello, gorgeous Liverpool.'

Nan chimes in, 'It's Thursday today and tomorrow's Good Friday. Happy Easter. It's time to go home.'

I start the car, pushing my foot on the clutch. Then I see him coming up the cliff steps from the beach. He's wearing a dark jacket, jeans. The breeze blows his curls across his face. He stands a few feet from the bonnet and smiles, his hands in his pockets. I switch off the ignition, undo my seat belt, slither from the X5 and run to meet him. He holds out his arms and I fill them. His mouth is against mine.

I kiss him back and say, 'I didn't expect to see you, Marcus.'

'I sent you a text.' His eyes shine. 'You're looking well, Georgie.'

I gaze up at him, into the ocean of his eyes. 'You, too.' I kiss him again. 'So you've come to say goodbye?'

'Yes.'

I take a deep breath. 'Well, goodbye then.'

He takes my fingers in his. 'We'll meet again.'

I pull a disbelieving face. 'I'll be in Liverpool. You're here.'

'I'll visit you.'

I turn to the car. I want to be the one to walk away. I don't want him to go, to leave me alone, staring into the distance. Then I come back.

'One thing . . .'

He pulls me to him, holds me against his chest. I feel the strength of his muscles.

'Anything.'

I take his hand, touch the tattoo on his wrist with my fingers and trace the S shape.

'Have a lovely Easter.'

He puts his mouth next to my ear. 'I don't really do Easter. This weekend, I'll be writing an article about parliamentary revelations and certain politicians as the four horsemen of the apocalypse.' I chortle and let go of his hand. 'But you have a great time, Georgie. I'll be thinking of you.'

I swivel round, laugh out loud. As I walk back to the car, I call to him, 'I'll be thinking of you, too.'

I settle in the seat and watch him walk across the path, turn down the steps to the beach, raise a hand in my direction and disappear.

Nan's little voice comes from the back of the car. 'He's such a lovely man.'

I smile to myself. 'He certainly is.'

She taps me on the shoulder. 'Good-looking. Nice manners and full of dignitas.'

'Dignity, Nan. Or gravitas.' And I start the engine.

Chapter Thirty-Seven

By the time we reach the M62, it's half past nine, pitch-dark and the lanes are full of criss-crossing traffic. I should be tired – we've been travelling for six hours. We stop at a mini-market, which is almost sold out of basic provisions. Bonnie picks out Prosecco, olives and capers, proclaiming them Easter essentials. I rifle through the classical section in a rack of CDs for anything by Rachmaninov. I can't find his Piano Concerto but I find one by Tchaikovsky and a copy of Beethoven's *Moonlight Sonata*, the music I recall seeing on Marcus' piano. I buy them and imagine him working at the computer in his cottage. Then we sit in queues of cars and lorries for ages.

But I don't mind the wait: my soul is soaring, I'm singing along to the radio. I'm in familiar territory and nearly home. I'll let Jade enjoy her life and return to mine. I know I won't hear from Marcus again, but I like my old life and I'll be fine. I'll have plenty to do to support Bonnie and Nan. They both have big changes coming. I've no idea what yet, but I know I'll help them.

Nan's dozing in the back and I'm pleased, because we've stopped four times for her to go to the toilet. Bonnie's head is on my shoulder, breathing softly. But I'm wide awake.

When we arrive at 5 Albert Drive, it's almost ten o'clock and yet I'm not at all tired. I have a smile on my face that I can't wipe off. I touch the bark of the hazel tree in my drive, catkins hanging fat as lambs' tails. I run my fingers over the door handle; once inside, I breathe in with delight as my eyes take in the sofa, the kettle. All these old familiar things are home, my old favourites, and I'm back.

Nan watches me and says, 'You can take the girl out of Liverpool, but you can't take Liverpool out of the girl.'

I grin. 'You sound like old Grandma Basham.'

There's a knock on the door. It's Amanda in a gold dress, grinning, and I throw my arms round her, scream and leap up and down. Rhys is just behind her, carrying several bottles of bubbly and portable party nibbles in a bag. Bonnie brings glasses while Nanny absorbs herself with the contours of Rhys' bicep.

'Could you just hold the bottle up for me? Oh, my, what an enormous muscle. Are you a Chippendale?'

Then it falls to me to relay the whole saga of Duncan Beddowes, while Amanda's mouth hangs open. I skip the part about Adie. Amanda knows from my texts about his disappearance. I don't mention Marcus at all; I focus on the spectacular rescue by Nanny with the spiraliser. Nan's face shines when Amanda cheers and claps her hands.

'Bravo, Nan. You deserve a medal.'

Rhys pours her more Prosecco and she winks at him. We chat until past midnight.

Then we sleep like tots, Nan in Jade's bed and Bonnie in the spare room. On Friday we wake up and pad downstairs, bare feet and in dressing gowns, and we nibble croissants in front of the television. At four o'clock we cook a roast together, all three of us. Bonnie makes gravy and Nan chops the vegetables. Afterwards, we sit with a tumbler of Irish cream, watching the film about the trendy prime minister who falls for his Cockney maid.

Nan leans forwards. 'Oh, I do like a bit of posh. Especially when he does that sexy bum-wiggling dance. What do you think, Georgina?'

I make a humming sound like an electric wire.

Bonnie says, 'He's nice. But not my type. I'm more of an Idris Elba woman.'

I consider the physical similarities to Femi Princewill and cover my smile. Marcus' face pops into my head and for a moment, I recall his searching expression, his ready smile. I remind myself that he's miles away, he's in the past; I can manage by myself. But something has softened in me and I have to admit, I miss him a little.

On Saturday morning it's raining. The Aigburth sky is the colour of concrete, but it's home and I don't mind at all. Liverpool is where I belong and I'm grateful for my heritage and my attachment to this wonderful city. The radio is on – *The Billy Butler Show*, Billy chattering about all things Scouse – while I make coffee, using my own things in my own kitchen space. Nan and Bonnie are tired after a hard day eating, drinking and talking yesterday, so we spend most of the day in front of the television staring as if hypnotised by the screen. For a moment my heart aches, because I know Jade is just a few miles away but I won't see her. She's texted me that she and Luis are in Manchester for the football game.

Nan goes to 'her room' to change and comes down in a football shirt with 'Basham' in huge letters across the back. It was a present from Luis that Jade had secreted in her case.

By three o'clock, she's in front of the screen, clutching a glass of Guinness, ready for the kick-off. While Nan shouts obscenities at the referee and at a tall player she particularly dislikes because he used to play for the opposing local team, the logic of which escapes me, I sort out the laundry, most of yesterday's washing-up, and even put a few twinkling lights up in the garden to celebrate that I'm home.

By half past four, I bring a cup of tea and a small chocolate egg for everyone. Nan's watching the screen, in hysterics. She fills her mouth with chocolate and bits fly out mixed with spittle.

'It's a penalty, a penalty. Can you believe it? What an idiot referee.'

'What's happened, Nan?'

I glance at Bonnie, whose eyes have glossed over; her head is in a magazine and she pushes a piece of chocolate into her mouth.

'One goal apiece. It's the last ten minutes and the ref – the moron – just gave the other team a penalty. Watch, Georgina, watch.'

I sit next to her, take her injured wrist in my hand gently to stop her waving it about, and we see a player with a sculpted haircut take a run at the goal. He slams it down the middle and somehow the goalkeeper falls on top of it; it whacks him in the stomach and he rolls over with it stuck to his belly.

'Save!' yells Nan.

Then Luis appears like lightning, picks the ball up on his foot and runs. Another player chases him, a big man with a shaven head, but Luis sprints away from him. On the other side, another player closes in and Luis dodges past him, does a little skip and boots the ball past the keeper and into the top corner of the net. Nan and I yell together, 'Goal!'

Bonnie looks up from her magazine and beats the

commentator to it. 'And it's another brilliant goal by wonder-kid Luis Delgado.'

'That's my lovely Louise,' Nanny beams.

An hour later, Bonnie has her coat on and my car keys in her hand. She's off to the airport to collect Demi and Kyle. It's only a short journey, but Bonnie's jittery.

'Come with me, Georgie. I'm not used to driving your car. What if I bump it?'

I stand; I'm about to reach for my coat, when a thought comes to me.

'You'll be fine. Honestly. This is the beginning of the new Bonnie. It's an easy drive. You can manage by yourself.'

Nanny wriggles in her seat. 'I've got an aching bum. I'll come with you, Bonnie. The exercise will do my hip good.'

I roll my eyes. 'You'll have to put the seat belt on.'

Nan makes a face behind her thick glasses. 'Of course I'd put my seat belt on, Georgina. What with all those drunk-drivers out there. I'd be mad not to wear one.'

I hug them both. 'Are you bringing Demi and Kyle back here?'

'No. I wondered if I could borrow your car overnight, so that I can take them back to Frodsham. We could spend some time at the house . . . it won't be easy, going back there, but being with Demi will help . . .' She turns to Nan. 'What about you, Nan? Will you come back with me? There's loads of room.'

Nan does her best Queen Elizabeth wave. 'Only if I can have half an hahr in the pahr shahr before I go to bed.'

Nanny's words take me back to our early days on the run: the trip to Edinburgh, to Brackley, the arguments, the laughs and the tears. I recall Marcus, his smile, his thoughtful expression; the warmth of his embrace stays with me and for a moment, I'm lost in thoughts, both pleasant and filled with regret.

Bonnie frowns. 'Will you be all right by yourself tonight, Georgie? You could come over for lunch tomorrow? I could fetch you in your car.'

I think about it and nod. 'Yes. It'll be nice to have a bit of time to myself. Go on, you go and get Demi. Don't be late.'

Then the house is quiet. I'm alone, stretching out my legs, smiling. The curtains are open at the French windows, letting in the twinkling fairy lights from the garden. I curl up in a chair with a glass of wine, put on an Aerosmith CD, play it really loud and close my eyes.

The music rumbles against the walls and I feel my body relax. I've had an exciting few weeks but now I'm home and happy. I recall Nan and our long talk last night. We all agreed that she'll move in with Bonnie. The house in Frodsham is too big for one and, anyway, there's Demi's extension, now completed apparently, which will suit Nan perfectly. When she returns from Australia, Demi will buy a house with Kyle on the Wirral. Then perhaps, after things have settled, Bonnie will sell her house, move closer to me, and Nan will move with her. We're all looking forward to happy times, spending quality time together.

My thoughts shift to Bonnie, how Adie'd held her back for so many years. Her new independence suits her. I remember the brazen way she asked Femi if he had a wife, how she coolly slipped the information about the where-abouts of Beddowes' money to the police. She's more resilient than I'd given her credit for; she's made of tough stuff. There's so much more to her than being Adie's trophy wife and she'll flourish now.

Trade at Beauty Within has been booming recently. I've three talented women working with me. Since I've been away, business has gone from strength to strength. I won't ever worry again about paying the mortgage if things continue this way. Amanda's done so well – she's keen to stay as manager and she's a much more skilful one than I could be. I might find a course on how to be a personal trainer and take over Jade's Gym. Georgie's Gym. It has a nice ring to it.

Then my favourite song comes on and in one leap, I'm on my feet, bouncing and bopping. It's Aerosmith, 'Dude Looks Like a Lady'. Bonnie and I danced to it at Demi's wedding. The beginning of March seems such a long time ago. I launch myself into the middle of the room. The lights in the garden flash green, red, yellow, and I imagine I'm at a live gig. I shake my hair, wave my arms, then the pelvis comes into play and I thrust it forwards and back and wiggle my bum. The guitar, bass and drums propel me and I'm singing out loud, my head thrown back, yelling at the top of my voice: '*Dude looks like a lady.*'

I stop dead. Someone's watching me through the French windows. A man in dark clothes, an overcoat. I freeze. My first thought is that Beddowes is outside – how can he be? Perhaps he's sent someone after me. My breath comes out in a gasp – I've spent too long enclosed, expecting the worst.

Then I pause and look at the man again. It's not Beddowes. The shadow is tall, slim, with curly hair. His hands are on his hips and he's laughing. I splutter through my lips.

'What on earth . . .?'

I run to the French windows and haul them wide. Marcus steps into the room and I fall into his arms.

We kiss for three minutes, five, then he chuckles. 'You're a great dancer, Georgie.'

'I didn't expect to see you,' I say and throw myself at him again.

He brushes my face with his fingers, pushes a strand of hair from my cheek. 'I'm here now. Is that okay with you?'

I flash my eyes. 'I thought you were writing the article about the four horsemen of the apocalypse. That didn't take long. It must have been a short revelation.'

'I finished it. It's emailed. Now I have some time off.' He strokes my hair as I lean against his chest. 'It only took me five hours to drive here. Not a difficult journey.'

'How did you find out where I live?' I hear the intrigue in my voice. I'm flattered.

'I typed you into the Internet, with the words Liverpool and beauty therapist. I clicked on a couple of choices and you came up straight away, along with the address for this place. So I put the postcode into the GPS and here I am.'

I'm suddenly awkward: I can't look at him. The next question is difficult and it takes a few seconds until I'm brave enough to ask. My head is on his chest.

'How long can you stay?'

His voice rumbles against my ears through his ribcage. 'I have my laptop in the car, a change of clothes. I can stay as long as you like.'

I feel a smile break out on my face, an unstoppable grin of anticipation. I don't want him to see the hopefulness, so I walk over to change the CD and pick up Beethoven. The simple opening notes of *Moonlight Sonata* drift from the speakers. We sit together on the sofa and he takes my hand.

'I love this music,' he breathes.

I'm pleased with my choice. I snuggle up to him, stroke the tattoo on his wrist and say, 'Tell me about Sarah.'

'She used to play this piece.' He closes his eyes. 'It was

one of her favourites. I can almost see her now, sitting at the old piano, practising. I still have it upstairs in the spare room, Sarah's piano.'

'Was she your first love? Your girlfriend?'

He meets my eyes. 'She was my sister. My twin.'

I listen to the music, the beautiful rise and fall of plaintive notes, and we're quiet for a moment. I imagine the girl with the cascading curls at the piano, her half-smile, her fingers moving softly and with empathy over the keys.

'What happened to her?'

'Car accident. She was at university with friends, four of them, driving back to the halls of residence. It was over thirty years ago. She was in the front passenger seat. Killed instantly. A drunk-driver was coming the other way; it was a rainy evening.'

'Marcus, I'm sorry.' I bring his fingers to my lips. The music has become hollow, sad, full of mourning. 'You had the tattoo done to remember her?'

He nods. 'My parents weren't pleased. My mother said it was morbid symbolism, an inappropriate echo of the past. My father cried when he saw I'd done it. But we were very close, Sarah and I.' His eyes are shining as he turns to me. 'And it helped me. It feels like she's always with me, that we're still connected.'

I lean back into the softness of the sofa and we're wrapped in each other's arms listening to the music build, a rise of repeated notes yet each separate, and the melody is heart-breakingly poignant. He pulls me closer and I let my eyelids rest, allow the music to sift, vibrate and diffuse around me. I can't help the sigh that shudders from somewhere deep. His mouth is by my ear, his voice gentle as an embrace.

'The past leaves its scars on all of us, Georgie. But we can't have those times back. They've gone. We can

351

remember with love but we have to stay alive ourselves. We only have this time, now.'

I pull myself away from him, stand and stretch out my hand. 'Dance with me, Marcus.'

'To Beethoven?'

I grin. 'Like you said. We only have now.'

He folds me in his arms and I breathe him in. I inhale the scent of a man, an equal, a dancing partner and who knows what else he could be? I don't know, not yet, but the air crackles with sparks of possibility. Our bodies are touching and time slows. We kiss, locked for a moment. Then I look up into his eyes.

'The thing that happened with Beddowes, it was horrific. I thought we were going to die. I couldn't think about a future. And the present was a very uncertain time for me. Life could've ended at any second. I couldn't think about a relationship with you. I wasn't even sure I had a future for myself.'

'And now, how do you feel? After such an awful experience.'

I consider it for a moment. 'What you were saying about letting go of past hurts makes sense. I can do that now. After Terry left, I decided not to trust a man again. Well, I suppose what I decided was that I wouldn't trust myself not to get hurt. I sort of closed my emotions down. It was easier.'

His lips brush my forehead. 'I understand that.'

'It was the same with Jade. I was frightened to let her go. I was terrified of being alone.'

His grip tightens round my waist. 'You don't come across as a person who has any fear whatsoever. I haven't seen that side of you, even with everything that you've been through. I admire your strength and courage. It's inspirational. You were magnetic, from the beginning, the first time I saw you, when I handed you the cereal from the top shelf. Your smile lit up the whole supermarket.' He chuckles, then his face becomes serious again. 'You have a gift, Georgie – the ability to make people laugh. You make me feel happy when I'm with you, truly happy. That's the first reason I wanted to get to know you. And that's why I'm here now.'

'I'm not frightened of anything any more.'

I remember for a moment, about Terry, how much I loved him, and how he went off with Alison and broke my heart. I picture him the last time I saw him, in Jade's living room, a sad-faced married man in a baggy jumper. Not the Terry I knew, but someone else, someone who's changed. I don't really know him now. But perhaps I will: perhaps we can be friends again and I can take the time to get to know Alison better. Terry saw something he admired in her: I can do that, too.

I gaze up into Marcus' shining eyes, his intelligent face, the raised inquisitive brows, the soft curls of dark hair speckled with silver. He's here now, and he can stay here – what did he say to me? – 'as long as you like'.

Marcus is so close that I can feel him breathing.

'Maybe I hung on to memories, Georgie. To hold on to Sarah. Maybe that's why my relationships failed. For too long, I was looking back and too focused on grieving to let the past go and embrace the present.' He pulls me against him, his eyes gleaming. 'Maybe it's time for that to end, for me to move forward, too.'

The music has stopped but we hold each other tightly in the embrace of the dance. The room is silent but heavy with expectation, as if the moment is full, waiting for something that's about to happen. He kisses me again; we share the same breath. I gaze up into his face and I've never felt more grounded, never calmer.

'You are absolutely right, Marcus. We have to live each day for the sheer fun of it. The span of life is too short to cling to what's gone. We have to enjoy it now, every minute that is now, and then the next minute.' Words flood back to me, wise words spoken by a wise woman I've learned to love and respect even more over the past few weeks. 'Because one day, the big clock on the mantelpiece will tick and then it won't tock. Or it'll tock and then it won't tick again. That'll be it.'

Marcus is impressed. 'That's so profound. Did you just make that up?'

I shake my head. 'Nanny Basham said it, while we were talking together one evening at Cliff Top. And she was so right. We need to live in each moment.'

He pulls me closer and my pulse quickens. We've both stopped breathing for a second. It's as if we've had the same thought, and it's made our blood leap.

'So, what do you say, Georgie? Time has brought us to this point. We've both been through a lot, learned a lot. Perhaps now it's time for us to think about each other, and that way we might even begin to think about ourselves. How can we move forward together? How can we make the most of this moment and then the next and the next and the next?'

I look up into his face, meeting his gaze. 'Marcus, I have a really good idea . . .'

Then I take his hand and give him that smile he likes so much, the one that lit up the entire supermarket. I tug him towards the door and upstairs towards my room.

Enjoyed *The Age of Misadventure*?
You'll love Judy Leigh's heartwarming
and hilarious debut.

Grab a glass of wine and escape to
France with this glorious novel,
that proves it's never too late to have
the time if your life . . .

Available in all good bookshops now.